Red Herring

Alisha Hayes

Red Herring

ISBN 978-1-4507-1459-4

For my husband, Nick.
You will never know how much your encouragement and support means to me.
&
For my parents.
Thank you for accepting the person I truly am, and for supporting the path I have chosen.

Table of Contents

Prologue

England
18 January, 2007

The streets of London are always blistering cold this time of year. Dark, damp, freezing and barren, they have an almost cruel-like way of consuming a person. If one can survive a winter there, they can survive anywhere. Each day and night that passes feels like a thousand years and it leaves a person hollow and dejected. Most people are driven mad during their first forty-eight hours on the street. They lose all sense of feeling and emotion. They become consumed with painful memories of their past lives, and more often then not, they are left to face their fears and demons alone.

There are over half a million people who call the streets of London their home: vagabonds, vagrants, hobos, junkies, rejects and prostitutes. They are mostly good people who have felt the wrath of an evil, Godless world. Down on their luck, they are simply looking for help; a friendly face and a hot meal. Ninety-five percent of these people will die whilst looking for this. They walk the streets not understanding why they are there; not understanding why no one will aid them. For they have been cast away by a society who thinks they are some form of mutated life—beast like, not worthy of their attention or concern. Passers-by forget that these people are still of man and they fear them as though they are an unspeakable, perfidious being; some sick, filthy animal whom cannot be trusted, whom deserves this fate.

I know these things because I was there. I have firsthand knowledge of what it is like to lose everything, to feel numb, to be treated like vermin. I know what it is like to be hungry, to have constant roaring pains, to be unclean and to have to fight for the makeshift shelter we squatters call home. Many nights I spent gazing up at the London sky wondering why God chose to punish me in such a merciless way. I can recall praying that it would all end and hoping that the Lord would take me away from what seemed a condemned life of misery. Death would have been better than this. But the Lord never came, and for many years I lived in a box, ate out of dumpsters, and drove myself to the brink of insanity with my idle thoughts of better times to come.

I got through the days and nights by dreaming of another place. I dreamt of a warm bed under a dry roof. Nothing fancy, just a small space to shelter me against Mother Nature. I thought of all the things I never got to do, of my stolen youth, and I vowed to one day get my life back. I saw many things on the streets, none of which were pleasant. There is pure evil out there. It lurks in every alley, around every corner, and it has a sickly sweet habit of consuming people. I have seen starvation. I have seen disease. I have seen murder, rape, and suicide. This monstrous beast we call the Universe harnesses these evils and it feeds itself upon them. It is ever mounting, and each time more vicious than the last.

I will never forget the twentieth day of February, nineteen ninety-four. It was the day I vowed to change this world. I pledged to make the rest of the world see that our governments and leaders were responsible for our downfall. We were not the cause of it; for we merely fell with it. The world's most prominent men and women were not willing to live harmoniously, as each sought to have unwavering power over their people. For this, we suffered. Nuclear attacks, cyclones, hurricanes, mass epidemics: each tragedy far worse than the last. And as each event unravelled and went overlooked, more men, women and children lost their homes, their families, their lives.

Suddenly, it seemed as though the streets had become flooded with people. Something had to be done. I begged the Lord for his help, but it never came. Things got worse. My fellow men were dying from disease and hunger right before my eyes. Women and children were being used in patriotic revenge missions. Smaller countries were losing half their population trying to fight losing battles against the United States, Britain and China. Death, destruction and disease had become a very natural being. This world was crumbling, and for mankind's sake, action needed to be taken.

Although my allegiance to Christ is immeasurable, I knew that he could not fix this world. I decided to shoulder the burden myself. I took the trouble out of God's hands and placed it into mine. I did this willingly, freely and without regret...

Chapter 1

Cunningham Street, London
20 February, 1994

The wheels of the old shopping cart could be heard from five blocks away. Its hollow thuds echoed across the barren streets; defeated, as its operator. A frenzied beat resonated off the decaying stone walls, sightlessly penetrating its way into the still night. I huddled inside an ancient boiler crate, lost in the depths of a cold, charcoal London.

My fourth winter on these streets; a feat I could hardly swallow.

Exposure...starvation...disease; fates that are met by most. How have I managed to escape such immutable forces of Mother Nature? Be it by luck, perseverance, or by the Lord's grace, with each new dawn I was truly grateful.

Lustful whispers and pleasurable moans seeped through the crate's flimsy walls, carrying with them the heavy burden of sin. Urine mingled with vomit clung to the bitter air like an indestructible parasite—a stench so powerful that it devoured all within its path. Placing a gloved hand over my nose, I withdrew further into my crumbling safeguard. I prayed for salvation.

Such pleas I was resigned to believe would never be answered: for in the absence of light, a wicked darkness had triumphed. Like a fiend, it mercilessly fed upon the weak, leaving nothing but soulless voids in its wake. Night after night I beseeched to the Heavens, only to be left unfulfilled. Had God left this place? This single, oppressive thought menacingly kept sleep just out of reach.

Red Herring

I was enveloped by the ever-present sounds of the allies: the gentlemen and the whore...the intense thumping from the club behind me...drunken laughter...hopeful catcalls...the looming wheels of the shopping cart. These consumed me; drowning me in their pitiful wombs. Perhaps tonight my deliverance *would* come.

I heard him enter the alley roughly half past three. A collector, he methodically pushed his cart over every inch of pebbled street. The radiant sea of white beneath his tired feet held great treasures, and he intended to find them.

Like myself, he had been left to battle the horrors our cruel society so impassively bestowed upon us. We were the calluses on the soles of the affluent. Leaches who sucked the beauty from every crevice of this great land: whatever ill fortune had been thrown our way was nothing less than warranted. The streets had yet to claim his old body, but his mind had been mercilessly stripped away some time ago. It was difficult to find justification in this.

The cart stopped nearby. I could not suppress a faint smile as I heard him mumble "What do we have here?" I listened mutedly as he eagerly dug through a trash bin. The dull clink of something dense penetrating the hamper's metal frame told me had found another treasure. After several minutes, the unbalanced wheels began to knock; he was moving once more. Despite the raw air, he would not render until he was satisfied with his cache.

"Oh yes, she will very much like you," he cooed. "Very much."

Although I could not see him, I knew his withered hands were lovingly cradling his latest find. A soft rustling confirmed that he had wrapped this prime jewel in old parchment before placing it amongst the rest.

If she only knew how much he loved her. Thirty-six years she had been gone. He took no notice to her prolonged absence. He continued to collect under the apparition that she was soon coming to see him. Each day that passed was in a chasm of blissful ignorance. Scrounging through what I was certain to be a pile of moulding cardboard boxes, he whistled cheerfully. Regardless of his increasingly frail physic, he was always in uplifted spirits. His old soul was completely at peace; nothing could bring him down. I jealously listened to his tune. What I wouldn't given to live the rest of my days in an effervesce of joyful indifference. It had been years since I had known happiness. The lingering bitter taste in my mouth had me convinced that anger, pain and sorrow were the only emotions I would ever know...

"Got you," he pacified. "Yes, I think my sweet Anneliese will adore you too." I took note of the familiar rustle as this new gem joined the ranks of those previous.

Cracking the cover of the crate, I poked my head out of the small fissure. Instantly I was met by a cold, wet darkness. Icy flakes pierced my ears and nose, numbing them upon contact. I could hear him clearly some forty feet away rummaging in the pile of trash the managers of the dance club had yet to dispose of. A squishing noise echoed through the alley as he began to wade through four feet of rubbish.

"I am over here, next to the dumpster." I called blindly. I always had trepidations about interrupting him whilst he was collecting. He had once told me that this was something he preferred to do quietly and in private. Uncertain of his unintelligible response, I withdrew into my haven. He would come when he was ready.

In the few moments it took for me to settle, a thunderous crash perforated the alleyway. I jolted so violently that the crate rocked unsteadily, my heart was nearly in arrest.

"Lazhítyes sabaka! Razrishaítye pazhálusta." The male voice was vicious; a tone so heartless it could have rivalled Satan himself.

"Lazhítyes sabaka! Razrisháítye pazhálusta." He savagely repeated. I clung to every syllable. This man was definitely Russian, clearly drunk, and very arrogant.

"I sssaid, lie ddown dog! Lettt mee passs." The callous words slithered off his tongue. I felt exploited, as though every ounce of purity had been pilfered from me. Liquor infused laughter erupted, dredging its way into my harbour. He was not alone. "Doooooo it. Nowwww! Or sssuff—ssuffer," he slurred.

I gently lifted the cover of the crate once more. Cautiously raising my head, I peered into semi-darkness. The back door to the club was wide open, a ray of light expounded four men as well as a cart full of rubbish.

Two giant-like fellows in black wool overcoats, sporting matching ushankas were holding the elbows of a man adorned in thick furs. At least a foot shorter than his mates, this man haphazardly carried a long staff in his left hand; upon the top, a red gemstone. A glare cascading off his knuckles came from the many gold rings he bore around them. He reeked of power and spawned fear. All the fourth man could do was stand frozen in a pile of debris, completely emasculated. Shamefully, I was in that very same vessel.

"Konsssstantin!" he barked. "Thi-thiss ssscum nee—eedsss a lesss—lesss—lesson in ressspect. What doo wee doo withh thossse whoo can-cannot follow ordersss?" His voice was playful, a wide grin etched on his face.

I wanted to call out, to say something authoritative; anything to make these men carry on about their business. I parted my lips, yet nothing came forth. I struggled to find the intonations deep within me. Pushing them to the surface, I tried once more. My lips moved, hot air expelled, but I was a voiceless shell.

A single shot pierced my eardrums, forever notching its terror within them. I watched helplessly as man and trash mound united. His limp figure crumbled into the vile pit; submerged.

"Vat iz vot ve doo.," the rough voice of Konstantin maliciously confirmed.

"Very goood. Now let usss go. Thee je-jet izz waiting for uss."

"Avter you, Vresident Golovin," the third man gushed.

"How very k-kind of y-you, Yuri," the short man scoffed. Using his staff as support, he staggered down the alley, his men in tow.

They found him nestled in a rotting mountain of trash along the backside of Cunningham Street. He had been shot execution style, his face mangled beyond recognition. The tatty clothes on his back coupled with his grubby skin, identified him immediately.

Just another vagrant., they had said. An unknown which would never be solved; such incidents were not worth a pound of their time.

"Let's wrap this up quickly lads," a guttural voice boomed. "I do not have the time, nor the patience to chase another dead-end street homicide. We have *real* crimes to solve. Have any of you seen my desk lately? Over six hundred unsolved murders in this city. Six hundred! We need not waste time on this mangy rat. Look at the state of him; his only companions were a needle and rubber band. A deal gone bad. The end."

Crouched within my protective sanctity, I had but two things on my mind: his name was Hans, and he had been my only friend.

Chapter 2

Federation Street Hostel, London
23 February, 1994

What makes a man good? The Laws of God dictate kindness, fellowship and purity as the blueprint to not only one's salvation, but as a personal measurement of one's self-worth. Loving thy neighbour, devotion to our Creator, unadulterated thoughts and actions...These are the markings of virtue; a one-way ticket into the kingdom of Heaven.

But how does one define kindness? Is it strictly twined by humanity, compassion, sympathy and generosity? Does one have the ability to mould each strand to his own partiality, despite their black and white interpretations?

Is unwavering devotion even plausible? Can one truly follow His laws to the letter, never running astray from the holy parchment which binds him? Not even in the direst of circumstance?

They say a man's deepest struggle is the one within. The fight pitting good against evil, the delicate balance between darkness and light. Our minds yearn for things which do not belong to us. Our body savagely quests for fulfilment. How do we filter the constant stream of ideas and emotion? Are we capable of sifting through the impurities, of peeling back the layers to expose only what has been deemed acceptable?

Am I to be condemned for my desire to seek vengeance? Shall I burn for my mere thoughts of it? Is my soul no longer worthy? There were far too many more questions than answers.

Red Herring

....

Who am I to leave this lie? I cannot simply walk away. A good man wouldn't turn the other cheek...or, when faced with his own eternal salvation, would he? In my eyes, there was only one solution: seek out, and expel the men who had done this to Hans. Yes, I should just let God sort them out. But what kind of a man does nothing? How can I carry on knowing what atrocity has occurred here?

Hans' death did not reach the public's ears. I was foolish to think that it would. The homeless in London were like an elephant within a glass room. Seen by all, but unheard. Hans deserved to be avenged. Even if his name and portrait never reached the obituary pages of the Times Global, even if there is never a single minute of punishment for his executioners, Hans was worthy of someone's time. His life, no matter how obscure and eccentric it may have been, did leave undying imprints upon the hearts he crossed paths with. His soul could not be neglected.

The torment I felt was asphyxiating. I wanted to be a good person, I wanted everlasting deliverance, yet I wanted my life to be meaningful and fulfilling. How can I have any of those things if I choose to sin? To act against another life...it is unpardonable. Will God forgive me? Will I be able to enter His kingdom without hesitation or judgment? Does it even matter, now that I've engrossed myself in such poisonous thoughts of revenge? Who was I to pass judgement anyway?

The days and nights blurred together in a chasm of profound thoughts and sickly indulgences. I had made up my mind; I was going to do whatever it took to bring these men to justice. I had accepted that I would be the lone man fighting for Hans' cause. It was a shame, but I could not change the outlook and preconceptions of others.

Playing God frightened me. It was iniquitous, and I was not worthy of such license. However, in His absence, I had convinced myself that doing His work would be commendable. I had decided long ago that I would rather die fighting for Hans than to suffer the fates which awaited me on the daily. I would not starve; I would not succumb to disease, nor exposure. I would die in combatant for something I cared about, and it would be on my terms. It would be with dignity.

But why stop with just Hans, something kept telling me. There were so many others like him whom had suffered, and many people who will continue to. Why not send a message? A message from God to all those who think they are above divinity's decrees. A message letting them know they cannot escape neither judgment nor punishment. We were always watching, and no longer would we remain dormant.

Entertaining such an idea was nothing short of ludicrous. I knew I was permitting my emotions to overtake my sanity, but I did not care. The more I stewed, the more I felt this was right. It needed to be done. These people had to be held accountable, and I was now acting in surrogate of the Lord as their adjudicator.

Hans would have said I was being irrational. He would have insisted I step out of the box: look inwards to see the big picture. He would have told me to be thankful that I was alive and to count my blessings. Hans also would have understood, and if I had asked, he would have been right by my side.

There was no set plan, no timeframe. There was no specific order, nor was there a list. The only thing of certainty was that there was no turning back. Gazing up into the sinister sky, I pledged my allegiance to Christ, and to Hans. I would stay true to the Lord, acting only out of inevitability, and I would not stop until either death rendered or God willed me. Where ever I ended up, I knew that it was preordained. No matter how bad it got, no matter what happened, there was reasoning behind it all. I would be encountering true evils, and there would be times of reclusive aloneness. None of this mattered, as I was prepared to do what ever it took to ensure the suffering would cease. My nightmares would become realities, gloom would consume me, my mind and body would become vulnerable; horrors which I had come to realize as irrefutable. But none of this carried substantive weight, as I would endure anything to ensure I served my Creator well. Mind set, I meticulously began my preparations.

....

The cross had not left my being in nearly thirty years. Given to me as a young boy, I had wound it tightly around my right wrist in oath that I would always carry it with me. Beautifully handcrafted of twenty-four carat yellow gold, each end had been scrupulously sculpted into tiny oak leaf points; a single canary diamond inlayed within the piece's centre. Rubbing my fingers over the glistening stone, I recalled a time of happiness. A time where nothing mattered. A time of love, amity and light. Such times have vanished for me; I was under constant cover of misery and despair.

How did I get to this point? What had gone wrong? Was I being punished? There had been times in my youth when my decisions had been questionable, and there are shames which I care to keep buried, but isn't that true of everyone? Mistakes and misfortune were common occurrences. Life, sometimes, was not fair. But to have thirty years of sorrow...What had singled me out? What had made me a marked man? My self perseverance was strong, but every man has his breaking point. I had nearly reached mine.

My heart was heavy as I trudged my way through the snow covered sidewalks. A bitter February afternoon, a mere four blocks yielded numb ears and toes. Tiny flakes plastered my head, matting my shaggy hair to the sides of my face and neck. As each fleck melted over my exposed flesh, an icy chill plunged deeper into my bones. Within minutes I lost all sense of feeling. Frankly, I welcomed the sensation. I gazed benignly at my battered black boots, taking no notice to the looming blizzard I was baring directly into. I had taken this path many times and knew it quite well. My destination was eighteen blocks into the west end of town. I had made this very trek several times per year in the past, always stopping short of reaching it. Today, however; I would go the entire distance despite how painful it would be.

The shop had not changed. Stunning white roman stone pillars accented an equally beautiful hand-chiselled limestone edifice; a cherry wood door with a single brass knocker balanced between two large blacked-out windows. The storefront was immaculate, a pearl amongst a heap of coal. Life around it was dead and decayed. Broken windowpanes, peeling paint, missing sandstone, rubbish piles: years worth of neglect had taken its toll on the establishments in this part of the city. Most were unoccupied, the odd one had been commandeered by squatters, others a front for lucrative drug and black market operations. Why the proprietor had chosen to remain in such a filthy place was beyond my comprehension. Perhaps, he too had made a commitment to someone long ago.

Paused under the landing, I removed the glove on my right hand. Instantly I felt the smooth, cool metal brush against my palm. I raised my arm, gazing at the piece. It was all I had. It was all that had sustained me these past twenty-seven years. Every time I had thoughts about death, and how badly I wanted the suffering to cease, all I had to do was hold the cross. It provided a comfort, a reason to keep on. It had become my pacifier, and I clung to its memories like a ravenous fiend.

I always knew the pendant held value. The diamond was nearly two carats, its clarity remarkable, like peering through glass. It was almost as ethereal as she had been.

I felt no shame as warm liquid began to leak from the corners of my eyes. I had given her my word. I had looked into her conquered eyes, in promise that I would never be rid of it. I had pledged to think of her often, and to find solace within the cross she had held so dear. I was letting her down. I knew this harsh reality, but I needed to do this. And I was certain she would have understood. For in my youth she had told me that within everyone's soul a vast darkness lingers, waiting for its purpose to be served. This was my purpose.

Unhitching the clasp, I unwound the thin gold chain from my wrist. A white ring of unexposed flesh stared back at me. I felt stripped. Resting the piece within my left palm, I elevated it to my chin. Liquid gushed from my eyes as I pushed my cracked lips onto the smooth stone.

"I have to do this," I whispered. "Please, forgive me."

Placing the pendant into my left trouser pocket, I wiped my eyes before lifting my right arm to the door's brass knocker.

....

The wispy shop-keep studied the diamond through his ancient loupe. His frail frame was practically swallowed by all the artefacts which surrounded him. A dozen glass cases were filled with gold, silver, diamonds and gemstones. Various jewellery boxes showcasing bracelets, rings, earrings and pendants were strewn about. A seven foot antique mahogany cabinet overflowing with wristwatches and broaches sat off in the left corner. Photographs from past excursions hung limply on the navy and gold papered walls. I stared blankly at the triumphant faces in each black and white photo. Some men flourished gems the size of baseballs. Others, a pan full of gold nuggets. Their travels had taken them to all parts of the world: Liberia, Canada, Brazil, South Africa, Sierra Leone, and Guinea. These places had been etched into the bottom right corners of several snapshots.

I combed the shop for nearly an hour in silence. The proprietor was engrossed in the diamond. A magnifier now stuck into his left eye, every few minutes I would hear him mutter how astonishing the stone was. Studying a lot of well worn pickaxes along the far east wall, I proceeded to let the man be. Once he was satisfied, he would beckon me. A gold plated I.D. tag caught my eye, bringing up sour reminiscences of my childhood. Swallowing dryly, I continued to pace the shop, however; I could not pull myself from the tag. I found myself going back to it time and time again.

"And where did you say you acquired this piece?" The old chap had a cynical look on his face.

"It was my mother's." I knew he pegged me for a poor bloke. That much was obvious. He had initially denied me entrance into his shop until I had shown him the pendant. This is not a hotel, he had spat.

"I see." He was eyeing me apprehensively. "Err...well, a lemon drop like this is rare. Very uncommon indeed."

I nodded my head in understanding.

"And the colour... I have never seen a canary stone so pure. Not a single hint of red, brown or green. Simply remarkable..." He trailed off, the magnifier jammed back into his eye.

What seemed an eternity passed before he spoke again. Having removed the diamond from the centre of the piece, he now wore a monocle in place of his magnifier, and was studying the stone under different angles of light.

"One point seven-six carats...colour, grade C plus. Clarity, IF or internally flawless. The cut is precise according to Tolkowski's weight ratio chart."

I did not know who Tolkowski was, nonetheless, it was apparent his chart held substantive credence with the jeweller.

"One hundred seventy-three thousand pounds." He peered intently at me, his clear blue eyes conclusive. "I can give you one hundred seventy-three thousand pounds."

Something told me this was a shoddy deal. I rubbed my wrist hesitantly. I glanced up at the shop-keep, he was stone faced. It was clear this offer would be the only one, and there was no room for negotiations. I pinched the bridge of my nose with my thumb and index finger, the gears inside my mind churning. I did not know where my path would take me. I had no sense of cost, no idea in terms of exchange rates. Would this amount be enough? What happens when these monies have been exhausted?

A bad-tempered tapping awakened me from my thoughts. The old man had emerged from behind the glass cases and was standing before me, his right foot rapping the floorboards, thick envelope in hand.

"Well?" He demanded.

Chewing my bottom lip, I could not take my eyes off the envelope. "Umm..." I began.

"Listen lad," he stiffened. "Yes, you could fetch more for this stone at auction. However; bare in mind you have no documentation proving that you acquired this gem from the proper chain of command. You say it was your mother's. I am inclined to believe you, yet I do not have to. If I so choose, I can confiscate this diamond and call the law. All, of course, in complaint that you are trying to sell me a stolen good. Do you want to part with it or not?"

The discussion and meditation were both over. I had mere seconds to make up my mind: take it or leave it. He was right, I could not prove the pendant had belonged to me. Given the state of my clothing, coupled with my grooming habits, it would be fairly easy to convince law enforcement that I had indeed illegally obtained the piece.

I nodded in confirmation. It was all I could do. My entire body had begun to gently convulse. I had betrayed her. Quickly wiping tears from my eyes, I snatched the envelope from his outstretched hand, deftly shoving it into my front trouser pocket. "Excellent." He beamed. I watched sickened as he bounced back behind the countertop. A huge smile was etched upon his wrinkled face. He carefully wrapped the diamond into a silk cloth before tucking it into his suit jacket pocket. For the first time, I had really taken notice to him. He was at least seventy years old, his thin white hair stuck out in every direction. Something told me he was about to take a long-term vacation.

"Do you want this? It is useless to me."

In between his thumb and index finger, he was haphazardly clutching the pendant. The golden chain glistened under the light; the cross although stripped, was still an object of splendour. Nodding my head, I stumbled towards the counter. Placing my hand under his, the pendant slipped effortlessly through his bony fingers into my adoring palm. I wasted no time returning it to its rightful place.

"If I may be frank, you could use a shave, a hair cut and a new wardrobe. I sincerely hope you use the monies wisely." The austerity in his voice was overpowered by the surprisingly softness of his eyes. Again, all I could do was nod.

"Good day to you Sir."

With remarkable speed, he had bowed me from his shop, the latching of the door's deadbolt delivering me back into my bitter reality.

The urge to spend had sunk in. What does a man do with one hundred seventy-three thousand pounds? Purchase a house? Perhaps an automobile? The wise would invest. I, having no desire to do any of these things, headed straight to a thrift store on Remy Lane.

Nearly sixty-five pounds later, I emerged with new-to-me boots, gloves, trousers, wool overcoat, toque and knit sweater. I also splurged a tad by purchasing a leather pocketbook, travel satchel and a golden pocket watch. All were essentials in my opinion.

I roamed the alleys until nightfall. I yearned for a warm bed, yet I could not bring myself to selfishly spend forty pounds on a room for the evening. There just seemed to be more important uses for the funds. Nevertheless, at half past seven, I succumbed to the elements and to the idea of at least relinquishing a few pounds to shelter myself. I was no use beaten down, and after the most peaceful, cosy evening I had had in years, I vowed to never sleep another night exposed. I had woken up in renewed spirits, ready to face the demons.

A positive energy filled me as I began to plan. I would transform myself into a herring of sorts. Blending in with the crowds and cultures as best to my abilities. Leaving it all up to obscurity. Nothing would be done the same way, and it would be in unconventional ways. I would also spread it all out. Perhaps it would take months, even years. That was up to God. I would take whatever He gave me and mould it to my benefit. I had convinced myself that I was not only ready, but the only man for this job. Strolling past a mangy young woman and her starving children, my first objective became clear. Fishing one hundred pounds from my pocketbook, I backtracked to the place where the young family sat huddled together. She glanced up at me, hazel eyes filled with despair. I took her scrawny hand and placed the pounds within her palm. Her children buried themselves deep into her chest; frightened.

"Please, get yourself and your children some food and clothing." I whispered.

She nodded, choking back tears. Mumbling into her chest, I gaped brazenly as she lifted her children to their feet. Smiling weakly, they proceeded to walk down the alley together.

I bore after them until they had left my sight. Setting out once more, I could not suppress my feelings of fulfilment. For once, I had been the giver. For once, I had seen the joy my kindness had brought to someone. It was the most euphoric sensation. I had given that young woman hope. I could see it written upon her face.

I could not stop giving. I found four more vagrants and gave them twenty pounds apiece. They too had the same optimistic looks in their eyes; one man even broke down and called me his saving grace. As pathetic as his sobs may have appeared, I knew that I had rescued him from fatality. The ones closest to the brink are the easiest to spot. He had lost faith, I could not blame him. I had been there many times. I had struggled with my Creator. I had pondered His love for me, and at one point, I had denounced Him. But there is peace and light for all of us; yet for the severely broken, it is sometimes difficult to see. Wandering aimlessly through the slums of London, a curious thought struck me: what better place to start than in my own backyard?

Chapter 3

Steele and Templar, London
9 May, 1994

Eighteen eighty-four: England at it's finest. Under Queen Victoria's reign, the British people bathed in a sixty-four year period of prosperity. Owning to its many colonies, the British Empire had strengthened substantially, allowing for vast profits and for the development of a sounder middle class of citizens. Industry, education, entertainment and socialism had changed the face of England, sky-rocketing it out of the agricultural rut in which it seemed to be wedged. Endless opportunities were available to those whom were willing to embrace them. Emphasis had been put on education, along with social congregations. The times had turned for the better, and for young Britons, the only path appeared to be upwards. To this day, the Victorian Era is thought to be the most momentous period in British history.

Things change. There is no use denying it, nor is there any point in trying to prevent it. As people grow, their wants and needs expand. A government rises and falls in accordance with whom is leading it, not based upon the types of people that inhibit it. A virtuous leader who does not understand his or her people's needs, can run a country into the ground practically overnight. In the case of Queen Victoria, she had a thorough understanding of what was needed, and facilitated those needs by expanding the Empire and introducing new opportunities to the working man. Her Majesty was far from perfect; however, she was capable and primarily responsible for uplifting Britain to where it belonged. Victoria laid the groundwork for her successors. She had set the bar, kept it there for over sixty years, and all that was required from the next person was maintenance. It would not be easy, nothing ever is. Nevertheless, an honest effort coupled with some give and take would have gone a long way.

England's current Prime Minister, Charles Benjamin Addams, had been around since the Stone Age. His methods were preservation instead of progression. He clung to the past, and governed England as though it were still in the early nineteen hundreds. Addams took what many Englanders called the "Refine the already refined" approach. He pumped tax dollars into what he declared to be "Historical Preservation Projects" and he gave large, undisclosed amounts of currency to "Overhaul England's higher standard of education facilities." In his speeches and on paper he made it look good, in all actuality, he was simply lining the pockets of those who did not need it. When accused of transgression, Addams' administration released a statement claiming it "Vital for England to rekindle its pristine past." And to achieve such pristine, we must "Refine those high points we so proudly covet, with hopes they will lay a foundation for our not-so-finer ones." In other words, our government planned to cut out the lower and middle classes completely. In doing so, they anticipated a set-by-example chain reaction from Britain's higher classes. Any fool could see right through Addams' plan. He was too blinded by what used to be, hence he was not capable of seeing what could be. Hans once told me it would be a cold day for a baboon's backside before Charles Benjamin Addams saw the error of his ways. As more and more people flooded the streets, as more children went hungry, as more disease spread, I too began to believe my late friend's words.

I will admit that Addams need not deserve to die. Overall, he was a decent man. His priorities were simply muddled. He did not understand our wants, therefore he was incapable of making greater-good decisions. He only had one desire; to restore England back to its days of glory. Did such a wish justify a death warrant? Probably not, however, Charles Addams was directly responsible for the problems which continually consumed the streets. Part of me felt he was also indirectly responsible for Hans' death. Or perhaps I just wanted him to be...

Had I thought this through? Yes... and no. When it came down to it, doing this was cut and dry. Either I fix things or I let them go. Of course, there is no guarantee my efforts will be beneficial. I could just be paving the way for something far more wicked. Even so, it would be cruel, not to mention quite selfish, to not at least try to make a difference. Use Addams as an example for all those in his legacy. Would it matter? I did not know. Would things worsen? That was also unforeseen. All I knew for certain was a result, good or bad, could not occur unless there was an action behind it. I could only pray that my efforts would not go unnoticed. I kept telling myself that this was the only way. And it truly was. I ran my fingers over the blood money I had recently acquired. What would my Mother say? I had made a promise to her. For as long as I could remember, I had never bound myself to something I could not honour. I felt ashamed, sinful even. So, this is what dishonour feels like.

....

Like the Royal Family, Addams had his own private army. Her Majesty's Armed Forces protected the Prime Minister three hundred sixty-five days a year. Never was he to be seen without a presence around him. Or so the general public thought.

Every Tuesday evening, from ten to midnight, Prime Minister Addams would venture into Cyprus Park. How he managed to escape the clutches of his Army, is neither here nor there. All I knew was that he engulfed himself in an intense game of chess each week, under cover of a baseball cap and shabby casual clothing. Rumour on the street had it that Jonathan, an eccentric vagrant, was Addams' estranged brother. Both men shared similar features;

eye colour, build and cleft chin. Though the men hardly spoke, they seemed to have an unusual bond, a bond that could hardly have formed for a weekly game of chess. They allowed spectators, usually consisting of Hans, myself and a few other tramps who called the park their home. For two hours we watched the men's mental warfare. Jonathan rarely lost, a fact he so proudly pointed out regularly.

My initial recognition of the Prime Minister occurred during a spectacular bloodbath, in which he was losing. I observed Addams, an unknown man at the time, place his index finger to his chin; a common mannerism to which I always associated to the Prime Minister. During interviews, Addams was prone to the characteristic should he find himself befuddled, or whilst contemplating a response. I recalled a particularly heated interview between a journalist from the Global Times Newspaper and himself. Addams had gotten into hot water, as the woman conducting the interview proved to be not only feisty, but more knowledgeable on Foreign Policy than he. His finger never left his chin, and a lot of "Ums" and "Errs" followed her inquiries. Jonathan's opponent had the same habit, and coupled with his uncanny likeness to the Prime Minister, it was easy to identify the man as such. Addams was unaware that his cover had been blown, nevertheless, he should have known that someone, somewhere would figure it out. It was only a matter of time.

As I watched Jonathan polish each piece adoringly, a wild idea struck me. When satisfied with their sheen, he carefully began to place the pieces into their individual slots within the set's case. Addams was always quick to depart as soon as the clock struck midnight. If a game was not-yet-complete, he left Jonathan with the task of recording each piece's position on the board and who would have the first move the following week. Just as Jonathan was about to latch the case, I stumbled hard into him. I watched as the pieces fell from the open case into the semi-darkness.

"Oh! Sorry old chap. I lost my balance" I said innocently.

Jonathan, already on his hands and knees, was attempting to retrieve the fallen pieces from within the dew spotted grass. Snatching an oil lamp from the tabletop, he shook his head and mumbled something intelligible as he continued his search.

"Let me help you with this," I said, squatting to his level. He waved me off, again mumbling incoherent phrases. "I insist. It is after all, my fault." My eyes had begun to scan the ground for the castle shaped piece. Using the Rook was the only way.

Jonathan was polishing each piece once more before placing them back into the case. I spotted the Rook behind his left heel, and quickly reached for it. I also grabbed a pawn which lain several inches to my left. Jonathan tore the piece from my hand.

"Said I 'ad it, Willie."

Rising, I quickly pocketed the Rook. "Alright, then. I shall see you next week." He nodded slightly before retuning to his loving pieces.

Hollowing out the Rook took more time and patience than I had anticipated. My pitiful Swiss Army knife barely scratched the surface of the resolute rosewood. A task made easy by way of a drill bit; unfortunately I did not have such a luxury. Perched under a streetlamp, I meticulously carved a cylinder into the underside of the piece. My fingers were cramped and decrepit looking from my laborious efforts. Nonetheless, I continued to shave away little by little. At least the cyanide had been easy to come by, I thought. The back doorknob to the toxic waste disposal facility on Mercy Street had been broken for the last several years. A forceful pull and turn combination had awarded Hans and I with a warm place to stay on many unbearable January nights. My heart ached as I reflected on those times. Sorrow consumed me, however, only just. In an instant, my veins pulsed with anger. Staring at the piece in my hand, I pierced the blade into it remorselessly, vowing not to stop until the hollow had been made.

At dawn I finally yielded. Plunging my left pinkie finger into the cylinder, I was disappointed to find that I had only penetrated two inches. Closing my knife, I stuck both it and the piece into my pocket. Upon rising, severe fatigue hit me. Steadying myself against the alley's cool brick, I attempted to shake it off. My legs felt like two tree trunks; heavy and stiff. Leaning flaccidly against the wall, I allowed myself to sink back down to the pavement. Exposed, I slept in that very spot.

The uneven wheels of Hans' cart had awoken me. In a fury, I sprang to life and ran after him. I searched all of our favourite sleeping grounds, but he was nowhere to be seen. Dejected, I trekked back to my workstation trying to make sense of what just happened. Every day for three years I had heard the dull clanging. I knew the sound; I knew he had been there...

It took me four days to carve out the inside of the Rook. As proof of my labour, I had a dozen tiny cuts in the palms of my hands. Using the thin blade of a small paper knife, I punctured a quarter inch slot in the top of the piece. After attaching the same blade to a wire spring, I forced the device into the bottom of the cylinder. If everything went as planned, a small amount of force on the pressurized spring would eject the blade through the slot I had created, hopefully penetrating the Prime Minister's flesh. This in itself would not harm Addams, but I was certain the cyanide caked on the blade tip would.

....

Did I have what it took? I was starting to think not. Cold sweats, vomiting and dizziness...I was a wreck; on the verge of madness. Every emotion of anger, fear, pain, and sorrow had run its course. It had left me weakened and vulnerable. The constant clanging of uneven wheels kept sleep at bay. I knew it to only be psychological, yet I still could not suppress the small ray of hope which ignited inside of me. Hans was still raw, for he had been the closest thing to family--something which had been unknown to me for nearly thirty years. He had made living on the streets much more tolerable. I knew I wasn't alone. I wasn't the only person to suffer at the hands of our merciless government. Hans was alongside me; where I always envisioned him to be.

I found myself in the middle of Cyprus Park, uncertain how I had gotten there. Everything around me was a hazy shade of grey. It was surreal, as though I was watching a black and white television program. An old tramp slugged past me sledging his feet like they were set in concrete. His transparent outline was supernatural; a paranormal state. I bore after him until he disappeared into the depths of the park. Part of me wanted to follow him, to make sure he was real. Another part of me was content to stand in this abyss of nothingness. There was no pain, no fear; only absolution.

A warming glow and the sweet smell of kerosene hung over me. Fluttering my eyelids, I could make out a shadowy figure billowing over me. Shoving an oil lamp into my face, Jonathan grasped my arm and pulled me upwards. I eased to my feet, my prior events flooding back to me at once.

"Saw ya fall, Willie. What 'appened?" He looked deeply saddened, most likely brought on by the loss of his Rook. Through his scraggly white beard I could definably see his lower lip trembling. His tired eyes were bloodshot; guilt swept over me as I envisioned him searching sleeplessly for his piece. Before I could respond, he had dropped to his knees and began weaving his gnarled hands through the dewy earth.

For a man of his age and physical condition, he worked rather deftly. Momentarily, all of Jonathan's concentration was focused on finding the missing piece. Instead of responding to him, I bent to his level to help aid in the search. I smoothed my hands over the lush grass in an effort to locate what I knew to be within my left trouser pocket.

Our search consumed the better part of an hour and covered nearly half the park's total acreage. Jonathan had taken to uttering incomprehensible rubbish as ten o'clock drew nearer. Between his outbursts I managed to catch the odd phrase. "Should call the law, 'Aven't missed a game in seven-teen years" and, "Conspiracy goin' on." I felt horrible as he was clearly at his wits end over the situation. For the first time realisation had set in: I was taking the life of someone's son, someone's brother, someone's father. Severing this bond would crush Jonathan. Like Hans was for me, Addams was all he had. What would his death do to him? Would Jonathan be able to carry forth? Or would he wallow in despair before going off the deep end himself? I became nauseated by such a thought. It was not my intention to harm the innocent. A foolish desire, as I now saw. My acts were bound to impact those directly associated with the Prime Minister.

I could not help the misery his death would cause those close to him. Nor could I allow myself to become consumed with his mourner's sentiments. Falling prey to such a vulnerability would compromise everything. I had to harden myself beyond caring about anyone but the objective. As much as Jonathan relished his weekly match-ups with his brother, as much as it pained me to take that away from him, I knew I had to. This also sickened me as compassion and kindness were my dictum. A grisly thought swept over me as I watched Jonathan's fully projected hysterics: Perhaps, I was masquerading my true self.

I am doing the right thing...I am doing the right thing...I am doing the right thing... Over and over I kept repeating these words. Jonathan had taken to sobbing uncontrollably under an oak tree, his limbs shaking with violent spasms. His twill trousers were soiled and damp from crawling on his hands and knees. He looked as though he had just emerged from the depths of the Thames. I watched with penitence as he tugged at his mangy hair and mumbled into the tree's matured bark. Reaching into my pocket, I felt the smooth rosewood graze my fingertips. There was still time to walk away...

"Willie! Willie! We 'ave to find it. 'E won't come if I don't 'ave it! Please Willie! You gotta 'elp me!" Jonathan's arms were suddenly enveloped tightly around my kneecaps. His eyes were wide and swimming with tears as he begged with everything he had.

A pathetic sight, I turned my head. "Please!" His words of desperation echoed into the night. "'E always said to keep it with me. 'E said 'Jonathan, this can be our only link and I am entrusting you with it.' That's what 'e said to me Willie, seventeen years ago. 'E is an important person and we can only be together when no one is watching 'im. It would be ill repute for 'is status if people found out 'bout me. 'E would be ruined. So ruined..." Jonathan's voice trailed off.

Clutching his shoulders, I pulled him upwards. "We will find it, Jonathan," I finalized. Releasing him, we continued the search together. I scanned the ground as I had done before. This time, I felt guiltless. Something Jonathan had said ignited a nerve: This can be our only link and I am entrusting you with it. I was repulsed by his exclamation. What kind of man would base a relationship upon a game piece? Jonathan stayed on the streets out of mere choice. He once told Hans and I that he would not trade this life for all the gold in the Queen's vault. Addams could not be persecuted for his brother's desire to execute his constitutional right, however, I could and would hang him for selfishly placing a limited acceptance upon their relationship. I gently removed the Rook from my pocket and placed it deep within the dewy grass. I meticulously rolled the piece several times over to ensure that it had indeed fallen there one week prior. When satisfied, I held the piece above my head and hollered to Jonathan from over my shoulder.

I offered to polish the Rook while Jonathan set up the board. More so out of fear than desire, I did not want Jonathan to be harmed should the mechanism expel prematurely. After five minutes of proper piece handling and cleaning instruction, he left me to it. Using the corner of my knit sweater, I carefully rubbed the piece until its sheen had been restored. Jonathan's mood had improved considerably. He was humming an old Al Bowlly tune as he wiped down the playing table. Addams was due to arrive in less than ten minutes, like a good host, Jonathan wanted to make sure everything was in proper order for his guest of honour. I placed the Rook gently on its allotted square, waiting for its approval. A hard slap to my back along with a low whistle told me I had done an exceptional polishing job.

Leaning against an ancient oak tree, I waited for Addams' arrival. Jonathan was compulsively removing every last spec of dirt from the playing area. I chuckled under my breath as he spat on the seating bench before scrubbing it vigorously with his shirt tail. Once satisfied with its cleanliness, Jonathan took to pacing the grounds. One hand stuffed in his trouser pocket, he solemnly treaded a path between the table and oak tree. By light of the oil lamp, I could see the trodden grass beneath his feet. He mumbled intelligibly, possible chess moves I suspected. On occasion I clearly heard him murmur a single letter coupled with an individual number. My nerves became angst-ridden the closer the hands on my pocket watch drew to ten o'clock. I stared impassively at the tiny golden hands. Time had always fascinated me. How it originated, how it functioned, how we set store by it. It befuddled me how something so minute was relied so heavily upon. Time dictated every second of ours lives. And why? The answer was quite simple; we permitted it to.

Addams strolled into the park at precisely ten. Tonight, he was dressed casually in a v-neck pull over and khaki trousers. His liberally grey streaked hair was tucked under a two-tone brown felt fedora. This attire was a step up from his usual baseball cap, flannel shirt and denim trousers. He and Jonathan exchanged dry pleasantries before taking their respective places opposite one another at the table. No words were uttered during the matches, it was an intense battle of the minds. Each move was recorded by Jonathan on a piece of parchment as the game progressed. Observation was crucial, a skill both brothers clearly had honed. The oil lamp's flames splashed fierce orange light upon the men's faces. Macabre shadows lined their brows and jaw lines, reminding me of old English authoritarians. A sense of importance had swelled around the playing area, as each brother strived to over-reach the other in the pecking order. Jonathan visibly had the upper hand, a position he was well accustomed to. In a series of grandly swept moves, he had confiscated Addams' Knight, Bishop and several Pawns.

Aggravation gushed from the mature serrations on Addams' face. His eyes narrowed and lips puckered as he helplessly watched Jonathan capture his Queen: a severe blow to not only his game play, but ego as well. Being somewhat of a wise man myself, I understood the wanton of excellence and the necessity to always come out on top of everyone else. Sometimes I wonder who we try to convince our intelligence to more, our peers or ourselves.

"Check," Jonathan said smoothly. From my post against the oak tree, I could see the position of Jonathan's Bishop a mere three squares in front of Addams' King. The usual etching of the pencil as he recorded each move could no longer be heard, as it had become drown out by the irritated grinding of Addams' teeth. I estimated the Prime Minister to have only three moves left. From the furious look on his face, he knew such to be true as well. Chewing his lower lip, Addams placed his left thumb and index finger around his King. In a movement so swift, he had single handily switched his King and Rook's position in a desperate, yet illegal attempt to castle.

"YA CAN'T DO THAT!" Jonathan roared. "YA CAN'T CASTLE WHEN YOU'RE IN CHECK! WHAT DO YA THINK YOU'RE DOIN?" Addams' expression was blank as Jonathan laid into him, finger stuck into his chest. "THE RULES DON'T ALLOW FOR THAT, YA SHOULD KNOW. IF THIS IS YOUR WAY OF TELLIN' ME YA GOTTA GO, YA COULDA JUST... WHAT THE—? 'EY! 'EY! WHAT'S— WHAT THE DEVIL?"

The Prime Minister was unresponsive; within seconds he began to sway over the table. His glossy eyes rolled back into their sockets, a white bubbly liquid oozing from the corners of his mouth. Jonathan hurled over the table just in time to feel the fabric of Addams' shirt slip through his scrawny outstretched fingers. Addams had fallen backwards and was seizing violently on the ground.

Although Jonathan's outcries had peaked my interest, they were unnecessary. I was less than four feet away from the Prime Minister when it happened. In the fleeting second it took for him to switch his King and queenside Rook, he had been cut and poisoned. Jonathan, full of anger, erupted prematurely causing for a mini diversion. He never saw the moment's pain upon on his brother's face. For this I was grateful. Each night since Hans' death, I had been haunted by his agonized features. Every time he died, a part of me went with him. Jonathan, being much weaker than myself, would not be able to sustain such torment. Of this, I was certain.

I listened to Jonathan scream in anguish for nearly five min-utes before it struck me—-I was in a park with a vagabond and his now dead brother. His high-ranking politician brother. Jonathan wailed like a child over Addams' limp silhouette. His sobs had begun to attract other tramps from within the depths of the trees.

The old man I saw earlier was the first to investigate. Still sledging his feet, he kneeled next to Jonathan and whispered into his left ear. Jonathan shook his head and flung his arms around the former Prime Minister. Tightening his grip, he wheezed into Addams' chest. "No, no, no, no." He cried. "No! NO!!!"

The old tramp reached out for Jonathan once more. Placing a withered hand on his left shoulder, "We must give him to the Lord my friend. He has departed and we must permit him to go home," the tramp soothed. "His soul no longer belongs here."

Jonathan nodded silently as he ran his fingers dolefully over his brother's pallid face. Addams looked peaceful; the cyanide's rapid effects had closeted any other type of expression. Jonathan removed a handkerchief from his trouser pocket and began to wipe the froth from Addams' lips and chin. Once satisfied with his brother's appearance, he nodded at the tramp. I watched numbly as the old man kneeled before Addams, grasping his right hand. He beckoned Jonathan to take hold of his left. The tramp closed his eyes and looked purposefully to the Heavens.

"Out of my hands and into the Lord's, I release this child of God. Father, please protect him." Releasing Addams' hands, the tramp rose. Clasping Jonathan firmly around the midsection, he pulled him upwards and eased him back onto the bench.

"Do you hear that my friend?" The tramp raised his right arm and pointed through the trees. "Do you hear it? It is help. Help is coming." He consoled Jonathan, "It will not be long now." He continued to pat Jonathan's arm in a nurturing manner. "Not to worry..." he mumbled.

The oil lamp flickered silently before extinguishing. The three of us were left to the shadows. My inner psyche was screaming run, however, my physical being would not render. I remained in the very spot I had been yielding prior to Addams' arrival; even as the light began to penetrate the trees. Several moments of silence passed, a heavy rustle among the thicket told me the law was very close. "Here they come," the tramp whispered. Again, I registered his words, knowing full well that I needed to depart. But here I stood; concrete. Blazing white light was bestowed upon us as a tall shadowy figure bore nearer.

"City of London Police. No-Nobody move." a male voice forewarned. His skittish tone had said it all. He was nothing more than a rookie. Tonight was most likely his first solo patrol. As he approached, my suspicions were confirmed. Less than five yards from us, he dropped his flashlight. In his haste to retrieve it, he fumbled it once more. When he arose, his helmet fell from his head. It bounced slightly, before rolling to a stop directly at my feet. The young officer hesitated before reaching down for it. I stifled a snigger as he placed it back onto his wavy blond hair in perfect position. I eyed him up; he may have been twenty-five, but no more than that. His appearance was very effeminate. His dark navy uniform had been neatly pressed, and his boots were as shiny as diamonds. The kid shone his light from face to face and finally briefly on Addams' cadaver.

Clearing his throat, "What is going on here?" he squawked. His attempt at authority had me quavering silently with laughter.

"It's... it's my brother, Sir." Jonathan pointed to the corpse on the ground.

Giddings stumbled over to Addams and knelt before him. "Sir, I am Officer Giddings. Do you need an ambulance?" He spoke rather loudly. I just about died. This blooming idiot had no idea he was talking to a dead man. "Sir?" he inquired again.

"Errr, Officer...this fellow has departed." The old tramp said softly. Jonathan had begun to lose control once more, pitifully rocking catatonically on the bench.

The puzzled look on the kid's face diminished as he placed his middle and index fingers on Addams' neck. "Bloody Hell!" He shrieked as he sprung to his feet. Dropping his flashlight, he grabbed it anxiously before turning towards the tramp. "This bloke is dead." The tramp inclined his head slightly as confirmation. In an abrupt convulsion, the kid vomited on his own boots. An amusing –yet pathetic– spectacle, I watched as he shook the old tramp off his arm, who had leapt up to aid him.

"I am fine. Please take your seat, Sir." Removing a hand-kerchief from his trousers, he wiped his mouth before turning to face us. His peripherals caught another glimpse of Addams; this time I had to take a step backwards to avoid the fountain of vomit. Instantly the tramp was at his side, a concerned look upon his face. Jonathan, in his own little world, was humming the children's tune "Ring Around the Rosie." This was a perfect opportunity to melt into the shadows. All three men were preoccupied...

Helping the kid to his feet, the tramp patted his arm. "It's alright lad. These things happen. Is this your first night alone?" He soothed.

Why am I still here?

"I said I was fine, Sir. And I don't recall telling anyone they could move." The kid was looking directly at me. Digging a pen and paper out of his jacket, he gulped and stiffened his shoulders. "Now, I am going to need statements from each of you. Nobody is to move until I say so. Got that?"

Get the Hell out of here, my subconscious warned. Grab the piece and go. Like stepping out of a trance, I had instantly become aware of my surroundings. My dormant body had been restarted, and panic had sunk it. My eyes began to scan the area for the Rook. In such little light, I might as well be looking for a glass bead.

"What's his deal?"

Snapping my neck to the left, I focused in on Giddings. He was pointing lazily at Jonathan with the end of his pen.

"The poor man is in shock, I'm afraid." To me, and to everyone else but this kid, Jonathan's behaviour was simple to deduce.

"That man on the ground was his brother." The tramp concluded. I followed his gaze as he rested his eyes momentarily on Addams.

"I see, what is your name?" Another idiotic question. One would think it would be more pertinent to find out who the man on the ground was and why he was in fact dead. I could tell by the tramp's frown that even he thought this Officer Giddings was a complete moron.

"My name is Philips. Rummy Philips" he said shifting on the bench. I can recall seeing him on numerous occasions in the past, but I never knew his name.

"And what are you doing here Mr. Rummy Philips?"

"I sleep in the park, just over there by those rocks." Rummy pointed behind him. "I heard someone yelling, so I came over here to check it out."

"I see. What did you find when you got here?" I had been giving the kid far too much credit. He was hopeless.

"When I got here, Jonathan, that's him" he nodded to his left, "he was yelling and hovering over that poor fellow. He was dead."

"Who are you and what are you doing here?"

It took me several seconds before I realized the kid was talking to me. I had been scanning the ground for the Rook, not really paying attention to anyone else.

"Is he deaf?"

At that exact moment, I found what I was searching for. When the kid shone his light back onto the tramp, I caught a brief glimpse of the piece lingering only inches from Addams' right heel. It took me less than two seconds to devise a plan: grab the damned thing and run.

"SIR, CAN YOU HEAR ME? ARE YOU ABLE TO READ LIPS?" Had it not been for the tight corner I was in, I would have blown up with laughter in the kid's face. Trumping the deaf man part up, I stared off into space.

"Perhaps I should write it down. Do you think he can read?"

I watched from the corner of my right eye as the kid scribbled on his notepad. Seizing this opportunity, I quickly stepped forward, stooped low, and snatched the piece before turning on my heel.

"GET BACK HERE SIR!!! I SAID GET BACK HERE!"

I was mere feet from the thicket when the triumphant grin got wiped off my face. The kid had begun to blow his whistle. I ran full speed into the trees, the high pitched screeching pursuing me. The fool had left Addams, Jonathan and Rummy in the park to chase me. This act of idiocy I had not planned on. I pushed myself through the trees, limbs slapping me mercilessly in the face, jagged rocks causing me to stagger.

"I AM A LAW ENFORCEMENT OFFICIAL. YOU WILL ADHERE TO MY WORDS!" The kid wailed on his whistle. "YOU WILL STOP THIS INSTANT!"

Out of the park and into the street, I continued at breakneck speed. The streets were empty at such an hour; however, the whistle had attracted my fellow vagabonds. Half a dozen men and women emerged from within dumpsters, from under benches, and even from inside unlocked automobiles. Confused, they all gawked in awe as I dashed past them, Officer Moron in my wake. Three kilometres; he was still hot on my heels. I took him down several alleys, through a playground, and into a crowded apartment complex, but I still could not shake him. You have barely gotten started and you've already screwed this up... Fatigue had hit me, nonetheless, I pressed forward. On Baklava Street, the kid aided another patrolman to cut me off at the next block. The plump man was surprised to see me bolt past his outstretched arms, his meagre attempt at a blockade. Idiot, I thought conceitedly. He tore after me, two thirds of a kilometre and he was spent. The kid however, kept on.

I stumbled over a pallet of Global Times newspapers on Schultz Avenue. Laying on my side, I panted fleetingly before I heard the footsteps rounding the corner. Jumping to my feet, I swung out into Arthur Street, a long paved stretch I prayed I could endure. Pushing with everything left in me, I pounded past the eighteenth century shops and boutiques without a moment's thought. A cat darted into my path, my left foot inches from kicking it as I hurtled through the air in an attempt to dodge it. I stumbled into a parked car, setting its security system into a tizzy. Sirens and yellow lights burst into the still night. The same cat hissed at me as I regained my balance and brushed past it. There was no way that alarm was going left unheard. You're finished, my subconscious surmised. Straining forth, I shook my inner-self off. There was an alley near the end of the street which led directly into China Town. God, I hoped my legs could carry me another two kilometres... Daring to look over my shoulder, I saw the kid's blurry figure some five hundred yards behind me. Through all the gasping and pains, I could finally see the ending light. I was almost free...

Freedom, as I soon found out, did not come without a price. Glancing back for but a mere second, my shins collided with something solid, sending me sailing gracefully onto the pavement. Blood trickled onto my tongue; its salty taste instantly nauseating. Wiping my bitten lower lip, I braced myself on what I soon realized to be another pallet of newspapers. Stabbing pain surged from my right ankle up into my thigh the moment I tried to stand. Clutching my leg with both hands, I stepped forward with minimal pressure. Gasping, I gritted my teeth as the pain rocketed through me. Closing my eyes, I leaned against the stack of papers. I couldn't hear the kid's footsteps but I knew he wasn't far. Defeat had begun to creep over me. Like a fish knowing it was hooked, I succumbed to my end.

Chapter 4

Schultz Avenue, London
14 May, 1994

"Are you alright, Sir?" A soft hand clasped my right arm. Alarmed, my reflexes withdrew sending new waves of pain tiding up my leg.

"Please let me assist you," she whispered. Seizing my right arm, the woman gently grabbed my left elbow pulling me upwards. "Up you go," she cooed. There was something very nurturing in her tone. She was strong, yet gentle.

"Come with me, I will get you fixed up. It is not very far." I leaned on her petite frame guiltlessly, as she steadied me.

"Quickly now," she pepped, steering me into a fissure nestled between two shops. She pushed me sideways into the tight space, "Stay here," she commanded softly.

I nodded, but knew she could not see my gesture. All was completely blackened.

Had it not been for the delicate echo of her footsteps, I would have guessed her to still be within arm's reach. Standing alone in a space half the size of a telephone booth, for the first time, genuine fear had surfaced.

Immobilized, I vividly recollected a time in my youth when I had been enclosed in a monumental tomb whilst playing a game of hide and seek with the children in my village. Not my brightest of ideas, however, at the age of six, nothing is usually said or done with much sense. Fighting the urge to panic, I decelerated my breathing and unclogged my mind. Keeping a level head and a steady heartbeat was vital. Anxiety could lead to insanity and near cardiac arrest as I found out some thirty-five years ago. I tightly shut my eyes in an attempt to find my serenity. A place where nothing mattered, a place of peace—complete mental control. Finding such a place never came without great effort. Horrifying memories from my youth resurfaced; from a phobia I was never able to quite shake.

Four slimy stone walls were closing in on me. Thick, musky air poisoned my lungs. Darkness had penetrated my soul. I was alone; fear resonated from every ounce of my being. No one knew where I was. I would never be found. I would never go home again...

Hyperventilation set in within minutes. My chest heaved with force as though my heart was palpitating through the flesh. Scenes from the tomb flashed before me. My childhood-self screaming frantically, digging my bloody fingernails into the resolute stone door. Darkness. Absolute darkness. In the hours that passed, I recall praying. I was too weakened to cry out for help, too lost in my own mind to even attempt to control the tsunami of negative thoughts.

Two grave diggers noticed a child's footprints at the base of an old monument. I was found nine hours after I went missing. Barely breathing, covered in my own vomit and perspiration, I was removed from the crypt and taken to the village doctor. To this day, I struggle to find freedom from that fear.

The woman had yet to return. I found myself praying that she would. She provided me with a comfort which I had assumed was long lost. There was something in her voice which was familiar to me. Even her scent reminded me of a buried past. I concentrated on her mystique; she had appeared from out of nowhere, offered a kind hand. I knew of only one other who would do such a thing. But that person had left me long ago.

Driving footsteps crashed upon my reverie. Arduous breathing and a high pitched whistle soon followed. I held my breath; as still as a ghost ship. Long forgotten were my past's trepidations. Momentarily, the kid would pass directly by me.

Was he aware of this small cavern? Were his senses acute enough to pick up on my presence? Suddenly, I found myself adrift in a sea of potentially new complications. And to think less than one hour ago, I was ready to scoff in his face. I squeezed my eyes more tightly together, straining the muscles in my temples. My crawling flesh told me he was close enough to touch. A blood-curdling whistle pierced my eardrums. I gasped, as the screeching reverberated off the stone walls.

"Do not move, Sir!" The kid hissed. He was wheezing heavily, his second blow much fainter. "I have a weapon and I will use it. Get up! -Slowly get up."

I was booked. The woman had given me a few moments of borrowed time, however, there was no use trying to run now. Using the stone in front of me as leverage, I slowly began to squeeze towards the fissure's opening.

"You there, Sir. Are you listening to me? I said get up off that pallet of newspapers. Now!"

Pallet of newspapers? What the hell was this kid banging on about?

"Oh! Are you talking to me young man?" A syrupy voice cooed. "I am sorry, I heard you saying 'Sir' and well, I thought 'He can't possibly be talking to me.' The woman giggled youthfully.

"Err, sorry Ma'am, I thought you were some... someone else. You haven't seen a man pass by here, have you?" His tone was optimistic. He was holding his desperations in well.

"A man you say? Why yes, I did see a man less than ten minutes ago. He was running rather quickly you see. Knocked me into a car! Just pushed me right into it! Set the alarm off and everything, but he just kept running. Can you believe that? No manners what-so-ever!" *Oh, she was good.* But why was she doing this for me?

"You did see him then?" He was bursting at the seams with excitement. "Fantastic! Which way did he go?"

"Oh, he kept on running down to the end. If you were to ask for my opinion, I think he was heading into China Town."

"China Town? You think so?"

"Yes, I would go there if I was running from someone. Why, wouldn't you?" *I loved this woman. I was completely in love with her.*

"Yes, seems logical. Thank you, Ma'am. Do you need me to whistle for a patrolman to take you to the hospital?"

"How sweet of you child, I will manage fine on my own. Thank you."

"Thank you!" The enthusiastic pounding of his fleeting footsteps ensured he would be chasing a fruitless dead end.

I wasted no time in emerging from the gap. Soon he would find out the woman was mistaken, or that he had been deliberately lied to. Ebbing my way onto the sidewalk, my leg instantly commenced to throbbing. Freedom tasted sweet. Between gulps of fresh air, I graciously muttered a "Thank you" to the woman. Glancing over at the pallet, I was taken aback to discover that I was completely alone.

What had just happened? I knew she was there. I knew what I heard and I knew what I saw. I cranked my neck in frantic search for my saviour, but she was nowhere the seen. Her voice loitered as I limply made my way towards shelter.

....

Utter chaos had broken out in all of England. Former Prime Minister Charles Addams was found dead in a park, murdered it was later confirmed, alongside another unknown man whom had evidently taken his own life. The Officer who had responded to the outcries that evening had been relieved of his duties, as he not only left an unsecured crime scene, but let their only suspect escape. Scotland Yard had taken over the case, and was actively following up on every single tip they were given. A tall, bearded man who may or may not be deaf was their only lead. Statistics show that roughly eight percent of the county's men were tall, deaf men. Over forty-five percent were just tall. It was unknown how many men in the country sported beards.

Re-folding the Times Global paper, I set it haphazardly in the empty seat next to me. In the week that had passed, I managed to elude the police by simply shaving and changing my sweater and trousers. I took shelter in a bed and breakfast on the outskirts of the city, where I left only once to purchase food. My heart ached for Jonathan. He was a beautiful soul, and an incredibly kind person. The loss of his life was a burden I would shoulder indefinitely.

Once my ankle was stable, I set out to purchase supplies. The journey could not stop. I had made a commitment to the Lord, and to myself. Someone had to finish this. Someone had to be the martyr. I was the sufferer for the cause, *our cause*, and in an oddly peaceful way, I was ok with it.

The train pulled into the station, engine hissing as it yielded next to the platform. Shouldering my travel bag, and clutching my freshly forged black market passport, I stepped forth into the queue. Placing my hand in my pocket, I felt the smooth curves of the Rook upon my fingertips. Cradling it lovingly within my palm, I removed it from its hollow. The moment I reached the edge of the platform, I bent low to retie my boot laces. My fingers limply released the piece. Coughing, I barely heard the deadened clink as it fell onto the tracks. Straightening up, I handed the attendant my ticket. He muttered before hitching his thumb over his shoulder. Grasping the rail, I began to climb the steps. Moscow would be unbearably cold; even still for this time of year, but for Hans, I would not surrender.

Chapter 5

Novosibirsk, Siberia
25 May, 1994

The sleeping land of Siberia is a vast region making up over seventy-five percent of Russia, covering approximately ten percent of our planet's total land surface. A tundra belt on the northern tip and a temperate forest region in the south, border the area in the middle consisting of taiga vegetation. This forestry life is one of the largest in the world, and one of only a few which have not been exploited. Rich in oil and natural gas, Siberia also has some of the world's most extensive deposits of lead, gold, nickel, zinc, coal and silver. Agriculture is restricted, leaving a high dependency on the fishing industry. Inhabitants of the south are able to grow barley, potatoes and wheat, owning to the area's textured black soil. A large number of sheep and cattle are also present. Population density is three people per square kilometre. Novosibirsk, the largest Siberian city has an approximate population of one million. There is remote access to its surrounding regions via rail, however the common consensus is to avoid the barren lands at all costs.

Whilst researching in Moscow, I learned that President Golovin had a cabin somewhere close to the northern fringe of Siberia, nestled along a small mountain range. This information was not hard to come by; everyone has a price. In Golovin's case, it was a disgruntled Práporshchik, a Warrant Officer among Britain's Military ranks, whom was quick to bleed out everything he knew. For fifty thousand Rubles, I was given a wealth of information on Golovin as well as his Genéral-Polkovnik and Genéral-Mayór, two men I assumed to be Konstantin and Yuri.

Red Herring

The young Officer had a loose tongue and truth be told, I suspect I could have acquired what I was after without payment.

"Golovin alvays has his Genéral-Mayór and Genéral-Polkovnik vith heim. Vey are mayates vrom hiss chialdhood. Vey are trayend too keil on ve svot. No quezteons axed. Ver iz eh cabeen ne-ear eh svall vountain rahange on ve norfthern teep of Siberia. Golovin iz ver. Eef yu ta-ache ve railvay too Novosibirsk, vrom ver yu caan vind sumvone going norfth. 'Ope yu ar up too hi-iking. Not too vany peepil go eento ve tundra vis vime uf vear. An you vill niheed varmer clofthes...an soop-lies. Vaybee a veam uf dawgs too..."

I did exactly as the Officer had instructed. At a used Military merchandise outlet, I purchased all the survival tools I thought to be pertinent to my excursion, along with a thermal sleeping bag, element withstanding tent, insulated combat boots, and a standard issue Russian service uniform. The Vladimir Lenin look-alike shopkeep spoke no English, and before I knew it, he had thrust half a dozen more items into my already overstuffed backpack. Subsequent to my fervent attempt to decline the items, I yielded my efforts before parting with nearly eighty-five hundred Rubles, and left his establishment. My arms now laden with snowshoes and a floor length fur parka complete with matching ushanka, scarf and gloves. Russian winters were long and bitter for the unprepared. I, being no stranger to the elements, took every measure to ensure that this would be the tropical vacation of my dreams.

....

I stepped onto the platform and squeezed my way down the narrow isle. The locomotive was bustling with people from all over: businessman, tourists, school children, Goths and bar maidens. Adorned in my Service uniform, I fit nicely into the ethnic melting pot. An out-of-tune mix of half a dozen languages caused static in my ears as I placed my backpack in the overhead compartment and began to search for a seat. A teenage girl with multi-coloured hair, wearing cut off denim bottoms over fishnet stockings took no notice to me when I slid into the vacant space next to her. Personal cassette player in hand, she was flailing her head in an untamed fashion to an even wilder conjunction of guitars and percussions. I gathered the high-pitched screeching coming out of her earphones to be vocals of some sort. I watched the sights whilst waiting for the train to take off. My pocket watch declared it to be half past noon. Retrieving my ticket from my left breast pocket, I attempted to find a departure time. After several moments of gazing into incomprehension, I stuffed the stub back into my pocket and resumed watching the passengers board. A flustered looking woman sashaying four small children rushed past me in a frenzy. Her strained bursts of Russian told me she had had better days. An elderly couple were chatting animatedly in the seats directly across from me. I was relieved to hear such English phrases as "The Moscow Kremlin," "Red Square" and "Ostankino Tower." Simply being misunderstood is frustrating in itself; to not understand those around you is completely maddening. I listened to their conversation guiltlessly. It was comforting to know that these South Africans felt the same way I did. The couple were headed to Novosibirsk to meet with their son whom was a missionary living amongst Koryaks somewhere in the Russian far east. I chuckled under my breath when the old woman told her husband he could stick an igloo straight up his arse for even suggesting they venture into Northern Siberia. The old man fired back with a few wise cracks involving her arse and a friendly tousle ensued. They continued to harp on one another until a sombre convoy of a dozen men stormed past us. They were all wearing the same stiff black suit, white shirt and red tie. Their leather shoes all matched as did their heavy black coats. The entire compartment had become aware of their presence, as an eerie silence crept through the already poorly ventilated air. Something sickly hung over the men. They were more than just well-dressed businessmen. Soviet Agents, Assassins, the Russian Mafia... God only knew who they were and what they were involved in. I kept my head on the straight and narrow whilst trying my best to flatten my breathing. The girl next to me was shaking violently, a confirmation that these men could make our beings nonexistent should they so choose. I grabbed her hand and held it tightly. Fear was pulsing through her fragile frame. A roaring hiss startled us both as the pistons decompressed and the train's engine came to life. I closed my eyes and exhaled as the beast slowly began to accelerate.

The men sat in silence; therefore, we sat in silence. I was unaware of how many kilometres we had travelled, had no indication of where we were, and no sense of which direction we were heading. I felt powerless, an emotion that I had always sworn to never relinquish. The girl next to me had fallen asleep with her outlandish tri-coloured head resting on my lap. Upon glancing around the compartment, I noticed that many of the passengers had begun to lean their heads on the windows and seatbacks. I closed my eyes attempting to find sleep, however the dozen "unknowns" behind me kept slumber miles upon miles at bay. I checked my pocket watch; twilight. The most picturesque time. The colours of the ending day melted into those of the beginning night. Always peaceful, it was as though Heaven was offering us a glimpse of what was to come. I watched the celestial transition until a black chasm filled the vast skies...

"Polkóvnik." A firm hand clasped my right shoulder. "Polkóvnik!" A guttural voice urged. I opened my eyes in semi-shock. The compartment was empty, and almost completely blackened. A trail of floor lighting was our only source of light. The young girl still lain in my lap, nevertheless the deep voice had started her awakening process. My eyes adjusted to the shadow next to me: neatly pressed black suit and a flowing trench coat. One of the men from the convoy.

"Novosibirsk." He said before removing his hand swiftly from my shoulder.

I helped the girl into a sitting position before sliding out of my seat. Stretching as much as possible, I lifted my arms upwards to the overhead compartment. A grunt and a nudge to my ribs stopped me short of opening the bin. The man handed me a neon green backpack and shouldered mine before nodding and stomping down the isle towards the exit. I accompanied the girl onto the platform, where she was quick to take her bag before running off. The man stood waiting some six feet away, puffing coolly on a cigarette. I turned towards him uncertain as to what I should expect. The rest of the convoy had dissipated. He was a lone man. If things turned for the worse, I was certain I could overtake him. I looked into his eyes. They were like glass. He reminded me of a young Joseph Stalin, defiant and confident. He nonchalantly handed me my backpack and the snowshoes which I had not noticed tucked under his left arm.

"Polkóvnik." He said once more, before saluting crisply and turning on his heel. I watched dumbfounded as he weaved his way down the platform and out of sight. Confused, I gathered my effects and departed.

....

As a young boy, I can recall hearing musher stories from a bloke by the name of Abooksigun. Known simply as Books by my father and his mates, the Native American grew up in Barrow, Alaska, a small village approximately eight hundred forty kilometres north of the Arctic Circle. Classified as a polar climate, the temperature barely reached ten Celsius and knew no darkness during the summer months. Books was one of Barrow's less than two thousand inhabitants, and one of only a few whom escaped it. Countless times over the last half dozen years, I have recollected his words. *If the cold don't kill a man, the white lands eventually will. I got out while I could, and won't go back for nothing. Nothing.*

A tradesman, Books enjoyed a simple life of hunting and expedition. Unmarried and childless, he spent all his time exploring the Alaskan lands and tending to his team of huskies. His eight canine companions were his lifeline. He said he put more trust into his team than in God himself. *Praying won't get you far out there. In those lands your dog's abilities are your only salvation. A smart team can get you home no matter where you may find yourself. A strong team can pull you from the depths of danger. And a compassionate team can give you joy like no other can. Dogs are like people. They have their own genetic mark-up and their own personas. The people in our lives have been handpicked by us based upon our own individual needs of companionship. In the case of team selection, I like to take that same approach. These dogs will be with me for the next ten to fourteen years, it's important we are able to spend the duration of their life together harmoniously...*

I studied the forty Siberian Huskies from a distance. I looked for all the things Books had said were important: temperament, strength, speed, solid interaction with people and their own kind, and their ability to promptly follow commands. The selection process truly was something to fret over. Each animal had his or her own personality, just as Books had stated, and what I figured would only take me several hours to work out, ended up taking almost two days.

After thirteen trial and errors, I settled on six dogs each whom I was confident could get the job done. My lead dogs were two highly trained twin sister's name Tatiana and Anastasia. Black and white with just a hint of auburn near the buttocks, both girls had unparalleled senses; often obeying commands before they had even been uttered from my lips. A collaboration of speed and endurance were utilized in selecting my swing dogs. I choose two marathon males, a red and white named Fedir and Lev, a particularly antsy black and white. I marvelled at their speed; it was like watching lightning. Within seconds they completed a hundred metre dash. Their endurance seemed supernatural, as they ran for hours showing no hint of fatigue. These boys were my pacesetters. Pasha and Pavel completed my team. Not the smartest in the lot, but these two auburn wheels had more individual strength than the rest of the team put together.

    With my team in hand, I set to work on my skills as a Musher. Five tries to get the dogs in their harnesses and another half dozens attempts to tie the gang lines together, I had accomplished the initial stage of mushing; preparing the team. Books' wealth of information made the process somewhat easier, although things such as this are always easier said than actually done. I rigged the toboggan in place, trying to recall why Books had said it was important to use this particular sleigh. Something to do with floating and deep snow came to mind... After placing my bags and snowshoes in the bed of the sleigh, I stood on the runners protruding out the back of it. I checked the braking system, in this case, a series of hooks attached to the sled via a rope. I prayed that I would not have to utilize them. Nonetheless, I prayed even harder that they would be functional. Grinding down on the sleigh's wooden handle, I inhaled deeply before barking a firm "Hike!" at my team. In less than a second they sprung to life, and I relaxed considerably as we began to glide gracefully across the white open lands.

    In two days' time, we had covered nearly five hundred kilometres. The days were depressingly long; the nights far worse. A cold front had moved in, dropping the temperature into the sub zeros. My team lay buried under two feet of snow, resting peacefully after a hard day's labour. After sixteen hours, four patch jobs, and a too close for comfort encounter with a territorial Siberian

Tiger, we stopped to set up camp; our final destination less than one hundred fifty kilometres north of us. The dogs had proven their worth; obeying my every command, and pushing themselves forth despite the sudden and often drastic change in the elements. I struggled more-so then they. I was accustomed to glacial climates, however, nothing compared to these unforgiving lands. Deceptively beautiful, this place was an alluring chocolate box. Soothing mountain ranges, glistening seas of white...Peaceful calm such as this was in a class all of its own, and how quickly I fell prey to the land's divine masquerade.

Captivated by the wonders around me, I had forgotten where I was and what purpose I was intended to serve. A mistake for the weak and inexperienced, I placed myself and my team within harm's clutches. Emerging from a Devil's playground pass on the northern fringe some nine hours prior, I permitted my emotions to overtake my senses, sending us into the hallow of a patiently waiting tiger. The beast barred his teeth whilst emitting the ghastliest roar. In the second it took for me to yell a commanding right turn, "Gee!" the cat had pounced. His agility was astounding, but not honed enough to outrun six severely frightened canines. Once we had what I felt was a wide enough girth, I slowed the team to a more reasonable speed, vowing to give the land the attentiveness it required...

Eight kilometres out, I smelled smoke. The final leg of the trip had taken nearly nine hours, as we found ourselves venturing across a vast ice field. Using the fan hitch for safety, I rigged the lines side-by-side, distributing the weight evenly. Books had told us many stories of impatient men whom had chosen not to implement safety procedures, but rather push their teams across the fields as quickly as possible. *Better safe than dead. In the two by two position, if one goes down, they all go down. Fanning them out when you are in weaker spots will keep the rest afloat should one slip into the cracks. Speed is for racing, not for expeditions or uncharted areas. Any fool should know that, but I suppose there are just some idiots who have to be idiots. Shame about the dogs though, they put as much trust in us as we do in them.*

At twilight I anchored the dog's lines into the ground and strapped on my snowshoes. I would be walking from here. Uncertain as to what Golovin may or may not have, I decided it would be wise to leave the dogs behind. Although travelling on foot would leave tracks, I was confident there would be no one following me back to the base camp.

....

The dimly lit cabin was less than what I had anticipated. Much less. It was squat and boxy, with a single window and crooked front door. Its spruce exterior was in shambles, many of the boards were warped, others had been poorly patched with an inferior grade lumber. Multiple footprints wound around the cabin onto a trail baring due east where a thicket of large trees congregated. Three snowmobiles were parked alongside the cabin's west wall, a timber pile a few feet from them. I cautiously approached the window and whilst stooping low, raised my head to peer inside. Laughter erupted from the corner of the room, where I saw the figures of three men sitting. Straining my eyes through the grimy glass, I watched as Golovin, Yuri and Konstantin played cards, a thick cloud of grey smoke hanging over them. They appeared to be currently unarmed and very much sauced. Empty bottles of vodka lined the floorboards beneath their feet. I studied them. From this distance they were like regular men. Just three mates relaxing over a game and enjoying imported cigars. I saw neither hatred nor arrogance upon their faces; they bore no signs of merciless executioners. Anyone whom stumbled upon this scene would have thought them to be expedition guides or friendly hunters. As normal as they seemed, I knew what they were and what they had done. I would not leave this land until they were dead.

....

The vodka ran dry after four hours. Heavily in the bottle, Yuri stumbled to the north wall, where he loaded the fireplace with more timber. Konstantin grabbed Golovin's left arm in an attempt to pull him off his chair, however, he also had had too much to drink and fell to the floor, leaving the President to gather himself. Golovin hoisted himself up, and using every object as a brace, he half walked, half crawled to the cot located on the east wall. Via a small miracle, Yuri managed to snuff all the lanterns before getting into bed himself. Konstantin remained sprawled on the floor as though he was adding to the room's décor. The only source of light came in the form of a soft glow from the cabin's fireplace. The dancing flames cast obscure shadows upon the walls, as though instructing me to what needed to be done.

Siphoning fuel from a half ton piece of steel without a hose was no easy feat. Almost impossible actually. Stealthily entering the cabin, I was able to find a large copper pot which would serve as a vapour collector. Yuri and Golovin were snoring heavily; Konstantin had swapped his place on the area rug for the spare cot. The floorboards sagged under my weight as I tiptoed towards the exit. I grasped the doorknob just as a raspy wheeze omitted from Golovin's bunk. My heart started and I dropped the pot, causing a dull thud to echo across the room. Frozen, I flattened myself against the wall in hopes that I had not aroused any suspicions. Konstantin rolled over, a quarter of his large frame hung over the edge of the tiny mattress. Releasing all the air in my lungs, I gently opened the door and took off towards the snowmobiles. The sky was crystal clear, too clear for what I was about to do, nonetheless,

I was determined to be rid of the President and his henchmen tonight.

Tipping the snowmobiles onto their sides was the easy part. Maintaining a steady position of the copper pot whilst tilting the machines as needed, was a bit more involved. After spilling half the gasoline out of the first one, I decided to take a short break to brainstorm. Fuel was what I needed, so it was imperative that I waste none. Dropping to my hands and knees, I used one of my snowshoes to dig a hole roughly the same diameter of the pot. I gently placed the basin into the hole before commencing where I had left off. I heard the gushing of the gasoline and the patter as it fell into the pot. *Success.* Within twenty minutes I had emptied the contents of all three tanks. Once I had removed the pot from its enclosure, I began to line the cabin's outer walls with the spare timber. Using half the fuel, I saturated the wood before entering the cabin once more.

All was quiet as I spread the gasoline near the cots, window, on the area rug, by the door and on the small pile of wood next to the fireplace. Opening the iron door, I used the ash shovel to scoop out the embers. I filled the pot to the brim, the vapour residue ignited briefly. One of the men grunted and mumbled something incomprehensive, but I ignored him. I needed to work fast. Starting from the south wall, I dropped several embers near, but not on the places I had covered with gasoline. I left the cabin, and quickly pushed the first snowmobile I came across up against the front door. Blockades such as this were necessary to keep the cabin's contents restrained. Under the window, I dumped liberal amounts of embers. The timber ignited instantly creating six foot high flames. Their second exit had been sealed. I spread the rest of the pot's contents, watching in a stoned-faced awe as the cabin became consumed by bright orange flames. The entire area surrounding me was lit up as though it were the middle of the day. The snow was a magnificent shade of peach; had it not been for the

nature of this mission, I would have enjoyed watching the flames'
metamorphosis. It was not long before the outcries, screaming and
banging started. I could hear the men pounding on the door, and
the shattering of the window pane. *Such a horrible way to die* I
thought to myself. Alas, this is what men such as they deserved.
They were merciless, and that fact sustained me as I listened to their
insufferable cries. Twenty minutes, the calm had returned and the
sleeping lands were so once more.

Upon returning to base camp, I found one of my dogs dead,
one missing and the remaining four injured. The ground was
splattered with crimson, soft whimpers were coming from a heart
broken, mauled over Tatiana. Anastasia lain by her side, rigid. Lev
had sustained injuries to his neck and snout, nothing serious. Fedir,
on the other hand, was bleeding out large amounts from his right
side. He along with Pavel, whom suffered an injury to his left ear,
were laying on what I soon realized was a half dead Siberian tiger:
the same tiger that had attempted to dethrone me three days prior.
It had tracked us to this point. I was amazed to see the beast go to
such lengths. The scenario began to play out before me. He most
likely killed Anastasia first, she was weaker. Lev, Fedir and Pavel
took him on and eventually brought him down. The mystery of
Pasha was soon solved as I found him curled up in my tent like a
scared child. He was unscratched, and would not leave my side as I
tended to Fedir. Pavel was content to have his single wound
cleaned by Tatiana, so I let him be and took to cleaning Lev up.
The cat's breathing was slow and calculated. There was a wild look
in his eyes, as though he was challenging me to touch him. I knelt
down and placed my hands around his velvety orange mane. A low
sigh came from within him. Sixty pounds of torque on his neck
and I whispered, "Sorry my friend." His glassy yellow eyes bore
lifelessly into mine.

The six of us made it back to Novosibirsk without any further incident. Fedir completed the journey in the sleigh, while the

others did what they could to get us back home safely. They were all broken by the loss of one of their own. I had never seen such shattered emotion come from an animal as I saw in Tatiana. Her ability to obey commands had weakened, as she often tried to backtrack to the place where I buried her sister and the cat. Lev and Pavel were my rocks; they kept plunging further and further and harder and harder. Pasha was now scared of his own shadow, and as I found out come nightfall, the dark as well. From six in the evening through to dawn, he never left my side. Sleeping in the tent, he whimpered as he strained to hold his bladder until the daylight hours. Several times I had attempted to tie him up, but he gnawed right through the leather leads, whining near the tent's opening until I permitted him to enter. I supposed an experience such as the one he endured would trigger any man's trepidations, however, he was clearly milking it for all it was worth. But I could not be mad at him. The fearful child buried deep within me most likely would have done the same thing.

Ten full days had passed since I left the city. The Turek I rented the team and equipment from was waiting for us. Before I could jump off the sleigh, he was unrigging the gang lines. Tatiana, Pasha, Pavel and Lev clamoured around the old man and began to howl as though they were in agony. His bony hands weaved lovingly through their manes in an effort to calm them. I cradled Fedir in my arms, he was severely weakened, but showing slight signs of improvement with each new dawn. Patting me solemnly on the back, the old man took Fedir from my arms and turned his heel.

"I—I— It was a—tig—tiger," I sputtered. "He is dead now." Close to tears, I watched benignly as the man and his dogs disappeared into his small cabin. I was not sure if I should follow, so I waited for him to return. He never emerged. Quavering, I gathered the last of my effects before heading back to the rail station.

Red Herring

Chapter 6

High winds and violent rain pounded the exterior of the Leiko. No longer did she glide with the grace of an ice dancer, but rather rocked unsteadily as though she had two left feet. Her prominent bow swayed weightlessly across the open seas as forty foot swells engulfed her stern. Stunned, she helplessly plummeted into the depths of the cold dark waters, regaining her balance but for a few minutes before plunging into the deep once more. Her entire three hundred fifty-six meter skeleton was submerged, the roaring of iron on iron was drowned out by the thunderous winds and rain from above. Her crew had long since abandoned her. Lifeboats were capsized in the distance. The fierce waves hurled them effortlessly thirty feet into the air; like they were made of flimsy pieces of cardboard. Her precious cargo was lost. The fifteen, twenty foot containers would be salvaged some time later, however too late, as their contents would have already suffered a dark and painful death.

....

Skiing was not my forte. In fact, I despised winter and anything connected to it. I disliked such mundane things as snowmen, tobogganing, hot cocoa, fur boots, even Christmas had lost its appeal. To me, these things meant colder weather, which meant heaps of snow and layers of ice; winds that would chill the bone and dampness that you could never quite shake off. Just thinking about it made me cringe...So why New Hampshire in the dead of winter? Had I lost my mind? For months I had been weighing my options: Three men, one shot versus the elements and of course, the risks. Everything about it was potentially problematic. Killing three people at the same time was a task in itself. Throw the weather, security, the public and my own trepidations into the mix, and I was quite sure I had concocted a recipe for disaster. My subconscious was screaming *Run! Take your time, separate them. It would be easier.* And I was certain it would be. Nonetheless, I could not force myself to regret or alter my decision–at least, not yet.

New Hampshire: known for its wealthy grandeur and historic significance, affluence flocks from every corner of the globe. Diplomats, actors, governors, industrialists... They were drawn to its seclusion, to its mystic, to its social symbolism––an epitomic sliver of paradise. Its inhabitants found themselves under the most beautiful horizons surrounded by a backdrop of astonishing landscapes. The widespread forestry and mountains, although rugged, were nature in its raw form. Evergreens and spruce trees that could have been rooted since the beginning of time towered over all else. Their branches sagging under the weight of the incandescent snow. Ranges encased by white stood self-righteously against the bright blue skies taut and proud as though protecting those beneath them. Bright sunlight cast divine reflections upon the glistening rivers and streams and wispy mist danced across the open plains. As magnificent as it was, the air was still bitter, as were the devilish winds. Shivering manically, I meandered through the streets. If the rest of me did not regret this, I knew my fingers and toes would.

The cargo ship which sank near the Bering Strait was said to be housing fifteen containers full of exotic plants, fruits and vegetables. After releasing eight containers in Fremantle, Australia, the next port of call was logged Anchorage, Alaska. The remaining containers would be dropped off, six of which would be exported into British Columbia, Canada. The remaining nine would stay on United States territory. Minor suspicions arose within the World

Trade Organization (WTO), when a General Agreement on Tariffs and Trades could not be located between the country of export, Japan, and the three countries of import. However, in the weeks following the ships' demise, a document signed by Takada Honjo Nakamura, Robert J. Redding, Pierre Gervais Moreau and Baradine Thompson surfaced, thus silencing the stir that perhaps something more sinister was aboard the ship. No one ever questioned how this vegetation could grow or survive the extreme temperatures of such northern climates. And no one ever questioned why the ships' crew had logged into Port Anchorage, however, their whereabouts thereafter became unknown.

As each country defended their trade practices, rumours continued to hit the tabloids. Illicit drugs and alcohol were being smuggled in. Prohibited weapons and knives were the general consensus. The Global Times, a British Newspaper, had gone as far as to stake a claim that Nakamura was exercising population control by selling children as slaves. An informant told a Japanese reporter, who in turn sold the story to the Times, that he had first hand knowledge of Takada's misdeeds. He claimed to have given the crew of the Leiko the order to abandon ship when it became apparent she was going down. He said the crew did not know of the container's contents. He instructed the men to leave the ship and save themselves. He assured them the Japanese government would take care of everything. They would salvage the ship and burden the cost of the lost cargo. The men did as instructed. Some time later they were found drifting in open waters by the United States National Guard. The men were picked up and taken to Anchorage, where pending immediate medical attention, a full report was filed. Everyone was released within seventy-two hours, but by direct orders from Takada himself, they were to be executed immediately before the WTO could formally question them. The crew of the Leiko never made it out of Alaska. The bodies of thirteen men now lay within the crevices of a vast glacier field.

Isolated, their families would never know what happened to them. A few short weeks after telling his story, the informant disappeared off the grid as well.

I was not keen on the idea of participating in winter activities. For weeks I had been trying to develop a more suitable plan-- an indoor plan. However, the only time Redding, Moreau and Thompson were together was when they met on the slopes. They stayed at different hotels and enjoyed varying tastes in cuisine. For a mere four hours each evening they would ride the chairlifts together, up to the top of Loon Mountain. Redding and Moreau were seasoned skiers, as their tempered climate permitted many months of practice. Thompson's squat frame could be seen lopping haphazardly down the slopes. He would remain uprooted for a few yards before his body reached its vertical limited. He would then cascade down the rest of the mountain in a jumbled mix of snow and metal. Leaning on my ski poles, I watched as he tried his hand at snowboarding. He was a disaster waiting to happen. Somehow his boot came loose as he tried to curve his body downwards into the slope. He managed to glide on his left foot momentarily before falling face first into the snow. In his attempt to regain his balance, he ended up losing the board completely. Still unable to stand properly, he collapsed allowing himself to roll down the mountain, only stopping when he became entwined with some bushes. I laughed uncontrollably, in my mind of course, as he lay there looking like a sausage covered in flour. Red in the face, he abruptly stood looking around sheepishly for witnesses. Redding and Moreau shook their heads in disgust as they came to a perfect halt at the end of the course. I would have given Thompson an eight out of ten just for entertainment purposes.

The diplomats' time on the slopes was supposed to be privatized. The mountain was shut down from eight to midnight each evening, enabling the comrades to enjoy the activities and one another's company without interruption. Security patrolled the perimeter of the peak along the tree line, however, even they were instructed to keep their distance. Nestled at the top of the mountain, a small station sat perched with a lone medical technician inside. Her duties were to watch the slopes for signs of injury. Should someone require her assistance, she would leave her post to assist them. I watched her from afar, rarely did she leave. She seemed bored by the happenings below. She watched benignly as Baradine Thompson fell on his arse night after night. I was fairly certain I could manipulate her into leaving her post. It was obvious she was itching for some action.

Overall, the three men were an odd assortment. At first sight, it was evident something was out of place. They did not fit together. President Redding's firm, arrogant nature and Prime Minister Moreau's professional, business-like mannerisms. Then there was Prime Minister Thompson; he was constantly out in left field. A close friendship was unlikely. In fact, it took me two minutes to sort out the who's-who roles they silently attempted to conceal. It was strictly a business relationship. All three were in the same trade, and I expected a vacation such as this would never have occurred had it not been for the loss of their cargo, and the rumours orbiting it. Redding and Moreau had close ties, as the United States and Canada dealt so closely with one another. Cordiality between the men was to be accepted, however, the closeness they portrayed here was simply incongruous. And Baradine Thompson? His hippie appearance, coupled by his space cadet tendencies; his own mother would be ashamed to be in his presence. Everything he touched crumbled to pieces. He was both politically and socially rejected by the entire United Nations. Ties with Australia had been cut based upon his inability to grasp concepts beyond one plus one equals two. Some countries, such as New Zealand, merely distanced themselves to ensure they would not be bound by the same rope. I suppose a laissez-faire attempt at running a nation may work. If, of course, that nation was the planet Pluto, and its inhabitants were all butterflies and pixies. Redding and Moreau could not stand the sight of him. Their noses were always upturned and their lips curled into an aghast sneer whenever Thompson's back was turned. It was quite clear he was the lowest of beings in their opinion.

Robert Jonas Redding ran the gamut. Dominant on sheer principle, the fifty-six year old from Greenwich, Connecticut grew up within the political ring. Five generations of Reddings had served in the Senate, Robert being the first to infiltrate the White House. A Yale graduate by chartable contributions, he always knew that his name would carry him anywhere. He served under the Eisenhower Administrations before being forced into the United States Military by his father and grandfather in nineteen sixty. Eight years, and several mysterious, yet overlooked absences later, Redding received an Honourable Discharge and a few medals for his services. He married a socialite from New England, and quickly produced two children. In nineteen seventy-seven he joined the ranks of the republicans once more, where he quickly climbed his way up the political ladder. Everything was effortless, as his family's name commanded such high respect. What he could not attain based upon his bloodline, he paid handsomely for. To this day, it is uncertain how much money his family shifted from their pockets into the hands of others to secure the White House.

Egotistical and arrogant, Redding prized himself on being "the most handsome and most in-shape President these United States have ever seen." His six-foot-one build was firm and toned. His square jaw line was always clean shaven and wrinkle free. A natural dirty blonde, Redding had been dying his hair jet black for years upon the ignorant opinion that a tall, dark and tanned man is what a woman truly wants. He frequently cheated on his wife. Affairs which she knew about, yet remained tied to him for monetary reasons. His children did everything in their power to dislodge themselves from him. *Mr. Perfect* as they called him, visited thrice per year, always smiling for the cameras whilst coddling his Grandchildren whom he knew nothing about, nor cared to know. They despised him for what he had become, and their mother for condoning it. But of course to the whole of America, the family was happily divided, as each child wanted to embark on his or her own journey.

At which point Redding entered into unforgivable sin with Moreau, Nakamura and Thompson is unknown. His reasoning for doing so was also murky and irrelevant to my cause. I cared not for the logic, but the act itself. Nakamura had some sort of lien on Redding. Perhaps the technology field, or automotive industry. None of that mattered to me anyway. Pierre Moreau was a coward whom shadowed everything Redding did. Canada was not run by the frog, but by the movements of the United States. Redding lapped it up, enjoying the intimidation he invoked on others. Moreau felt that his country needed the United States to survive. Trade, imports and exports; the U.S. was a vital thread to the livelihood of those in the north. Always very professional, Moreau was a kind, courteous, respectful leader. Had it not been for his lily-livered approach towards the United States, he would have been a model diplomat.

Pierre was a family man, his Roman Catholic background had instilled the highest of morals in him. He cradled Canada in his hands as though it were his child; shaping and moulding her into the prosperous, proud country he knew she could be. Moreau was well liked. He had created ties with Russia and China; ties that no one thought possible. He was having peace talks with Iran and Croatia, and it was reported that things were going well between the countries. He laboured vehemently for globalization. His goal was to bring every country up to par. Increase the standard of living, provide everyone with the same opportunities. A far cry some thought, but nonetheless, his efforts were to be admired. Redding would rather exploit the third world's resources before building a wall and drowning them all. As strong a leader as he was, Moreau could not shake the influence of Redding. Every stone remained unturned until he consulted the United States President. Every decision was made by Redding, tailored towards *his* leadership and *his* country. Moreau was spineless, and he deserved whatever fate he may meet.

What started out as a joke, a bit of fun in the eyes of some of Australia's politicians, ended up being the country's worst nightmare. His wardrobe and hair style were twenty years too late. His ideals were foolish and implausible. He was fat, awkward and in most cases dim-witted. He was Baradine Bradey Thompson, and he was Australia's leader. Known throughout the Cabinet as the "Jester," his childlike ways and blatant disregard for his own personal appearance had labelled him an oddity. A misfit whose family name had secured his future, Thompson was a free spirited nitwit, and *he* thought nothing different of it. While the rest of the country was loathing his very existence, he was out wheeling and dealing with Mongolia and Greenland. His schemes never benefited Australia, in fact they just further landed the country in debt and tarnished its good name.

During a warming period in the early nineteen nineties, Baradine decided to cool the country's more popular beaches and lakes by importing ice from Greenland. It cost the Australian economy over one billion dollars, and the cooling affects were nonexistent. In nineteen ninety-three, he imported three dozen Eurasian Wolves from Mongolia to help control the population of black and brown rats. Although he assured his countrymen that the wolves would be unable to breed, "things happen," as he called it, and now the shores of Melbourne and Sydney were frequented by packs of carnivorous canines. One can imagine how something as scandalous as buying Japanese children would be pinned on Baradine Thompson. His idiotic past had fit the bill to a tee.

Impersonating security personnel would be all too easy. The black attire, ear piece, boots and can of mace could be found at any sporting goods store. The hip holster as well, however, I was having difficulties with the firearm. I was uncertain as to what they carried, and was resigned to just going without one. I would be under cover of darkness anyway. The slopes were faintly lit, but the trees around them were nearly a pitch-black void. I was confident I could take my place near Thompson's favourite landing bush without being seen. He would be first. That was the only thing which was set in stone. Baradine was a wanderer, he did his own thing and was not particularly aware of his surroundings. A strange accident would not be questioned. At least not by Redding or Moreau, they would be silently thanking those responsible.

After days of contemplating and nights of sleeplessness, I decided to go in blind. No weapon, no mace, I would work with what I had. My own attire would have to suffice, and my prayers would have to sustain me. I had spent nearly a thousand dollars on food, transportation and mountain passes. Coupled with the eleven hundred American dollars for the flight over, I could not justify any unnecessary expenses. I had only just begun. So much more was in store for me, it would be foolish to exhaust my finances so early. Truth be told, I was worried about whether or not I would be able to complete this journey. It was not going to be like checkers. I could not simply jump from one country to the next. There were so many hidden expenses that I had not really thought about; so much time that would be wasted away in between targets. Conservation was going to supersede all else.

....

The basement of the old church was dreadful. The single kerosene heater had burnt out just past midnight, leaving myself and twenty-nine others inside a dungeon of frigid air. Frost rose off the cement foundation and seeped through the brick walls. The thread bare blankets did nothing to take the edge off, only expose us further. I lay curled up into a small ball, numb. My rime breath was short and laborious. I had spent the day on the slopes plotting my coordinates and double checking the security features. Hungry, frostbitten and tired, I trudged my way through flurries and rain to the church I had been calling home. A community outreach organization, the congregation did what they could for those in need. They supplied and prepared meals thrice per day, and had converted half of the basement into lodging quarters. Thirty steel cots had been placed in the room, each complete with a pillow, fitted sheet and wool blanket. There was no heat or electricity, however the room served its purpose by providing shelter from the elements. Stagnantly cold, I would rather be curled up in a bed with the chills, than on the snow covered ground. I was grateful for their hospitality.

Each night brought the same song and dance. I would toss and turn for several hours, unable to sleep despite being wholly exhausted. At times I would slip in and out of consciousness, but only to be waken by the creaking of a mattress as its occupant rolled over, or by the cries of cold, hungry children. The resigned breathing of my neighbour was heartbreaking. She had spent the last three nights in the cot next to mine. Her gray hair was matted and filthy. Her trousers were frayed, their original colour unknown. She wore a men's tan leather jacket and tennis shoes which looked as though they had once been a dog's chew toy. Deep grooves were embedded into her face, her finger tips were black with frostbite. She had not left the cot since she first arrived. She never ate or drank anything. The look in her eyes was submissive. I had seen that look before. It had been some time, but I knew that unbreakable, glassy stare of hopelessness. I could not mistake the eyes of someone begging for death.

....

"So *what* exactly do you propose we do about our little problem?" A curt, clipped voice inquired impassively. "I cannot be implicated in such an atrocity. If my cabinet ever uncovered any of this..." His voice trailed away as the men trekked towards the chairlifts. I followed, slinking through the trees, closer to the shadowy figures I knew to be Redding and Moreau.

"I suppose we *could* dispose of him," Moreau continued. "What with all the predicaments he gets himself into, no one would question an accident sustained abroad. I know a man whom could do it quietly. With no mess," he added reassuringly.

I strained my ears as the two men clamoured onto the chairlifts. Impeded by the thinning trees, I could go no further. Although night had blanketed itself around us, luminous moonlight was cast upon the snow-covered slopes. They were alone tonight, as Thompson was recovering from the minor injuries he sustained the previous evening.

Once situated, I watched Redding lean his billowing frame towards Moreau's.

"I too know a guy Pierre. Do not worry my friend, I have already made the necessary arrangements. He will be here in two days time." Distaste flowed in his words, menace flickering within his eyes. Redding slumped back into his chair before casually releasing the lift's start lever. I watched the pulleys strain as Redding and Moreau began to slowly ascend out of sight.

Chapter 7

Lincoln, New Hampshire
11 February, 1995

Two days. I had a mere forty-eight hours to execute three deaths. Rationale told me to let Redding and Moreau deal with Thompson. Nonetheless, my sentiments would not allow Baradine's death to be on any terms but my own. He would die for the atrocities he had committed, not as a means for keeping them buried.

Sleep had abandoned me. The church basement had been transformed into an arctic Hell. A paradox in itself, however, there was no other way to describe it. I tried for hours to rest, yet it evaded me. I stared wide-eyed into the darkness, listening to the gasps and wheezes coming from my neighbouring cots. Redding's words were all I could think about. I have already made the necessary arrangements. He will be here in two days time... I had no sense of what I was going to do. No direction what-so-ever. My mind struggled to find some sort of an epiphany–a kernel of inspiration I could quickly mould into a reality. I was tired and frustrated, a useless combination when one is trying to get things accomplished. Alas, rendering my plight for slumber, I threw back the blanket and sat upright on the edge of the cot. The icy stone floor engulfed me, sending insufferable chills up my legs into my spine. Deciding a walk may warm me up, I waded through the sea of cots. Silence wafted among their occupants, nevertheless, I knew every person in the room to be wide awake.

The church had to be pushing three hundred years old. Its handsomely hued rosewood flooring groaned under the weight of my feet, the cracked stained glass rattled violently against even the slightest of breezes. The concrete walls were crumbling in places, as the many fills and patches no longer withstood the hands of time. I walked swiftly down the aisle, quivering as cold air descended from the rafters. At the head, Christ was elegantly displayed before me. High above all else, His limbs nailed to a bronzed cross; the sacrifice He bestowed upon us. I kneeled before my Creator, allowing His aura to consume me. My grace through faith in Him had carried me to this point as I knew it would. I thanked Him for His sacrifice, for blessing me with this body, and I prayed in repentance of my sins. I asked for guidance, a nudge towards which path I should take. He would shed light, He had yet to fail me. I need not look for His sign, it would show itself when the time was just.

The wind howled like a caged beast as I continued to wander throughout the church. Walking kept me warm, for which I was grateful; yet my prowling activities did nothing for my insomnia. I tested my faith by entering the landing which led up to the second story balcony. From below, I could tell it was not in use. I was positive it was mostly out of fear, the stone support pillars had large chunks missing from them, and the wooden guardrail was severely damaged, splintered in two in some places. I climbed the deteriorating stairs, praying my foolishness would not get me killed. Three steps from the top, I heard a snap as my right foot sank below my left. Splinters jabbed into my ankle as I manoeuvred my foot out of the hole. I clutched the railing to steady myself before leaping onto the topmost step. With that heart stopping jolt, I vowed to pay more attention. The Lord overseas all, but He cannot save the stubbornly injudicious. There is such a thing as fool's faith...

My footsteps were muffled by layers upon layers of dust, at least six inches of it. Each step caused it to stir around me, within seconds asphyxiation had begun to set in. Coughing into my sleeve, I peered at the open space before me. A lone pew was propped against the wall to my right. To my left, a dozen or so boxes lain haphazardly upon the floor. An even thicker layer of dust covered them. Moth eaten robes hung limply from a coat rack behind me. Shabby and discoloured, it was difficult to determine which century they hailed from. A frieze of The Last Supper had been spectacularly painted on the wall directly in front of me. Christ and His Apostles glistened extraordinarily despite the dim light. I eased towards the mural, raising my hand to Christ's beautiful face. It felt warm; comforting. I studied the image. The look of surprise in Andrew, Bartholomew and James, son of Alphaeus' eyes...The unmistakable anger etched upon Peter's face... Philip's yearning for an explanation... All in response to Christ's claim that one of the twelve men would one day betray Him. This painting was not just a mere image of fine brush strokes and primary colours, but of something far more consequential. It depicted real emotion--hatred, jealousy, revelation, sorrow. Feelings even Christ himself could not restrain. History had painted some of the Apostles to be almost as perfect as Jesus. Always divine, never an ill-wisher, or seeker of things they could not attain. They were humble, kind and of pure thoughts. I marvelled at how time and time again we continued to only see what we wanted to see. How we forced ourselves to believe that divinity meant purity. In truth, no one, not even the keepers of the Kingdom could escape the realm which housed our deepest, most desperate desires. I smiled blissfully. Christ's men were only just that, men.

I could not shake the mural. I was uncertain why, but for some unknown reason, I felt as though I was supposed to find significance within it. Sitting cross legged on the balcony, I stared benignly from face to face, searching. I did not know what I was searching for, but it had to be there. It just had to be. The tranquillity of the space made for peaceful thinking. And it was surprisingly warm. I had not taken immediate notice to the change in atmosphere. My skin was balmy, my knitted sweater and twill trousers encased my body like a furnace. My initial reaction was I was catching the flu. Wonderful. Just what I needed now. I had but a mere thirty-one hours left. This was not a good time for my immune system to go into hibernation.

I was floating up the stairs leading to the balcony. My right foot sank into the third stair from the top. Releasing it, I supported my weight on the railing and glided gingerly onto the landing. The room before me was spacious. I took notice to a single pew, some dozen boxes, and a coat rack housing old fashioned robes. Curiously, I drifted towards the robes.

"No." A voice was telling me. "Those are not what you seek." I wanted to make my way to the edge of the balcony, to peer down at the scene below.

"No you do not," the voice said. "Keep searching." I was confused. What was I looking for? The pew, boxes and robes were all that were here. What else is there? I wanted to leave.

"But you must not," the voice urged. Ignoring it completely, I turned to leave. One step towards the landing and I had become frozen. Literally. I peered down at my feet in horror. They were firmly set into heavy blocks of ice. A cold like no other swept over me. I tried to move, but was rooted to the spot. I gasped in horror at the white glass sheathing my legs. Ice was ascending to my knees. Slowly, everything was turning numb.

"You asked for my guidance."

I don't know what I'm supposed to be looking for! What is it you want me to find? Please, I beseech you... you're killing me.

"I would never harm one of my children." An invisible hand cranked my neck sideways. My eyes locked onto a painting– Leonardo da Vinci's 'The Last Supper'. I optimistically scanned the life-like figures of Jesus and His Apostles, but found nothing extraordinary. I sighed, this is just a mural. I have seen it thousands of times.

"You are not looking hard enough." But his words of encouragement were not necessary, I had found what I was searching for. Two seats to Jesus' left sat Thomas the Greater. The claims of one of the Apostles' betrayal had clearly stunned him. His face bore a grave shock and his arms were raised in the air in what appeared to be disbelief. In fact, his index finger was pointing straight upwards... I tilted my head towards the rafters, seeing for the first time an enclosed scuttle hole.

I was not frozen to the floor, but I was still cold. There were no blocks of ice and there was no voice. Or was there? It was a dream. Just a dream I rationalized. There had been no revelation from Christ. He had not penetrated my mind, nor had He solidified me to the floor. I had simply fallen asleep whilst staring pointlessly at the da Vinci painting. Frustrated, I leapt to my feet. Dawn was approaching and I did not want to be caught roaming part of the church which I was not permitted. As I stepped onto the landing a curious sensation arose in the pit of my stomach. I stepped backwards, glancing up into the rafters. A covered hole, large enough to accommodate a medium sized man, was set into the ceiling between two joists. Perhaps it was not just a dream.

Tottering threateningly on top of the coat rack's flimsy metal frame, I stretched my arms upwards as far as I could muster, my finger tips grazing the ledge of the cubby's opening. The cover was ever so slightly out of my reach. I scanned the balcony for anything I could use as leverage; something I could prod up into the hole. I only lacked a mere six inches. Deflated, I knew I could search for hours, but yield nothing. It had more than likely been years since someone had set foot up here and chances were, they knew nothing of the hidden cubby. Watch over me again as I attempt to do something extremely foolish, I beseeched the Lord as I leapt carelessly into to the rafters. The impact of my jump sent the rack crashing to the floor, causing a thick cloud of dust to swell around me. I sucked in my breath, and gritted my teeth. My fingers hungrily clutched the ledge of the opening; my legs dangling at least ten feet from the floor. I had no place to go but upwards. Surely a fall from this height wouldn't kill me, but it would leave me severely handicapped.

I gripped the ledge laboriously with my right hand whilst pushing on the hole's cover with my left. I never thought it would be so testing to hold my own weight. Hanging in the balance, my fingertips had begun to throb. Time had glued the cubby's cover steadfast. I pushed with everything I had, but nothing was rendered. I tried again, straining every muscle to not only budge the lid, but continue to hold on. Sunlight was peeping through the windows below. It would not be long before the Priest, Sisters and Bishops arrived. What would they make of a man hanging from the topmost beams of their place of worship? Surely, I would have a mountain of explaining to do, of which would most likely lead to the American police being contacted. Grunting and pushing with every ounce of strength I had left in me, I was determined to get up into the space. I could not be seen.

"Good Morning Sister Ava." I heard a crisp voice from below. Cranking my neck, I could just barely make out the heads of a man with dark hair and the black veil belonging to a Nun.

"And a very good morning to you as well Bishop," a soft voice chirped. This is not good, not good at all. I continued to push on the cover, praying for a miracle. Perspiration was now lining my brow and my palms had begun to slip. I could allow myself to fall and then hide amongst the boxes should someone attempt to investigate. The Bishop and Sister were having an animated conversation below. How long would it be before one of them let their eyes wander upwards? Five minutes, maybe ten. Could I even hold on that much longer? The sensation in my fingers was telling me no.

"Well as you know Sister, nothing is definite. However, should we receive the funding..." The Bishop's voice trailed away.

I peered down at the spot where they had initially been conversing, but their figures were no longer there. Panicking, I had a decision to make: fall or be seen. I could not keep this up all day, and it was evident I was not going to get into the cubby. I weighed my landing options below. I had hoped to position myself under the robes, but that was crushed when it became apparent that the coat rack would break my fall. The pew could do some serious damage, as would the floor. My only option was to swing myself into the boxes. They were stacked some three feet high, so I would have cushion. That is, of course, unless they were full of books or some other solid object.

"Shall we go take a look?" The Bishop inquired. A look? Where? I prayed he was not insinuating coming up into the balcony. I searched for their figures. His voice had sounded much closer than before. I was certain they were directly under me.

"Bishop, I do not recommend anyone set foot up there. It would be extremely foolish. This sanctuary is three hundred twenty-two years old. As you can see, everything is crumbling. Two sisters and myself carried some boxes up there in nineteen seventy-four, the three of us thought we would never live to tell the tale. The old floor is rotting, as are the support beams. Just last week another beam fell. I hated to send someone up there, but it needed to be removed. As I was telling the coven, I do not know if it would be worth it to salvage this old place." The sister sighed. "And what a shame that would be. It pains me to see His house in such a state. Perhaps it's time we cut our losses. There is no one left but us, and we are not spring chickens."

My fingers gave way and I felt the cool air sweeping beneath me. Within seconds my knees and chest had gelled with the fragile cardboard. A dull thud echoed in my wake, and I was thankful for the boxes "softer" contents. My weight had spilt the crates open, but overall, I thought the fall was grand. My body had imprinted itself on the boxes, and I became cocooned within them. As I lain with my eyes closed, I thanked the Lord for my good fortune.

"Did you just hear something, Sister? It sounded as though something has fallen, a loud crunching noise."

"Oh, uh no, I did not hear anything, Bishop. Then again, I have been here fifty-five years. This place, its scent, its sounds, they have all grown on me. And I suspect my hearing is not as sharp as it used to be." The Nun chortled. "I am sure it was just the pillars and walls settling. They will do that from time to time. Eventually you will get used to it."

Their voices trailed away, however, I continued to lay on the balcony for some time. Eyes closed, ears open, I tried to make sense of what had just happened. The dream...the painting...the fall. Everything had to be connected somehow. I was just not seeing it. Sunlight cascaded through the windows, the shuffle of foot traffic and voices rose up to where I was resting. Things would come full circle. I was put in this position for a reason, and like a puzzle, I now had to make everything fit.

I spent hours analyzing every part of the dream. I had given up on The Last Supper. Some of history's most respected symbolists have told us there are many hidden messages within the painting. Whether there was truth to this, whether da Vinci was trying to inform the future by inventively etching it into the past, I do not know. I was resigned to think that the mural was placed upon the wall as a means for the person or persons whom created the cubby to secretly pass its existence down through the church's generations. Perhaps it held some significance in the past, but here in the now, I found it to be of little importance.

One can go mad trying to find things that are just not there. Many men have done just that in their quest for answers. Heaving myself up off of my makeshift lounge, I stood staring up at the cubby whilst stretching my back and legs. For falling over twelve feet, I was in excellent shape. No aches to speak of. My neck and shoulders rotated without hesitation. Bent at the waist, I begun to straighten and sort the boxes back out. It would be rude of me to leave their contents half spewing onto the floor. The three top-most boxes contained an assortment of robes, candles and literature dating back to early nineteen hundreds. I folded the red and silver robes with care before gently placing them back into their shell. Setting the boxes aside, I began to reform the crates on the bottom. Two boxes were jammed packed with books; their tattered covers illegible. The only damage sustained was in the corners of the cardboard. The third box was crushed beyond repair. Split open at every corner, the box was a jumbled mix of paper and long thin wire. Although moisture had marred the thin metal, I instantly recognized it to be piano wire. Appearing frail, it was deceitful in a sense that it was made of high tempered carbon steel. Subject to repeated tightening and slacking, this wire could withstand even the heaviest of blows, and more often than not, it could do more damage to the pianist than what that player could do to it.

Holding the curvaceous steel within my fingers I tested its tension by wrapping it tightly around my index. I watched the blood drain from my finger as the wire bore grooves into it. Each pull constricting the skin and bones closer to the breaking point. A wild idea popped into my mind. An idea full of snow, cables and chairlifts. I looked up above me. I was not meant to enter the hidden space, I was meant to draw inspiration from it. Or so I convinced myself that my theatrics were such.

....

Soft music descended from the peek of the mountain. I gazed into the darkness until I saw a tiny spot of light. The medic had arrived and had begun preparing for her shift. She too had a routine. Usually the predictability of an individual I found to be frustrating, but for tonight's purpose, it was welcomed. The young woman arrived exactly forty-five minutes before the Diplomats. She would enter her station, turn on the music and proceed to make coffee. Once brewed, she would pour herself a cup, doctor it with cream and sugar before settling into her post. Although her taste in dance music was not shared by myself, I was grateful for her frequent bursts of drum rolls and her crazed whirlwind of flying hair and body parts. It was clear she was not on high alert until Redding, Moreau and Thompson arrived. Even then, I suspected she could give a damn less about them, as her amusement in Thompson's skiing atrocities had grown significantly.

After begging the Lord for forgiveness, I commandeered a dozen strings of wire from the church. Looping all but one of the strands together, I had created a cable of sorts. My plans were to string it between two pine trees located on either side of Thompson's favourite landing bush. When the force of Baradine's weight collided with the cable, it would crush his throat/jugular region. I did not relish the thought of causing him so much pain, but there was no other way. Uncertain as to how things were going to pan out, I had planned to linger close by, the remaining wire at the ready in case I needed to take a more direct approach to things. Redding and Moreau had become immune to Baradine's various "ouches" and groans. They merely laughed into the night before sashaying up the mountain. Thompson would easily go down. Within minutes I had prepared the area for him.

Stressing the chairlift cable in such a short period of time was unlikely. Finding steel cutters sturdy enough to handle the cable's resistance was but a mere fantasy. The simplest means had turned out to be the most difficult to achieve. I toyed with the idea of loosening the chairs from the line, but I knew there was not enough time to slacken each one of them. The medic would surely spot someone tampering with the chairs, and if for some miracle she remained oblivious, I risked having the chair fall out from under me. I had two alternatives: separate the men and take care of them individually with the wire, or tamper with the lift's levy mechanism. I knew nothing of mechanics, and the former would be virtually impossible as the men were inseparable. Nevertheless, I would attempt anything to ensure they did not leave the slopes tonight.

The dark sky was saturated with clouds. A crescent of a white moon was barely visible through the thicket of haze. Fresh snow blanketed the ground, with the threat of more over the next several days. Crouching behind the bulky pines, I waited for Thompson. The comrades had only just arrived. Trudging towards the chairlifts in silence, Redding and Moreau were cautious to keep several strides behind Thompson. I was appalled by their arrogance. I stand corrected, Redding's arrogance. Moreau was merely acting as his puppeteer had instructed. Nonetheless, he chose to allow his country and his mind to be run by such scum.

The men were minuscule by the time they reached the top of the mountain. Redding and Moreau's shadowy figures departed to the ski courses, while Thompson walked a short distance to the amateur's course. I heard the gentle conveyor of the lift churning up the mountain, and vaguely wondered if I could possibly manage to slacken each chair without occurrence. A breeze had surfaced, perhaps if it strengthened I could use it to my advantage...

Almost thirty minutes passed before Baradine came slopping down the mountain. He truly was a disgrace, but his oblivion was his glory. My eyes watched him predatorily; the wire clasped in my hands should I need it. Sixty feet from the trees he attempted some sort of midair turn. His lump figure swayed uncontrollably as he came crashing back down onto the course. His board tittered menacingly on its side for several feet before settling. Baradine laughed, grabbed his chest and looked genuinely pleased with himself. Tonight, I would have given him an eleven out of ten.

With snow expelling around him, Baradine continued to stay on course; picking up speed. I bent at the waist, ready to strike. Hitting the wire was imminent, as he had not mastered how to stop the board without falling down or colliding with something. I watched hungrily as he came closer and closer, taking no heed to what was in store for him. He was less than a dozen feet away, when a rustle startled me. The wire fell to the ground, as I heard a gargle escape from Baradine's throat. He had been clotheslined and had fallen backwards into a sea of luminescent snow. Wasting no time, I retrieved the single wire from the ground, and left my post to dismember the cable from between the trees. Baradine had not moved an inch. I peered at his limp figure for a few seconds. His face bore the signs of a wild shock. I am sorry, but this is what fate your sins have caused you to meet. Stuffing the wiring into my jacket, I slunk back into the trees.

I waited, watching both Redding and Moreau's movements down the mountain.

The two were separated for roughly five minutes whilst one would start the course, end it and then wait for the other to follow. Manipulating this short window of time to my advantage was going to be difficult, but I was confident it was doable. Haste was a necessity as I would need to overpower one before the other reached the base. Pierre would be the easiest. A weak mind was usually coupled with an even weaker body. His physical strength had been pretty much shattered under the weight of Redding's control. Moreau was so enslaved he might even enjoy the pain.

An exhaust of snow billowed after Redding's perfect pikes and turns. He was truly something to look at. Years of practice and private lessons had moulded him into an Olympic worthy candidate. He glided with the grace of a ballerina. Every turn was precisely calibrated; his body hugged the mountain as though they were inseparable lovers. I was star struck by such eloquence. I was unable to shift my eyes from him. On the slopes, his arrogance was justified. Moreau joined him at the end of the course where they rested momentarily.

"He will be here tonight," Redding said causally. "I spoke to him before I left the chalet. His plane was due to land at nineteen hundred hours."

"Are you certain he is the one?" There was a hint of panic in Moreau's voice. This news had shaken him. "I mean to say, are you certain he is capable of, uh, disposing of the problem without any further incident?"

Redding glanced up at the mountain, his expression bored. "Not to worry Pierre, no one will ever know he existed. Once he is finished with Thompson, I will be finished with him." Clamping his hand on Moreau's shoulder, he nudged him towards the lifts. "Now come, I expect he will be here soon and we want to make sure that cute young thing up top the mountain sees us."

The information that Redding's executioner would be terminated as soon as he completed tonight's job did not surprise me. In fact, I expected no less from the President. Corruption and cover ups had become such a real thing, one would be hard pressed to find someone who still had faith in the governors of our humanity. Generations of politicians and the arrogance accompanied with it, had permitted Redding to get anything he wanted. He was a man with no recourse. Nothing he did was above my amazement. Frankly, I would be shocked if plans to dispose of Pierre were not in the works. After all, Moreau needed Redding more than Redding needed him. Finding a new puppet would come as easy as killing the old one.

News of the executioner's arrival should have jump-started me. Instead, I continued to skulk within the trees. I was uncertain what I was waiting for. Both men had come down the mountain thrice in the past thirty minutes. Moreau even skidded to a halt ten feet in front of me. I could have effortlessly overpowered him. What are you waiting for, the voice inside my head was demanding.

I don't know, I thought. I watched absent of mind as the two men clamoured onto the lift once more. Redding appeared to be at his leisure, however Moreau was anxious. I would have bet my life as to what was running in his thoughts. Was he going to be leaving the slopes tonight? Or did Redding have plans for him as well? Redding may not have plans for you, but I do. A wave of confidence blew over me and I vowed to act on whomever should venture my way next.

Moreau's eyes darted from side to side as he stood leaning on his poles waiting for Redding. He was fidgety and nervous, something I could use to my advantage. I stealthy crouched out from behind the trees, untwining the wire between my hands. Moreau shifted his weight and coughed slightly. Fear in its raw form. Snow had begun to fall at an alarming rate. My tracks were already being covered by pearly white mounds. Coughing again, Moreau looked up the mountain. I mimicked him, just barely making out Redding's figure some three hundred yards away. I was so close to Pierre I could smell his cologne; violet leaf and rosemary. His breathing was unsteady, a silent sign of a pending panic attack. Raising the wire high above his head, I cautiously checked Redding's position one last time. He was scarcely visible, as a whirlwind of snow had created a semi shield between us. Moreau moved forward as I hastily drew the wire down onto his throat, constricting it vigorously. His mouth was wide open as though to scream, yet nothing but breathless gurgles came out. He thrashed his arms attempting to pull my hands from the wire, but the steel was much too powerful. As his windpipe crushed and his last hope for breath died away, he closed his eyes and succumbed peacefully to his inevitability.

I had no time to move the body out of Redding's view. He was barrelling down on me at an incredible speed, completely lost in his own grandeur. Anchored behind the trees once more, I sat ready to pounce on him as soon as he reached the end of the course.

Redding exited out of the last turn and arched his body for the final stretch. The wind had begun to pick up, blinding me momentarily in a mini blizzard. As the air cleared, I looked up to see Redding's shocked expression as he tried to manoeuvre around the limp figure of Moreau. But it was too late, and he collided with the Prime Minister's corpse. Infuriated, Redding hastily removed his skis and groped inside his jacket pocket. He took no notice to the dead man he just pulled himself off of. I curiously watched him remove a small cellular device and vehemently punch in a series of numbers. His heavy breathing and sideways glances at Moreau sustained him whilst he waited for his party to answer.

"Mr. King," he said softly. "Did I, or did I not compensate you to take care of an Australian problem?" Redding listened in silence for several seconds his eyes fixed on Moreau.

Prodding the Prime Minister in the leg, he fumed "Then please explain to me why I have just ran into the corpse of a Canadian?" There was silence as he considered what his party was saying.

"Well you have created an even greater problem for me, Sir. How do you expect me to explain why two of my colleagues were found dead on Loon Mountain, yet I managed to survive?" Redding's voice had escalated. He bent at the waist, shifted the telephone to his left shoulder and touched Moreau's neck with his free hand. "Oh yes Mr. King he is very dead. Where are you?" he demanded.

Gathering his poles and skis, he moved closer to the trees, distancing himself from Moreau. No doubt he was trying to shield himself from the medic's view. "What are you talking about?" he snapped into the phone. "Do not attempt to bullshit me, Mr. King. I am not a man whom you can play these games with. I gave you orders for Thompson and Thompson only. Moreau was to come later. I made that quite clear. Did I not? Just get the Hell out of here. The money will be wired as soon as I return to my suite."

Snapping the phone shut, Redding walked over to Moreau and squatted beside him. His expression was callous, something straight out of Hell. Sneering he hissed over Moreau's body; "You were nothing but a coward and a fool. I did not want you dead so soon, but, well... C'est la vie."

Unable to control my rage, I pounced. I had the wire at the ready and I was prepared to fight this man to the death. The moment I strapped the steel around his throat, he elbowed me in the ribs. His reflexes were sharp, his second blow sent agonizing sensations of pain pulsing through my body. I continued my hold on the wire as Redding kicked me in the groin and used his elbows to jab any part of my body available to him. I lost my balance and we both toppled backwards onto the snow. The weight of Redding was crushing me as I struggled to maintain my grip. He smashed my nose with the back of his head. A sea of blood ran into my mouth, flooding my throat. Gagging, I felt the wire slip and Redding rolled off of me. He jumped to his feet like a cat, ski pole in hand. I scrambled upwards, blood dripping off my lips and chin.

"I told you not to play games Mr. King. You will not win." He raised the pole but stopped mid swing as comprehension dawned on him. Astonishment washed over his face, causing him to take a step backwards.

"Who the Hell are you?" he demanded.

What an absurd thing to ask. I thought to myself. His ski pole was still in mid air, obviously he felt he had the upper hand. He was not concerned by my presence. Out of the corner of my eye, I spotted his other pole. Stealthy dropping to the ground, I rolled towards it, clutching it firmly in my hands. In the second it took for me to acquire my new weapon, Redding had regrouped and attempted a swing in my direction. His pole connected with the ground, and I saw my opportunity. I raised the metal staff to shoulder level and brought it crashing down onto the back of his skull. He fell to his knees and swayed as though inebriated. His eye lids began to droop and his arrogant smirk disappeared. His body gave way, collapsing face first onto the ground. I watched as the snow around him immediately turned a sickly crimson. I pinched my nose with my left hand, the bleeding had stopped. The pain was subsiding, my body was slowly rejuvenating itself. I peered around our battlefield in search of dark spots in the snow. I could not leave my blood nor the wire behind. When I was satisfied my tracks were covered, I meandered drowsily into the trees. A frosty cot awaited me.

I did not get very far when a violent blow threw me against a vast tree trunk. I sunk to the ground, only to be lifted effortlessly to my feet. A man closing in on seven feet tall had me pinned, the tip of his shiny blade caressing my chin and neck. I stood stalk still wondering if the late President had even met this Mr. King. I, for one, had lost my bravery in the presence of someone so large. I knew there to be a mammoth of bulk under his dark jacket. His head was the size of a small boulder, deep indentations upon his skin served as proof that he had known battle. The handle of the knife was lost somewhere in the clefts of his enormous hands. He could and would crush me without hesitation or breaking a sweat.

"Listen to me very carefully, and you may get to keep your life," he whispered. There was a hint of an accent which he laboriously attempted to hide: Ukrainian... this was just perfect. I was dead already. Out of all the nationalities to be involved with, I had to fall prey to a Ukrainian. It was not in their nature to be forgiving. I could beg, plead, even offer compensation, but none of that would matter. They knew one thing: sufferance. And how I would suffer. His last words hung sickly in the air... and you may get to keep your life. He was toying with me, throwing me a bit of rope. I knew his game, and I knew the outcome. I would listen, but I would not concede to him.

"You murdered Redding, the Aussie and the Canadian." It was a statement more than a question. I relinquished nothing.

"Why?" he demanded. Pressing the blade into my left cheek, his right hand firmly clasped over my chin. I could taste his putrid breath on my lips. Using his marbled body, he crushed me deeper into the tree trunk. I heard the grinding of the bark as my back wore down on it.

"Not a talker, huh?" he soothed. "Well that suits me just fine. Truth be told, I prefer the more silent type." He ran the blade over the tip of my chin. "See, when the time comes, the quiet ones always plead the hardest." The words floated off his tongue like liquid velvet. "And you will beg," he whispered into my ear.

In the moment it took for him to shift his weight, I sprang. With the force of a hurricane, I drove my left knee into his groin. Instantly he bent doubled, gasping in pain. He reached for me but I had already escaped his grasp. From behind, I kicked him forcefully in the shin, just enough to incapacitate him momentarily. He groaned as his leg gave way. Stooped over on the ground using the trunk as support, I gave him one last blow in the ribcage. As my heavy foot connected with his right side, I heard the unmistakable snap of freshly fractured bone. His eyes grew wide as he suppressed what would have been a piercing howl of pain. I wasted no time. He had already begun to recover; the predator within would not allow me to escape. The snow fall was now coming down even more rapidly. Each imprint upon the earth taking only seconds to vanish. I blindly weaved through the trees, yielding for nothing. I came within yards of Redding's outer wall security patrol. By the time the guard had taken notice to my presence, I had burrowed deeper into the trees. My breathing was shallow and painstaking. Each gulp sucked the life out of my lungs. On the verge of passing out, my legs were like jelly. My head felt as though it was full of helium. Certain I had not seen the last of Mr. King, I pressed on; cold, exhausted and drenched with blood and sweat.

I slipped past a guard posted at the entrance of the mountain. Slowing down, I weakened my strides and concentrated on regulating my breathing. The icy streets were nearly vacant as I paced myself back to the Church. Surprisingly, I thought not of what just happened, but of where my next journey may begin. I would have to stay in the church for the time being. Once the bodies were discovered, the entire country would be put on high alert. This was just the beginning of what was to come.

In a few hours time, the whole of North America would be brusquely awakened, and I expected nothing less than fearful, cataclysmic chaos. The United States were known for their over-hyped, outlandishly barmy behaviour in face of even the slightest acts of pandemonium. Never mind the continuous bloodshed in Africa, forget the millions of starving people in the Middle East and to Hell with all the sick and diseased. None of that mattered so long as an ocean kept it at bay. America only cared for their own. Soon enough every newspaper and broadcasting company around the globe would be harnessing the pleas and outcries of this hypocritical, self-righteous country. All the stories I had heard about this "promised land" as a child were false. I had seen the true face of America: she was one pompous, conniving bitch.

Several blocks from the church I heard him. Unaware of his own futile stealth movements, he no doubt presumed he had me cornered. The vast streets of white may have muffled his footsteps, and the snow flurries blurred his figure, but his raspy breath could not be muted. I quickened my pace, not daring to look over my shoulder. Judging from the cogent gasps, he was no more than two or three car lengths behind me. Amending my plans to return to the church, I hastened past it without giving the crumbling sanctuary a second glance. This man was a beast, visions of his potential carnage flooded my mind. He would not hesitate to slaughter an entire basement of innocent people. Of this I was certain. Losing him would perhaps be my most difficult endeavour. I had better chances of out running a grizzly. Even the police could be easily fooled, but not this man. Years of training and self-discipline had taught him patience. He would hunt me to the ends of the earth if need be; only yielding when he found what he was searching for or death swept over him. Moving as swiftly as my legs could carry me, I frantically reached into the depths of my mind with hopes of finding some sort of fruition; a pre-formulated plan for my escape; plans that were slumbering, waiting for me to awaken them. As I bolted into the crosswalk, a wave of red and blue lights hit me. Taken aback, I stumbled onto the curb in a cyclone of shock. A dozen law enforcement officials blazed past me, cherry tops booming, taking no heed to my haphazard figure. Shaken I lumbered to my feet. As though mummified, I watched their taillights until they were mere specs of amber in the vast darkness.

Lingering on the curb had been extremely foolish. Once again, I could hear Mr. King from somewhere in the shadows. Like a feather, his chafed-like breath floated through the air; penetrating the still night. Deciding to take the first street I came upon, I turned a sharp right, finding myself in an alleyway between a sporting goods shop and an antiques dealer. As quietly as possible I slunk behind a trash dumpster, praying I had lost him. The smell coming from within the bin was nauseating. If Mr. King was tracking me by scent, I was certain the trail had stopped here. Clasping my hands over my nose and mouth I stood jelly-legged hoping the Ukrainian and the urge to vomit would both soon pass. Severely weakened, I strained to push past the fatigue and pain. I had no place to go and an assassin on my backside. The temperature had dropped drastically in just a matter of minutes. Rigid air had descended, bringing with it razor-like bursts of wind. The snow had now transformed into jagged pellets of ice. They fell from the blackened Heavens with a merciless fury, like jagged pieces of shrapnel from hundreds of thousands of grenades. Moreover, here I am, wide open in a lone manned trench. There was no way I was going to climb into that dumpster. Logic told me to take shelter, however, my stomach was telling me to run like a gazelle to the nearest lavatory. I really need to find a place to stay. I suppose I could backtrack to the church or find a bed and breakfast for the evening. It had to be drawing near midnight, if not later, so my choices were limited. The church was always open; even if there were no cots available, I could camp out in the balcony. Treading very softly, I poked out from behind the dumpster. I listened for any sounds out of the ordinary, yet the sleepy town was just that, sleepy. No traffic, no people. The only thing lingering in the air was the woody scent of cedar burning fireplaces. Visibility was minimal: I was confident I could sneak past an entire infantry. My fingers scraped the rough brick wall as I felt my way out of the alley. Bearing westwards, I tucked my head into my jacket, and prepared for the quick sprint back to the church.

"Do you think you can outrun me?" I gasped in horror as the raspy voice wrapped around me. "Really, do you think you have a chance?"

He was close. Not close enough to hear his breathing, but close enough to be alarmed by his words. The church was out of play again. I could run and hide all night, but with no where to go, everything I did was sickeningly futile. I was grasping at straws. Nonetheless, no matter how feeble my attempts to escape were, I needed to keep running at least until dawn. If I could just keep him at bay until day break, I could then lose him in all the hubbub that would stir up when the town awakens. Tucking in, I jetted full throttle to my right. It was silly, as I knew my heavy footsteps would be heard by his well-trained ear. But I took no heed to it and continued to pound the snowy pavement with retribution. Two yellow orbs shone directly in front of me. I ran towards it, not knowing why this little bit of light was so appealing. As I drew nearer, a low rumbling fused in my ears and I smelt carbon in the air. A sliver of light followed by animated chatter erupting from somewhere up ahead. A tidy queue of shadows had assembled and comprehension dawned on me. A bus station. I slowed my pace, calming myself as much as I could. I needed to be on that bus, period. I did not have a ticket, nor was I certain where to get one. I contemplated my options whilst watching the scene before me. The bus, I noticed, was idling in front of a hotel. The fifty or sixty people in queue all seemed to know one another. Their voices had the same thick drawl; like molasses. I caught several words and phrases. It was past one in the morning... A hefty woman was complaining that she did not have makeup on. Another person was trying to sooth a few angry passengers; the weather was due to get worse, so they needed to leave now to ensure they would not get caught in the pending storm. I watched the catatonic passengers carelessly throw their bags into the sidelong luggage compartment before trudging onto the old beast. There appeared to be no ticket inspector; the driver was just as zombie-like as the rest of the lot. Testing my luck, I joined the queue.

Chapter 8

Honey Bayou, Louisiana
16 July, 1995

"Say, Willie, you want some of this here hog head cheese?"
Nauseated by the thought of such a thing, I declined politely. There were some things I simply downright refused to eat. It was mid July on a Sunday afternoon, and I had found myself smouldering under the glaring orange sun. Sweating moonshine from every pore in my body, I savagely gulped the clear liquid. An acquired taste, I drank it for the sole purpose of staying hydrated. My head felt heavy in comparison to my light-weight body. The entire town had turned out for my send-off party. Picnic tables were overloaded with mouth watering goodies and a live band played joyfully. Laughter filled my ears as I watched many tangled bodies dance under the sun's scorching rays. I tried my best to relish what little time I had. I had been here over five months and it was now time to move on.

When I exited off the bus some eighteen hours after it departed Lincoln, I thought I had entered the ninth gate of Hell. Met by blinding sunlight and stifling heat, I was thrown back against the beast's metal frame in a tempest of shock. My eyes adjusted to the scenery before me: Grotesquely shaped trees draped with pea green moss, swampy marshlands overgrown with mysterious vegetation, and acres upon acres of dark soil. A dozen of the same squat, boxy buildings stood decaying in the blistering sun. Long ago forgotten, they were in dire need of new paint, doors and windows. Or even better, a demolition crew. A single paved roadway ran through the heart of what I was assuming to be a small village. The peeling signs on the windows made it difficult to

determine exactly where I was and *what* this was. Several cars lined
the curb in front of the odd building, but aside from this, the place
was a dreary hole. It was as though an eternal slumber spell had
been placed upon it. I looked around speculating of how often this
place saw outsiders. What did people in these parts do for a living?
There was nothing here but dying fixtures and a fuel station with
rusty pumps. I gawked at the fields surrounding the village. They
appeared to be freshly cultivated; perhaps the residents relied on the
cash crop industry. It was hard to imagine this place generating
income from any other commerce. In fact, it was hard to imagine
anyone living here willingly...

The bus had emptied and its passengers waited as their luggage was pulled from the side compartment. I only had my travel
bag, so I stood in the sidelines watching everyone else. A dozen
women gathered their effects, talking animatedly of a church
potluck and tonight's eating agenda. My eyes followed their backs
as they bounced down the street. I gawked at them until they
entered a building next to the fuel station. It was shabby, in need
of fresh white paint, but well kempt compared to the rest of the
places surrounding it. I strained my eyes until I found what I was
looking for; a small steeple. Maybe I would get lucky and be
permitted a place to stay for the evening.

The bus ride was long, far too long. We broke down outside of Memphis according to a hefty man whom used to be trucker
in those parts. After four hours of idling, we were back on the
road. The low rumbling of the beast was tiresome, so I quickly
found myself in the deepest of sleeps. Had I been awake, perhaps I
would have a better insight as to where I was. Of three things I was
certain; I was hot, I was tired, and I was deep within the south. My
stomach had begun to grumble, my mouth cotton dry. If this place
had a church and gas station, surely there had to be a place to dine
somewhere. Five men sashayed past me mumbling anxiously about
needing a couple shots of whiskey apiece. "The whole damn

bottle" I heard one of them sigh. I followed in their wake as they walked steadfast towards the place where their whiskey was calling.

With a population of two hundred sixty-eight people, Honey Bayou, Louisiana was a mere spec on the map. There were no signs on the Interstate leading motorists towards it, and there were no official roads linking it to any other part of the state. A cousin of a cousin trucked in fuel every three months from Baton Rouge. Every six weeks the owners of Duster's Waterhole made the four hour drive into the city for more whiskey, beer and peanuts. Hettie and Mac Thibodeaux, entrepreneurs of the town's only restaurant/grocery store, were closed weekly on Sundays and for religious holidays. Any other day of the week, one could dine and/or shop from dawn until dusk. Twice per month a vendor from upstate brought in canned items; dairy, meat and flour products, which the Thibodeaux's proudly stocked on their shelves. Prices were reasonable, and the honour system was utilized for the local folk.

The village had a post office which ran once per week. Always on Wednesday. Your letter's destination would be achieved in seven to ten days, provided the larger town of Routtier received all correspondence before four in the afternoon. There was no formal delivery man, all mail was sorted and placed into regions. A representative from each region would pick up the items and deliver it to his or her neighbours. Honesty was widely relied upon, and I was shocked to see that it still counted for something. While I was paying cash for my supplies, others were signing promissory notes to pay the balance within fourteen or thirty days time. It did not take long for the locals to realize I was an outsider. Wanting to keep to myself, I attempted to maintain a quiet campsite among some trees on the periphery of the village. Nonetheless, I was a product of everyone's interest, and it was not long before the villager's came calling.

Red Herring

Half a dozen men invaded my campsite on a particularly humid evening some four days after I had arrived. Sitting crossed legged staring into the hazy orange-purple horizon, I casually stirred my rice and beans whilst they cooked over the amber flames. I had done nothing but sleep and sweat since I had gotten here. I had little appetite and the heat, coupled with the calming sounds of the marshlands, kept drowsiness within my clutches. The men did not come quietly. I heard them approaching, yet I was too exhausted to do anything about it. As they stalked through the knee high grass, I kept my eyes on the setting sun. I was certain they had come to ask me to leave. And due to their large numbers, I was sure they assumed I was going to put up a fight. The closer they got, the more evident their mental states became. Drenched in the scent of beer and fish, I braced myself for what I knew was going to be a drunken battle of wits and swift movements. Needless to say, I was shocked when the men invited me to Duster's bar for a couple shots of "juice."

It is profound how a simple spur-of-the-moment whim can transform into something life altering. I had no intentions of mingling with the locals, nor did I intend to make such a splash upon the little town. From the very moment I crossed the threshold into Duster's bar, I had become one of them. My background, no matter how different, was not put into the light. My life's history, despite my questionable actions, was not concerned for. I was welcomed as though I had once been a lost child whom had finally found his way back home. They cared not for my life, but for what quality of life I had had.

Although they marvelled at such things as my place of birth, my travels, my education, and my accent, they seemed truly saddened by my choice to remain unwed and childless. Many of the residents were in agony over my lack of family, and the constant verve which kept these things out of my reach. Their lives were slow paced, nothing was planned, and with the exception of the sugarcane harvest, nothing was done on a strict time schedule. The days were long and lazy. Most businesses opened and closed at whatever time their owners felt practical. Meals were served whenever the entire family managed to collaborate at the table. Every evening, the men met at Duster's where they talked of family, the cane and a man they seemed to revere by the name of John Deere. The women gathered at the church, where their UCW (United Church Women) group cooked meals for the town's sick, quilted, and planned shopping trips into the city.

There were about seventy five children in the town, all of which had good, strong upbringings. They remained to be seen, only coming to and from school, as modern technology had kept them in their homes. I was surprised to learn that almost everyone had satellite television and a telephone; everything just seemed so backwards in the Honey Bayou. The people were friendly and helpful. There was a hint of age to them, as though time was only pressing things upon them at its own pace. They upheld tradition, their family and their name were the dearest of all. It was rare to see such passion for things which the world had long since deemed inconsequential. Three months had lapsed since my arrival to the town. Each day was something new, something I had never seen, heard of, or done before. If it were not for the heat, I could have spent the rest of my days there.

Red, the barber, had insisted from our very first meeting that I bunk with him. He had recently lost his wife Carla, and was in dire need of company. He sent two young men up to my campsite to retrieve my bag, whilst he escorted me to his home some five miles outside of Honey Bayou. A single dirt road ran through a thicket of trees. I can recall wondering if such a road was leading me to my demise. I had just met these people, they had been more than willing to extend meal and housing invitations. I was uncertain what I was getting myself into, and although the pit of my stomach was churning, the organ in my chest was telling me not to fear them.

The ride to Red's home was the most insightful and interesting fifteen minutes of my life. He was a bubbly man whom had grown up in the Bayou. His family held a permanent residence there, as did everyone who lived in the town. They welcomed guests, however, unless one married into the family, they were not permitted to live on their lands. I learned that the deepest parts of Louisiana had been settled some three hundred years ago by several hundred French-Canadian families whom had been asked to leave Nova Scotia. After being forced out of various places in the United States, they all eventually settled in the swamplands, where they lived off the land, and remained in close ties with one another. Once part of the French Colonial Empire known as Acadia, these Cajuns, as they now prefer to be called, were forced into exile for reasons unknown.

Over time, the families branched off to other parts of the state, some going as far as Southeast Texas. Roughly two hundred years ago, eight families made the journey to what is now the Honey Bayou. Spanned over twenty thousand acres, the families built a central come and go station and fanned out around it. A single roadway was constructed linking each individual plantation to the town's central point, but not to one another. Those with the surname Boudreaux, Chauvin, Dubois, Guillot, Hebert, Mouton, Savoie and Thibodeaux were welcome to create a homestead on their appointed acreage. The families co-existed in peace; with each knowing their boundaries. However governed by the state's laws, the families also lived by their own rules of sovereignty. With the exception of a handful of independent businesses in town, all eight families shared an invested interest in the sugarcane fields. Everything was divided eight ways, the labour, the profits, and of course, the losses. The eldest member of each family served as a member of a special board created to act and judge upon things that were in the best interest of the entire town. I was in awe over their harmonious acts towards one another and the land they harvested. Never had I seen such an alliance of individuals whom truly just wanted to live their lives as well and as long as God permitted them. They worked with what they had, nothing more. Several times on the ride to Red's home he reminded me what I was missing: good friends and a great family.

"If ya ain't got family and ya ain't got friends, ya aint got nothing," he finalized.

Almost all the homes resembled one another: boxy, with a front porch, painted various shades of white or brown. Simplicity at it's finest. The odd home had pillars, a shed or garage and a second story. According to Red, these homes were built with money that was embezzled from the cane crops in fifty-six, fifty-seven and fifty-eight. Several of the board members decided to take more than their fair share, and instead of sticking the money away somewhere, they built grander homes. Red said they did this to flex their power over non-board members. Nonetheless, the families have since moved past the incident, and no one thinks twice of the "dirty homes" as Red called them. In my opinion, I believed him to still be bitter, as his family nearly starved in those three years.

Each day, we toured through the region, Red kept a steady stream of commentary flowing. There was nearly twenty-thousand acres of cane field, and he intended I see every corner of it. We crawled down the road, windows open, his old seventy-eight Ford pickup had no air conditioning. I was sweating after the first five minutes. My t-shirt was stuck to my back and I could feel the perspiration sliding down my chest and arms. Red looked quite comfortable in his patched work pants and long sleeve cotton pullover. I suspected anything less than twenty Celsius would be cool to him. For mid July, it was abnormally hot. I suppose it was the average here, but to my tempered body, I was frying like an egg. The days seemed to pass exceptionally slower compared to when I had initially arrived. The cooler weather made for more activities, whether it be long leisure walks, or lending a hand around various homesteads. The heat was exhausting on its own, throw in any sort of activity, and I was down for the count quite quickly.

"See those chutes stickin' up outta the soil?" Red pointed out towards the fields casually.

"Mmm. Yes, I do," I said as I strained my eyes until I saw the little greenish-brown stalks he had been talking about. Just barely twelve inches in height, I could make out the thousands upon thousands of chutes which had been planted in precise rows. They seemed to carry on for miles. *No wonder the entire town was a part of this operation.*

"How tall will they get? And how do you know when to harvest it? Does it come from seeds?" I inquired excitedly. I'm sure my questions were foolish, but to someone who knew nothing about the operation, it was fascinating.

Bumping along, thoroughly enthused Red began to ramble off the entire mechanics of this operation.

"Ya see, cane is bred from cuttin's. Every cuttin' must have one bud on it, and we plant those by hand. It's long, hard work, but someone's got to do it, ya know. When it's planted we harvest it 'bout three times. See the cane keeps sendin' up new stalks called ratoons. After a while, the cane stops growin' and we have to replant. We usually get 'bout six harvests before we have to plant again."

I nodded in understanding, my eyes fixed on the fields. I always thought sugarcane was grown in Brazil, Asia and Africa. I never would have believed anyone who told me it was grown and harvested in the United States. Nonetheless, I supposed the climate could sustain it.

"Did ya hear me, Willie?" Red tapped me on the shoulder. He was pointing towards the open fields. "I was sayin', we do all the cuttin' by hand. Everyone who is able helps out. Some boys have jobs in Routtier and Baton Rouge, so they help on their days off. It's a big operation I will tell ya. When we get ready to harvest we set the field on fire. This is-- "

"What?" I chortled. "You set the field on fire? But why?" Something told me Red was feeding me a load of tripe.

"Yep. We set the field on fire. It kills all the snakes and bugs. Makes it easy for gettin' down the rows too 'cause it clears all the dead leaves."

"That doesn't harm the stalks? I mean, won't the crop catch fire?"

"Nope, it sure won't. We get a lot of rain and we irrigate too. The stalks and roots have so much water in them they won't catch. So after we do that, we take cane knives, some folk use machetes, but I like the knife, it makes for a smooth cut, so yeah, we take the knives and cut the stalk. But you have to cut it just above the soil. Some operations have automatic harvesters, but we have no use for them. Too costly when they break down, and besides, honest labour ain't ever killed anyone. Though some of these young kids will do anything to get outta workin'. Yep. They just don't work like they used to. In my day, we were forced to cut five hundred kilograms an hour or suffer a beatin'. I did six forty-five once." Red smiled proudly at nothing in particular.

Something told me there was a story behind such a large number. No one in their right mind would willingly work that fast and hard for one hour. I whistled lowly. "Wow Red. Six forty-five. That is rather impressive." I wanted to hear more and stroking his ego would keep him talking. The heat had reached its peak, I was sweating like a pig, but my interest was far too great to be concerned with anything else.

"That was back in forty-two. I was eighteen years old. Me, Rusty Guillot, Beaver Dubois and my second cousin Lucky Hebert had a bet goin' on to see who could cut the most in one hour. See, we all liked the same shotgun that Ollie Savoie was sellin'. Every day when we got paid, we'd go to Ollie's an' try to buy it without the other knowin'. Finally ole Ollie got tired of us and said whoever could cut the most cane in one hour, he'd give it to. Lucky, we called him that 'cause he got ran over by Miss Bama Thibodeaux two times, anyway, he cut six thirty-seven and we thought it was over. But I kept goin'. I wanted that shotgun more than anythin'. Twelve gauge Winchester, ninety-seven model repeater. She was beautiful."

Judging from the triumph on Red's face, he had won that shotgun. "You won. I know you did."

"Yep and Ollie's youngest daughter Carla to boot. Lucky was something' mad too. But I didn't give a coon's ass. Between us, Willie, cuttin' that much almost killed me. Lord, I miss that gun. Lost her in the swamplands fifteen years ago. Shame too, cause she was somethin' else."

Red smiled so widely, it touched his eyes. The walk down memory lane had clearly done wonders for his old soul.

"So what happens after it's cut? It's the sugar you want, so how do you get it?"

"We remove the leaves, then load the cane on a truck and take it to the mill. When we cut the stalk, the sugar starts to ooze out, so we have to quickly load it up and take it away. The mill puts the stalks on a conveyor where the rest of the sugar is squeezed out. The stalk is thrown out after that, usually into big dumpsters. When the dumpsters are full, they are left to rot in the fields. And let me tell ya Willie, rottin' cane smells worse than any dung I've ever smelled." Red turned his nose up in disgust.

After an entire morning of cane education, we decided to go into town for lunch. Red had an appetite for Hettie's crawfish, which were the best in the state, he claimed. I had been to Hettie and Mac's on one prior occasion; when I first arrived in town. I purchased thirty dollars in supplies before quickly ducking out of the spotlight. I recall Hettie talking more loudly than necessary, her eyes trained on me in the most peculiar fashion. Her hands fumbled under the cash register countertop; most likely in search of the shotgun she kept under there just for instances like mine. I handed Hettie two twenty dollar bills along with nine cents. As she presented me with my change, she yelled over her shoulder, "I need a bagger in here. Now!" She hand wrote me a ticket, and passed it to me with a friendly, yet apprehensive smile. "Just one moment, Sir. My husband is on his way to bag these items up for ya," she had said. I simply nodded not wanting to frighten her any more than what she was.

After several moments of uncomfortable silence, Mac emerged from somewhere in the back. It was my turn to step back. The man before me was massive. His features were boyish for his age, his frame, however, was as big and as a wide as a door. His arms were thicker than my thighs, his broad chest could have served as a dining table. He thundered towards the counter, the old floorboards sagging under his weight. He eyed me up, his penetrating stare sending chills coursing through my veins. He kept his eyes on me as he blindly stuffed the paper bags with my items.

"Not from around here are ya." His voice was so forceful, I had to fight the urge to run out of the place. I was willing to starve if it meant I wouldn't have to cross paths with Mac ever again. He finished bagging my items and in one swift movement I had thanked them, more so Hettie than Mac, grabbed the bags and was gone.

Today, Mac greeted me with a bear hug that could have crushed a small whale. His boyish face was uplifted into the most warming expression. He escorted Red and I to a table near the window before leaving to fetch us some sweet tea. I had never had cold brew tea before, so it was quite a shock when Red offered me a glass. He had laughed for days at the thought of drinking hot tea with cream and sugar. Mac brought our tea, which I doctored with sugar before it sucking down. It was an odd taste at first, but once one got used to it, it was rather addictive.

"What are we havin' today, Mac?" Red asked. "There ain't no menus here, so we eat whatever Hettie and her daughter Willow cook up," he said glancing sideways at me.

"Sorry old man, no crawfish today. The girls are makin' chicken fricassee."

Once Mac left, I turned to ask Red what exactly a chicken fricassee was. Before, I even got the "what is" out, Red laughed.

"It's a chicken breast with gravy and vegetables served over rice. Mmm, Willie it's good. Hettie uses a lot of red pepper and onion in hers. Sometimes she adds hard boiled eggs to it. You'll enjoy it."

We ate in silence, something that everyone seemed to do. No matter what time of the day it was, no matter what may have happened, nothing takes a man away from his food down here. I asked Red why this was once, and he told me that so much passion and care goes into each dish; it would be a shame to let meaningless chitchat ruin the hard work that went into preparing it. I had never thought of it that way before, nonetheless, one bite of Hettie and Willow's fricassee, and I immediately understood what Red had been talking about. It was so good, I savoured every single mouthful of it. After stuffing myself to the brim, I had the overwhelming urge to take a nap. I was exhausted. Red said that fatigue sets in after a particularly excellent meal. Once again, I thought he was full of it. Yawning, I patted my stomach; something I was surprised to see everyone else doing as well. Red pulled his wallet from his pocket and tossed a few bills on the table.

"I'm buyin' today, you buy tomorrow," he said. I nodded my head slowly. My entire body felt anchored to the chair I was in. Red stood up after a few moments and started to head towards the door. I had no choice but to follow. He was, after all, my ride and newest best friend.

"Hey wait! Professor! Err Mr. Willie, wait!" I was at the door when I heard a woman calling my name. I spun around to see a tall, wispy young lady standing before me. Her blonde hair reached her waist, her round face pretty and friendly.

"Oh, good! I thought I was goin' to have to chase after you," she gushed. "My Ma wants to invite you over to our house for Etoufee and Beignets. She said don't worry about not knowing what it is, she doesn't expect you to. And she also said my Daddy will pick you up at Red's tonight."

"O...k.," I droned. "Sounds wonderful." *Why was I talking so slowly?* I must have sounded like an idiot to her.

"I'll let Ma know yer comin'. See you tonight Professor," she beamed.

Red wasn't too happy about not receiving an invite, none-theless, he was humming in his rocker on his front porch, his old shepherd George next to him when Mac arrived. It was twilight and still as hot and humid as though it were noon. I bade Red goodbye and hopped into Mac's pickup. Instantly, I had begun to sweat. Or, perhaps I had just never stopped. I wiped my brow with my hand, and leaned my head closer to the open window. The air was luke warm, but it felt great on my balmy skin.

"If ya put yer window up, I'll turn the AC on for ya." Mac fidgeted with the dials on the dash for several seconds before air started blasting through the vents. I rolled my window up, and closed my eyes. The cold; I never thought I'd long for it as much as I did just now.

"Hettie is sure pleased yer comin' over. She's been dyin' to make something with the alligator we have in the freeze."

"You have an alligator in your freezer?" I was not shocked by this news, more or less curious. "A real alligator?"

Mac slapped his knee and laughed so loudly, I thought my eardrums were going to burst. His booming chortles bounced off the walls of the cab. "Yep, a real alligator. I know what yer thinkin' though. It's just the meat. Two of the Mouton boys and Ducky Chauvin ran into it while huntin' last November. They were deep in the swamps. Came across it, was just going to leave it alone, but the sucker had marked them and was makin' it's way to land. Ducky shot it, and the other two boys skinned it. They thought Hettie would enjoy some of the meat since she loves cookin'. Gave it to her as a Christmas present. It sure was nice of them. Alligator is expensive."

Once again, I should have been shocked by the news of three boys giving a middle-aged woman an alligator for a Christmas gift, but I was not. Things were done in a different fashion here. From the way Mac went on to describe how pleased Hettie was, I guessed receiving an alligator ranked right up there with getting a new car or receiving a diamond necklace.

The Thibodeaux residence was beautiful. The same boxy shape as Red's place, but it had blue paint, a brown roof and a red front door. Vibrant coloured impatiens and golden marigolds lined the stone walkway leading up to their porch. Under the front windows, bright green shrubs and foliage lived harmoniously. The front windows cascaded with rose bushes, and the porch was lined with white rope lighting. Getting out of the pickup, I closed the door, and followed Mac up the walkway. I climbed the stairs to the porch, for the first time hearing soft music.

"Heh, the old girl's gone all out for ya," Mac said shaking his head. He opened the front door and bowed me inside.

Although nothing matched and the décor was fifty years passed, Hettie and Mac's place had a warm, welcoming feel. The family room was cluttered with mismatched furniture, and the walls were plastered with knickknacks and family portraits. Willow through the years took up half a wall to herself, a life's journey which was far from complete. A magnificent fireplace was shelled into the north wall, it's mantle draped with a pale blue silk cloth. Upon it a massive stuffed catfish was proudly displayed. In the far corner of the room, along the west wall, an antique sewing table served as a home for an equally ancient radio. Through a single speaker, a majestic accordion played. I was drawn to the beautiful sound. It was like nothing I had ever experienced before. It was so elegant, music for the soul, yet there was a hint of twang to it.

"Do you like it?" a female voice inquired. Waking me from my trance, I saw that Willow had joined at my side.

"It is breathtaking. Surreal even," I spewed.

Willow smiled, humming along. "It's our music. I mean the Cajuns. Keep listening, it gets better, my fourth cousin Snippy joins in on the washboard."

"Snippy? That's an odd name..." A fierce rapping fused with the accordion, sending me into a euphoric state. I had the sudden urge to take Willow by the arm and waltz her around the room. It had been years since I let my body go thoughtless and free-spirited.

"It's just a nickname," Willow said. "His real name is Jason. Like Willow, everyone just calls me that because I'm really tall and thin. And of course my hair is everywhere. Like the weeping willow tree actually. My real name is Rachael."

I eyed her curiously, "Willow suits you," I said smiling. "Everyone else in town, they have strange names as well; those are just nicknames?"

"Yep," she replied. "My Daddy's name is Raymond, but everyone calls him Mac because he's as big as a semi-truck. You know, the Mac trucks? Anyway, my Ma's name is Ella, but everyone calls her Hettie because she has eight sisters and my crazy Granny called her and my Auntie the same name. But I guess if I had sixteen kids, I'd be crazy in the head too." She laughed sweetly before returning to the music.

"So everyone has a nickname then?"

"Yeah, except for Mr. Dubois. He said there is no way in Hell he was going to be called anything but his proper name. He's pretty old. Like eighty-five or ninety. We call him Mr. GA, when he's not around."

I was confused, "Mr. GA?"

"Mr. Grouchy Ass," she whispered. "But don't tell my Ma and Daddy I said the 'a' word because I'm not allowed to swear. Hell is ok though because it's a place."

I made a zipping motion across my lips. "You're secret is safe with me young lady."

"Thanks Professor," she grinned.

"Professor, I'm assuming, is the nickname you have given me?"

Raising her index finger to her temple, she said "Because you talk so smart. My Daddy said you're--"

"Willow, can you please bring Mr. Willie into the kitchen?" I heard Hettie yell from somewhere in the house.

"Coming Ma," she said, gripping my arm and steering me out of the room.

"Good evening, Willie," Hettie gushed, pecking my cheek. "Mac's getting the gator from the freezer, then you and I are gonna prepare it. How does that sound?"

"Errr...great. I must tell you this though; I don't know what I'm doing." I can honestly say I was scared, yet thrilled for what I was certain to be an eventful evening.

"Oh never mind that. I'll show you what to do. It's very easy to work with. I'm so excited. I've been waitin' for a special occasion to cook it up!" She bustled around the tiny kitchen like a pro. And that was saying something, as this room was laden down with hundreds of knickknacks also. A small oval table in the centre of the room had been set with four places, a fresh vase of marigolds serving as a conversation piece. Apart from the range and refrigerator, there were no other luxuries to speak of. The countertops were littered with spice racks and cookbooks. Clearly, Hettie enjoyed her craft.

"So how much longer do you plan on stayin?" she asked whilst gently kneading the cream coloured dough she was tending to.

"I'm not sure. A few weeks, maybe a month. I should be on my way shortly," I replied. In actuality, I shouldn't have stayed this long, but it was easy to get lost here. Time had just slipped away.

Hettie rolled out the batter and began to cut it into four inch squares, cutting a slit in the centre of each piece. "Well, we hate to see you go, but you will let me when you plan to leave, so we can give you a proper send off. It's tradition to throw a big party when someone leaves. An entire day of food and dancin'. You will love it."

"I will let you know what my plans are. This place is astonishing. I'm afraid if I don't leave soon, I never will and I have many more stops to make." Nobody ever questioned what brought me here. They had assumed I was on a North American tour, and had simply gotten on the wrong bus in New Hampshire.

The dough crackled as Hettie dropped each piece into a pan of cooking oil. "Yes," she sighed. "It is easy to stay. We are a world of our own, and although it may not be modern, nor idealistic, to the ones who call this home, it's perfect. And we wouldn't have it any other way."

I was in awe over her change in vocabulary. I had thought she was born here just like everyone else had been. "You are not from here?" I asked politely. For a moment she had sounded regretful, so I was treading carefully.

She smiled, and stuck her finger to her nose. "No, I am not." Her words were clipped, nasal even. Laughing, she turned her attention to the frying dough. "I was born in Casper Springs, New Hampshire. I met Mac in nineteen seventy-one while I was attending Grad School in Baton Rouge."

"Did he attend University there as well?"

"Yes, he was in several of my night courses. His family wished for him to stay in the Bayou, but he had aspirations of becoming a chef, as did I. He attended classes without their knowledge. We started dating in seventy-two. We would have graduated together had it not been for the death of his parents. He was willed the store and restaurant. I wanted him to sell, but he couldn't part with the family business. His great-great-great grandparents had been the first proprietors in the town." She scooped the fried dough onto a plate of paper towels. "I'm sure you can guess how the rest of the story goes. Mac asked me to move here, we got married, had Willow and I got lost in Louisiana."

"Do you see your family often?" I asked.

"Every February, a busload of us make the trip up to New Hampshire. They spend all their time enjoying the winter sports and eating non-traditional foods. I drink hot tea and savour every second I have with my siblings. It's become a bit of tradition for us all. Well, the ones who are brave enough to go out into the cold. This past February was our fifteenth year going north. It's always a great time. Can I offer you a beignet?" she asked sprinkling icing sugar on the pastries.

"I would love a French doughnut. I haven't had one since I left Paris," I replied.

Alligator Etoufee was quite possibly the most delicious thing I had ever eaten. Another gravy over rice dish, the onion, garlic, tomato and green pepper gelled nicely with the black pepper and cayenne infused meat. Served with a fresh garden salad and a thick slice of homemade French bread, I mopped my plate clean.

Willow and Mac laughed as I scarfed down every single morsel and nodded ferociously when asked if I desired a second helping.

"Say, Mr. Willie, what do you have all over your arms?" Willow inquired with a low giggle.

Blushing, I attempted to peel the hardened mixture off of my arm. I cringed as fine hairs came off with it. Willow giggled and Mac roared so thunderously, the entire table shook.

"You two leave him be now," Hettie scolded.

"Yes Ma," Willow said, coughing into her napkin. Through my peripherals, I could see a grin on her lips.

"Sorry sweetheart." Mac hung his head. He too was smiling.

"Just soak real good in warm water when you get back to Red's place," Hettie advised. "It will take a few minutes to dissolve, but it will peel right off."

I was not much of a cook as it turned out. Hettie had placed me in charge of concocting some sort of roux gravy from flower and water. After writing the instructions down on a piece of parchment, she left me to it. Using the heavy cast iron skillet she had placed out for me, I poured cooking oil into the pan and placed it on the burner. I added a quarter cup of flour, and using a paddle, I stirred it continuously until the mixture achieved the colour of peanut butter brittle. In the meantime, Hettie chopped the garlic, pepper and onion. She added the vegetables and I kept stirring as per her instructions. After five more minutes of stirring, I slowly began to pour the water into the pan. Hettie had strict instructions to pour *slowly*, and to constantly keep stirring. I suppose I was not stirring slowly enough because the moment the water hit the pan, it exploded all over. I jumped back, dropping the cup of water onto the floor, my face, arms and shirt covered in a gooey mess. Hettie covered the pan before tossing it into the stainless steel sink. She immediately began to wipe the cabinets and countertop down. I tried to help her, but there was little room for the two of us. After twenty minutes of cleaning up my mess, she took her kitchen back by subtlety telling me to have a seat at the table.

Mac, Hettie and myself were finishing up the rest of the beignets and chatting about my travel when the phone rang. Willow, who had retreated to her bedroom for the evening, came skidding into the kitchen screaming "I got it! I got it!" excitedly. Hettie and Mac rolled their eyes as she inhaled and exhaled quickly before picking up the receiver. She let out an exasperated "Hello." She listened but did not join in the conversation.

"Probably that Boudreaux boy. He calls every night. What's his name again sweetheart?" Mac asked.

"Burg, and we should be thanking the Lord she's interested in him. I don't know what I'd do if my baby started dating one of the Chauvin or Guillot boys."

Mac nodded his head and snorted just as Willow hung up.

"Daddy, Muddy Savoie wants you to meet him in town. He said to bring Martha. A man has been asking about Mr. Willie, he even beat up Boots Dubois thinking he was hidin' him."

My heart stopped. I had to clamp my jaw shut. How? There was no way he could track me here. *Just no way.* All eyes were on me, as I attempted to regain my composure. "What?" I heard Mac ask his daughter. Willow began to repeat her telephone conversation, but I heard little of it. My mind churned to find an explanation of how this could have happened. He could have tracked the bus by its plate number, or maybe he followed me all the way down here and had just been hiding out these past five months, waiting for an opportunity. But there had been plenty of those. My gut wrenched as I thought of a more sadistic possibility...

"Willie!" Mac roared. "Listen to me. What's goin' on?"

I quickly searched the depths of my mind for a feasible story. "I umm...well it's hard...err, you see..."

"Just spit it out will ya! Who is this sumbitch? What in Hell does he want?" Mac looked furious and Hettie and Willow were just plain scared. I looked from face to face. They had been so kind and hospitable. It was wrong to lie to them, but I didn't have any other choice.

"When I was in New Hampshire, I ran into this bloke by the name of Mr. King. For some reason I had upset him, I do not know what I did. He cornered me in the woods near the ski slopes and threatened to kill me. I got away, but not before he struck a few blows. I was running away from him when I saw the bus. Everyone looked so tired, I figured it was my only way to escape him, so I hopped on. I am deeply sorry Hettie. I didn't know where else to go and he was closing in on me."

I closed my eyes, fighting the urge to weep like a child. When I had looked up, Mac was standing over me, shotgun at the ready. He placed a colossal hand on my shoulder. "Do me a favour and stay here with my girls. I will round up the Guillot's and Mouton's and whoever else I can find. Don't worry, we take care of our family in these parts." Mac was out the door and in his truck before I could utter a single word.

Within two hours he had returned. His shotgun smelled strongly of gunpowder, and he was covered from head to toe in mud. "Problem solved." He muttered, "Goodnight."

Hettie drove me home in silence. Red was waiting on the porch, a faithful George at his side. After a short recap of the nights' events, we went into the house to retire for the evening. As I lain in bed, I made a mental note to inform Hettie that I would be leaving in two days time.

Global Times
Australia: Tragic Loss, or Plotted Murder/Suicide?

The Australian government has released a statement proclaiming the innocence of now deceased Ex-Prime Minister, Baradine Bradey Thompson. For the past five months, suspicions that the former Prime Minister murdered his two colleagues, former President of the United States, Robert J. Redding and former Prime Minister of Canada, Pierre Gervais Moreau before taking his own life, have run the gamut.

As the entire globe knows, the three friends were spotted vacationing together at a winter resort in Lincoln, New Hampshire this past February. Sources say the men appeared to be in good spirits and enjoying the winter activities. In the early morning hours of Thursday, February 13th, security personnel found their lifeless bodies at the base of the Loon Mountain.

The body of Ex-President Robert Redding, had been savagely beaten, while Ex-Prime Minister Pierre Moreau had been mercifully suffocated. Pathology reports from Langley, Virginia have confirmed that these two men were murdered first, which has raised grave speculations that a known-to-be-jealous former Prime Minister Thompson is responsible.

A close friend of all three men can recall countless occasions when Ex-Prime Minister Thompson had shown animosity towards the deceased, whom were more respected and more successful them himself. Former President Redding's successor, President Edmond Arthur Allin IV, recently released a statement, within it, harsh words for the country of Australia:

"We have experienced a profound loss. In these times we must unite as one, should we ever hope to conquer our enemies, and move past this grave tragedy that has left us all exposed. As for the country of Australia, its leader's sinful acts against two of the world's most esteemed visionaries, have shown cause for our

Union, as well as the dominions of Canada and Japan to sever ties with the entire continent, along with any country who shows alliance to it. I strongly urge the rest of the world to take into account what has been done, and what has been lost."

Calls to the office of Thompson's successor, Prime Minister Jeffery Murphy Aarons, have been unreturned, leaving one to conclude only the worst.

Chapter 9

Himalayas, Northern Pakistan
25 October, 1995

Snow capped mountains could be seen across the horizon for miles. The sacred peaks rose towards the Heavens, stopping just short of reaching them. The chilly air was dense, but pure, and a crisp scent floated around me. Once I became used to breathing at such a high altitude, I felt as though I had been reborn--like I was using my fragile lungs for the first time. The unpolluted air was addictive. I greedily gulped it down as though it were a non-replenishable resource. I knew I was being unreasonable, the air at this level would remain chaste for an eternity. My anxiety was facilitating my fiend. I hungrily continued to suck down all the air around me. Only when my lungs were on the verge of bursting, and hyperventilation was closing in, did I cease. It took me a few moments to regain my composure.

Some twenty-six hours prior, I was trapped between a chatty Turk and a sweaty, rotund woman of whose descent was unknown to me. Like a giddy schoolgirl, the middle aged Turk stammered on and on. Within the first two hours of our eight hour flight, I had heard his entire life story. I knew that he was flying from Wales to Karachi, where he would be spending ten days on a business, possibly a pleasure trip as well. He had a son whom was nineteen, and a homosexual. He and his wife had sent him to the United States for higher education with the hopes that he may never return. His youngest two children were eleven and nine. Both Girls; his angels. According to him, they faired their strikingly beautiful mother, both were accomplished violinists. He had high hopes for their future.

Red Herring

I felt as though I was inside a rubber tube that had been constricted by a million pairs of hands. The woman next to me was far too large for the plane's petite seating. Each passing minute caused her to perspire more profusely. I watched appalled as she struggled in her chair, noticeably uncomfortable. Several times she mumbled unintelligibly to the stewardess, whom always responded with a shake of her head, no. I felt like a loaded gun, I truly despised flying; the cost, the anxiety it brought on, and the Turk breathing unceasingly next to me. No matter how hard I tried to show my disinterest in his thirty-one year old Macaw parrot, or his mother's cornucopia of health issues, he kept blubbering on, oblivious to my stale, incandescent "hms" and "ahs".

We landed in Karachi Jinnah International Airport; I swiftly gathered my bag before making a beeline into customs. Whilst in Wales, I had fabricated a new passport, an even better forge than my previous. Today, I was Marcos Gaccio Rossi. Born in Eastern Scotland, raised in Central Italy since the age of two. I did not have the physique nor complexion to pull off someone of true Italian descent. If they asked any questions, my mother was a genuine Italian. However, luck was on my side, without hesitation, I was admitted into the country, and steered towards the exit.

As a young boy, I had heard stories about the remote villages in Northern Pakistan. Bordering the Himalayas, these small isolated covens existed in extreme poverty, yet provided the perfect antidote to anyone's troubles. It was easy to get lost in these diminutive clefts. As long as you had a little money to purchase fruits and vegetables from the locals, one could find themselves a perfect hide-a-way. Seven bus rides and almost twenty painstaking kilometres of foot travel later, I found myself on the outskirts of a village nestled in the base of the mountains. I marvelled at how intact the scenery was. Everything looked like it had just been placed there; as though God had only just created it. Perfect. Trees were plentiful, each one had its own shade of the most dramatic bright green. They swayed gracefully, a light breeze flowing through their rustling tops. The sky was a flawless pale blue. I had never seen the Heavens look so divine: Even the brown earth and slate-grey mountains had their own astonishing characteristics. The range looked mystically cold, yet the clay below it radiated warmth.

My first impression of the village was that it something straight out of a Mark Twain tale. A single, worn dirt path stretching approximately two hundred yards served as the coven's 'main street.' Scrawny chickens ran loose throughout the dusty land. Anorexic looking cattle were tethered haphazardly to large stakes protruding three feet above the ground. A single water pump was situated in the middle of the village, its bronze handle shone brightly in the sunlight. Slightly elevated, and surprisingly well kempt, it was as though this were something of worship. Forty or so dome shaped objects stood soldierly side-by-side. An uneven brown texture covered their exterior walls, all the way up onto their rooftops. Small openings draped with greenery and cloth served as entrances into what I realized were homes. I walked several yards to the first dwelling, and gently placed my hand upon it. The texture was rough, and it crumbled ever so slightly as I smoothed my hand over it. Mud had made these walls. As I made my way through the village, I could not help but notice the one thing it was lacking; inhabitants.

My initial thought was that it had been deserted, perhaps by choice, perhaps not. It was not until I saw the embers in several fire pits did I realize that *someone* was or had been here. I wanted to inspect the homes, but for some strange reason, I could not bring myself to enter them: possibly out of respect, possibly out of trepidation. Either way, I continued my inspection of the village on high alert. A makeshift paddock contained an ancient gray mule. Its sad brown eyes pierced my own as I cautiously walked towards its coffer. A few rusty bicycles along with a rickety wooden buggy sat mouldering next to the animal. I was uncertain how long things had been this way. Surely not for any length of time, the mule looked decrepit, not starved. The dirt floor of the paddock contained no nutrients, so it must be getting food from another source.

The wind blew a gentle breeze causing dust to pick up across the path. It tousled my hair and whistled forcefully in my ears, but not enough to drown out the unmistakable sound of a child's laughter. Not knowing where it had come from, I wheeled around wildly. In my frantic attempt to pinpoint its location, I lost my balance and fell grandly onto my buttocks. More laughter ensued, this time by more than one voice. Gingerly I jumped to my feet, my defences heightened. I could feel their penetrating stares on me, some out of curiosity, others out of fright. They had seen me coming and had retreated to the safety of their homes. Despite being certain the villagers would not harm me, I decided to offer my intent to do them no harm as a precautionary measure. Clearing my throat as though preparing for a speech, I spoke in very clear, articulate English:

"I have no intentions of harming anyone in your village. I plan to set up camp just inside those trees." I pointed towards the woodlands, "I have come in search of food, which I can give you payment for, and I offer my hand in friendship."

I waited, unsure if anyone spoke English, as I did not know a lick of Urdu. The sun beat down on my back. Within five minutes, I was sweating through my clothing. The breeze had died down. I was amazed by how quickly the climate shifted here. Naturally it was cooler at the base of the mountains, however, I did not expect this sort of heat in mid October. I had heard rumours of warm days and extremely cold nights, a reality that was now incontrovertible.

A rustle came from somewhere behind me. I reeled around to come face-to-face with a wizened man. His white hair stuck out in every direction. It was wispy, and reminded me of cotton candy. The loose leathery skin upon his face resembled that of a peeled plum, spongy and delicate. The gentlest of touch would have left him bruised. His eyes bore into my soul. I could see his interest, he was clearly not afraid, yet until he figured me out, he would not give me a shred of empathy. I remained steadfast, not wanting to upset the fragile balance of his analysis. He turned away from me, retreating. I took that as a subtle hint to leave. As though reading my thoughts, he once again faced me and extended his right arm. I felt his brittle fingers push my midsection. Instantly, I froze. He said something intelligible; I parted my lips to tell him that I did not understand.

"Err..." I began slowly. I hesitated as it had become clear that he was not talking to me. A woman, as old and as frail as he, appeared from the doorway of the dome I had touched. She was covered from head to toe in a bright yellow muslin material. Her pace was slow, yet for someone as aged as she, she moved rather gracefully. Her arms were laden with a woven basket chalked full of fruits and vegetables. Although I could not see the rest of her facial features, her eyes showed the same curiosity the old man's had. He took the basket from her, she quickly withdrew. I knew from my readings that as part of their culture, woman were not to be seen nor accepted by the general public. I hardly considered myself public, yet this is what these people knew.

"How long will you stay?"

I gasped. His English was impeccable, raspy with age, yet eloquent. Feeling foolish for my reaction, I quickly regained my composure.

"Uh," I cleared my throat, "I am uncertain at this point. A few weeks, maybe a month... I do not know."

He nodded in understanding. "We do not have electricity nor do we have running water. There is a pump with a wash basin should you require it, and bicycles should you need to ride into a larger village to obtain supplies we do not have. Fruits and vegetables are plentiful as are chickens."

It was my turn to nod in agreement. I had never dreamed of such acceptance. "Thank you... so much." I murmured.

"Take this basket. We do not require payment, only your trust and alliance. You can stay in the village should you please. I am certain you be will more comfortable here, however, that is your decision to make."

Again, I expelled a gracious "Thank you."

He nodded and turned his heel. As he walked away, I announced, "I am Wilhelm." He did not hesitate. "Thought you ought to know..." I muttered as he disappeared out of sight.

Not wishing to jeopardize my welcome, I decided to stay at the base of the mountains. There were hundreds of fissures to shelter me against the elements. I chose a roomy space between two sister peaks. The inner cavern was chilly, the coarse wintry floor did not look appealing, nor did the damp walls, nonetheless, I would make do. Leaving my effects behind, I left my new home in search of tinder and greenery. I slowly ebbed my way over the jaded boulders, and out across the uneven ground into the foothills of the trees. An ocean of green engulfed me. I was in a thicket of vastness. It swallowed me whole, sucking my senses away from me. I heard nothing, saw only varying shades of green, even my sense of smell had become void. It was as though I had been completely cut off from reality. There were no birds, no traces of larger animals, nor insects. I was alone. Something I was used to, however, it still seemed very odd. I felt like I had discovered some sort of alien planet, which held a life different from that of our own. I was invading on them, probing into their lifestyle, taking in their habitat, all in the means of sharing my new-found knowledge with my kind. Shaking my head foolishly, I began to gather as many twigs and as much foliage as my arms could carry. Although it was just a woodland, I could not liberate myself from the potent feelings which cautioned I should not be here.

Staggering back down to reality, my eyes scurried over the mountains and across the dry land into the village. Part of me needed to be sure of my surroundings. Normally a very rational man, I could not fathom a reason as to why I had felt so oddly insecure whilst among the trees. Perhaps being alone on foreign soil had started to take its toll on me. Or perhaps, I was losing my mind. The latter would not have surprised me in the least. I had accepted long ago that I must have some sort of defect. Mental, physical, I was unsure which, possibly both. It took a crazy, yet strong man to do the things which I have done. I was not going to let my intelligence and personal will take all the credit. There had to be lunacy lurking somewhere.

Once back inside the cavern, I began my feeble attempts to build a fire without the aid of matches. The villagers had already shown me great hospitality, I did not want to impress my neediness on them by asking for a few embers from their fire pit. After four hours of deceitful sparks, but no flame, I resigned my efforts. Putting my concentration elsewhere, I began to intertwine the foliage. My fingers were numb, so I worked fast. The end result was nothing to be proud of, alas it was usable. It would have taken mass amounts to make a cushion suitable enough for sleeping upon and I also had to factor in keeping warm. Adorned in every article of clothing I owned, and a secondary 'blanket' type weave, I settled in to my new bed and attempted sleep.

Death would have been more bearable. The mountain was not as weatherproof as I had hoped, as each tiny crack within its walls brought not only noise, but bitter drafts. I was using everything within my grasp to keep warm. The twigs were now serving as a layer of insulation. Rocks encircled my body; a pathetic effort to keep the draft at bay. Freezing to death would have been welcome. The longer I convulsed, the more I wished some wild animal would rip me to pieces. Chills rocketed into my bones, my joints became numb, sleep was unavoidable. I stared blindly into the darkness, my eyes were glacial, two frozen little ice cubes. I prayed for daylight or death, whichever would come first. I didn't care, so long as I didn't have to endure this any further.

The laughter had returned. High pitched, yet muffled at the same time. My eyes were swollen, too tired to open, so I lain in silence listening. I was certain it was a young child, perhaps even two of them. I heard footsteps scraping across the boulders at the base of the peak. For each step, a dull thud ensued. Too stiff to move, I made no attempt to see what was going on. After the night I had just had, an assassin could have picked me off without much effort. I had no intentions of stirring anytime soon. Considerably warmer now, I tuned out whatever was now making a rattling noise and allowed myself to drift away.

The twigs and rocks were a bad idea. Rolling over to a more comfortable position yielded only injuries, as jagged stones gouged into my ribcage. I pushed myself up into a sitting position, only to be jabbed in the buttocks by several twigs. Of all the desperate things to do... If I wouldn't have been so uneasy about returning to the woods, I would have had a warm, comfortable night. After stretching cautiously, I rummaged in the basket for something to settle my hunger. I devoured two mangos, or rather ravaged them. Their sweet juices barely satisfied my thirst. Like a starving beast, I craved so much more.

Each day a new gift was bestowed upon me. My first twenty-four hours yielded a copper pot which contained half a dozen orange embers. My nights had been nothing less than wonderful since. Within the next seventy-two hours, I had mysteriously acquired a loaf of bread, two canteens of water, a blanket made of what appeared to be hemp, and a man's green button down shirt. I had my suspicions as to who was leaving me these things, however, I could never catch the culprit in his or her act of kindness. The deeds seemed to be coupled with the sounds of laughter. I tried to keep my distance from the village as much as possible. I was oblivious to its inhabitants, yet I still felt uncomfortable using their water supply and taking their fruits and vegetables. My days were spent gathering tinder and stoking my fire.

As much as I enjoyed the time to myself, part of me yearned for the humidity and bliss that I experienced in Honey Bayou. I had never been so limitless. I believed the stories of violence, control and poverty. One glance throughout the village confirmed the horrors that this country suppresses. It was difficult to tell if the villagers were happy. If this was the only life they knew, I imagined it would be hard to see the bigger picture. Nonetheless, they must have known that this...their lives as they knew it, was not right. I brusquely poked the fire's orange embers thinking of ways I could kill President Zafar Amini. I ran down my usual list: poison, bomb, sniper rifle...etcetera, etcetera. Why the United States Armed Forces did not kill the putrid swine in the early nineteen-nineties was beyond me. They could have saved everyone a world of trouble. I supposed it never crossed their minds, they had their eyes on resources then...

I heard the dull thud once again; quickly I snapped out of my reverie and scrambled for the peak's opening. There was no laughter, yet I could hear the calculated steps of someone crossing over the boulders. I peered out the hole. Two small children were making their way towards me; heads down, concentrating on their steps. The young boy was roughly twelve years old. His brown skin was smudged with dirt, his hair matted to his head. He wore a ragged pair of beige pants and a matching shirt. He was carrying another woven basket full of fruit. The girl had long black hair which was platted in a gold barrette. She also wore ragged clothing; however, her pale yellow shirt was more embellished than the young boy's. The boy shifted away from her and I immediately saw the source of the thudding. The girl was walking with a makeshift set of crutches; her left pant leg had been hemmed up to her knee. She was missing a limb. I watched in awe as the two climbed towards me. The boy would stop every few feet to help the girl. She always shook him off and carried on without any assistance. *So these two were my Robin Hood.* I felt grateful and shameful at the same time. They were giving me things which clearly they could use themselves.

When they reached the opening, the boy placed the basket on a flat rock. His hand was inches from my foot. I wanted to thank them, but I was at a loss for words. Clearly the children did not want to be seen. I didn't want to make a spectacle, nonetheless, it would have been rude to not acknowledge their kindness.

"Thank you," I said gently.

I heard the girl gasp. She said something in Urdu before taking off as fast as her crutches would allow her. The boy looked after her, but did not follow. He had a curious expression on his face, as though he wanted to ask me something. I poked my head out to get a better look at him. He had big brown eyes and eyelashes that touched his cheeks when he blinked. His lips were thin, his jaw strong and prominent. I knew that look: he was trying to show his bravery. I could not help but smile. He was no more than twelve years old, yet he stared me down just as the old man in the village had.

"Are you from America?"

I was slightly taken aback by his English. I was certain he did not learn it in school. From what I saw, education was nonexistent. His eyes were fixed on me. A proud, but defiant look upon his face.

"No, I am not." No point lying to the boy. I had already told the old man and whoever else was listening my name, so it wouldn't hurt if they knew what country I hailed from.

"Then where?" He demanded more than asked.

"England," I replied.

He studied me for a few moments as though trying to find truth in my words. The girl had stopped some six feet down the mountain, she rolled her eyes and shook her head in what I was certain was irritation. He spotted me looking at her; his features instantly darkened.

"Is that your sister?" I asked.

Lightning flashed in his eyes, but before he could respond, I cheerfully said "Tell her thank you again for the food and clothing. And you as well, thank you for your kindness." I retreated into the cavern, hoping he understood my words to be compassionate as opposed to immoral. His voice followed me in.

"Can I come back tomorrow?"

I hesitated. "Err, sure. I will be here."

The boy returned at dawn, his arms filled with bread and mangos.

"My Mother wanted you to have these."

I took the items and uttered my thanks. I had expected him in midmorning or afternoon; my eyes were still adjusting to the creeping daylight, my joints popped loudly with renewed function.

"I'm Nouman. I'm thirteen."

He seemed very proud of himself. For his age, and for his ability to comprehend English. I was sure he was probably only one of two children whom understood and spoke it.

"My sister said you are welcome. She was too scared to come. She's fifteen, her name is Sanari. She does not like too many people."

"I understand. It is a pleasure meeting you. I am Wilhelm." My lips curled into a wide grin, "But you probably already knew that, right?" The boy stared back at me, his teeth were dazzling white against his brown skin.

Nodding his head furiously, he said, "Yes, I know. I heard you tell Rehan."

I understood Rehan to be the old man whom I had spoken to when I first arrived in the village.

"Why are you here?" Like yesterday, he demanded an answer as opposed to asking for one. It was impossible not to like the kid. His eyes danced like gypsies, and his smile could light up even the darkest of places.

"I am visiting your country. I have never been here before, so I plan to hike around for a while." I hated to lie to the boy, but I highly doubted he would understand my true reasons for being here.

His eyes scrutinized me for a few moments. I knew he was trying to find the truth. It was a terrible lie, even this thirteen year old had figured that out.

"Why Tindki? Why our village? There are hundreds of better places to visit." He fiddled benignly with a loose string on his pants. I noticed his hands were course and bore many cuts and bruises. He had hands as old as my own. Perhaps I was misreading the boy.

"I got off the bus in Islamabad and continued heading North. This is where I ended up. I will not be here much longer though. I just wanted to see the Himalayas. They are Heavenly."

Deciding a change of subject was in order, I grabbed two mangos from the basket, tossed him one and asked "Do you go to school around here?" I hoped I sounded interested and inconspicuous.

The boy weighed the fruit in his hands and replied, "No." He took a small bite, and continued, "No one goes to school here. We are taught how to read and write by our mothers, but that is only if they know how themselves."

"I see. I assumed you went to school. Your English is perfect, where did you learn to speak it?" This was the truth. I was truly impressed with his grasp of the English language.

"My father taught my mother, sister and I." He said this in an offhand manner, as something like this occurred quite regularly. "He went to school in America for a while. Before he met my Mother. Before my sister and I."

I had many questions for this boy. Why had his father returned from the United States? The quality of living and standard of care was much better than here. What made him come back? I never got to ask him anything, for bloodcurdling screams rang out from somewhere below us. It was noticeably a woman, and she was plainly afraid for her life. I dropped my mango and bolted towards the exit. I was almost outside when the boy's soft voice echoed, "You cannot help them." He sighed heavily. "No one can. You will only make the men angry."

I only half-registered what he was saying. The screams had gotten worse; they had, in fact quadrupled. Fear, agony, pain... I could hear it all so vividly. I had to know what or who was causing these woman such pain. I stepped out onto the landing, immediately a force pulled me backwards.

"You cannot be seen! They will kill you!" The boy had his small hands around my waist and was tugging me back in. "Please! You do not understand..." His voice was pleading, he was genuinely frightened.

Gone were the dancing gypsies in his eyes. His lips were taut, as was the rest of him. I permitted him to steer me back to the fire. His grip did not lax until I held up my hands in surrender. He released me, but kept a stern eye in my direction. I could not help but chuckle under my breath. He was a mere thirteen.

After several minutes I sat down. The boy mimicked me. He drew his knees to his chest, tightly wrapping his arms around them. His features were so broken. I noticed for the first time just how pale he was. Whatever was happening in the village was clearly heinous. I wanted to ask him what was going on, but he was so young and already so frightened, I didn't want to dredge up any more sediment. The screams had not subsided, and I could have sworn I heard shots from a pistol mingled amongst them. From the expression on the boy's face, he had heard it too.

All afternoon he sat in the same position. He would not eat the bread I had lain out for him; his canteen of water was left untouched. I thought he was in shock. He definitely looked it. His skin was ashen, and his right hand twitched ever so slightly. His breathing was strained, laborious. This was not normal behaviour for a child.

"They did that to my sister. To her leg." It was a mere whisper. He still had not moved an inch, yet his eyes were glassy, his lips parted. Staring at the wall, he spoke in hushed tones once more.

"Those men work for Zafar Amini. He sends them into the villages to bring back young girls. Some he marries, some he makes his slaves, others he just kills for pleasure. When the men arrive, they invade every home in the village and force the daughters to line up side by side. Any girl under twelve is excused, but not without promises to come back when they are of age. Not every girl is chosen to go with them. They have to meet Zafar's standards. Pretty is all he wants. No deformities. The girls that are chosen are forced into a truck and taken away. They never return. Their families rarely try to stop the men: mostly because they are cowards." He scoffed, his eyes full of disgust as his words lingered. Visibly, his family had stood up to the force.

"Two years ago they came to Tindki. There were only nine girls of age then, my sister one of them. Since we live in the east end of the village, and furthest away, she was last in line. My mother cried as they took her outside. She knew Sanari would never return. My father pleaded with the men, telling them she was only eleven. One man grabbed my sister and pulled down her shalwar, that would be pants to you. He pointed excitedly at my sister's private area, and told my father that the hair upon it proved she was of age. Mortified, my sister began to cry, the man slapped her and told her that she needed to hold her tongue; or she would suffer greatly. The first two girls were turned away because they were disfigured. One had a large birthmark covering half her face from the nose down; the other had a growth on her neck. My mother tried to shield me from view, but during her weak moment I saw everything. The girl before Sanari was ignored completely, she ran back to her family with arms wide open. The same man who had humiliated my sister was then inches away from her face, rubbing his hands on her cheeks, and grinning widely. *He* wanted her badly. That much was obvious. I watched with fury as he touched every part of her body. She cringed as he cupped her breasts and placed his hands on her bottom."

The boy swallowed dryly. For the first time, he reached for the canteen. Hastily unscrewing the cap, he chugged half the water down in two gulps. Crossing his legs, he fiddled with the canteen's cap for a few seconds before continuing his narrative.

"Another man spoke harshly and pushed my sister towards the truck. My mother screamed and sunk to her knees. She began to pray to Allah. She recited every verse from the Chapters of Al-lkhlas. She begged Allah to spare her. She pulled me next to her and through her tears asked me to pray with everything I had left in me. Together we beseeched that Sanari be left with us. There was none comparable to our Allah, he would answer our prayers. Through the shrieking and banging we prayed. My mother's voice was heard over all as she continued to plead."

"I heard a loud pop, and my sister's cries of pain. My father ran into our home calling for gauzes and water. My mother did not move she was lost in prayer, so I followed my father's frantic movements. He shoved a pot of water into my arms and pushed me out the door. The men were gone, however, my sister lay in the dirt, blood all around her. Rehan was by her side praying and soothing her. He was clutching Sanari's leg, his hands covered in blood. My sister's fingers were dug into the ground, and she was howling in pain. My father took the water from me and carefully poured it over her kneecap. Sanari screamed in anguish. Immediately I saw what had caused her pain. A small bullet was lodged in her knee. She was bleeding uncontrollably. My father sent me to fetch more water while Rehan called for someone to get the mule and wagon ready. When I went back into the house, my mother was laying on her side. She was talking crazy, and reaching for my ankles as I walked past her. When I returned, Sanari had been loaded into the wagon and gauzes had been wrapped tightly around her leg. There was cloth placed in her mouth to muffle her cries. My father took the water and told me to look after my mother. He left with Rehan and two other men from the village. I did not see my sister nor my father for almost three months."

"We thought they were dead. My mother was beside herself. She would not cook, clean or wash our clothing. I tended to our garden and chickens while the other woman in the village brought us meals and washed our things. My mother did nothing but recite from Quran. She refused meals and would not even get up to bathe herself. Rehan and the other men had still not returned, and there had been no messages brought to us from other villages; we were under a constant cloud of darkness. In mid July they returned. I was feeding the chickens when I heard the hooves of the mule and the churning of the wagon approaching. Rehan was sitting on top, my father and the other men in the wagon. I threw the feed aimlessly towards the birds and ran to greet my father. He looked like he had aged one hundred years. His eyes had dark circles under them and his clothes hung from his frame. When I did not see Sanari, fear immediately settled in my gut. Rehan halted the mule and stepped down from the platform. My father got out of the wagon and came towards me. He could barely walk. He asked me to heat up some water and make up a bed. I ran into the house shouting to my mother that my father had returned. She was so lost inside her own mind, she did not respond to me. I did everything he asked of me, and when I met him in the doorway, he was cradling Sanari. My eyes lit up and he smiled weakly at me. She was sleeping, I could see her chest moving up and down, so I knew everything would be fine. As soon as my mother saw my father and sister she snapped out of her coma. It was like nothing had ever changed. She cooked a huge meal for us all and busied herself taking care of Sanari. My father took me aside and explained that she had been taken to the hospital in Islamabad where she had to have an operation to remove the bullet. He also told me that she would need support to help her walk for the rest of her life. When I told him that was okay, I would help her, he said that she would be with us until Allah took her. She would never be able to marry or do things that young woman her age should be doing. I told him I did not understand, nor did I care. Sanari was alive, that was all that mattered. He smiled, placed his arm on my shoulder and told me I was a good boy. He said that Sanari would need me more than anything now and he was proud that I was so willing to help her. I just thought she was going to be sore for a while. But then he told me that the operation she had was to remove part of her leg."

"I still did not care. I would take care of her. She was my sister and I loved her. When she came around, we had wood supports for her. It took her a while to get used to using them. She cried a lot and was very bitter, but with time she got over it. She still does not like my help, but she accepts it without much complaint. I have asked her what happened while I was praying with our mother but she will not speak of it. Hafiz, the boy who lives next to us, later told me that my father fought with the men. He said that he would not allow them to take Sanari. They would have to kill him if they wanted her. Pagah, the man who had been touching my sister, grabbed his gun and pointed it at my father. Hafiz said that as Pagah pulled the trigger, Sanari stepped in front of my father and the bullet hit her in the leg. As soon as Pagah realized that she was disfigured, he no longer wanted her. The men got into their truck and left the village."

It took me a while to notice that the boy had stopped speaking. My blood was boiling. I could not fathom what I had just heard. Such atrocities. In the past there had been rumours that such behaviour still existed throughout the middle east, but I never dreamed proof would be sitting a mere six feet away from me. I was foolish to think that the violence had been somewhat controlled. There were laws in place to stop this kind of blatant disregard for another human life. These people were not only suffering from poverty and cruelty, but they were having everything stripped away from them. Pieces were being torn from their hearts. Zafar was a monster; stealing children, raping them, killing them. Who would allow such things to happen? Who would want to see such things happen? I wanted Zafar dead more than anything.

....

My bond with the boy had grown. So much that I was now spending my days and most nights with him. I had not been down to the village to meet his family, but they graciously sent provisions with him. He told me all about his life, which incidentally wasn't much of one. He had never seen the city, only the neighbouring village of Kubar. He spent his days helping his father with chores, and working on the lessons his mother planned for him. I was amazed by how easy it was to converse with him. Despite our cultural and age differences, we had much in common. After several weeks Sanari found comfort in the cavern and started to frequent the place as much as her brother had. Although she never spoke of what happened to her, she knew that I had been brought up to speed by Nouman. She eyed him reproachfully when she felt he had gone too far with his narratives. He was a natural born talker. I hardly had to say anything. He would ask the odd question about my travels and childhood, but most of the time was spent discussing his dreams, hopes and future. He yearned to go to university in America like his father, Aamir, had. However, with no formal education, he knew that would never be a realization. Aamir was raised in Islamabad, so he had many opportunities and took every one of them. He only returned to Pakistan because his mother and father had prearranged his marriage to Aisha, Nouman's mother. Nouman said he knew his father missed America terribly, but he also did not regret his decision to marry his mother.

Nouman walked next to me bending down every few yards to collect tinder. He had become my sidekick. We ate meals together, prayed together, me to my God, him to Allah, and we swapped family tales passed down by our descendants. His family did not seem to mind his absence so long as he did his lessons and chores. Oddly I did not seem to mind his company. Nouman's father had trekked up in the mountains one afternoon to formally introduce himself, and to extend an invitation to dinner. I accepted graciously and we exchanged pleasantries. He was perhaps ten years younger than I, still youthful in the face, but his body was worn. Nouman was a spitting image of him. As I washed my face and hands before I left, Nouman's voice echoed from outside. He came into the cavern carrying an armful of cloth which he dumped onto my makeshift cot.

"My father asked me to give these to you. He said the villagers will be more accepting of your presence if you are wearing the proper clothing. The kameez may be a bit too tight, but my mother can take some of the fabric out for you. She is good with a needle and thread. The shalwar should fit you almost perfectly."

The shirt and pants were brown and reminded me of loose flowing hospital garb. Nouman waited outside as I changed into the outfit. Together we walked down to the village. He chatted animatedly about a girl he was interested in, and I just listened as twilight fell up on us. A long row of burning fires lit the path to Nouman's place. Most of the villagers were loitering around their homes, tending to their fires, conversing with their neighbours. For some strange reason, I was nervous. My stomach was doing back flips. A gentle breeze kept us comfortable, yet I was sweating by the time we reached the edge of the village. Nouman stopped in front of the door, and pulled the cloth covering aside before bowing me inside. Oil lamps and candles lit the inside of their home. It was as small as it had looked. The kitchen area was to my left. There was no stove, or refrigerator. Just a wooden counter top cluttered with spices and jugs of water. A single lopsided table and four chairs were set in the centre of the room. Two small shabby writing tablets were to my right; a doorway draped in cloth led to what I assumed was a bedroom directly in front of me. No photos hung on the walls, no artwork or knickknacks. This is what poverty truly was like.

I heard the unstable thud of Sanari approaching. She was dazzling in a vibrant pink shirt and matching bottoms. The material was rather shiny, I guessed it to be chiffon or silk. She smiled stiffly and said hello to me before busying herself with something on the countertop. I watched as she filled a woven basket with spices and five plates. She left as quickly as she had arrived. Aamir came from the other part of the house to greet me. He shook my hand and offered me a glass of water. He too was wearing a shiny shirt and pants. His were a darker colour, perhaps navy blue, made from the same material as Sanari's. I glanced at Nouman, but he was no longer next to me. I had been so engrossed with Aamir's attire that I had not noticed his absence. He returned shortly and was also wearing new clothing. The pale golden material shone against his skin like diamonds. Then understanding hit me; they were all wearing dress garments.

Sanari returned and spoke sharp Urdu to Nouman. He chuckled and chased after her. Within seconds he was back carrying two plates in each hand, followed by Sanari and a woman I guessed to be their mother. I gasped when I first laid eyes upon her. She was beautiful; perhaps the most beautiful woman I had ever seen. Her long dark hair touched her waist and was pulled back behind her. Her eyes were dark like the rest of them, but her skin was the colour of milk chocolate. She had full lips, and a very youthful heart shaped face. She could have passed for eighteen years old. Her purple shalwar and kameez sparkled, the gemstone embellishments across her chest were striking against her features. She smiled at me, a row of perfect white teeth protruded between her lips. Her arms were laden with three plates and a basket hung from her right arm. I could smell curry and chicken. It was intoxicating, and my mouth was suddenly watering. The plates were carefully set down on the table, the basket in the centre of everything. I wanted to eat the whole table. Nouman saw the look upon my face and chuckled. Sanari shot him a look of disgusted. Aisha did not speak, rather she poured water into glasses and placed each one in front of a corresponding plate. Sanari said something to Aisha who merely nodded in agreement. Nouman played translator.

"Father went to borrow a chair from Hafiz's family. We are very fortunate; most families eat off of a raised surface with cushions on the floor. When he returns we will pray, then eat. It will not be too much longer." I could tell he added the last bit in for my stomach's benefit. I was certain both Sanari and Aisha could hear it grumbling from four feet away.

Aamir brought the extra chair, and we all sat down at the table. We were elbow to elbow, but no one seemed to mind. The four of them prayed while I thanked the Lord for the meal I was about to receive, and for such good company. Nouman's mother spoke for the first time, explaining that she had prepared Quarma, a rice dish cooked with curried chicken which was to be eaten with Naan. Flat bread, as I knew it by. It was absolutely wonderful. There was no talking throughout the meal; everyone was concentrating on their food. I ate three helpings, and was eyeing Sanari's as well. She saw me looking at her plate, mumbled dryly, before earnestly shovelling the rest of her chicken into her mouth. She was an odd, but sweet girl. After dinner, Nouman and Sanari cleared the table and took the dishes out to be washed. Aamir explained that there was a basin and a secondary fire pit used for cooking in their backyard. Aisha stood organizing her spices and wiping down the countertop. She didn't speak whilst attending these duties. I was beginning to think she did not approve of me. Aamir must have read my mind because he apologetically looked at me and said, "Aisha is normally very sunny and cheerful. She is shy and meeting new people is somewhat of a discomfort to her. Do not worry, she will lighten up with time."

Aisha's back stiffened, and Aamir winked at me just as she was turning to face us. She gave him a chagrin look that could have rivalled Sanari's. Aamir simply smiled and blew her a kiss. It was evident that the normal code of conduct did not apply within their home.

....

"Why can I not go with you?" Nouman demanded. His lips were depressed into a frown, his brow furrowed. Miserable eyes penetrated my own, reminding me of a scolded dog. He had been watching me pack up my things from a distance.

I sighed heavily. "I told you, Nouman, you cannot go where I am going because you are too young."

"Where are you going then?" His voice was rising. More so out of outrage then of gloom.

"You are too young to understand. Please just trust me. You cannot go where I am going, and you cannot know where I am going."

Nouman spat on the stone floor.

"That is horseshit! We are friends. You know everything about me and my family. You *are* one of us now. I am not too young. In case you have not noticed, I can handle quite a bit. I am going with you."

I stooped at the waist to where my eyes were level with his. I gazed at his youthfulness. Innocence was drawn on every line of his skin. This is the only thing that stopped me from taking him. "No, you are not," I breathed.

He glared back, hands on his hips, his jaw set. "Yes, I am."

I was resigned. It was a losing battle. Ever since I had told him I was leaving we had been having the same dead-end conversation. He wasn't going. He was a child. He needed to be with his family and friends. He was just too young to understand what I was going to do. Although he would be grateful, he would not see past it but as a mere act of vengeance. I did not want him to think that way. It was much more than that. I wanted to take him with me, but I knew he would not be able to grasp that killing Zafar Amini was a necessity. He needed to understand that hate could not be the ruler of one's mind and decisions. His sister's wounds ran too deep, and until he was old enough to sort out hate from need, he would be kept in the dark.

"Please, Wilhelm," he begged.

I had heard those words so many times in the last three days. As he wrapped his emotions around every syllable, I struggled to find reasons to make him stay. I shook my head every time. I had seen him go through every emotional phase there was: anger, sadness, hysterics, even excitement when he thought that I was showing weakness and may allow him to come with me. But I held firm. At least until I could no longer stand my ground...

We had been arguing for six hours. I was tired, Nouman was tired, yet our pride would not allow us to render.

"ENOUGH!" I boomed at him. "SIT DOWN, NOW!"

Nouman was taken aback, but obliged, and sat in his usual place by the fire. I exhaled slowly as I sat as well. I placed my head in my hands in an attempt to regain my composure. I felt horrible for yelling at him, but my mind and emotions were frayed. Slowly, I resumed even breathing. I looked over at Nouman. He was fidgeting with some pebbles on the floor. I had to tell him.

"First of all, I am not giving in that easily. Out of friendship and compassion, I am going to explain to you why you cannot accompany me to Islamabad. I want you to understand that what I am telling you is very real, and I am only telling you because I feel our bond is strong enough to sustain such a blow. "

He nodded, but kept his head down.

"You asked me why I am here. Why Tindki? Obviously you know that I am running from something, and that I am hiding something. You have known that since the first time we met. I am here because I needed a place to stay whilst I figured out how I was going to kill Zafar Amini."

Nouman's eyes were wide. He mouthed the words *Kill Zafar Amini* to himself.

"You are an assassin," he concluded more than asked. His body language showed no indifference to it. We could have been chatting about automobiles.

"Yes, and no. I do not kill out of spite, I kill out of sheer longing for a better life. A better life for you, for your family, for all else who suffers. I kill because I must, not because I want to. There *is* a difference." I wasn't sure whom I was trying to convince more, him or myself.

"You see, I have lived worse off than you. I have experience true suffering. I have seen it etched into the faces of my peers. The leaders of this world preach humility and harmony, yet they spawn hate, lies and torment whenever the opportunity arises. Take for instance, my friend Hans. He was killed by a Russian diplomat and his two guards for simply not understanding their language. He did nothing wrong, but for some reason, these heathens marked him as their prey. I watched one of the diplomat's men execute him without a second thought. He just took out his pistol and shot him between the eyes. Hans never had a hope nor a prayer. Do you know of Takada Nakamura? He is the Prime Minister of Japan. He poisoned over one hundred thousand of his own countrymen and blamed it on the Afghans and Iraqis. As if that was not bad enough, he decided to take population control into his own hands by making a deal with the United States, Canada and Australia. He sent boatloads of children overseas, where they were bought and forced into slavery and God only knows what other horrors. Recently, a boat sunk off the coast of Alaska. Roughly two thousand children were on that boat. They perished in the deep waters. Just think of all those families who have suffered. They will never know what happened to their children. Takada will die next."

Nouman never spoke. He let me speak without interruption. When I finished, he jumped up and said, "When do we leave?" Not exactly the reaction I was hoping for. He must have seen it on my face, because he quickly defended himself.

"I am going. You said I need to understand the difference between hate and necessity. How will I ever know if I cannot be permitted to witness it in its true form? We can lie to my mother and father. Tell them you want a tour guide, someone who speaks the language, and knows the customs. Which *is* what you need. You will be killed for sure if you do not take me with you."

I pinched the bridge of my nose with my thumb and index finger. He had a valid point, but I just could not drag him into this. If something went awry and he was harmed, or worse killed... thoughts I did not want to think. Nonetheless, everything he was saying made sense. I was torn between what was logical, and what was easiest. I sat in silence pondering on what I should do. My gut told me yes, my head told me no. Sighing deeply, I looked over at Nouman. He was still standing, his eyes full of anticipation.

"You will ask both your mother and father first. You will tell them that I have asked if you can go with me for no more than a couple of weeks into Islamabad. I want to see the city, and I need someone who can help me get around. If they say no, their word is final."

Before I could finish, he was gone. I heard him stumble on the rocks on his way down. I prayed this decision would not haunt me forever.

....

The old Mercedes bounced violently along the dirt road. Nouman sat in the passenger seat next to me in his glory. The smug expression had yet to leave his face. Aamir was just as excited as Nouman for our 'trip.' He gathered a knapsack full of provisions for both Nouman and I, and had given us the names and addresses of a few old friends should we need assistance while we were in the city. Aisha was not too keen on the idea of Nouman leaving, but in the end, she stuffed the largest basket she could find with bread and mangos before sending Nouman on his way. Aamir followed him up the mountain. Nouman was wise to give me warning by talking as loudly as possible on their way up. Without acknowledgment, they had entered the cavern together. Aamir was beaming with delight as he gave me a road map and a set of keys.

"Walk directly into the trees until you find a small clearing," he had said. "There you will find an old Mercedes covered in moss and leaves. I tweaked it a little bit as soon as Nouman mentioned the trip. It should run no problem. Aisha and the other villagers do not know about it. When I moved here, I was supposed to give up all 'outside' technology. The car belonged to my father, so I've kept it hidden all these years. I took it out about a month ago, everything seemed operational. Just watch the clutch."

He bent down to hug Nouman whose eyes were huge with astonishment. Aamir shook my hand and wished us a safe, pleasurable trip. I thanked him for his kindness and promised to bring Nouman back in roughly fourteen days time.

The drive was uneventful. Nouman, for once, was speechless as he had never experienced anything like this before. He knew what a car was, had seen the truck Zafar's men brought into the village, but he had never ridden in one before. There were so many things he knew of, but had not experienced. First on the agenda was permitting him a few of life's finer delights.

At dusk we found ourselves on the outskirts of Islamabad. Other than a few short stops to consult the map, relieve ourselves and refuel, we had made excellent timing. Nouman anticipated that we would be driving for "at least three days." His comprehension of car versus mule was a little off. Nouman had never eaten in a restaurant, never stayed in a hotel, nor saw a female wearing jeans, or men "talking into black rectangles." I tried not to laugh at his ignorance, it was not his fault.

The first three days were spent educating him on all the things he had no concept of. I took him to the local library to show him how to work a computer. He was instantly addicted, and asked the librarian if he could take the machine home for a month. She laughed whole-heartedly before telling him no, but he was more than welcome to come back and use it anytime he desired. I showed him how to work a telephone. He was amazed by how we could be talking to someone who was not next to us. To make sure it was a real thing, he called half a dozen strangers and marvelled at how the "thing" worked. They all hung up on him. He was positively delighted about it. He had his first taste of chocolate ice cream, and said that he would never feel the same way about his mother's cooking ever again. I laughed as he tried to figure out how the microwave in our hotel room worked. He pushed every button and read the manual twice before finally chalking it up to some alien technology. He still struggled with the concept of electricity. He did not understand running water, nor the shower or commode, but he was grateful for them both. He later said that he could get used to such things *if* he had to.

On our fifth day in the city, we finally got down to business. The weather was chilly, and a light drizzle was coming down. While Nouman was taking another hour long shower, I went to the nearest convenience store to purchase more ice cream and chocolate bars. Nouman's face lit up like Christmas lights when I told him that chocolate was simply a flavour that was put into the ice cream. There were different kinds of both. So far he had taken a liking to strawberry and vanilla. He much more preferred the chocolate on it's own in the form of a candy bar. He enjoyed it with peanuts and caramel as well. I bought several items for myself: a small note pad, all the local newspapers and matches. I will never again freeze because I could not manage to rub two sticks together.

Nouman was taking six showers a day and flushing the commode just for fun. I took the telephone away from him before he could start calling random numbers again. He was slightly disappointed, but I explained to him that the hotel charges extra to use the telephone, and it's usually more than a few Rupees. I kept him busy scanning the newspapers for any type of events that Zafar may be attending or any cities he may intend on visiting. This brought nothing but dead-ends as there was little about the President's movements being published. Nouman wanted to storm into Karachi with guns blazing. I will admit after eight days of nothing, it sounded like a solid plan to me. Nouman was getting anxious. He had considered everything from strapping a bomb to himself in a suicide attempt to stealing a "gigantic truck" and crashing it into

Zafar and his men when they exited their office building after work. Either way I looked at it, a trip to the capitol was inevitable.

We loaded up early on the ninth day and headed south for Karachi. Nouman was in renewed spirits. All the way he threw out crazy ideas.

"Let's pay someone to do it. My father gave me some Rupees before we left. How much do you think it would cost?"

He was serious, yet between the two of us, we did not even come close to funding a professional hit. "Too much," I mumbled. He sank into the seat, his eyes closed in concentration.

"Don't worry, we will figure it out. Once we get closer to his building, we will know what is plausible and what is not."

Arms crossed in front of his chest, Nouman put his feet up on the dash and muttered, "I still say we shoot him. That's my vote."

I chuckled. "This is not a democracy. There will be no vote."

Yawning, Nouman put his head on the seat and closed his eyes. "I know. But if it was, my vote would be to shoot him."

"Do you even know what a democracy is?"

"No."

Shooting him was in fact our only option. As day ten came to a close, panic sunk in. While Nouman was enjoying his eighth shower of the day, I took a stroll of down town Karachi, in particular the administrative building where I knew Zafar's office was located. The building was entirely made of glass, and at least forty stories high. A map of the structure coupled with a public tour told me that floors forty-five through forty-eight were the private offices of the President and his cabinet. Metal detectors and guards with pistols protected the entrance and exits to the building. This, of course, was a given. As the tour ended and we shuffled towards the exit, I had one thing on my mind: the building ten blocks away.

Nouman was waiting for me when I returned. Television remote in hand, he hit the "mute" button as I entered the room and took my sweater off.

"Well?" he inquired.

I simply smiled at him and went into the bathroom.

"You are happy. What is going on?" He yelled through the door.

I washed my face and unbolted the latch. I heard an "Ow" as the door collided with something solid. Nouman stood several feet away hopping on his right leg, his left foot clutched in his hands. I sat down on the bed, and took my shoes off. Nouman hobbled over to me, and put his hands on his hips, his lips turned up into a triumphant grin.

"We are going to shoot him, aren't we?"

I simply nodded in affirmation.

Chapter 10

Karachi, Pakistan
17 December, 1995

Locating a weapon was not as difficult as I had thought it would be. Nouman had a way with words. In no time we found the shadiest places of the city and had coaxed a name and address out of a deranged drug addict. The Middle -Eastern black market was large and powerful. One could obtain anything they dreamed of. This excited, yet scared me, and I made sure Nouman understood that obtaining things illegally was not acceptable. Of course, his cheek and tongue pointed out that I was doing just that.

I needed something powerful. A rifle was what could send a two hundred fifty grain bullet sailing at about three thousand feet per second. I needed a muzzle energy of at least four thousand pounds. In more comprehensible terms, I needed to knock a markhor down from two kilometres away. This would not be a problem the arms dealer said. He told me I could become the proud owner of a .338 Lapua magnum for a mere four hundred thousand Pakistan Rupees, or five thousand U.S. dollars. I told him he must be joking, and turned to leave his shop. He hesitated begrudgingly before hissing that he could go no lower than two hundred, ten thousand Rupees. I smiled, and told him we had a deal. I paid the man and left swiftly with my purchase.

I told Nouman to keep the car running. He sat perched behind the wheel, his eyes darting anxiously to and fro. I was not keen on taking Aamir's car into such a crooked place, but it would have been difficult to conceal such a large rifle whilst walking down the street. I hastily placed the gun in the back seat, and took over Nouman's place in the driver's seat. I drove extra cautiously to the hotel, making Nouman take note of every street sign. We parked near the back of the lot where light was minimal. I sent Nouman up to the room to get a sheet off of the bed. When he returned some ten minutes later, I gently wrapped the rifle within it. Using Nouman as my lookout, we climbed the stairs to the seventh floor.

Once inside the room, Nouman placed the "Do Not Disturb" sign on the door and bolted it shut. I closed the blinds and foolishly checked under the beds before unwrapping the rifle. Nouman let out a low whistle as he admired the weapon from a distance. I could tell it both intrigued and scared him. I felt the same way. The body was sleek and entirely black. The barrel was as long as my arm, weighing over ten pounds. I ran my fingers over the trigger. The dealer told me it was a four bullet, bolt action capable of hitting a two thousand yard target. When I inquired about ammunition, he sold me a box of 416 Rigby case which he claimed was necked down to a thirty calibre. None of that made any difference to me, so long as I could pick the ace from ten blocks away.

"What do we do now?" Nouman's voice sounded like it was an ocean away. I turned to look at him. He was ghostly white, and standing with his arms wrapped around his chest. The reality of it all had finally sunk in.

The one great thing about the wealthy and powerful is that they are predictable. They want everyone to know just how good they have it; how the rest of us will never fit into their world of class and spoils. Zafar in his arrogance had left himself wide open. He drove to work each morning in an imported Chevrolet Corvette. The Stingray's curvaceous body and bright yellow paint job stood out against all else. He was always alone, as he preferred to arrive with panache. This gave me an additional, more likely plausible window of opportunity. From the time it took him to exit his car and walk into the building, I could have killed him at least a dozen times over.

Nouman came up with codes names for us; Rex and Charlie. These were the names of his father's old schoolmates from America. Not exactly something I would have chosen, but he was happy with it. Any time we left the hotel, we transformed ourselves into them. I was an American tourist, Nouman was my guide. We were careful to visit hot tourist spots, such as the Mohatta Palace and Masjid-e-Tooba, the world's largest dome mosque. With a disposable camera I had purchased, we took a few photos to further facilitate the lie. Since carrying an assault rifle in the streets would surely not go unnoticed, I took Nouman into a music shop to purchase a less conspicuous carrier for it; a guitar case. Nouman was excited when I presented him with the instrument, for I only needed the crate it came in. The inner lining was removable and hollow, a perfect hiding spot for the Lapua.

Together we walked to the Okmni Hotel, and took the elevator to the fiftieth floor. Two days prior, I had discovered that the building ten blocks from Zafar's office was a massive hotel suite. This was just too perfect. With so many people bustling around, no one would ever suspect us. Nouman or myself always kept the key from our hotel in plain view, as it was the same colour white. No on ever questioned our comings or goings. Once on the top level, we had to sneak through an elegant walnut door next to the elevator. It led to a set of brass handled stairs which lead out onto the rooftop. Sometimes the door was unlocked, sometimes we had to jiggle it with a nail file. Nouman proved quite the expert at breaking and entering. The smug look always remained on his face for several minutes after the fact.

As murky as our plan was, we at least had one. If we were caught on the roof, our excuse was that I was teaching the boy how to play the guitar. Not as foreign an instrument as it was to Nouman, I still had no idea what I was doing, so I told Nouman to simply mimic the hand placement and strumming patterns that he saw on the television. However, this was not necessary as no one ever bothered us.

The night before, I couldn't sleep. Judging from the uneven breathing floating across the room, Nouman couldn't sleep either. I pushed myself up on my elbows and softly called his name through the darkness.

After some time he responded with an equally soft, "Yes?"

"Are you alright?" I inquired. I heard the bed springs creak as he rolled over in an effort to turn on the lamp. He was wide awake.

"I am fine," he muttered unconvincingly. "What about you?"

"I'm fine too. You don't have to do this, you know. You can stay here. I won't be long."

I wanted to give him another option. Lately he had been showing signs of trepidation. It wouldn't be right to make him stand by my side whilst I killed a man.

He mumbled something incomprehensive, yawned and said, "I know. I want to be there though. Like you said before, it is important I learn the difference..." His voice trailed off right around the same time my eyes closed.

....

The gentle strum of the guitar hummed in my ears. It was five in the morning, Nouman and I were perched on the rooftop, waiting. Zafar always arrived early on Thursdays; usually between a quarter after five and five thirty. I kept adjusting the scope on the Lapua. It was amazing how powerful the rifle was. I could clearly see the 'false' target as though it were a mere two feet in front of me. I had high hopes as I waited patiently for the President to arrive. We would take things nice and slow. Nouman wanted to wait with the car running, but I knew that would only draw attention to us. Instead, we had agreed on taking our time. Once we exited the building, we would return to our hotel where we would take a few photos, have breakfast in a nearby restaurant, and then be on our way home. If we acted too hurriedly or too anxious, we would be blown.

"Rex?" he said.

"Yes Charlie?" I responded.

"Thank you."

"You're welcome," I said not quite sure what he was thanking me for, but it would have been rude of me to not acknowledge his gratitude.

Minutes ticked by in silence as we waited for Zafar. Nouman had since given up his strumming, the guitar lay forgotten by his side. He was on his hands and knees next to me, his eyes penetrating the breaking dawn like a defensive animal. I kept my eye stuffed into the scope, index finger at the ready. My biggest fear was not the weapon itself, but rather the improper functioning of it. I loaded and unloaded it at least thirty times, more out of my own insecurities than anything else. Holding the butt tight to my shoulder, I grasped the barrel with my right hand. My left hand was the trigger finger. I tried to sort of imitate the actors I had seen in movies. I'm certain I looked foolish, yet Nouman seemed indifferent to my discomfort.

"Rex?" Nouman whispered.

I kept my concentration, "Yes Charlie?" I responded.

"How do you do it?"

"Do what?" I breathed unsteadily. As much as I enjoyed his company, now was not the time for idle chitchat.

"How do you do it without hate?"

Talking more so into the scope, I replied absentmindedly, "You just have to. You have to get past it."

"But how? How do you get past it? Hate is a very strong emotion. I feel it every day. I do not want to, but it is there."

I mulled over his words for a while. I had always thought myself to be an unbiased person. I was taught to act out of compassion, not out of abhorrence. Was there truly a way to get past the feeling? Or was it always lingering in some benign part of me? I had never thought about it much. I despised the people I killed, but I always let the necessity of their death rule over all else. Perhaps I had been kidding myself...

"Everyone feels and measures hate differently, Nouman. That is to say, each person has a different mindset. I do feel hate for the wicked, yet I bury my negative feelings to ensure that I am acting out of an unbiased manner. You see, if I allowed myself to become consumed with hate, I would not be able to see the fine lines between revenge and necessity. They are very fine lines as they sometimes tend to intertwine. You have to be able to separate the two, it is sometimes difficult, but it can be done. I think of the necessity before I think of the hate."

I hesitated. "Err, does that make sense to you?"

"Yes. I can hate something so much, but--" I thrust my hand up to silence him.

"What is it? Is Zafar coming?" His eyes swam with apprehension as he strained to see across the orange-hazed horizon.

I inclined my head with confirmation. That was the only function my tightened muscles could relinquish. The yellow corvette had just entered the parking lot. It felt strange watching Zafar through the scope, unable to hear what was going on. I suddenly became aware of just how tense my neck and shoulders were. A thin layer of perspiration urbanized over my face, chest and arms. The weight of the rifle felt like a thousand pound sandbag in my arms, my right limb quivered, on the verge of buckling.

I followed Zafar out of his car and along the paved stone path that led to his office. His perfectly tailored tan overcoat billowed around him as he strode up the walkway. Even his stride was arrogant: high and taut. As Zafar closed in on my 'false target,' I increased pressure on the trigger. My index finger felt marbleized, as though rigamortis had set in. Nouman's heavy breathing beat on my ear drums... or perhaps it was my own. Everything seemed glossy. I pressed my right eye as far onto the scope as possible. The pain as it crushed against my cheek and brow bones was a mere blur. Zafar was only a few feet from where I needed him to be. My right arm shook violently under the weight of the rifle. My brain felt like it was submerged in water. I was slowly losing oxygen, everything was shutting down. I tried to concentrate on Zafar... he was so close... I watched numbly as he stopped to adjust his maroon silk tie... *Why didn't I take a shot just then?* I was going under, succumbing to unconsciousness. Zafar drew further from my false target, but he was still within range. I tried to curl my finger around the trigger, but it just didn't want to. My brain was screaming for oxygen. I faintly registered the burning in my lungs. *Pull the trigger! Do it now...* someone said. The voice was comforting, angelic even. I obliged it, feeling my body give way as a shattering force knocked me into a dark, frozen abyss.

....

Jasmine and lavender filled my nostrils. The scent was delicate and wonderful. Hushed indecipherable tones floated over me. A woman, and perhaps a young boy. Opening my eyes sent a dull ache straight to my brain. Everything came flooding back at once. Nouman and I on the roof waiting, rifle in hand, heavy breathing, shaking limbs, perspiration... I turned my head towards the voices, my neck screaming in protest. Despite the pain, I had to smile; Nouman stood nose to nose with a very large woman, his finger in her face. In her mid fifties, the woman stood erect, hands on her hips, shaking her head furiously. Sending a fury of Urdu all around us, Nouman forcefully pointed his index finger at an object behind the woman. She defiantly shook her head once more whilst shoving a small white card in Nouman's face. He ripped the card from her hand and threw it across the room. Infuriated, the woman shouted at him before turning her heel. I heard a door slam with so much gusto I thought it had come off its hinges.

"What was that all about?" I inquired groggily.

Nouman was temporarily out of sight, but when he returned, I saw the guitar case, my travel bag, and his knapsack within his arms. He dropped everything at the foot of my bed and with great effort, began to pull me upright.

"Rex! Rex! We have to go now. Before that lady comes back! You have to get up!"

I peered at him, my expression befuddled. This was our room, we had paid for it, what was the problem?

"Come on Rex!" he urged, his voice set in panic.

I glanced to my right at the clock radio on the night stand, and was mystified to see that it was not there. There was no nightstand. Slowly my eyes started to adjust to my surroundings: the way too expensive oil painting above the writing desk, the window that had suddenly gotten ten feet larger, the plush arm-chair that shouldn't be next to the bed. Realization dawned on me; we were not in the same room, let alone hotel.

Pushing past the pain, I jumped out of bed, panic stricken, only half-conscious. Nouman was in the midst of shouldering his knapsack as I grabbed my bag and the guitar case. I half threw him out the door, and together we made a beeline towards the stairs. The Okmni Hotel security would be alerted to our presence momentarily, we did not have much time. We hit the stairs running, my legs felt like jelly, my chest on fire. On the seventh floor we met a maid sitting on the steps. Nouman and I both jumped over her, the coffee in her hands and furious shouts ignored. We entered the lobby quietly. The front entrance was some fifty yards in front of us. Nouman nudged me in the ribs, titling his head towards the front desk. The woman from the room was talking to security personnel, her back to us, but her hands animated. She stuck her left hand up over her head, then dropped it to shoulder level. She was clearly describing us.

"Run as fast as you can. If we get separated, we'll meet up at the car. If I'm not there in one hour's time--I gave Nouman the keys--then you go. You get in the car, follow the map and go straight home. Tell your mother and father we parted ways ten kilometres from the village. Be sure to thank them for me."

I fished my pocketbook out of my trousers and thrust twenty thousand Rupees into his hand as well.

"This will get you home. Don't forget to stop for fuel, and make sure you pay attention to all the road signs."

Nouman's expression was puzzled. He looked at the keys and money in his hands as though they were foreign objects.

"But...but...what about you?"

I smiled weakly, "I will be fine. This is just a precaution. We cannot be seen together now. The staff will be looking for us as a pair. You leave first, walk slowly out the door, once you get into the street, run to the car."

He did not seem convinced, tears swelled in his eyes. I touched his shoulder. "Don't worry, everything will be just fine. Now go, I will see you shortly."

Nouman stuffed the keys and Rupees into his knapsack and he took the guitar from my hands.

"Go," I whispered softly.

Tears streaming down his cheek, he left the cover of the stairwell, and I watched anxiously as he disappeared out the main entrance.

One...two....three... I counted the seconds as they passed. The lobby was nearly empty, so I was forced to wait. *Three hundred ninety-six...three hundred ninety-seven, three hundred ninety-eight...* Ten minutes into it, I lost count. I was surprised no one had found me crouched in the stairwell. Perhaps they were up in the room searching for clues to our identity. The logical thing would have been to check the restrooms, stairwells and elevator shafts. Maybe luck was on our side. I stuck my head out into the lobby; no one was paying any attention. A bellhop was wheeling a brass cart of luggage towards the elevator, with a woman in thick furs nipping at his heels. The check-in counter was empty. The host was no where in sight. Two men loitered in velvet armchairs, one reading the New York Post, the other engrossed in a magazine. *Now is as good a time as any.* I readjusted my bag, pulled the door handle and stepped out into what I hoped wasn't the limelight.

I was halfway to freedom when I heard excited shouts followed by heavy soles hitting the marble tiled floor. I didn't have to look to know what was going on. The woman from the room had spotted me, and was directing security my way. I bolted towards the exit, skidding abruptly into large revolving glass doors. I threw myself into them, pushing my way towards the street. I heard frantic shouts from the men chasing me, more than likely telling the pedestrians to seize me. I turned left almost colliding with a young man on a bicycle, I ignored his furious outburst.

I continued east as fast as my legs could carry me, the hotel security only several yards behind me. Completely ignoring all traffic signs, I thrust myself into oncoming traffic. An orchestra of horns and protests erupted all around me, but I kept going. My lungs were stinging with the most painful burning sensation. It was as though someone had lit a match inside of me. I wanted to stop, but the dogs were on my heels. I could see our hotel's parking garage in the distance; the light at the end of the tunnel. I hoped Nouman would have the engine running.

Further and further I pushed myself. My chest heaved like an overworked mule. At any moment I expected the muscles in my heart to contract into arrest. I was gasping for breath as I rounded the corner into the garage. I could see the Mercedes sitting idly thirty feet in front of me. Ten feet away, my legs locked up and I fell to my knees. I was forced onto my stomach as something solid hooked into my ribcage. Immediately, white hot pain engulfed my left side, causing my quest for air to become even more desperate. I felt pressure on my back and shoulders as the cool barrel of a pistol prod my right temple. Cold sweat dripped into my eyes as I lain helpless on the pavement. There was a crisp click in my ears as the hammer was cocked. I closed my eyes trying to imagine another place. *My mother... my place of birth... Nouman's wide, beautiful smile...* anything to take me out of this momentary Hell. I would not beg, I would not repent, I knew where I was going. I just hoped it would be painless.

A crash followed by a muffled groan caused me to open my eyes. It took me a few seconds to realize that the pressure had been alleviated from my back, with the pistol resting six inches from my cheek. More crashing ensued. It sounded as though something wooden was connecting with something as equally solid. Ignoring the throb in my ribs, I scrambled to my feet. As dimly lit as the garage was, I could make out a smaller figure hovering over top of a much larger one. The smaller form had something big and bulky in his hands: a guitar case. I stumbled over to where he was, the guard lain curled on his side whimpering in pain. Nouman looked at me menacingly before bringing the case down onto the man once more.

"That!" he gritted his teeth, "Is for trying to kill my friend."

He wielded the case high above his head once more. "And this, is for..." I grabbed his left arm.

"Hey!" he protested. "Let go! I was not finished."

His livid eyes penetrated the pathetic figure at his feet.

"Enough," I sighed. "You have done enough. He isn't going anywhere for quite a while. We on the other hand, need to get out of here."

I saw a man some twenty feet away. His expression was horrified as he frantically pushed buttons on his mobile device.

"Now," I commanded.

Nouman seemed like he wanted to protest, but once he heard the sirens approaching, he thought better of staying, and hurdled towards the car. Throwing the guitar carelessly into the backseat, he jumped in the passenger seat without further hesitation. I already had the engine running. We sped towards the exit, and turned right onto the highway. I pushed down on the gas, leaning off the clutch. I broke every traffic sign as we left the wailing sirens behind us.

It turns out I did manage to hit my target. Nouman said the rifle expelled and within seconds, all Hell erupted. Traffic stopped, patrons were in the streets, Zafar's men could be heard shouting over the hordes of spectators. Orange flares were sent sailing high above the city; medics and law enforcement were everywhere. Utter chaos had broken out, and I missed it all. Not knowing what else to do, Nouman half drug, half carried me down two flights of stairs. He saw a cleaning crew about to enter a suite when an idea hit him. He left me and ran towards the women claiming that he and his family had just been in the room and his mother had sent him back in search of an opal bracelet she had lost. The women said they had not found one, but at his request they went to double check. He stood next to the writing desk as they searched everything for him. When the women were not looking, he took the key the previous tenant had left behind. The women searched for twenty minutes, but found nothing. Crestfallen, Nouman left the room dragging his feet, pouting at the thought of having to tell his mother her bracelet was not found.

When the crew had entered another room, Nouman quickly drug me and all of our things into the empty suite. We stayed there for the next two nights as I slipped in and out of consciousness. Nouman said I was delirious, talking crazy, sweating and shaking.

He wanted to call a doctor, but the city was still in an uproar over Zafar's assassination. He left only at night to get food. On day three, Nouman was surprised by a woman claiming that she was appointed to the room we were in. Nouman argued with her, saying that his father, myself, was ill, but she would not give in. She threatened to notify the hotel staff if we did not leave her room immediately. Nouman called her bluff. From the events that took place thereafter, it was quite obvious she was not bluffing.

We arrived back in the village five days behind schedule. I was surprised when Nouman's family greeted us with warm smiles and inquiries about our trip. Nouman told them all about the city, showed them photographs he had developed, and explained to his sceptical mother and sister about computers, telephones, hot showers and commodes. When Aamir noticed my discomfort, Nouman told him I tripped and fell down three flights of stairs. His mother made a huge fuss about it, which I was grateful for. The fewer questions they asked the better. I wanted to go up into the mountains, but Aisha would not allow it. She put cool cloths and a brownish paste on my side and made up a cot for me in their home. She would not permit me to lift a single finger, and the weeks that followed were aggravating, yet peaceful.

Nouman and I barely had time to talk in private. Aisha or Aamir were always in the vicinity, and when they weren't, Sanari was nipping at her brother's heels to let me rest. One sunny afternoon I insisted that Nouman join me outside for some fresh air. We walked to the edge of the village and sprawled out in a nearby field. I had been replaying the impending conversation over and over in my head for the past two weeks. In a few days time, I would be leaving. I did not know how to convey this to Nouman. He was capable of handling truths and realities, but I knew from the look in his eyes that he had become too attached. As had I. I never anticipated feeling what I did for the boy. I never intended to get close to anyone, yet like in Louisiana, my loneliness had triumphed.

Nouman sat silently whilst picking at a blade of grass. He had not said too much since we returned. Perhaps he was still in shock over everything. I knew I was. Not just Zafar, but how Nouman reacted when I had fallen. He was sort of a natural and this frightened me. I wasn't sure if he truly understood the means behind the motive. The look in his eyes whilst he was attacking the security guard... I had never seen such loathsomeness. His brown orbs had been replaced by black coals. His sweet smile was twisted into a sickening grin. I felt nauseated by it all. I should not have taken him with me. I should not have told him anything about me. I should have simply stayed in the mountain and ignored him.

Nouman watched longingly as some children his age kicked a tattered red ball back and forth. Shirt and shoeless, the children's happy laughter echoed across the field. Impoverished as they were, they still found things to make them happy, to take them away from their pitiable lives. They had no clue what was beyond the exterior of Tindki; the opportunities, the technology, the means to a better life. They probably thought this was it. And assuming it was like this everywhere, there was no point in trying to get out.

Aamir had been the lucky one. He knew what was beyond these walls. He had experienced it first hand. He had tasted the unlimited freedom. I found myself angered by the fact that he chose to remain silent about it. If these children knew, if they only knew what they could have...

The ball came sailing towards us, and with a soft thud, it landed on the grass. One of the children shouted something at Nouman. He picked up the ball, tossing it between his hands. I watched as he strode over to the group of children. He returned the ball, hunched his shoulders and sat back down next to me. He looked heart-rending. He should be playing with his friends. What had I done to him?

"Can I come with you?"

I had been expecting this. When I didn't answer, he got up and walked away. I watched as he joined his friends. They were happy to have him, yet his face showed nothing but despair.

Climbing to my feet, I went back to Nouman's home to collect my things. I was certain he already knew my answer, so I felt that it was best to leave now. My heart ached at the thought of causing him any more pain. I could feel Nouman's penetrating stare in my wake. Within minutes he was at my side. Everything I owned could be fit into my travel bag, so packing did not take but five minutes. Nouman brooded in the doorway, his expression flat.

"Are you leaving now?" he asked.

I nodded, unable to meet his gaze.

"But I have not packed yet. I have not told my family I am leaving." His tone sounded hopeful, but his body was deflated in defeat.

"I'm sorry, but you cannot come with me. I wish you could. I want you to, but you must stay here."

I shouldered my bag, shifting uncomfortably.

"Let us go find your family. I want to thank them for their hospitality."

Nouman followed me in silence, his footsteps thunderous. I knew this was not going to end well for either of us. I thanked Aamir and Aisha for their kindness; both were delighted to have me as their guest and relished the day when I could return. Sanari leaned on her crutches, her expression bland. She made no effort to acknowledge my gratitude towards her. Nouman sulked mutedly a few feet away: I could tell his behaviour was somewhat worrisome for his family. Their expressions became stricken, sympathetic even. They obviously had known this day would come and had made every effort to prepare themselves for it. *How do you prepare for something like this?* I thought to myself as I watched Aisha's compassionate eyes lock onto those of her mourning child.

After promising Aamir I would write to them every now and then, apparently they received post once every two to three months; we shook hands before parting in front of their home. Nouman was still at my side. Together we walked down the dirt path to the outskirts of the village. His expression had not changed. Through my peripheral vision I could see tears leaking from the corner of his left eye. Once we reached the end of the path, I stopped. Nothing could have prepared me for this moment. I had never experienced such raw emotion before. I looked at Nouman; words could no longer express the anguish I felt as I watched him cry. His milky tears were flowing down his cheeks, dripping onto his bare feet. He looked at me, his angelic face saturated with deep sorrow. Slowly he bent his body. I thought he was feeling faint, so I placed a hand under him, but he got on his hands and knees before me.

"Please." His voice was a hoarse whisper. "Please can I come with you?"

He was begging, beseeching me. If it were not for his fallen expression and slumped figure, he would have seemed pathetic, a jester in the eyes of spectators. But this was no joke, he was tormented. And I was the cause of it.

I collapsed to my knees next to him. Not knowing what else to do, I placed my arms around him. His limp frame convulsed as he clutched my neck and chest. His howls penetrated the land around us, shattering everything within their path. I wanted to die. It was more than what I deserved. Bringing a child into... this. What kind of sadistic, irresponsible being would drag a thirteen year old into a life of violence and sin? I felt sickened by my very own existence. I should be burned at the stake.

Nouman clung to me. His sobs were barely audible as he buried his head deeper into my chest. His voice was a soft murmur as he continued to beg.

"Please."

I could do nothing to console him. Nothing I said would make things better, nor right. I pulled his body away from mine. He was so broken, so limp, it was like manipulating a string puppet. I placed his hands into mine, anf bore into his eyes. It was as though he had died. Paler than I had ever seen him, his lips were rigid and cracked; his eyes looked like black holes in their sockets.

"Nouman," I whispered, "please listen to me. Please try to understand what I am about to say."

It was hard to tell if he was absorbing anything I was saying. He stared past me into nothingness; unchanged, incomprehensive.

"Nouman, I want you to come with me, I truly do. I would love nothing more than to have you by my side. But this is not your burden.... This is not your fight. Everything I am doing, it's...it's not right. It's not right to bring you into this life. I want you to grow up, I want you to be happy, to know normalcy, to have strong morals, to be loved unconditionally. I want you to have things that my path will not permit me to have. You do not know how much I suffer. Being alone, shouldering this weight... I am thankful for you and your family. You took away some of my pain. I need you to be au fait with my words, I do not expect you to agree with them, but I need you to accept them."

I firmly held his hands in mine, eyes fixated directly into his. His chin dropped to his chest as he whispered, "Okay."

Warm liquid trickled down my cheeks, jutting across my jaw line as I formed my next words. It had always been difficult for me to express exactly how I felt. Even as a child, I struggled with feelings that were not directly aimed towards my mother. When it came to her, I could say anything, not that I had to. But with others, I always stopped short of expressing what was really behind my protected emotive barrier.

"I am so proud of you. You stood next to me and fought an evil that was beyond the capabilities of most men. You showed me great loyalty in risking your own life to ensure that mine would carry on. Our bond is one that I will cherish and revere until my dying day. I pray you can find solace in knowing that I will always carry that with me."

Nouman nodded his head and wiped his eyes on the hem of his sleeve. I could see that my words had sunk in. He had understood them and was resigning.

"Will you come back when everything is done? You can live with me, I will take care of you."

His voice faltered and he choked, fresh tears swimming in his eyes. "Even if it is only for a second, will you come back?" he pleaded.

Despite the obstinate plan I had for myself once the aftermaths had calmed, I knew that I could not damage this child's heart any further. My lie was so cruel, yet necessary in that I must not cause him another ounce of pain. I closed my eyes, *Forgive me,* I asked the Lord. My eyelids fluttered and my lips trembled as I looked into Nouman's sweet, innocent face and breathed the words I knew were untrue.

"I will."

A wide smile spread upon his face. Not quite reaching his eyes, but his spirits had been heightened considerably. I stood up, his hands still in my own. I peered across the horizon, the mountains were so peaceful, the forest calm. I glanced over my shoulder at the village. It was quiet: welcoming in its own eerie way. I could have stayed there forever. It would have been easy. I could have lived in a bubble of ignorance, never knowing or caring again for the horrors beyond it. Immune from the clouds of evil. Unnoticed. I released his hands.

"Goodbye," I whispered softly.

My guilt consumed me as I set out onto the beaten path; outside the protective bubble, and into the horrors that were my world.

Chapter 11

Tokyo, Japan
17 January, 1996

If someone were to have asked me as a child what I anticipated seeing myself doing twenty-five years in the future, I would have said a doctor or an accountant. As far as my personal life, I would have foreseen myself to be married with several children by now. Who would have thought my path would stray so far from my childhood aspirations? For years, I had always believed that we make our own fate; that no one holds the keys to our future but ourselves. We may have some guidance or divine intervention along the way, nonetheless, what we do with our God-given gift is up to us.

Reflecting upon the last thirty years of my own life, I cannot help but wonder if everything I have done was in preparation for ambitions that do not exist. What if every move we make is predetermined? What if our paths have been chosen for us? Despite how sinful it is to take the life of another, what if this is what I am suppose to do? Maybe God chose me. Not because there was no other man for the job, but because He knew my loyalty to Him was authentic. I would not, nor could not, accept any other reasoning for why I am here... for why I had taken the lives of eight people, and for the life I was about to take. Perhaps He knew that He could not rely upon anyone else. Being unable to fix mankind Himself, He chose a worthy soldier. After all, why should we depend on Him to correct the mistakes we have made? What if He was leaving things up to us, simply waiting for someone to take the reins? He would never let His children hang themselves, but maybe this was something that needed to be done; a lesson we all needed to learn.

The Russian and his two men were sheer acts of vengeance. They had to pay dues for what they did to Hans. Although I was in no position to be the payer, those men did not deserve to relish their gifts. In time, I would endure the consequences of my heinous actions. As for the rest, and what was surely to come, I was following the path the Lord had lit for me. I would do His bidding whenever it may be and wherever it may take me. Thus far, He had yet to steer me wrong. Addams, Redding, Moreau, Thompson, Amini: they were all worthy of the punishment they have been given. No longer did people have to suffer at their hands.

Takada Nakamura solicited the services of his own country's youth in exchange for population control and some classic foreign automobiles. I never had a doubt in my mind that the stories published about the man were false. The executive officer who gave the order to the captain of the Leiko disappeared as suddenly as his claims were made. The entire crew also promptly vanished, yet all thirty-three men were accounted for when they logged into a port in Anchorage, Alaska. Nakamura had since cut off all ties with the United States, Canada and Australia. All imports, exports and trade agreements had become null and void. In the age of globalization, why do such things? Japan's economic solidity depended on their ability to manufacture products for the rest of the world. Why would Takada put an end to such a sure thing? The answer was simple: Fear.

Tokyo was animated. The streets were so crowded, the sidewalks became maze-like as one had to zigzag their way in and around hundreds of vendors and herds of tourists. An odd assortment of people had taken to the streets; some dressed up like ancient warriors, others like sacred animals. Children selling hand painted ornaments were bobbing happily after potential patrons. The smell of freshly prepared domburi wafted in the air. As I weaved my way through the sea of people, I had but only one thing on my mind, Nouman.

Never had I wanted to wrap someone in my arms as much as I wanted to him. I wanted to scoop him up and take him as far away from such cruelties and inhumanities as possible. I tried not to think of the sadness in his eyes, or the frown chiselled across his face. I have prayed for him every night since we parted, constant tears of guilt filled my eyes and my heart had not stopped aching. What had I left him to? He was living in a place where civility had been lost; where there were true evils. What would happen to him? Would he grow up to be the men whom we had hunted? Would he even grow up? I cringed at such a thought. Going into this I had envisioned changing the face of mankind. For the first time, I had thoughts that such changes may never occur for him and his family.

I did not have a clear plan for Takada yet. I knew that the streets would be my harness. The hustle and bustle would cover any tracks I may make, and the hundreds of restaurants and shops could provide refuge if need be. There was no way Japanese law enforcement could detain the thousands of people who loitered the storefronts. Nor could they sort through all the tourists who dillydallied whilst taking photographs and hording around souvenir wagons. I knew I would find my safe house there. Sitting in a shabby, faintly lit eatery, I began to formulate a plan for the Prime Minister. Over a bowl of piping hot curry rice, or kare raisu to the locals, I mulled over possible scenarios. On a tattered piece of parchment I had made my list. Poison was out; I did not want to get close to such filth. A sniper rifle was also out of the question, as that provided a connection to my previous target, Zafar Amini. The time involved in planning an execution was tedious. Every time I thought I had a viable, fool proof strategy, it turned out to have many holes and imperfections in it.

After a months' worth of brainstorming, I had created what I was sure to be a solid foundation plan. There was room for error, as with anything, but I was certain I could pull it off. I religiously monitored the newspapers and television broadcasts for the slightest bit of information on Takada. Two things were common knowledge: he was always seen with the same miserable aid by his side, and he always made his entrances and exits from a black Lexus. As unhappy as he appeared, it was rumoured the aid was a life long friend, so there was no chance he could be compromised. I decided to stick with what I knew, thus the Lexus had become my target.

As crude as it seemed, I figured it was best to execute Takada as short and as sweet as possible. I was not one hundred percent sure how I was going to do that, but I had several ideas. These ideas, of course, depended on how accessible the Lexus was to the public. Cutting the brake lines would be the simplest route, however, there was no guarantee that the impact would be hard enough to take a life. Possibly the driver of the car, but the passengers were shoddy at best. A bomb would take too long to construct. Every second counted, and time was something I knew I wouldn't have a lot of.

....

The young man handed me my bag of fireworks and bowed me happily out of his shop. I meandered through the masses towards an isolated diner I had stumbled upon a few weeks prior. The place was perfect to conduct my work. It was situated inside an alley, away from the streets and all the passers-by. I initially used it as a shortcut in between a park I frequented and the cheap hotel I was staying in. One evening whilst on my way back to my room, I saw an old chap exit out into the alley carrying a carton of food. He nodded at me before mounting a rickety bicycle and pedalling away.

Overcome with curiosity, I foolishly grabbed the door handle and stuck my head inside. Makeshift tables and crates were set up in the middle of a small dingy room. The place was lit by candles and smelled strongly of mushrooms. Two men sat eating rice in one corner of the room, and an ancient woman was sipping tea from an eggcup in the other. Thinking this was some sort of private affair, I turned to leave when a woman, equally as old as the one I had just seen, appeared out of nowhere and beckoned me to sit down. Deciding it would be rude of me to decline her invitation, I took a seat a few tables away from the men in the corner. She instantly appeared with an eggcup of tea and a wooden bowl full of domburi.

The atmosphere was unhurried, the old woman sipped her single cup of tea for over an hour, and the men ate leisurely while conversing in hushed Japanese. When they were finished, they left a few Yen on the table and exited quietly. I sat for hours that night, taking in my surroundings, contemplating everything that still needed to be done. The smell of mushrooms grew on me, as well as the domburi. Night after night I found myself slipping out of the darkness and into my own private haven. The best thing about this place: its lack of wait staff. Everyone who showed up received the same food and drink. The woman did not linger, nor did she return. You could take as much time as you needed. You would never be asked to leave. I scanned the room for a price list, but there was none, so I assumed that one could leave as much as they desired for payment of their meal. I always left six hundred fifty yen, the equivalent to five Great Britain Pounds.

I placed my bag of goods on the table where I could examine them more closely. One of the great things about Japan was its endless festivities. Every event, no matter how big or small, always included some sort of pyrotechnics. It was easy to locate a shop selling every type of firecracker on the market, and it would have been foolish of me to not take advantage of this, if for no other use than for a small diversion. Young children could be seen at night running around waving lit sparklers high above their heads. Parents would set off a few noisemakers as pre-bedtime entertainment. Colourful dragons and serpents lit up the sky almost nightly. No one ever complained about it, so I knew I would not stand out whilst walking the streets with a sack full of fireworks.

I had told the clerk that I was looking for something with a little kick. He did not speak much English, but he understood "big bang" and happily steered me towards a display filled with brightly coloured rockets and cylinders. He hastily grabbed a neon green tube and pointed at the two foot fuse.

"Make big bang," he had said smiling excitedly.

I returned his enthusiasm by pointing at it and saying "More." It may take a lot of big bangs to pull this one off.

Slowly I began to formulate a plan. I spent many days, and most of my nights, chewing over how I could possibly make things work in my favour. There was no one to manipulate, no one to buy, no way to get inside access to Takada or his Lexus. When I attempted to pay a visit to his administration building a few days prior, I was obstructed by a massive wall of soldiers firmly shouldering AK47s, hundreds of security procedures, and at least fifty guards patrolling the perimeter with rabid-looking Doberman Pincers. There was no way in, and I was certain, no way out.

Takada never left his building. From sunup to sundown he was inside with his cabinet. I had played with the idea of trying to manipulate one of his employees, but that thought quickly dissolved once I saw how they were cut. His entire administration had been dyed in the same wool as he was; arrogant, self-indulgent and ruthless. I knew I would have better luck trying to tickle a sleeping grizzly than to get one of his own people to turn on him.

I had been in the city for almost three months but still had nothing solid. My original plans to take advantage of the crowded streets had fallen through once winter set in. Tourism diminished considerably, thus my chances of being able to blend in were now very slim. Once spring rolled around, foot traffic would pick up once again, but I did not have that kind of time available to me. Four weeks of carefully watching Takada's building had yielded nothing. No habits, no breaks, the man simply stayed inside for fourteen hours each day. I was resigned, and knew I had to move on. There was no way I could get past all his security personnel. And even if I did, what good would it do? Takada was not a foolish man, he probably had his own private army standing outside his office door.

Another wasted day, I thought as I trekked back to my room. Surely *something* had to happen in my favour soon. I was now concentrating on Takada as he moved throughout the city. The Lexus had a set route, at a set time, and rarely was there any deviation. Nine traffic lights, three left turns, twenty-two minutes before Takada exited from the rear passenger door and was escorted into his penthouse. My timeframe was short and traffic was rather light. I had ill feelings about the whole situation.

I needed to get out of Tokyo as soon as possible. The landlord at the hotel was beginning to ask questions. His English was passable and I could tell that he did not believe one word I had been telling him. I paid him the required amount of yen on time each week, and in my opinion, that should have been good enough to secure my privacy. I was still frequenting the restaurant, however, the place had become more crowded than usual. Not wanting to draw attention to myself, I simply ate and left. The isolation factor was what took me there, now I didn't even have that. So, I took to roaming the streets.

On a particularly calm evening, I set out to find clarity, and perhaps an epiphany. Twenty minutes into my therapeutic walking session, I was jolted by screams of alarm. They pierced the chilly evening air, and within seconds a thick smoky haze settled all around me. Harsh Japanese cut through the darkness as heavy footsteps rushed past me. Commotion had erupted. The entire neighbourhood was awake, and as the smoke cleared, I saw a crowd of people gathering around a smouldering object across the street. As I approached the crowd, the smell of gunpowder and burnt rubber filled my nostrils. A moped lain in sweltering disarray against the curb. The seat was in flames, and its tires were liquefying. Rapid Japanese followed by pointing and scared children's voices ensued; it did not take me long to realize what had happened. Some of the neighbourhood children had lost control of a firecracker; it struck the moped causing it to blow. Several more minutes of gawking, and the site before me became stale. I walked away from the hubbub on cloud nine, for I now knew *what* needed to be done.

Twenty-two minutes. One can accomplish many things in this time, however, when broken down to exactly that much time, when everything has to be spot on, twenty-two minutes suddenly becomes ten seconds. So much rode on my ability to manipulate my surroundings; to outrun the hands of time. I had walked Takada's route at least a fifty times. I studied the foot traffic at all nine intersections and I made note of which stops yielded heavy congestion. As much as I did not wish to harm others, I had come to accept that there may be some injuries, or possibly a few additional casualties. Takada's aid and driver would be in the car with him. There was simply no way around this. He had guards at his office as well as in and around his home. As it seemed, the only time he was not in the presence of heavily armed men was when he travelled from his office to his penthouse. Like it or not, I was forced to make the streets my playground. Hopefully they will serve a dual purpose by becoming my shadow of cover as well.

My aim had to be precise. A balance of distance and delicacy would be imperative. I had been practicing my accuracy every day for almost two weeks. Squished between a trash bin and a brick wall, I would locate a car, wait for it to idol at the light, then toss a small rock under its frame. When the traffic cleared, I would try to locate the rock. The first dozen attempts were feeble, as either I would overthrow or apply too much downward pressure causing them to roll. By my twentieth time, I had pretty much mastered it. The key was to use soft hands and release slowly. The rocks were landing dead centre; no one seemed to take heed to what I was doing. Each day brought an even bigger smile to my face.

....

Takada's Lexus was approaching. The rumbling of many exhausts coupled with the heavy footsteps of passers-by palpitated through my body. My left arm was slightly numb; I could feel my heartbeat on the very tips of my fingers. Eleven cars back, I bowed my head in silent prayer. My biggest fear was hitting a green light, or else missing my mark completely. Beads of sweat lined my forehead, suddenly I was very warm. Inhaling slowly, I tried to regroup. I could not help being nervous, so much was at stake. I could not have chosen a better day; overcast, with no winds to speak of. God had blessed me with such perfect conditions. Under cloud cover I was virtually invisible. The only obstacle I faced was conquering my own self-doubts.

Six cars in the queue, the Lexus idled benignly waiting for the go ahead. I watched fascinated as pedestrians walked nonchalantly past its sleek frame. A man of such power and influence was a mere eight feet from them, yet they showed indifference to it, and simply carried on about their business. I was amazed by how self-engrossed people could be. Takada was within their reach on a daily basis. They had all protested and rallied for his resignation. They called for his imprisonment and made death threats against him. And here he was, right under their noses, in the most vulnerable position.

I fumbled for the book of matches in my trouser's pocket. My hands were still shaking despite every attempt to calm myself. My surroundings blurred together, and all I saw was the Lexus. No sounds entered my ears, the passers-by were mere shadows and had become insignificant. Retrieving the firecracker from my breast pocket, I concentrated on my mark. I had only seconds to ignite, set my aim and release it. I flipped the matchbook open and sightlessly tore a stick out. I rubbed my thumb over its cardboard body, feeling its roughly textured tip. I struck it forcefully against the book, it immediately ignited. Raising the firecracker towards the flame, I stole one last glance above before jabbing the fiery stick onto the cylinder's fuse. Within seconds I had contact, a low hissing and gentle vibration had erupted within my hand. Poking my head out from behind the trash bin, I raised my left arm...

A forced knocked my arm towards the ground. Irate bursts of blood-chilling Japanese enveloped around me. Petrified and confused, I tried to move, but a swift kick to my gut immobilized me. A strong pair of hands crushed down on my windpipe, instantly I felt all the air being sucked out of my lungs. Gasping for breath, I fearfully looked upwards into what I was certain were the eyes of my imminent downfall. He was young, but venomous. His callous hands had slackened around my neck only just, however, his firm stature pinned me to the pavement effortlessly. Starry-eyed from the lack of oxygen to my brain, I was able to make out knee high trekker boots, black cargo pants and a matching long sleeve button down shirt. A wide belt around his waist glistened with metal. His unforgiving eyes were burning. I knew what he was thinking... knew what he was about to do... and *he* knew that I knew it. He leaned in close, his breath was thick with stale alcohol. I shut my eyes firmly, silently praying for my soul.

"Koko e kite kudasai." I opened my eyes; the young man had released me and was billowing over my shattered form. Upon regaining my cogence, I focused on all the shiny metal harnessed on his belt. Knives...at least a dozen of them. Some were jaded and very large, others were small and razor-like. Judging from their worn handles, he had used these knives many times, and had used them well. Within seconds he could have had me carved up like a holiday turkey. What ever this man wanted, he would get it.

"Koko e kite kudasai." His words were harsh, incoherent, I tried to speak to let him know that I did not understand him, but he seized my arm and pulled me upwards.

"Ugokasu," he hissed as he dragged my limp frame in his wake.

I attempted to steady myself against the concrete wall of the alley, but the man would not stand for this. He kept tugging my arm, forcing me to fumble after him. No one seemed to take notice to us. Nor did anyone pay attention to the loud raucous the firecracker had caused. As the smell of gunpowder infused smoke filled the air, passers-by just stole a quick glance at the awry noise-maker before shuffling on. The man continued to drag me down the alley; his pace had quickened once the cover of smoke lifted. My legs were sore from squatting and my gut was aching. Insufferable sensations were being rocketed into my back and kidneys. I tried to stop to catch my breath, I tried to tell the man that I needed a few seconds, but he would not adhere.

Waiting for us at the end of the alley was a beige van. It sat idling in the street, its tinted windows shielded any passengers from view.

"Demashō, Tsuitekite kudasai." In a matter of seconds I was bound, gagged and blindfolded. He jabbed me in the back, causing me to trip and miss the step up into the van. Cursing through the gag, I blindly entered the vehicle. More stale alcohol met my nostrils; I could also faintly smell ammonia.

Using my body as a sensory system, I fumbled my way around in search of a place to sit. A robust pull yanked my feet out from under me and I fell forcefully to the floorboards. The van took off in a whirlwind of speed, my body convulsed as it weaved in and out of traffic. The rear wheels squealed, the exhaust deafening. I had no sense of direction; no control. We rode in silence. The rumbling of the exhaust and the occasional honking from automobiles around us were the only sounds that sustained me. We came to an abrupt halt, the van door crashed open, I was pulled from the floorboards and once again dragged against my will.

I saw nothing, felt only the uneven pavement beneath my feet. Although I was senseless, the place had a familiarity to it. The smell in the air; the noises surrounding me --I had been here before. I was certain of that much. I heard a stern knock ahead of me, followed by the eerie rasp of an ancient door. I was heaved over the sill and immediately forced to take a seat on a wooden box. *I'm alive thus far, perhaps I will live for another day.* Still gagged and blind folded, it took me a few minutes to realize that I had regained use of my hands. I touched the box beneath me, thanking the Lord that it was a crate of sorts and not my impending place of rest. I sat in silence as soft murmurs discharged to my right. No one seemed to be attentive to my presence; after a few minutes of stillness, I uncovered my eyes and removed the cloth from my mouth.

The room was packed. In all my time of coming to the place, I had never seen more than a dozen people. The shabby tables were littered with parchment; every crate was spoken for. There were also a fair number of people standing around peering over shoulders and conversing quietly within circles. Confused as to what was going on, I remained seated and dimwittedly waited for someone to notice me. For reasons even unknown to me, I could not bring myself to leave the place. Just minutes before, I was within an inch of having my windpipe crushed, now I had been given the chance to run, yet my body was deaden. Who *were* these people? They were an odd assortment: some young, some old, both men and women, wearing all types of attire. From a woman wearing hospital garb, to a middle-aged man in an expensive business suit; these people could have been doctors or bankers. Completely staggered, I tried to get a handle on what may be happening around me. I spotted my kidnapper at a table to my left. He was in the thick of things, speaking rigid Japanese and pointing firmly at some documents in front of him. All eyes seemed to be on him, so I assumed he was their leader. I stared mesmerized at the scene before me. Was this some sort of society? Why had they not killed me? For all they knew, I could be fluent in Japanese: I could expose whatever it is they were doing. A young woman in knee high boots and a mini skirt pointed at me. All movement and conversation stopped. The young man slowly rose from his chair and walked towards me. *This is it,* I thought to myself. Once again I closed my eyes and began to pray.

"A firecracker. That was your big plan? A child's toy? Open your eyes you fool, no one here is going to harm you."

I apprehensively lifted my eyelids. Was this some sort of a joke? *I was dead.* This man was merely toying with me. They were giving me hope. A hope of living, which they presumed in turn would give them complete control over me. They were throwing me a tiny bone, a morsel of food; and they were all expecting me to graciously lap it up before succumbing to their every desire. I remained planted on the crate. If this was God's will, then so be it.

The young man had not taken his eyes off me, I returned his stare as defiantly as I could. I would not beg, I would not plead, I would not go gentle. Nonplussed, he reached into his breast pocket and produced a discoloured piece of paper. Tossing it meaninglessly on the floor, he snickered,

"You should have stuck with the sniper rifle. At least then you *may* have hit something. What were you expecting to happen with that rocket? Even if you did manage to position it under Takada's car, the guards behind him would have been all over it as well as yourself within seconds. We thought that you were really going to pull off something big. We sat back and left you to it. Our attempts have failed us many a times. This is what we waited almost five months for? A big bang and a few seconds of smoke?"

A few scoffs and chuckles echoed in the room. The men and women were still staring at me, yet their faces were not of hatred, but of disgust. The young man walked back to the table he had been occupying and started collecting up his documents. No one moved, or spoke. His back to me, he continued.

"For ten years we have been trying to get to Takada. Ten years of letdowns. Ten years of suffering. Ten years we will never get back." He approached me and thrust the stack of papers into my lap. I was amazed to see a blueprint of Takada's administration building peering up at me. "We have shot him...stabbed him...poisoned him...even blew up his home, yet he will not cease. We have tried everything in our power to take him down. Nothing has worked. Then you came along. We do not know who you are, however, we have our theories." The young man bent over and retrieved the piece of paper he had tossed aside. "We have been watching you ever since we found this next to your corner table."

Unfolding the parchment, I saw my own handwriting scrawled all across the page. I was too shocked to speak. These people *knew* what I was. They had been *watching* me. They knew what *my plans* were.

"You brought us revived hope," he continued. "For a few short moments we were able to picture our lives without Takada Nakamura in it. But you, like ourselves, have failed." He breathed a tormented sigh and hung his head. Several people were sniffling while others stifled cries.

"I am sorry," I whispered. I did not know what else to say to these people. I bowed my head; I could no longer bare to see the deep grooves of anguish upon their faces. The ancient woman whom had always brought me tea and domburi was crying silently on the shoulder of a much younger lady. Others were shaking violently in attempts to control their own emotions. At that moment, everything I had done had come full circle. My feeble plan for Takada; my spectacular failure. I had clouted these people in the face with my childish ways. Never in my life had I been so ashamed. Everything they had worked for, all the sweat and blood they had poured into perfecting their devices. I came along, and in an effort to make things better, I made it worse. Hope was now bygone in their hearts... as was I.

....

Sonni and his small army of radicals had called the isolated café home for nearly twelve years. Once a sworn protector of Prime Minister Nakamura, Sonni had witnessed many atrocities, and had first hand knowledge of Takada's misdeeds. Several years into his post, he had come up close and personal with the magnitude of Takada's power-thirsty ways. The Prime Minister personally had asked Sonni to dispose of one of his own; his childhood friend, Junichi. Takada called upon him, accused Junichi of being a traitor, and in turn told Sonni that it was his duty, his *honour* even, to kill all those who imposed a threat against Japan. Friend or not, it had to be done. Sonni could not bare the thought of his life-long friend being a traitor. He refused to accept such accusations, so he went to Junichi's home to speak to him. To his surprise, Junichi had been told the same thing by Takada, but it was Sonni whom the Prime Minister had labelled a turncoat. Together, the two men made the swift decision to leave with their families. For reasons only known to Takada, both men had been marked. If they did not kill one another, they were certain the military would gladly step in to finish the job.

The café was a front. Both men needed a place to hide their families, and they needed some source of income. Sonni's grandmother, Chiku, came up with the idea of creating a low profile eatery. While Sonni and Junichi were in the backroom making plans and strategizing, she and the others were cooking domburi and keeping an eye out for any suspicious activity. Thus far, they had yet to be found, although the government knew they still walked among the living. Takada was so certain of this, he had offered one hundred million Yen apiece for their capture. Dead or alive: it did not matter to him, so long as they were in his hands. Some four years ago, Takada had the gift of Junichi bestowed upon him. Sonni had not rested since.

The two men's first attempt on Takada eleven years prior had been as close as they had come. Each attempt thereafter yielded nothing but shattered hopes and great disappointment. Takada had become somewhat invincible; nothing they did was successful. Bluntly put, the bastard just did not want to die. And now he was more protected then ever. Although Sonni showed the face of a dignified leader, he was beginning to accept defeat within his heart. All that sustained him were Junichi and the children. He had to keep fighting for them, no matter what it took, no matter what the cost. But how do you keep going when there is nothing left to hold on to? When there is no chance of winning; when defeat is almighty...when it is imminent. Somehow you must. You must pull every ounce of courage from the deepest of crevices within you; and you must allow it to become more important than what you fear. Sonni had become a true master of this. He told me his courage did not replace his fear, he chose to make Junichi and the children more important than his fear of Takada, his fear of death.

On a warm evening, some three days prior to my departure, I took a long walk with Sonni. He approached me shortly after dinner, and extended an invitation to join him just after twilight. Although tried from a full day of machinating, I agreed. We met in the alleyway, and after exchanging polite nods, we set out into the idling streets. The loitering patrons and commuters had taken to their homes for the evening, leaving just Sonni and myself to wander at our leisure. The air had not cooled, although the sun had long since disappeared into the horizon. The charcoal sky was starless, the moon hidden under heavy cloud cover.

We walked in silence, Sonni's distressed breathing and our wispy footsteps were the only sounds which infiltrated my ears. I knew he was in agony. For the past several weeks he had not been his usual self. A buoyant, yet dignified leader, Sonni's disposition had changed drastically. He had become a recluse, only coming out of his room for meetings and meals. His words of encouragement had become lacklustre. Gone was the gleam of hope in his eyes. He was giving up.

Our feet carried us to the west end of the city, or what was left of it. The rundown flats had seen better days. Many rooftops were covered with canvas material and many windows had been knocked out. The smell of sewage hung thick in the air, a stench that instantly nauseated me. Sonni, however, seemed to be immune to it. As we walked deeper into the streets, I could hear the soft cries of women and children, the harsh words of men, and the buzzing of televisions and cooling fans. The sidewalks were littered with trash making them inaccessible. Street lamps had been broken, and as we walked past the endless graffiti strewn buildings, I could not help but feel a sense of homecoming for Sonni. Something in my gut told me that this is where he had once raised his family. The silence hung between us as we continued our journey. I had many questions for him, but held them in. It was he whom had extended the invitation, if he wanted to speak, he would do so.

Sonni abruptly stopped. Fearing that something was not right, I swivelled in every direction in search of what had caused his sudden behaviour. I turned to face him, but he was no longer standing before me. He was sitting on the curb with his knees firmly set against his chest, gazing resolutely into the night.

Clearing away clutter with my foot, I sat down next to him. Minutes ticked by before he spoke.

"Junichi and I grew up here." His voice was a mere whisper, and his tone was cumbersome. "As children we had dreamt of becoming fighter pilots. We made plans to live together, to raise our families together...to die together. We pledged our eternal allegiance to one another right on this very spot. 'Death before dishonour.' We had heard that line in an American war film. It's meaning was so true, for us anyway."

I stared at my feet and simply nodded, knowing full well that it was I who should be honoured by his openness. One's past was usually more difficult to relish than one's feelings. Although for me, they were both on even playing fields. It had taken everything Sonni had to tell me this. The least I could do was let him speak with dignity. He swallowed dryly, and with a great sigh, he looked towards the Heavens.

"I'm not much of a believer, but Junichi always was. I fear the day when we may meet again. To have to look him in the eyes and tell him that I have failed..." His voice broke as he trailed off.

I continued to stare at my feet. All words had escaped me. I knew how he felt, yet I could not muster the courage to share that with him. He sniffed softly, and judging from his quick movement, he had also wiped his face. A small group of adolescents passed us, their undaunted laughter settled eerily upon the air. We watched in silence as they exchanged jokes and playful punches. Once out of sight, Sonni spoke once more.

"I have made one final plan. I am going to enter Takada's office building, and I am going to sacrifice myself. I have already set everything into place. I have purchased enough ST grenades with enough C4 to blow his entire establishment to pieces. This *is* the only way. I have thought this through for many years. I had hoped that it would never come to this, but things have come full circle, and this is what I must do."

"What about your family?" I whispered. I had heard these words before. Nouman's innocent voice filled my head; my eyes flooded with tears.

"They know of what must be done. Although they do not like it, they understand it. My wife will be taken care of. My children also. We keep good company, I am certain they will be safe."

Sonni's voice was on the verge of cracking. My heart ached for him. He obviously did not want to do this, but he had convinced himself that he had to. I sat speechless as I knew nothing I could say would enlighten him, nor change his mind. I looked upwards into the Heavens for guidance, for some sort of sign from the Lord: anything He could offer as a means for Sonni to spare himself. But the blank vast sky offered no solution, so I knew this was what fate God had intended for my young friend. "Will you promise me something?" Sonni murmured.

I inclined my head, and uttered a firm "Yes."

"It is of the greatest importance. I feel that I can trust you, but I need to hear the words upon your lips."

"Yes, I promise. Whatever it is, you have my word."

Sighing deeply, Sonni placed a gentle hand on my shoulder, "Should I not succeed, but die trying, will you please find a way back here to..." he inhaled, "...to finish this?"

His touch was delicate, almost as though he thought I was a fragile porcelain doll. I could feel his anguish, it was like a chain reaction. Every part of my body had become sensitive to his lingering pain. Not daring to look directly at him, partially out of fear that my own emotions would not hold up, and of slight discomfort--I fixated myself with my feet, and breathed a barely audible "Yes."

Sonni seemed to have said all he wanted to say. We both remained rooted to the curb, my legs and buttocks on the verge of numbness. Midnight had urbanized around us. The innate feelings of anxiety that came with being out at such an hour huddled over me. No matter how hard I tried to shake it, reason told me that it was almost always unwise to be loafing in the dark streets at this hour. Sonni, however, seemed to be oblivious to this, and continued to hold his post. The clouds shifted revealing a perfectly chiselled moon. Its opaque form hovered over us like a watchmen, a beacon amidst the darkness. I found myself staring benignly at the orb, wondering what it would be like to have a family, to have people in my life who truly cared about me. Unconditionally...unwavering.

Apart from Hans, everything that I had done thus far had been for the benefit of strangers. And although it was rewarding in itself, I could not help but wonder what it must feel like to truly sacrifice everything you had for a single being, or in Sonni's case, four single beings; to give up your life so willingly, as though it were merely an apple versus orange decision. Sonni had clearly thought this through. I, being a man of humility, could only sit back and revere him.

"How many more men are you planning to kill?"

His words took me by surprise. We had been sitting in silence for so long, I had not anticipated another conversation to strike up between us. I could feel his gaze upon me. It was a genuine question, blunt, and since we were both in the career path, it was quite acceptable.

"I do not know. I have not thought that far into the future." It was the truth, I did not know where this journey would take me. Perhaps there would be a dozen more, or perhaps none. I was the beholder of God's compass, and He was the needle. Where ever He pointed me, I would go willingly.

"Why do you do this? I mean to say, I am avenging Junichi and all the families who have suffered by Takada's hand. But you... you have not spoken of a family or friends, who or what are you fighting for?"

The clouds re-shifted over the moon, leaving us blanketed in darkness once more. A gentle breeze materialized from nowhere. It was balmy, yet tolerable. I knew what had brought me to this point. Although my rationale may not be clear to others, to me it was black and white.

"I do this because no one else will." I could feel Sonni's eyes on me. Absorbing what I had just said.

After several moments he whispered, "You are a selfless man, and you will one day be rewarded for your humanity." Sonni rose swiftly, "Shall we go back now?"

Thankful for the enveloping darkness, I less than gracefully pushed my stiff form up off of the curb. Sonni fumbled in his trouser pocket as we began to walk back to the café. I heard the unmistakable striking of a match and saw its momentarily orange glare. Smooth tobacco smoke immediately filled my nostrils. I glanced at Sonni, a pink-orange glow protruding from his lips.

"I did not know you smoked?" It was more of a question than a statement.

Savouring the bouquet, Sonni inhaled long and slowly. After several seconds, he tilted his head upwards to release the excess smoke. The moon's position was once again in our favour. There was a thin smile etched upon his youthful face. "I don't... at least my wife doesn't think I do." With that, he tossed the cigarette aside and continued walking, leaving me to follow in his wake.

....

The time came for me to leave; a solemn affair as I had become very attached to Sonni and his band of misfits. I should have learned from my experience with Nouman not to allow myself to get close to anyone. But knowing that I wasn't alone in this fight, the peace that came from having others who felt the same as I; it roped me in and I became vulnerable to my own needs for close-ness and friendship.

I firmly grasped Sonni's hand and pulled him into a tight one arm embrace. Neither of us spoke, in fact, no words had been exchanged between us since the night we took the walk together. Conversation was not necessary, we knew and understood what each other had to do. As I pulled away from him, I felt his hand grab mine. His long cool fingers swiftly placed something in my palm before quickly turning away from me. I gazed stupidly at the small piece of parchment in my right hand for several moments before unfolding it. I stared benignly at Sonni's immaculate pen-manship. Two words were carefully scribed in black ink:

Karras. Greece.

My lips curled into a delicate smile as I folded the parch-ment and placed it into my weathered travel bag. I made my way into the streets, anticipating nothing but my next expedition.

Chapter 12

Ionian Islands: Corfu, Greece
27 April, 1996

Water trickled steadily down the mossy concrete walls; soaking my hair, pattering mind numbingly at my feet. Sulphur seeped up through the damp wood floor; the smell of dry rot was asphyxiating. Days, perhaps even weeks, had passed since my capture. I had no concept of time, as each futile glance above was into a pitch black abyss...

An amalgamation of machine and man rushed past me. Like a rampaging beast completely out of touch with its surroundings, I was forced to jump into the nearest doorway to avoid being struck down. I braced myself in the doorway momentarily, I had run for at least two kilometres. My breath was short and I could feel my heart pulsating within my chest. Each breath more weakening than the last. I knew I had not lost them, they would come. Maybe not tonight, maybe not tomorrow, but they would find me. There was no way off this island; no other place to go.

When I was a child, my mother had once told me that God tests everyone's faith just once. As the days ran into nights, I found myself more devout than ever before. I would not allow myself to accept this fate. Being held in this damp, icy hole with no source of light and very little food and water, I was left to drown in my own vastly subsistence. With each passing minute, the waves of insanity became more rampant. Maybe this was my test: to let my faith conquer all else.

I sought shelter inside an old broken down Volkswagen, however, sleep was but an aspiration. I stayed on constant alert throughout the night. The city was abuzz with the news of Prime Minster Alexious Theodoridis Karras' death. Although, no two stories were the same in their entirety, most of Corfu's residents had the substance of it correct. Despite rumours that the Prime Minister had been shot, stabbed and pummelled to death, the Hellenic Police force were indeed searching for a middle aged, brown haired, Caucasian male that was spotted fleeing the scene. This man was not of Greek descent, most likely European or American. The island had been put on lockdown, with no one being granted the permission to leave or enter Corfu until the threat had been contained. The Special Anti-Terrorist Unit was crawling over every inch of the city. The use of extreme prejudice was permissible if need be. No one, black, white, Greek or Indian was above suspicion. Getting out of this city was going to be painstaking; it could be days, weeks or months until the lockdown was lifted. However, I would be patient, as I knew they could not keep people in or out forever. As I let the night wrap itself around me, I braced myself for the tribulations that would surely come.

A single hand pushed two fist-sized chunks of hardened bread through the small crack in the wooden door. For a few glorious seconds I was able to see a sliver of light; the most comforting feeling in the world. There *was* something beyond this place, and there *was* hope. Although there were three of us in the cell, the guards could smell that one of us had passed. They would not remove the body until only bones were left. Rotting flesh was putrid, beyond nauseating. It got into your system and stayed there for some time afterwards. Swavek Grocholski, my cellmate, had been in this hole for thirty-three years and he had yet to shake the smell.

As I knew they would, they came for me. It took them nine days to hunt me down, and when they found me hiding near a riverbed, I was tired and broken to the point of immobility. I simply allowed them to take me. Nine days without food or clean water. Nine days with minimal sleep and constant thoughts of paranoia. I was beaten down, too exhausted to process rational thoughts. Part of me was angered for permitting them to take me so gently; for being so weak. The other part was relieved.

I was transported to the Hellenic Headquarters where I was stripped of my clothing and forced to undergo a very physical form of Chinese water torture in efforts of achieving a confession. For seven days and nights I was battered mentally and physically. The more I denied the Hellenic, the more the violence escalated. I gave them nothing in return. Their fruitless efforts caused me to be engulfed in a constant sea of pain, but I did not render, not ever. I had the Lord, and I knew He would protect me.

When the beatings would cease, I was subject to more brute water torture. Strapped to a gurney, my entire body would become constricted, and I was forced to endure hours upon hours of tiny droplets of water pecking at my forehead. The drops themselves were painless; the general idea was to push me into insanity. Each icy bead was perfectly timed. Just enough to make you regain your senses, then drip, and you found yourself slipping once more.

Swavek Grocholski was a Polish entrepreneur whom had found himself in the wrong place at the wrong time. He and his brother Stashu had travelled to Corfu in the late nineteen fifties in hopes of finding love and prosperity. They had dreams of opening up a Polish cuisine restaurant together. Swavek was excellent with finances and customer service, his brother Stashu was an exceptional chef. The two brothers found a small space for rent, and within four months of arrival, they were living their dream.

They struggled to make ends meet from the very beginning. Word spread rapidly around the island that two Polish boys had opened up a new diner, however, very few customers frequented their establishment. Some people would come out of sheer curiosity, yet they had no steady clientele. The islanders thought it was an insult for two Polish men to not only invade their city, but also slap their heritage in the face by offering uncustomary foods.

After four years of complaints, and unwillingness to accept these men, the residents of Corfu rallied around the government in one final attempt to exile the two brothers. On August the twenty-sixth, nineteen sixty-three, the Greek police, better known as the Hellenic, burst into their restaurant and with no reason, took them both away. Swavek had not been outside these walls since, and like his brother Stashu, he will probably never see anything beyond them again. I continued to tell Swavek to keep his faith in the Lord; He would see him through this.

Confess and it will all be over, they had said. Tell us what we want to know and you shall be free of this, they had said. Gazing at them through my swollen eyes, blood dripping off my lips, I whispered 'No'. The beatings continued, this time more fierce then ever. I was whipped and electrocuted. When that did not work, I was then forced to endure the weight of many bags of rocks upon my chest. I knew they would not kill me, for they thought I possessed the information they so terribly yearned for. They grew tired of my silence and told me I would be sent to the hole until I chose to loosen my tongue. Here I am.

He never asked me what I had done to be placed in here. Perhaps he already knew. Some say that if you listen hard enough, you can see a man's soul through his words. Maybe Swavek was one of these men. Regardless of what he may or may not have been, I was grateful for his companionship. He did not have much to speak of, but his presence meant more to me than he would ever know.

There was mumbling outside our cell door. Hushed tones in fluent Greek, the voices of a man and a woman were barely audible. I heard Swavek rustling some few feet away from me. The voices continued, however, the woman was becoming more vocal. After several minutes of what was clearly an argument back and forth, everything went silent once more. I closed my eyes in an attempt to fall back asleep. It wasn't difficult, we were in total darkness at all times, and there was nothing else for us to do. I felt something cold and scaly grasp my arm. Swavek's frail voice whispered through the black murkiness.

"The woman has come for you Wilhelm, but the Hellenic will not let her take you. She has left for now, but not without informing the Hellenic that she will be back. She said they will release you upon her return."

My eyes snapped open. Surely this was but a dream. I was certain Swavek had misinterpreted what he had heard. After all, he had spent the past three decades in this place. He was an old man now, time and isolation had to be taking affect upon his mind. I merely sighed and attempted to put his words out of my mind.

The woman had not returned. I expected this, but nonetheless, tried to stay positive. I had been praying for strength and salvation constantly. I would not accept defeat; I would get through this. Swavek had not spoken a word since he told me about my potential release. Perhaps he felt guilty for getting my hopes up. I blamed him for nothing. In fact, there was part of me that had sprung to life. It was as though a fire had ignited within my body; it was a warm feeling. It brought hope. And although deep down I knew she was not coming, I still held on to that spark with everything I had.

....

The voices were back. Clearly the woman had returned, and once again she was conversing almost mutedly with the Hellenic. I felt Swavek's frail body brush past my own as he crawled towards the door to listen. He was inches away when the door swung wide open. A sudden showering of white sunlight blinded us both. It was calming and warm. I looked at Swavek and he looked at me. His long grizzly mane was completely white and his face was almost entirely obscured with matted hair. He had the most beautiful green eyes, tears could be seen leaking through the corners of them. The Hellenic entered the cell and jerked me upwards by my left arm. He was as strong as an ox, or perhaps I was just that weak.

"Come," he mumbled in crude English as he dragged me towards the door. Mystified, I struggled to gain my balance, ultimately allowing the man to drag me across the floor. I was almost over the threshold when Swavek's soft voice whispered from behind me.

"Did he suffer?"

I turned to face him. He was looking at me in the most quizzical way. "Who?" I whispered.

His lips parted slightly, "Karras."

"No," I replied softly, fully aware that the Hellenic had released my arm, as though unable to fathom what he was hearing.

Swavek closed his eyes and leaned his head back against the wall. "Pity. It was he who put me here."

I stared momentarily at him, completely in awe of the man before me. I was seeing him for the first time. This was a man who had received a terrible fate. Brought on by a country who could not accept difference. This man had nothing left, yet as I turned to leave the cell, I could see the hint of a smile upon his face. The Hellenic shut the door and locked it. We were in a brightly lit stone corridor.

"You take," he spoke. He was pointing at a brown paper bag some few feet away. "Take," he repeated.

I held firm, unsure what may be in store for me. The Hellenic grabbed the bag and pulled some cloth, along with my weathered satchel out of it.

"Clothes and bag, you take," he said once more before thrusting the bundle into my arms. For the first time, I glanced at my own clothing. My trousers were dingy and threadbare. My shirt was frayed and I had no shoes upon my feet. I glanced at the Hellenic, his features were hardened, but his eyes were soft.

He pointed down the corridor. "The woman said, 'Carry on.' "

Chapter 13

Paris, France
03 June, 1997

Every Spring the who's-who of French politicians and aristocrats host a night-long Gala to benefit the millions of sick and hungry children in Africa. In reality, the event is nothing more than a wealth extravaganza. The most exquisite foods, fashions, wines, jewels and automobiles make an appearance. A very formal affair, only France's most powerful and prestigious warrant an invite. The pedigrees of those in attendance could rival monarchs. Mostly business tycoons, heirs and heiresses, each guest is required to have a net worth of at least five hundred million francs. Old money or new money, it did not matter, so long as their pocketbooks were deep and their surname renown.

One year in the making: as each Gala closed, preparations for the following year begin. A staff of over eight hundred labourers is necessary to perform various tasks: caterers, musicians, wait staff, interior decorators, florists, valet and security personnel. There are assistants to assistants, and under-secretaries to those individuals. It is almost ludicrous in the sense that so many people are needed to ensure an even flow. Receiving an invitation gives one supreme bragging rights, as only one hundred twenty-five requests of attendance are mailed out. Those bestowed with such an honour take nothing for granted, as an annual invitation is not guaranteed. Economic and social factors play an enormous role, and in recent years the polices have been revised to permit the attendance of the current President and Heads of State. This, of course, did not sit well with all of the non-political attendees. They feel strongly that old traditions should be upheld, past policies should remain firm. However, the general consensus is that the event's board of directors do not want to piss off the French government. The funny thing about the wealthy; they have the means to purchase whatever they please, yet they are the first to complain about any small increase in expenses or taxes.

....

At the time when Savard Guillory LeBlanc initially stepped into the political arena, he had nothing but a single grey business suit and two hundred francs in his bank account. He walked to work, packed a brown bag lunch and watched every penny as though it were his last. His wife of fifteen years had left him grandly on the night of their anniversary. He arrived in their sitting room to find it barren; everything had been stripped from the once quaint living space. A panicked inspection of their home yielded more empty rooms. It did not take Savard long to realize what had happened. His new job had demanded almost all of his time, and what he thought was meaningless threats from his wife, turned out to be a cold, hard reality.

The divorce was a bloodbath. Savard had managed to scrape together fifteen hundred francs for an attorney to aid him. His wife's father had paid fifty thousand to contract services from the most successful attorney in all of Paris. At one thousand francs per hour and a firm which could start its own football team, Savard knew he had no chance. She got the house, the Audi, the furnishings, the electronics, the artwork, and the dog. *His dog.* The once love of his life, can't live without her, had gotten everything. He was left with nothing but his clothes and an old rawhide bone that had once belonged to his German Pointer, Benoît.

Savard became consumed with his work. It was not a hard task, as he already devoted fourteen hours each day to it. His ex-wife was always on his mind, but he found it hard to think of anything other than sleep after pulling a month worth of twenty hour shifts. Slowly, she drifted out of his thoughts and Savard began to pick up the pieces. Now, some eight years later, he had finally gotten his personal and social life back on track. He rose grandly into the monarchs of the French government; had his own private jet, penthouse, along with vacation homes in Aspen and Queensland. Savard had made something out of nothing; if only the bitch could see him now. He had heard rumours that her father's Fortune 500 company had declared bankruptcy. Each time a new scrap of information reached his ears, he would smile sweetly. He was not one to relish the past, it did not do good to hold grudges, but he hoped Geneviève was living in squalor somewhere alongside her father.

It is no easy feat to hold an entire country within ones' hands. As delicate as a newborn child, yet as harden as stone. Every decision that was made had at least a dozen consequences; some more desirable than others. An equilibrium of politics and economics was crucial, as each fuelled the other's fire. The spongy exterior of the country's governmental infrastructure proved easy to manipulate, yet its colonised fossil core was not so willing to embrace change. The general populous was unwilling to accept change, as old law and old traditions were believed to be the best polices. Savard laboured endlessly to ensure a delicate balanced was achieved, yet at times, this was just not possible. There were so many intricacies; like a thousand piece puzzle. Each piece had to be studied and then connected to another. In most cases, everything fit together beautifully. There was, however, always a piece that just did not seem to fit properly. Bottom line: cover-ups, disposals, and set-ups were necessary to ensure the stability and balance within the French government. There was no honour. There were no complete truths, only half certainties. Everything that was done, no matter how heinous, was done to protect the country's political and economic sectors. Things were taken care of quietly and with some attempt at dignity.

Overall, Savard LeBlanc thought he had done an exceptional job at running this country. His predecessor had sent France into the ground with his empty promises and failed attempts of prosperity. And when Savard took office, he was once again left to pick up the pieces. He was not trusted and his words meant nothing. He was unanimously the single most hated man throughout the entire country. His first eighteen months as newly elected President were something straight out of a horror show. Death threats, bombings, rebellions coupled with an uncooperative administration; Savard was stressed to the max and wanted nothing more than for it to all cease. Several times he considered putting in his resignation. *Let the next poor bastard deal with this mess.* But like a throng, he hung onto what seemed to be invisible rays of hope, crossed his fingers that the country would turn for the better, and he would make it out alive.

It became apparent quite early into the Presidency that charm, honesty and decorum would not secure stability or prosperity within the country's walls. Savard's 'honesty is the best policy,' policy had been made a mockery of. Soon he realized that his own administration was comprised of some of the most crooked politicians this side of the Seine River. Despite their ungodly character and questionable business practices, these men and women always seemed to get the job done. And, surprisingly, with minimal damage. He found himself leaning on them, as they had a solution to everything Savard had thrown their way. "We accidentally nuked five thousand of our own service members. What do you suggest we do?" he had asked them. The solution was simple: leak information that a nuclear warhead was stolen by Middle East Militants and blame the attack upon them. If that did not work, point the finger at some of France's high-profile war criminals. The rest of society will be so outraged by the thought that their own countrymen blew the shit out of their sworn protectors, they will wash our hands of the problem and of some scumbags for us. Solutions were found and problems were taken care of instantaneously.

"A fifteen year old girl has accused our cabinet minister of molestation. What do we do?" Dispose of the girl they had suggested. Within four hours of that conversation, the child was dead.

"The public is in an uproar about education reform. They don't feel we are doing enough. What do we do?" Throw a few million francs their way just to shut them up, then in six months time, increase taxes by seven percent.

Savard knew he was going to Hell for what he had let occur. Yet he had foolishly convinced himself that everything they had done was for the benefit and well being of France. He operated under the delusion that he *was* still a good man. A good man who simply had to make sacrifices. France was now one of the most prestigious and wealthy countries in the world, a small price to pay to achieve such greatness. And tonight, everything he had worked for, all of the choices he had made for the good of this country, would come full circle, and the class, the wealth and the opulence that *is* France would be spectacled and revered. Tonight was the annual Gala held in benefit for the starving children in Africa. As President of the Republic of France, Savard warranted an automatic invite. He would join the ranks of France's most prestigious. This event made world headlines. Tonight France would shine.

"Where the HELL is my tuxedo Victoire? I'm expected to make an appearance in less than two hours time. What is the big hold up?"

"It is on its way, Sir. There is traffic on Rue Balzac. Your eveningwear will be here momentarily."

"It damn well better be. I have laboured too hard over the course of the past nine months. All in preparation of tonight's event. I will not be made a fool of."

"Yes, Sir, understood."

Victoire strutted with purpose through the elegant white French doors and out of the President's private study. Shutting the doors softly, she exhaled and leaned her slender frame against the aged hardwood. *God I wish someone would just put that man out of his misery...* The vibrant ringing of her mobile device echoed from within her trousers pocket. Answering it with a swift "Ello" and a quick glance into the bronzed mirror on her left, she immediately sprang to life.

....

Lovers walked hand in hand down the streets, tender music could be heard seeping through open two story windows. Beauty bled from every crevice of the city. There was not a single grotesque site. Even the homeless and beggars had a mystic splendour about them. Oblivious to her surroundings, Victoire ran full force into the sea of people loitering the sidewalks. At twenty-nine, she was in the best shape of her life, and she was thankful for this. Seconds after she assured the President his evening attire was on the way, she had received a call from one of her many assistants who informed her that the car carrying the President's garments had broken down. Acquiring the tuxedo was now solely in her hands. She hiked up Rue Carte, past all the bistros and boutiques in a whirlwind of speed and fury. The people in the streets were mere blurs and their conversations buzzed incomprehensibly in her ears. She made a sharp left turn into an alley between her favourite café and shoe boutique. On a normal day, she would have stopped for a latte and a little shoe shopping therapy. Panting like a thirsty dog, Victoire pushed herself further and further. Her peep-toe, chocolate Christian Louboutin heels pounded the pavement with the force of a jackhammer. With each thud she cringed, hoping that there would be no damage to the pieces of art she wore upon her feet. *That bastard better be thankful. These heels cost more than his Tuxedo...*

The passengers seated inside the President's black Bentley were on the edge. Perspiration the size of marbles ran down their brows, and every few seconds they darted their eyes sharply in every direction.

"Où est-elle?" the most anxious of the two colleagues kept frantically inquiring. *Where is she?*

Wringing his hands nervously, the man spotted a thin young woman with long flowing black hair walking towards their car. Jumping slightly, his lips parted to reveal a toothy grin, but instantly sank into a frown, as the young woman kept walking past.

Pressing his palm hopelessly upon the tinted glass, he gasped exasperated, "Elle a dit qu'elle serait ici! Où est-elle? Je ne la vois pas." *She said she would be here! Where is she? I do not see her.*

Breathing a sigh of defeat, he glanced at his deflated colleague before closing his own eyes. Surely they would be terminated. The President was not a merciful man. He got what he wanted, no matter what the cost. The fact that these recent events were beyond their knowledge and control would mean nothing to him, even after everything they did for LeBlanc and his administration. All the personal favours and unethical practices: they were but mere fallout men. Unappreciated and downgraded, as they were once political fish whom had failed to survive within the tank full of sharks.

A forceful knock upon the car's passenger window followed by the angered shouts of a panic-stricken woman caused both men to hit the roof. A severely beaten down Victoire was frantically hitting her fists on the window and cursing wildly as she clutched the car door handle.

"VITE! VITE! DONNEZ-LE MOI!" *Quick! Quick! Give it to me!* Her screams caused passers-by to shuffle past her in a confused, apprehensive fury.

The driver unlocked the rear passenger door, within seconds Victoire had ripped the garment bag off the seat, and without a word, vanished. Exhaling gradually, the two colleagues glanced at one another before chuckling nervously. They may survive to serve the President another day.

"Merde!" She spat as her left heel snapped in two. Removing her shoes altogether, Victoire tucked the garment bag under one arm, her weathered Louboutins under the other, and once again, she set out as fast as her legs could carry her. Her entire body was about to collapse, her legs felt like jelly and she was certain her lungs had reached the point of explosion. Beating the same path as she came, Victoire ran into a swarm of tourists in front of the Arc De Triomphe, which stopped her dead in her tracks. *Condamnez-le!* Damn it, she thought. Tourists were the only downside to living in this country. It was full of them. Normally she did not mind the cloud of people, she enjoyed watching their reactions to the breathtaking sites that make up Paris. However, not today. She bullied her way through a group of Chinese men and woman, all the outcries in their native tongue went unacknowledged. She broke the threshold, thinking only seven more block to go...

....

Limousines, Ferraris and Rolls-Royces littered the drive in front of Louvre Palace. Once a fortress built by Philip II in the twelfth century, the Palace now played host to the infamous Louvre Museum; the world's most frequented art museum. Its rich history and thirty-five thousand plus artefacts made it an ideal location to hold Galas and benefits for the most important aristocrats throughout France. With natural beauty that could rival the Northern Lights and Machu Picchu, the palace was adorned in art spanning back hundreds of centuries and an elegant divinity lingered in the air.

Haughtily, Savard stepped out of his vintage Rolls-Royce, immediately relishing the air around him. Wealth. And a ton of it. His chauffeur closed the door behind him; instantaneously he was surrounded by a team of security guards whom had exited from the sport utility vehicle behind him. A plush golden carpet lined with white rope lighting guided their way to the entrance of the Palace. The sky was dark, the moon's yellow orb was the only visible source of light from above. The Louvre Pyramid's six hundred and seventy-three panes of glass sparkled like diamonds, giving it the most stunning mystique. However, Savard paid no attention to such beauties; he was concerned with his grand entrance. He had paid all the right people to ensure his initial appearance did not go unnoticed. With the ever graceful and astonishing Victoire at his side, they ascended over the threshold into the bright spotlight.

The violinists received their cue from the waiter who had received his from the doorman. *When you see me touch my right ear, stop the music.* It did not take the band long to realize whom they would be ending the overture for. No one was as arrogant as the President, and anyone with an ounce of self-respect would not even dream to make an infantile request such as this one. Nonetheless, they obliged, and when they saw the smartly dressed waiter raise his right hand to his ear, all became silent.

Savard and Victoire lingered momentarily under the marble archway. He had instructed her to show no emotion apart from a slight smile. Although she thought this to be absolute ridiculousness, she knew the consequences if she disobeyed him. Just one hour prior, she had witnessed him terminate two of her colleagues for 'disloyalty'. *As though they could have foreseen their transportation breaking down.* Alas, Savard did not see things as most logical individuals did. Victoire smiled satisfyingly; not a single person had taken notice to their entrance. She could feel the President's arm stiffen around hers as they stepped into the ballroom. He released her, the musicians' second cue to pick up where they had left off.

When you have so much affluence under one roof, there is only one thing on everyone's mind: to out do the person standing next to you. In all actuality, half a million francs worth of decorations, flowers, fine food and wine were minute. The wealthy made their own sophistication. The most dingy of places could be transformed into something luxurious when enough 'money' was congregated there. The thousands of golden baubles dangling from the ceiling, the bright white Egyptian cotton linens covering the round tables, the perfectly handpicked purple and white orchids, all tied together with historic artefacts from across the globe... no one took notice. The pâté, the foie gras, the sushi; all fine foods these people had thrown at them everyday. Even France's most expensive wines become dull and tasteless after one had sipped them long enough.

The Gala was in full swing. The band beautifully launched into Carlos Gardel's Por Una Cabeza, and the dance floor immediately became congested with couples passionately melding to the tango. Under the light of the baubles, diamonds and gemstones dangling from the intertwined bodies glistened, creating the most exasperating phenomenon. Savard made his rounds. First the CEO of France's most prominent natural resource company. The two men conversed for several minutes, however when the CEO refused to 'kiss ass,' Savard moved on.

He chatted nonchalantly with Adrienne Côté, a popular shoe and handbag designer, until he grew tired of hearing her ideas for her new fall collection. Waiters weaved between the circular tables carrying golden trays laden with tall glasses of wine and an array of finger foods. Savard snatched a glass of Pétrus from a passing waiter, and in two gulps, had consumed the entire beverage. *Where the Hell is Victoire?* He thought angrily. He demanded that she remain within ten feet of him at all times, yet she was nowhere in sight. If it had not been for her intellect and beauty, he would have fired her long ago. She was simply pretty face. Savard's advisor had suggested he hire a personal assistant whose charm and beauty could be used to their advantage. Victoire had been under his employment for the past three years and it had paid off ten fold. No matter how bad the situation was, he could send Victoire to speak to the media on his behalf. Time and time again they lapped up what she had to say and found comfort in her words. Savard would do anything to keep her sweet, slender and beautiful. *Anything.*

In nineteen ninety-five, Victoire had tearfully informed the President that she was pregnant. She could not have been happier. She was not married to the unborn child's father, but the couple were making plans to wed in the weeks to come. Savard was beside himself. He could not have his "golden face" be seen as a sinner, nor out of shape. He quietly arranged for Victoire to have an abortion, and for her troubles, he gave her a hundred thousand franc bonus. Although, their relationship had never quite been the same since, it was a small price to pay to keep your country's civility.

He spotted her some fifty feet away, talking animatedly to a young man ornamented in platinum chains and diamond earrings. He was wearing a very handsome Armani suit, however, the effect was ruined by the black baseball cap upon his head and black and white tennis shoes on his feet. Savard had no clue who this young man was, but he could tell by Victoire's body language, that he was someone of importance. He made a rather swift beeline for the two, almost knocking a waiter clear onto the marble floor.

"Excusez-Moi," mumbled Savard.

The man simply nodded his head, straightened the jumbled glasses on his tray, and carried on about the floor. *Such rude behaviour from people these days. Did he not know who I am?* Savard smoothed his white tuxedo jacket and continued towards Victoire.

The young man she was with turned out to be Rémi Villon, a music mogul Savard had never heard of. Victoire introduced the two men, and surprisingly, Savard and the young man hit it off. Despite his odd choice in fashion, Rémi was knowledgeable on numerous topics ranging from healthcare reform to public works.

"Car je disais juste le Président LeBlanc, je suis satisfait avec ce que vous et votre administration a fait pour l'éducation de distircts d'école, sans compter le programme de musique. Je le sens très important que la notre jeunesse soit bien arrondie dans les arts..." But Savard only partially processed what his newest supporter was saying. He had become slightly disoriented as the air around him seemed to thicken with every breath. Savard politely excused himself under pretence of needing to speak with someone whom he had just spotted across the room. Making his way through the crowd, Leblanc's legs began to spasm and ache with every step. As he shook Villon's hand, his extended arm suddenly jerked and a blinding pain shot up the length of his arm to his shoulder.

His attempts to hide this quickly became feeble as his entire body was soon ravished with ever-escalating convulsions and vicious pain. Victoire rushed to his side to aid him. "Monsieur, êtes-vous se sentant bien? *Sir, are you feeling alright?*

Savard mumbled incoherently that he must have eaten some spoiled pâté. He tried to smile but his face merely contorted grotesquely with the effort. His throat was closing, he gulped fiendishly for air. LeBlanc's legs finally gave way under his weight and he fell to the floor like a ton a bricks. As he lay there, flopping around like a fish out of water, Victoire once again voiced her concern and commanded Rémi to get help for the President.

However, it was too late, for within just a few short minutes, he was dead.

It did not take long for the guests to realize that something had happened. The music stopped and every single person in the room had crowded around LeBlanc's lifeless form. Victoire showed as much emotion as she could muster whilst yelling frantically for a doctor, for the police, for anyone who would listen. Just hours before she had made a wish for someone to put Savard LeBlanc out of his misery; as far as she was concerned, he deserved this fate. The ex-President's security team had arrived on the scene and began to create a barrier around Savard. They aggressively kept all the spectators at bay.

I lingered for a few moments before slipping into the caterer's passage. The tunnel went under the Palace and the Louvre Museum for two kilometres. I could not stop for fear that someone may have seen me. I was certain I was spotted bumping into the President just minutes before his death. At the base of the passage I tossed the access badge I had purchased from a young man a few days prior to the event into a crevice in the stone wall. I bent the needle off the syringe I stuck into Savard on the rough rocks as well. Just as the crooked chemist had said, the strychnine took less time to take effect than it would for a man to tie his shoe. Nonetheless, the job was done.

Under the blackened sky, I walked the streets of Paris. Every available law enforcement officer was currently at Louvre Palace, there was no one to chase me. I had idol time on my hands and the next train to anywhere was not due to depart for several hours. My only thoughts were of *where to next?* When the formidable woman at the ticket inquired as to where I was going, I responded "Vous décidez." *You decide.*

Chapter 14

Madrid, Spain
26 August, 1998

Alejandro sat patiently waiting behind the wheel of his new grey Mercedes. Seven months prior, his superior had surprised him with the lavish gift. Top of the line with leather seats, the automobile come equipped with all the latest high tech gadgets: GPS navigation, satellite radio and a built-in mobile device. It was expensive and classy; something that Alejandro would have never been able to afford on his petty salary. Him and his new vehicle were the talk of the office. *He must be kissing some serious ass,* they had said. *He is manipulating the President into buying things for him. He's brainwashing the President. He's fornicating with the President.*

Alejandro had heard it all. His colleagues were not exactly discreet, and more often than not, he was within complete earshot when they would make their snide remarks. It was such a vicious circle. Alejandro's name was tarnished and he was subject to daily torture and ridicule. His mother had told him to stand up for himself, to defend his name. Alejandro just could not do that. As much as he yearned to set the record straight, he was bound to secrecy by the President himself, and he knew that if he ever spoke ill of his superior, he would not live to see the age of twenty-seven.

Truth be told, the Mercedes was one of the many 'hush-hush' gifts Alejandro had received throughout his tenure as personal assistant to the President. He acquired the position fresh out of college. Young, naive, but nonetheless eager to learn, Alejandro was taken under the President's wing instantly, and within six months, he had become his most trusted confidant. He asked for his opinion on matters of national and global interest. He permitted Alejandro to sit in on meeting with diplomats and leaders from other countries. He had even been invited to the President's home over the holiday season. Alejandro had the perfect job, and his future in government appeared to be very bright.

Coming from a less-privileged family, Alejandro and his two sisters did not have very much. He grew up in a two bedroom apartment in the southern region of Madrid. It was very impoverished, slums were everywhere, as were drug dealers, prostitutes and gangs. His mother worked ten hours a day as a maid for a wealthy family on the outskirts of the city. She made six thousand pesetas a week, yet she slaved like a dog. Alejandro's father had a mobile shoeshine business which he operated out of a single black handbag. Each morning he would gather his brushes, cloths and array of polishes and head downtown to the busy streets of Madrid. He would work sixteen to eighteen hour days. He earned roughly twelve thousand pesetas per month. They struggled to make ends meet. Sometimes it would be days between meals. They used minimal water and electricity, and when Alejandro's mother had time, she handmade all their clothing. Despite their hard times, the family was very close. They appreciated everything they had. There was always someone in their community who had less than they did. They thanked the Lord for each day they spent with one another; their faith and family were their salvation.

Alejandro knew at a very young age that he was different. He knew things that all the other children his age did not, and his capabilities were significantly higher. His parents called his intelligence a gift; they laboured fruitlessly by harnessing and encouraging Alejandro to take advantage of his gift. To leave the south city, to become something great. By age fourteen, Alejandro had surpassed every academic record set forth by individuals three to four years his senior. He excelled in mathematics, literature and the sciences. He was skilled in debate, his knowledge of the past was profound, and his eagerness to learn more was inspiring. He could never get enough knowledge. He fed off of it. There was always something new to learn: some new scientific fact, a more intense mathematic theory...History had been written and rewritten. Documents resurfaced changing the face of what we had once known. Alejandro kept up-to-date with every single change within the mathematical, scientific, political and historical societies.

College was paid in full by the Spanish government. His family could not have been prouder. His father had always said that Alejandro's intelligence and ambition could buy him a new life. And indeed it had. By age twenty, he had graduated with honours from the University of Madrid: School of Business. He also attended U of M Technical Institute during the evenings, where he obtained a degree in computer science. Alejandro was first noticed by the President four years prior when the technical assistance company Alejandro had worked for had been hired to solve problems that arose with the government's old, deteriorating computers. The President was so impressed with the way Alejandro presented himself and the effort he put into his job, he offered him a position in his office; effective immediately. Alejandro jumped at the opportunity to work so closely to such a highly respected government official. The decision was an easy one to make.

Now, four years later, Alejandro had begun to question whether or not he had made the correct decision. Week after week he sat waiting for the President to emerge from the hotel, under cover of cloak and dagger. Alejandro knew that what his superior was doing wrong, but he had been sworn to silence. His career had been threatened, along with his life, and his family's, should he ever speak the truth. The President had given Alejandro a two hundred fifty thousand peseta bonus the first year he was under his employment. The second year, he purchased a small condominium for Alejandro's family to live in. It was all done as a reminder to

Alejandro: to solidify their secret. "I purchase you a few things, you in turn keep your mouth shut." The President's exact words. The previous year, Alejandro had informed the President that he was taking another position located in New Zealand as the senior manager of technical services. The President wrote Alejandro a cheque for a million pesetas and sent him and his family to Tahiti for fourteen days of rest and relaxation, all expenses paid. It was quite obvious the President did not want his aide to leave.

The Mercedes truly was magnificent. Alejandro could not deny that his superior had great taste, and he knew the art of the bribe. His behaviour sickened and repulsed Alejandro. Countless times he wished he could make the President stop, but he knew that nothing could be done. He had contemplated killing the man himself, yet his faith and morality could not allow him to commit such a treacherous act. He sought the Lord's guidance. Alejandro prayed for the victims' safety, and he prayed for his soul. One day he would face judgment for what he has done.

....

In nineteen ninety-two, one Gomez Salazar Cervino joined the ranks of the Spanish government when he was inaugurated as President under His Majesty Carlos Zapatero IV. Not the most attractive man, most intelligent or the most polished, Gomez Cervino's appointment was rumoured to be linked to Spain's Royal Family. Although his fellow Spaniards would have preferred his running mate, Luis H. Ramirez, the King and his handpicked government ran the gamut. If a candidate was akin to the King, their future was bright and golden. Ramirez was more qualified to serve as President and he was more professional, yet Cervino's family had strong ties to the Zapateros, thus making an official election pointless. The number of ballots received meant nothing, as the outcome was predetermined.

Cervino did as he was told as dictated by the King. He was merely a puppet; a handsomely paid puppet. King Zapatero wanted someone whom he could control, someone whom could be easily manipulated and moulded to do his bidding. He had found everything he could ever hope for in Gomez Cervino. Ambitious to the point of over zealousness, not too bright, and eager to please, President Cervino was appointed the King's unofficial fallout man. He ran the country recklessly through the President, knowing that his bloodline would be his protection, and Cervino in turn would be the marked man.

After two years of playing Cervino's puppeteer, and after a decade of dishonourable rule, the reign of King Carlos Zapatero IV had come to an abrupt end--a very abrupt end. Found dead in a pool of his own blood, King Carlos died by his own hand when he "accidentally" punctured himself with one of his many handcrafted swords. His fascination for forearms and rapiers could be traced back to his childhood. Blind in one eye, he was far from being a skilled marksman, and as a child, he was always injuring himself whilst brandishing his swords. The Royal Family launched a muted investigation; six weeks after King Carlo's death a formal statement noting cause of death was made to the public. The King was sent off in style, and then easily forgotten as Spain now had a new Queen.

Unlike her brother, Cipriana Zapatero II chose to take a backseat approach with regards to her government. She terminated her entire staff and held an emergency election in which she allowed the people to determine who should take office. Every name was counted, no ballot was tossed aside. Majority rule, period. She knew of her brother's antics and had full knowledge of what Gomez Cervino had been used for. Spain was calling for the President's impeachment, yet she could not bring him to tribunal for doing as he had been instructed. Cervino had showed his loyalty to his King, and for that, the Queen felt he deserved a second chance. Giving President Cervino full power over Spain's economic and political issues would test his strength and encourage him to take a more positive and righteous approach to running the country. To the Queen's amazement, Cervino took on the role with renewed enthusiasm. He made some key changes in his own staff and began to listen to what his people had to say.

Gomez Salazar Cervino was not a cruel or greedy man. In fact, he was very fond of his fellow Spaniards and a perfect role model for young children. The Cervino family was known to be kind, caring and giving people. They were neighbourly, never fought with anyone and attended Mass twice per week. Always together; warm smiles upon their faces. Yes, the President would sometimes become befuddled during debates and interviews, but that was to be expected: he was only human. Not all of his choices were great and he received his fair share of backlash. Nonetheless, he always took criticism and setbacks in stride. Unlike his predecessors, President Cervino learned from his errors and he made an effort to improve. He was a great man, perfect in almost every way. He had family, friends, supporters...Queen Cipriana had recently bestowed a high honour upon him for his outstanding devotion and humanitarian efforts. She said he was the new face of Spain; that she was proud to call him the leader of her government. Unfortunately, the face Spain saw was not the true one. They saw but a mere mask as the face beneath it was much darker and sickening. It was not a face of kindness or nobility, but that of a hungry predator.

....

On a cold winter night in mid December, nineteen ninety-five, I inadvertently overheard a conversation between a Priest and a young woman. Held up in a church on the outskirts of Dublin, I took shelter from the raging snow storm outside the cathedral's walls. I had just returned from a warm furlough in Louisiana, and wished nothing more than to be back in the south. Ireland was a bastard during the winter months. I had become stranded there as all air travel had been suspended. I bore the elements for several hours in search of a hotel, but due to all the flight delays, every place I went to was filled to maximum capacity. Chilled to the bone, I saw a queue of people in front of an old Catholic church, and quickly took my place in line.

Midnight Mass had ended at half past one, and as the pews were clearing out, the Priest announced that there would be confessions until four. I decided to linger in the back row of the cathedral nearest the confessionals under pretence that I was waiting my turn to speak to the Father. I noticed a young Latino woman sitting several rows ahead of me and I wondered vaguely if she had been a stranded passenger as well. The line-up was long, so I curled up in the pew and attempted to get some rest. At some point I dozed off. When I awoke, it was to the sound of soft crying. I peered towards the confessional; it was empty, the queue of people had diminished. The crying continued followed by kind words of comfort from a male voice. I cautiously poked my head above the pew directly in front of me. The same Latino woman from the hours prior sat sobbing gently into her hands, the Priest next to her.

"Do you swear you won't tell anyone?" I heard her say in passable English.

She turned her head towards the Priest, tears streaming down her cheeks. I remember how young she looked. No more than sixteen or seventeen. She was so scared and lost. I had wondered where her mother and father were and why they were not here to comfort her. I silently listened to their conversation under cover of the pews and dim lanterns. The young girl said her name was Yolanda and she had been born in Spain. At the age of eleven, her father—a poor brick layer, sold her to an old woman whom she knew only by Senora La Reina from Madrid. She was forced to live in the dirty, rat infested cellar of Senora La Reina's home. There were approximately twenty other girls whom lived there as well; all very young. All had been sold by their families. Yolanda told the Priest that she and the other girls had to "work" for food and water. When the Priest inquired what "work" meant, the poor girl broke down, and began to sob violently on the pew in front of them.

After several minutes of uncontrollable weeping, Yolanda informed the Priest that she and the other girls were forced into sex, oral and penetration, with much older men. Senora La Reina would make all the arrangements ahead of time. A girl was chosen as per the client's wishes based upon age, hair colour, breast size, number of men the girl had been with, and so forth. The chosen girl would be blindfolded and taken to a bathtub where she would be forced to sit in boiling water to be cleaned. Some girls had their private area shaved if the client wanted it. Others were forced to endure vaginal cleaning with a long rough bristle brush. From the washroom, the girls would be taken to the "dress up," room as Senora La Reina called it. They would wear whatever outfit the client had instructed. Their hair and makeup would also be done exactly per the client's wishes. Yolanda told the Priest that they never saw any of their surroundings other than the cellar walls and the bedroom area of hotel suites. She said the men were rough and a lot of the girls were beaten by the men for not performing up to their standards or for crying. Some girls who left Senora La Reina's cellar never returned. I was repulsed by Yolanda's account of what had happened to her. I was absolutely sickened to think that countless young girls were being violated in such a manner: their youth striped from them without remorse or hesitation.

When the Priest inquired as to how Yolanda broke away from Senora La Reina, she said that the rules were simple: A girl works until she is sixteen years of age, and then she is relieved of the cellar. Senora La Reina would give the girls the equivalent to twenty-five pounds and then under threat of killing them if they talked, they would be released. The girls would be taken, blindfolded, to some remote location before being abandoned. Yolanda said she was taken to a village approximately one hundred and fifty kilometres outside of Madrid. She was thrown from the vehicle, and as a reminder not to contact authorities, the people whom dropped of her off beat her half to death and stripped her of her clothing. Passed out, bloody and naked, Yolanda lain in a ravine for what she claimed was two nights before a young boy and his grandfather found her. They took her to their home where she was nursed back to health and treated with kindness. Until that night in mid December, she had never told a soul what had happened to her.

Despite the trauma, abuse, the infringement of her body, and the terror Senora La Reina and these men impressed upon her, she was quite calm. Through her tears and sometimes incoherent murmurs, I found out about a man whom Yolanda called El Travieso. *The Wicked One.* Although this was just a nickname for a menacing man, I could feel the fear pulsating around Yolanda. She was truly frightened by this man. And when she spoke of him it was in whispered tones, as though he may hear. She told the Priest this man was a well respected figure and his rank within the Spanish government was high. She said he called Senora La Reina once per week to request a girl. He was not a picky man, he did not care what age the girl was, nor what she looked like as long as the girl obeyed him. Yolanda had been forced into intercourse with him at least fifty times over the course of her enslavement. She claimed this man was the most savage of them all. He sodomized the girls, beat them, urinated on them, tied them up and whipped them. Yolanda said she was certain he had killed girls before. Countless times he had forced Yolanda to perform oral sex, and if she slipped to where he felt teeth, she would receive a beating. The stories were horrible, this man was a beast. He would leave the girls in the hotel room to bleed from every orifice of their body; some had broken bones or punctured lungs. The damage inflicted upon these girls was so severe that the vast majority of them would never be able to have children of their own. I, along with the Priest, lost control and broke down in tears when Yolanda said that she would never know what it was like to be a mother.

To this very day, I am still disgusted by Yolanda's words, and the horrific images of her suffering will forever be burned into my mind. I had never planned to travel to Spain. The current President had turned a new leaf in recent years, and I had faith that he would remain a great ruler. After hearing Yolanda's story, I ached to avenge her and all the other girls whom had suffered at the hands of Senora La Reina. I figured my chances at finding El Travieso were slim, nevertheless, it would be heartless of me not to try. I arrived in Madrid with nothing but a name and a general idea of where to start my search.

I checked into a cheap villa-style hotel, which I quickly realised was infested with drug dealers and whores. The outside of the building was nothing to praise; a red flag as to what the inside must be like, however, my funds would not allow me to stay anywhere swanky. On the way to my room, I was propositioned by a young woman dressed scantily clad in only a pair of red panties. Her long black hair was matted with oil and filth. She had track marks from excessive heroin usage on both arms, bloodshot hazel eyes, and beneath her grungy flesh, bones protruded sickeningly. As pathetic as she was, I could not help but feel sorry for her. She was a drugged out whore with no place to go but downwards. I was a firm believer in second chances, but something about this woman told me that she had reached the point of no return long ago. As I entered my room, I found myself wondering if she had been one of Senora La Reina's girls in the past.

My search for El Travieso started in the very establishment I was staying in. For six days I watched the traffic coming in and out of the hotel, however, I saw no young girls or suspicious looking men enter the building. Two weeks brought nothing but more drug dealers and prostitutes, so I checked out and moved on. I found a business directory inside a telephone booth several blocks from the hotel. I leafed through it until I found the hotel listings; there were seventy-four listings for hotels in the municipality of Madrid. I was instantly crestfallen. There was no way I could afford to check out all these places, not to mention the time it would take to do so. I was seconds away from forgetting all about Spain, Senora La Reina and El Travieso. I attempted to convince myself that I need not be bothered with them and their sordid affairs. My thoughts strayed to Yolanda... to her innocent eyes...so young and so full of fear. I gripped the directory tightly whilst ripping the page from its spine.

To find El Travieso, I needed to think as he did. If he truly was high amongst the ranks of the Spanish government, he would take every step necessary to conceal his fetish. If word ever got out about his sick behaviour, he would be stripped of whatever title he held; his life would be over. This man would be killed in prison on sheer principle of what he was. It was common knowledge that a child molester never lived long enough to stand trial. A mere accusation of such behaviour would get a man murdered. El Travieso would be cautious, meticulous and egotistical. He would not take a young girl into a slum or a crack hotel. I was certain he would choose posh places in more highly trafficked areas. A man within government would not dare step into a rat hole. Even as clandestine as he was, his ego would not allow him to be seen in lower class areas. Being somewhat of an intelligent man, I was confident I had El Travieso pegged. I did not know his identity as of yet, but I knew from the directory that he probably would only frequent twenty hotels within the city. Although it appeared as though I had a wealth of information, in reality, I was grasping at straws. Keeping an eye on twenty hotels would be a huge challenge, however, not knowing when to expect El Travieso to show up would be crippling.

....

Seven painstaking months of searching finally yielded what I was looking for. After comparing photographs, automobiles, and young girls from twenty hotels throughout Madrid, I was beyond certain that I had a match. Although this man wore different disguises and was careful to never be seen leaving in the same attire he had entered the hotel in, he had made one fatal mistake: he was still arrogant enough to have a driver take him to his engagements. The same wiry young man took a thoroughly disguised older gentleman to a different hotel each week. It took me five months to catch onto this. I had documented every person and every automobile in and around the hotels. I attempted to establish some sort of pattern, but as I was one man keeping an eye on twenty places, it was very difficult to string anything together.

The first five months were hit and miss. I had begun to think I would never find him. In early January, my luck changed when I caught a break. For three weeks straight I saw the same grey Mercedes. It was at a different hotel each time, however, the driver perched behind the wheel was unmistakable. In his mid to late twenties, the young man sat each week reading the newspaper or conversing on his mobile device whilst waiting for his passenger to return. The look on his face was what gave him away. He appeared to be an intelligent person--reading only the financials and the economic sections of the paper. Despite this, his eyes were constantly darting to and fro and he had the continuous look of a guilty person upon his face. I knew that look. I had seen it many times throughout my youth. He had knowledge of the misdeeds being committed.

I attempted to follow the Mercedes from Villa Brazos one dreary afternoon, but my efforts were futile as the congestion of people throughout the city made it difficult to manoeuvre. The man and his driver were spotted at three of the most prestigious hotels in all of the municipality. I was positive he operated only at these places. The other hotels were posh, but they lacked the grandeur and importance which Villa Brazos, Lolita and Grande Lujo had. It was rather idiotic of this man to frequent places such as these. I am sure he thought it was a great idea; all three establishments were hectic, yet he did not see through his own arrogance. All it would take was one person to recognize his voice, his stature or some odd habit and his cover would be blown. Then again, my own ego and arrogance was telling me that I had the right person. I could be wrong about everything, but in the back of my mind I knew I wasn't. I suppose everyone is entitled to a little self-superciliousness every now and then.

I religiously watched the television and combed every single inch of the city's daily newspaper, Informador de Madrid, over the course of the next two weeks. If this El Travieso was anyone worth mentioning, his face would appear in the media at some point. I had captured a photograph of the man, unfortunately, his heavy beard and black bottle cap glasses obscured his true features. He had a medium build and was fairly slender. Those two specifications, coupled with the grey Mercedes and young driver, were the only things I had to compare the politicians on the television and in the papers to.

Sitting cross-legged on the squashy bed, I absentmindedly clicked the television remote from one channel to the next. I watched transfixed as the hazy grey transition screen lingered just long enough to be an annoyance. My confidence had been lowered significantly and frustration was starting to boil in my veins. Channel 24-ESPN La Liga....Channel 41-Baile por el Luna, some type of Spanish soap opera...Channel 77-Lugares a Visitar, the equivalent to the British Travel Channel. I flipped through all ninety-nine channels for two hours, yielding nothing. I was beginning to wonder if Madrid's residents even cared about the happenings throughout the rest of the country. Surely there must be something happening in Spain's parliament that was noteworthy. It was damn near unheard of for the media to refrain from reporting political issues. Whether it be some sort of new legislature, an honorary event, or a public appearance; the media was usually right in the thick of things and making mountains out of mole hills and exploiting the private lives of the more well-known government figures.

Sighing heavily, I stretched my arms above my head, interlocking my fingers together. I bent towards the bed, slowly, straining my back muscles. I had been staying in the same hotel for nearly eight months now. I could feel myself beginning to come undone. It was maddening to be so close; every piece was in place, except the last one. I searched three quarters of the city in the hopes of locating the grey Mercedes. To my surprise, there were a lot of them, but none piloted by the wiry young man. Hopefully tomorrow would yield better results. I had plans to tour the Parliament Buildings. I doubted the forty-five minute public tour would be beneficial, but I was running out of options. Glancing at the clock, I yawned sleepily. It was already past midnight. Another day wasted. I pushed the red power button on the remote and watched in frustration as the television screen faded to black. Pulling the thin sheet back, I sprawled out on the mattress, sinking several inches towards the floor. *No wonder my back has been bothering me...*

I was disturbed from my slumber when I heard a stern knock followed by what sounded like a forceful kick at the door. I was instantly sent into an alerted shock. Although highly aggravated, I stumbled out of the bed and drowsily walked the ten feet to the door. Sliding back the chain lock, I opened the door several inches. Maximo, the saint/drug dealer occupying the room next to mine was standing stupidly on the doorstep holding a rosary in his left hand and a glass pipe in his right.

"Señor Wilhelm, it is time," he said thickly.

I peered at him through the slits of my eyelids. He looked dishevelled, as though he was fending sleep. His brown skin was waxy, and as he fumbled with the white collar around his neck, I saw unmistakable needle marks. I closed the door and lurched my way into the washroom. Splashing water on my face, I glanced at my pocket watch resting on the tank of the toilet: four forty-one in the morning. Maximo was starting early today.

Once a Father of the Spanish Church, Maximo Dueñas was sent into exile by the Vatican for breaking the rules of Priesthood. His holy order of abstinence proved too much for him to handle. Maximo was caught by a Bishop inside a confession booth having intercourse with two women who, it later turned out, were both married. He was immediately stripped of his title and forced to leave the Church. How he ended up in a rundown hotel selling and using drugs is unknown, as his recollection of his own past is very murky at best. Nevertheless, every Sunday and Wednesday morning he could be heard pounding on his fellow tenants' doors in an attempt to awaken them for Mass.

Maximo had a congregation set up in his room and those who happened to be in attendance were never disappointed. Being a religious man myself, and being someone who reveres the Lord, I can honestly say that I appear to be Atheist when standing up against Maximo and his words of power. When he was coherent, he would spend hours shut up in his room writing his weekly sermons. Often there were times when I could hear him rehearsing. His voice was stern, yet full of love and compassion. Drug dealer or not, he truly did love our Lord.

When Maximo first approached me to extend an invitation to his weekly Mass, I was sceptical. I had been raised Catholic, been taught the virtues of the Lord and I had been forced into good behaviour on the principle of going to Hell if I sinned. In my eyes, a drug dealer was not worthy to do God's work. I remembered thinking that he was a mockery, a slap in the face to Christianity. I was so outraged by Maximo's blatant disregard for our Lord and Saviour that I decided to attended his sermon just so I could give him a piece of my mind. Needless to say, I was pleasantly surprised when he delivered the most exhilarating sermon I had ever heard. Maximo made me experience Christ in ways I never dreamed possible. I was hooked, and week after week I found myself pulling up a chair.

After the sermon, Maximo and I would stroll down to Pájaro Cantante Restaurante, a local café where we would sit quaintly sipping té whilst discussing today's world issues. He and I agreed upon many things and I found his company to not only be intriguing, but refreshing. His disorderly past meant nothing to me and his dodgy present was irrelevant to our friendship. Everyone makes mistakes; something I learned at a very young age. My mother was a firm believer in trial and error: forget and forgive. She said that we all needed to find our own path, and in doing such, mistakes were expected and in her eyes, accepted. Maximo may not be living the most desirable life, but his allegiance to Christ had guaranteed him riches and prosperity in Heaven. I commended him on his continuous efforts of spreading God's word. I could not even begin to imagine what it must be like to be in the position he was in, I could only assume it was dreadful. Maximo seemed happy though; he had God in one hand and his pipe in the other. Not my idea of happiness, but I suppose one man's worst nightmare is another man's dream come true.

We conversed until sunup before parting just outside the café's entrance. It was a chilly morning and I was eager to return to the warmth of my room. Maximo mumbled something about a young woman he fancied and I watched him shuffle down the street before disappearing into an alleyway. I zipped my sweater completely up and stuffed my hands into my trouser pockets. Not quite as cold as a winter in the United Kingdom, I had been spoiled by Spain's tropic-like temperatures. The wind picked up, causing me to hasten my steps. I was within fifty feet of the hotel when I was thrown aback in my tracks. A makeshift stand containing several bundles of the Informador de Madrid was blocking my path. I peered down at the black and white front page image. Smiling sheepishly back at me was the driver of the grey Mercedes and to his left, the beaming President Gomez Salazar Cervino. *El Travieso.*

I had never been so sickened in my life. Gomez Cervino, the President of Spain *was* El Travieso. In recent years, I had thought he turned over a new leaf. He was doing wonders for the Spanish economy. Tourism was at its highest peek in over a decade, trade practices were proving prosperous, and the country's unemployment rate was down twenty-two percent. Cervino was shaping up to be a great leader. He had been praised a hero by his fellow countrymen and his new democracy was being revered as one the most efficient governmental structures in all of South-Western Europe. I, like the rest of the country, had fallen for the dim-witted Spaniard's larking.

It is expected that every man has skeletons in his closet; ghosts from the past that do not necessarily have impact on the present. Yet if you throw an ordinary man into the limelight, his seemingly irrelevant past comes back to haunt him sooner or later. Some secrets are just too damning to keep buried, yet in most cases, remain such. Whereas others that are of a less harmful nature tend to resurface. No man, no matter how great he may or may not be, deserves to have his privacies put into the public eye. However, there comes a time when a past so destructive must be brought up, or put to bed in the case of President Cervino.

Past political issues of adultery and indiscretions have shown us that any misdeeds committed by a government official will either be protected or stay buried within the government itself. Cervino's sick fetish would remain a secret regardless if he was living or not. And I was certain he knew this. Why else would he be so bold as to frequent the same hotels and have his own personal assistant drive him to his little rendezvous? In his mind, he was protected and completely invincible. As long as he thought this way, young girls would continue being victimized. Why give him the opportunity to keep stealing innocence? In my eyes, he needed to die. There was just no other way. Even in death his government would make justifications for his sick, perverse behaviour. He did not deserve to live, and when I saw a young girl exiting his hotel suite covered in bruises, blood running down her inner thighs, barely able to stand, I made a vow that Gomez Salazar Cervino would not go gently.

....

"¿Qué nivel del piso?" *What floor level?* I inquired softly.

The young girl next to me held out ten fingers and squeaked sheepishly, "Diez." She was shaking like a leaf. Her light brown skin was clammy and tears were leaking from the corners of her eyes. I knew she was making the trek up to Cervino's suite. His driver Alejandro was waiting in the grey Mercedes across the street. This poor child was about to experience something far worse than Hell itself. The elevator climbed upwards. With each passing level, the young girl became more frightened. She was biting her lip and wiping her eyes with the back of her hand. I peered at her over the top of the bouquet of flowers I was holding. She was losing it: the poor girl knew what fate awaited her.

Under pretence of being a florist delivering a bulky arrangement of purple orchids, I had managed to obscure my face whilst walking through the hotel lobby to the elevators. I spotted the young girl entering the building and hastily followed her. One week prior I found myself in the same position, riding the elevator with a different scared little girl. I had been a flower delivery man then as well. I rode with her to the top floor, level thirty-two. I never exited the elevator with her and every night since, I had been praying for her and praying for forgiveness. Today, I would not make the same mistake. Cervino's reign was over. After today, he would no longer be able to hurt another child.

The soft beep indicated that we had reached our destination. The doors opened and I watched the young girl step over the threshold hesitantly. I followed her at a short distance. She walked several yards before stopping in front of room ten-nineteen. She pulled what appeared to be a plastic key card from her pocket. *Now or never,* I thought to myself. She was seconds away from sticking the card into the door's slot... I gulped dryly and took the plunge.

"¿Senorita, podemos hablar?" I whispered in her ear...

Chapter 15

Prague, Czechoslovakia
19 April, 1999

The silver dagger sliced into my finger as though it were a stick of soft butter. Instantly, I felt white hot pain as a sea of deep red engulfed my forefinger. Applying a liberal amount of pressure to the cut, I deliriously cranked the bathroom faucet on and thrust my bloody finger into the icy stream. After flushing the wound thoroughly, I saturated it with peroxide and wrapped it tightly in a bandage. Then I waited. If any of the hemlock's poison seeped into my fleshy wound, I would know in less than thirty minutes. Contamination did not take long to spread and the poison would pulse through my bloodstream in a matter of minutes, even seconds, depending on how mature the plant was.

The roots of the hemlock had to be cut with precision, as they, along with the stem are the most dangerous. A member of the parsley family, hemlock is often mistaken for wild carrots. More often than not, the results are deadly. The only visual distinction between the two is the lack of tiny hairs on the hemlock's leaves and stems. Once the plant has been crushed, a pungent odour emitted from it gives away its true identity. This fatal poison was originally a native of Western Africa, Northern Asia and Europe. In the 1800's, it was exported from Europe to North America to be used as a garden ornamental. Today, the plant can be found primarily in large, moist areas. Pastures and meadows are an ideal breeding ground.

Hemlock's role throughout history has been renowned. Native Americans used the root and stem juices to poison the tips of their arrowheads. It was even rumoured to be given to Jesus

Christ during his crucifixion. Ancient Greece used the plant to poison prisoners; Socrates being the most famed individual to meet this fate. Although in recent years the plant has proven to be helpful in the treatment of some medical illnesses, if consumed or used irresponsibly, the consequences are dire.

After ninety minutes of trepidation and fright, I determined that I would indeed survive another day. I carefully finished extracting the juices, placed the transparent liquid into a small glass vile and corked it tightly. I took every precaution whilst cleaning up the chopped roots and stems. I wiped every surface in the bathroom thoroughly with peroxide and bleach. The toxicity of hemlock was nothing to take lightly, and I would have to monitor my health for the next forty-eight hours. Nausea, paralyses, dizziness and bloating were telltale symptoms of poisoning. And although my exposure to the plant was minimal, if untreated, my condition could become chronic or peril. Such a rudimentary way to die, yet very effective as hemlock poisoning is difficult to trace in the bloodstream.

My decision to poison Ivana Vladislava in such a manner derived from the ways in which she treated her countrymen. I felt it was only fitting she die a crude, weak-natured death. For so long she had trampled on those beneath her. Her people and her country meant nothing to her. She wanted power, complete control over everything within her grasp. She wanted to be seen as strong, domineering, and resilient. Nothing could touch her. How ironic it would be for her to die at the hands of some impoverished drifter. A nobody. And how sweet it would be to watch her lose control; to succumb to weakness.

From my previous six weeks of surveillance, I knew that Ivana had a well organized daily routine. At precisely five minutes to six o'clock each morning, she would enter her administrative building's parking complex. Her ruby red BMW convertible could be spotted a kilometre in the distance. Just as fierce and flashy as its owner, the magnificent piece of German engineering embraced the pavement passionately. The automobile bolted from one spot to the next; smoothly, swiftly. Without cause or concern, Ivana could drive. She gripped the steering wheel firmly with her left hand whilst shifting effortlessly with her right. Never a single moment of hesitation. Man and machine truly were one. Each morning I watched sickeningly as she indulged herself in luxury. Prada, Gucci, Versace: she wore only the most exquisite fashion labels. Diamonds and gemstones hung from her earlobes, draped elegantly around her neck and shone brightly upon her fingers. Everything about her emanated beauty. She was stunning from head to toe. It was a shame such radiance was about to go to waste.

By ten o'clock, she was ready for a thirty minute break. Her office was located on the sixth floor. She had a balcony all to herself. Ivana would slip through the white French doors, remove her stiletto heels and stretch out leisurely on a leather lounge sofa. After fifteen minutes of relaxation, she would pour herself a single glass of Chianti red wine and savour it for an additional fifteen minutes. Heaven only knew what she did with herself through the day: she never left her office. By the time noon rolled around, she could be spotted once again on her balcony enjoying a succulent catered lunch. At one thirty, Ivan would retreat to her office quarters in anticipation of her afternoon delight. Around that time frame a massage therapist could be seen entering the heavily guarded revolving doors leading into her administrative building. What went on behind the tinted glass was a complete mystery as only selected individuals were permitted access to the building. I found it quite odd that every single person who crossed the threshold wore latex gloves. For no man, woman or child could be spotted without sporting a pair of these white rubber germ protectors. Surely Ivana was not that neurotic. What was the point of such behaviour? Soaps and antibacterial gels would have been a more humane route. Then again, Ivana knew nothing of compassion or kindness. I expected nothing less than malevolence from her.

Being pampered and coddled endlessly must have been considered laborious in Ivana's eyes. After her ninety minute massage, she would make her way back out onto the balcony where another thirty minute break was relished. This time she would enjoy a cigarette with her Chianti and make a ten minute telephone call. It was always ten minutes and *always* animated. Ivana would flail her arms wildly and pace back and forth like a maniac. In some instances, she could be heard contemptuously speaking in Czech. Her features twisted like some ugly beast. I thanked God I was not on the receiving end of such a telephone call. To be treated that way, every day, it must have been horrible for the person on the other end. I had always assumed she was speaking to the same individual day after day.

Ivana's BMW would come to life at exactly five minutes past six every evening. She was the last of her administration to leave and always the first to arrive. Her regiment was so strict, she never fell a moment behind. It was compulsive in its nature: so tedious. If she had applied such efforts into the way she ran Czechoslovakia, perhaps she would not be facing such a tragic, yet well deserved fate.

I determined very early into my surveillance that the massage therapist would be my ticket into Ivana's office. Somehow I would have to persuade one of the therapists to assist me. I was uncertain how I was going to do that, but I knew one thing: Czech Koruna would come into play. And a lot of it. Gone were the days when people did things for others without the prospect of monetary gain. Selflessness had long since been replaced by selfishness, and it had become a pandemic. To find a soul that was truly pure, truly in it to help others out of sheer empathetic desire, was like finding a cure for cancer. I was simply stretching my arms out to something that was just not there. And that reality saddened me.

Prague would top any world traveller's list as the most exquisite city in all of Europe. For over one thousand years, the inhabitants of Czechoslovakia have laboured to preserve its rich history. Elements from each historical era can be seen throughout the streets. Located in central Bohemia, nestled on the Vltava River, Prague is a melting pot of architecture. Art Nouveau, Gothic, Neo-Classical, Baroque and Renaissance are just a tiny sample of the structural designs found throughout the city. The Astronomical Clock, Lennon Wall, Charles Bridge and Prague Castle are must sees, and the country's cultural festivals are rumoured to be the finest events in all of Eastern Europe.

Although to some I may be considered well travelled, in reality, I have not seen much of anything. Sure, I had trekked all across Europe, sweltered in the Middle East heat, survived the Russian tundra and basked in Japan's electronic age. I have lived as the Cajuns in Louisiana and as the impoverished villagers of Pakistan do. I have eaten things beyond most people's wildest dreams and I have laboured like a slave. Not because I wanted to, but because I *had* to.

The fact that my pedigree includes visits to such picturesque and pristine countries means nothing, for I have not relished in their splendour nor engulfed myself in their rich history. Seeing something in passing, or only for a few moments, cannot be compared to actually standing before it or within it. I longed for that opportunity. I dwelled up on it. Every new target brought a new country, a new city. My heart ached to explore every inch of these places. I had toyed with the idea of laying low for a few years, possibly returning to my place of birth where I could easily find work at the fishing docks. I would be able to save up enough money to do more than just "pass through." Nevertheless, there was work to be done and there would be a time and place to "see and do" once my mission was complete.

Like clockwork, I watched Ivana arrive at exactly five minutes to six the following morning. She exited her car with arrogance and strutted with her nose in the air towards her office entrance. This time she was adorned in a tight fitting brown Armani business suit, coupled with four inch bronze heels. Her Gucci handbag swung freely from her right forearm and her silky black hair was tied behind her head in a loose roll. Such beauty and elegance...

....

When Ivana Simona Vladislava secured the Presidency in nineteen ninety-five, she had big plans for the country of Czechoslovakia. Preserve the past, enrich the present and move forward into the twenty-first century together as one nation. Her motto spread across the entire region of the Czech Republic and before long, Ivana Vladislava had become a household name: Someone who offered hope, who was passionate about her country and her fellow man. She won the Presidential election by a landslide, beating out her five male candidates. She was the first female to ever take office and the first woman to be looked upon as a symbol of reverence. The precedent was set; a new age of women's independence had been born.

President Vladislava's first two years in office were astronomical. A serious change in the wind had occurred. She laboured endlessly to ensure the youth of her country received a proper education. She increased the medical budget by almost thirty-five percent and had personally overseen the construction of one hundred shelters for the needy throughout Czechoslovakia. She appeared to be very selfless in her nature. Always giving, never taking. Ivana was a true humanitarian, a gift given to her people from Christ himself. She could do no wrong. Every decision she made was for the greater good, weighing all of her options before jumping the gun. She wanted her people's opinion and if the general population was not in accordance, she found other avenues to get them what they needed. She cut taxes, she saved lives and violence had become almost non-existent. Czechoslovakia had never been so prosperous or so united. Simply put, Ivana Simona Vladislava was the best thing that had ever happened to the country. She was also the worst.

Every governmental structure must have its checks and balances. One simply cannot rob from Peter to pay Paul. This was exactly what President Vladislava had done. Within twenty-four months it had caught up to her and the country began to crumble. She may have cut taxes, but to do so, she took away from other organizations she deemed less important. The Czechoslovakian Military took a massive hit when President Vladislava decided to increase the medical budget and build more shelters. A very empathetic thing to do, however, she left her country wide open to attack as weapons and defence were put on the back burner. Although the education of youth is important, no economy can survive without the utilization of the trade industry. Importing and exporting practices had ceased as Ivana felt it unnecessary to sell her country's resources. Inflation was up over one hundred and twenty-five percent by mid nineteen ninety-seven and the unemployment rate went through the roof. Like a true coward, President Vladislava blamed everyone but herself for the sudden downfall. She blamed the British, the Russians, the Germans, the Americans...You name it, she pointed her finger at it.

People rebelled. They wanted answers and they looked towards their President for a solution. Ivana ran for cover: she sat back while the walls deteriorated around Czechoslovakia. She did nothing to prevent her countrymen from losing everything. During the aftermath, Ivana emerged metamorphosed into a cold hearted, arrogant, egotistical beast. She was no longer President Vladislava the humanitarian, the gift from God. She was President Vladislava the wicked, the spawn of the devil himself. She imprisoned her fellow man for treason... for not displaying their support to her government... for breathing. She spat on everyone beneath her and left them to fend for themselves. The shelters were full to maximum capacity; young children walked the streets trafficking drugs and selling their innocence to feed their families. The military roamed the streets of Prague instilling fear into anyone they came across, forcing them to give up what little money they had. Violence was insurmountable, each day brought more death and destruction throughout the country. Vladislava simply sat higher on her horse––untouchable and unconcerned. Any force that tried to withstand her government was taken down. Completely eliminated. She showed no mercy. She was in total control. Killing her would be the country's only salvation.

....

I waited seven and a half hours for him to arrive. His white van entered the parking complex at exactly fifteen minutes past one o'clock. He jumped out of the driver's seat and made his way towards the rear of the vehicle. I watched him open the back doors and remove a black leather bag, foldable table and fresh linens. He was a tall and lean man. His face bore the signs of a hardworking individual: someone just trying to get by. His neatly pressed sky-blue uniform hung from his frame as though he had recently lost a lot of weight. His dark hair was streaked generously with grey and when he walked, it was with a slight limp. He was my man.

I abandoned my post and ran gingerly towards him. For nine weeks I had been waiting on this man. He was the one, I could feel it. If I could persuade anyone into relinquishing their supplies and uniform, it would be him. I slowed to a walking pace as I entered the parking complex and weaved through the lot to where he was standing leisurely smoking a cigarette. I approached him cautiously, smiling weakly. He nodded and returned my smile with one of his own. Up close he looked beaten down. Deep groves were embedded into his pallid face and he shook ever so slightly: perhaps the onset of Parkinson's disease or Multiple Scoliosis. Looking into his tired eyes, I made the quick decision to be blunt with him.

"Do you speak English?" I inquired.

His expression was blank. *Perfect.* His face was inquisitive as though he was studying me. Or perhaps it was just incomprehension. He took a long drag on his cigarette, tossed it on the ground and whilst stamping it out, he nodded.

"You do speak English?" I asked him once more.

This time he nodded more sternly. His heavy accented voice emitted a low "Yez."

"Are you working on President Vladislava today?" I inquired bluntly.

Once again, he nodded. The man showed no signs of curiosity. He just stood before me, completely calm. I hesitated for a moment. There was just no easy way to break the ice. I could beat around the bush and waste precious time or I could tell this man my plans straightaway in the hopes that he will not have a melt down and attract law enforcement.

Throwing caution to the wind I blurted, "I will give you five thousand Koruna for all of your equipment and your uniform." My voice was shaky, my hands were twitching rigidly, yet he stood stalk still.

"Just give me your table, bag, uniform, linens and walk away. Leave the van as well. You will not have any further use of it."

He was peering at me blankly, like he received such offers on a daily basis. I removed an envelope from the left pocket of my faded trousers. "The Koruna," I said removing the money from its safe house and fanning the colourful bills out before him.

He continued to stare at me, completely unaffected by the words I had just spoken and seemingly oblivious to the Koruna.

"Take it," I whispered whilst pushing the stack into his hands. "Please take it. All I ask for is your co-operation. I need your equipment and uniform. This is very important. No one will ever know we spoke. Take the Koruna and leave this place. Go north, go south, it does not matter as long as you and your family get out of Czechoslovakia."

He still had not spoken. For a moment I wondered if he had been lying when he said he spoke English. He turned to face Ivana's office. His hands were clutching the Koruna for dear life. Based upon these actions, I knew he had understood every word I had spoken. He was absorbing and contemplating everything I had just said. He looked at me. I began to plead with him.

"Please, I know you are not happy here. I can see your struggle; it is written across your face. I am offering you a way out. An opportunity for you and your family to start a new life. A life without fear... a life without hardship... a life without Ivana Vladislava. Please...I am beseeching you. It is time for Ivana to meet her maker. She must face our Lord and have judgment passed down upon her. Ivana must reap what she has sewn... Please help me."

I continued to look at him, pleading with my eyes for his assistance. He kept glancing from the Koruna to Ivana's administrative building. The fact that he could not decide what to do proved decent people still existed in this world and that my efforts have not been futile. A man of true virtue would find it difficult to choose between the honourable path and the less troublesome one. I had nothing but the utmost respect for this gentlemen standing before me. If he would have walked away from me, I would have accepted his inability to choose.

Suddenly he pivoted on his right leg and opened the doors to the van. He stretched his arms towards a cardboard box and removed a light blue material from within it. He withdrew himself and gently closed the doors, thrusting what I instantly recognized as a spare uniform into my hands. With his left foot, he pushed the table, bag of supplies and linens towards me.

"Set up thee tayball at one forty-five then leef thee room. She will ring thee bell when she is ready for you. Speak when spokhen to. Massaj lasts one hour thirty meenits."

Completely expressionless, he lit another cigarette and stole one last glance at Ivana's lair before limping away, a trail of grey cigarette smoke following in his wake.

Her skin was flawless; milky white, smooth to the touch. She had the body of a Goddess; sleek, curvaceous and sensual. Her features were like none other. Soft green eyes, high cheekbones and full lips. At first sight she appeared elegant, compassionate and very much an independent woman. She was iconic in her beauty: a woman to be worshiped. It was difficult to digest that I must kill her.

She was spread out before me like a work of art. Her body's curves hugged the table as though the two were a single conjoined being. Black hair flowed freely over her shoulders, cascading onto her back. A white terry cloth was snugly stretched over her buttocks, silhouetting its shapely nature. She could have been a muse, an idol to be moulded and sculpted to any artist's liking. In essence, a female David.

I laid my hands on her bodice, only to instantly feel the real woman within. Her beauty had evaporated. Her blood was cold and a malicious toxicity pulsed through her veins. My fingertips became absorbed with wickedness and impurity. Not even the latex could mask such caustic energy. It was like acid, eating its way through her flesh and onto mine. I wanted nothing more than for it to be over; for her to be dead and for me to be as far away from her impiety as possible.

She looked peaceful laying on the table, yet I knew she was calculating and critiquing my every move. She was a woman who commanded respect and she enjoyed the power and privilege which was bestowed upon her. She feasted on the fear of others; it made her stronger... more vindictive... more hungry. I reached for the leather bag containing the scented oils. I gently removed the cork stopper from a bottle of vanilla jasmine liquid and slowly poured it onto the arch of her back. The smell was intoxicating and she moaned with pleasure as I began to rub the scent into her skin.

"Delat svou praci dobre nebo budu mit vas vyhodili," she whispered callously. She had raised her head a few inches to look at me. Her eyes were full of contempt. Her expression was something straight out of Hell: grotesque and unkind.

"Samozrejme," I whispered. *Of course.* And with that I continued to rub the hemlock laced oil into her bodice, praying it would soon take affect...

Chapter 16

Cardiff, Wales
13 May, 1999

After leaving three Pounds on the table, I rose, stretching gingerly before placing my jacket on. My stomach about to burst at the seams, I sledged to the counter, fishing my pocketbook out of my trousers.

"How much?" I inquired lazily to the young lad working the register. His fingers worked deftly, rapidly striking the metal keys whilst rambling off the contents of my meal.

"Eleven Pounds please, Sir," he replied cheerfully.

Removing a twenty banknote, I absentmindedly placed it within his outstretched hand. Transfixed on the parchment resting on the countertop directly below my right hand, I could not take my eyes off of the most recent Times Global headline.

ANOTHER FAILED ATTEMPT: EX-NAKAMURA HENCHMEN ERADICATES ADMINISTRATIVE OFFICE. PRIME MINISTER SURVIVES.

I need not read the article which followed as I knew precisely what had occurred and what I must do.

....

When I was a child, my father would amuse me with tales that had been passed down by his father and grandfather. Old German war stories involving my great grandfather, a wizened Colonel and a past prominent chancellor to Germany. Although I had never met my great grandfather or my great grandmother, I pledged to one day travel to Germany in search of them. As a young boy, I was vulnerable to almost anything. My father, on the other hand, was the only exception. I learned at a very young age to ignore his "drunken madness" as my mother would call it. I was forced to face a grave truth: he was untrustworthy and dishonest. He filled both mine and my mother's heads and hearts with empty promises and shattered hopes. However, through all the lies and countless disappointments, there were times when I felt that a shadow of truth lingered behind his words.

At age twenty, I ventured to Germany with hopes of locating my kin. For almost two days I trekked through snowy, ice-capped mountains and dense woodlands in search of a small cabin rumoured to be the home of Radulfus and Katharina Miller. An ancient barman who operated a pub in the village at the base of the mountains told me that the Miller's were strange folk who were only seen once a year. They quickly and quietly came down from their homestead with huge handcrafted sleighs in tow to gather twelve months worth of supplies, and within a blink of an eye, they were gone once again. The barman also told me that in thirty-six years, he had never seen Radulfus Miller make the trip into the village alone. Six winters prior, in nineteen seventy-three, Katharina Miller had not come down with him. In subsequent years, she had not been seen either. The villagers assumed she had passed on.

I never had a clear plan as to how I would introduce myself once I arrived at the cabin. When I did think about my reunion with my great grandparents, I had envisioned myself being graciously welcomed into their home. I wanted to know everything about their lives; I saw myself sitting next to them, listening quaintly to their tales and adventures. I would eventually find a way to inquire about the stories my father had told me. Alas, it was nice to dream. That is all my envisions turned out to be.

Alisha Hayes

Chapter 17

Luxembourg, Germany
22 December, 1999

I crept slowly on my elbows and knees through the thick, muddy marsh. My eyes frantically darted in every direction in search of the enemy. I was sixteen years old, fighting a man's battle. Every breath I took could have been my last. All around me the perished and wounded lay strewn about. Outcries of agony and sorrow filled my ears. A glaring orange glow followed by a suffocating heat and wind engulfed me and I was instantly forced face down into the muddy marsh by a rough pair of hands.

"Keep yer eyes open an' head down boy! Yeh could 'ave been killed!" hissed my Colonel.

Spitting out the muck I had just been forced to eat, I looked ahead and saw the source of the commotion. The abandoned church we had been hiding out in had gone up in flames. In just a few short minutes the smoke had travelled to our area, filling my lungs and nostrils, choking me.

"Shut the Hell up boy! Yer givin' away our position! They're comin' right at us!"

I raised my head cautiously, squinting towards the woodlands ahead of me. Emerging from the smoke and fog-infused clearing were several hundred tall looming figures. Flames from the blaze cast great black shadows, making their silhouettes giant-like. They moved towards us with speed and agility. Gracefully--yet with dominance. My eyes were full of smoke and I was silently gagging into the sleeve of my soiled uniform.

Between gasps I softly whispered to my Colonel, "Shall we continue to remain in this position?"

With a confident nod, he swallowed and beckoned me as he began to creep further into the marsh. Almost completely submerged, we yielded to listen for the approaching enemy. At thirty paces their features were clearly visible in the firelight. Old men with scars and determined looks upon their faces. Young men, like myself, who were trying to show bravery, despite the blatant looks of terror dancing in their eyes and etched across their tightly stretched lips. They drew nearer; I saw the gleam of metal around the waists and shoulders. Suddenly their presence seemed very real. They had guns, massive guns. Part of me wanted to kill myself right there. I knew I was dead anyway. It might as well be by my own hand than that of the enemy.

"Did you hear that? They are speaking Hungarian! Look at their uniforms! It's the Hungarian Army Colonel! Ha-Ha! Let's get the Hell outta of here!"

"No!" cried my Colonel. "Get down yeh arse! Get down now!"

I glanced to my left to see my Colonel forcefully pulling a young Private by his arm back down into the muck.

"But—but—Col—Colonel, it's the Hungarians. Our sworn allies. Why are we concealing ourselves from them? We need them!" the Private said frantically.

"Listen to me yeh fool! Yeh don't think they won't kill us the first chance they get? 'Old yer positions 'til I give yeh the signal to shoot."

"To shoot? Why—wh—why the Hell are we shooting them? They are on our side!" I stammered.

" 'Old yer tongue Miller. Don't talk 'bout somethin' yeh don't understand," my Colonel said insolently. Clutched in his muddy hand was a brown lemon shaped object: unmistakably a grenade. "I'm goin' to pull the pin an' when I do, yer to fire. Shoot to kill, men. We 'ave our orders."

Befuddled and even more terrified, I pleadingly looked at my commander. "Orders? I do not understand. Who would give orders to kill our allies? Colonel, you must have misinterpreted the information. This is not possible. Who told you to do this?"

"I 'ave orders from Kanzler Laudenbach 'imself to kill anyone we come across. Shoulder yer weapons and shoot on my command."

"They are innocent Colonel. German allies. We must not." My voice was a mere shaking whisper, my body was convulsing with fear. "Think about what you are doing Colonel. We cannot kill them. Our qualms are not with them. The Private is right, we need them to aid us against the British and Americans, our true enemies."

"I will not ask yeh again. Shoulder yer weapon 'nd obey my commands. Insubordination is punishable by death need I 'mind ya."

Like a tiger, the Colonel's movements were swift and unpredictable. Within seconds I heard an explosion and the stunned shrieks of the Hungarians. Rapid gunfire commenced behind and in front of me. I slowly raised my weapon and helplessly pulled the trigger...

The Colonel did not survive the attack. He was shot in the abdomen by one of our own and he eventually bled to death. Myself, along with two Privates, dragged the Colonel into the woodlands where we took cover until the gunfire ceased. He clutched my arm tightly and with great effort, told us his story. He said that Laudenbach had personally ordered for the attacks on any militia; allies or known enemies. The Colonel said Laudenbach had a plan for a perfect world, a perfect race. This war was his opportunity to weed out the imperfections, to purge the world of racial and religious minorities. Laudenbach had a master plan and many people within his government were clinging on to his every word. He had followers, thousands of supporters, and he would stop at nothing to gain complete control over mankind. He not only wanted to play God, he wanted to be God...

The Colonel died in my arms. He was overcome with remorse and apologized until he could no longer speak. His last moments were in vain as he gazed into my eyes repulsed and saddened by his own actions. I sincerely believe he felt guilty for what we had done. We all felt guilty. We killed our country's sworn allies and we did it shame-

lessly, with minimal protest. Reflecting back, I should have refused to shoulder my weapon. Being killed for insubordination would have been less dishonourable than to have to live with my grave mistake. In later years, I thanked the Lord my commander died that night. Colonel Hitler's name was a mockery throughout Germany after word spread of what he had ordered us to do. He would have been forced disgracefully into exile if he had known what his grandson was to later become. The terror his own spawn caused; the lives he stole, the evil he proliferated.

It was rumoured Laudenbach himself took the Colonel's grandson under his wing to spite him . He planted his idealisms in the grandson's young mind, and when he had failed to create the perfect race, he placed the task into Adolph Hitler's sculpted hands. Many people chose to believe that it was the Colonel whom had this idea. The Colonel wanted to purge the world of all things abnormal. He wanted a perfect religion encased within the perfect race. It was quite easy for those who were not present in the woodland that night to point the finger at the Colonel. Laudenbach made a public statement placing him, as well as his "minions," at fault. Those of us who were really there, who knew the truth, were of course not believed. I do not deny partaking in this travesty; however, I do deny that the Colonel was the supreme creator of such immorality. He was merely a pawn which Laudenbach could dispose of and shift blame upon should his plan of racial and religious purification fail.

For sixty-two years I have lived with this guilt: a guilt which has consumed me. The shame I feel when I reflect back upon the events of the twenty-ninth of September, nineteen seventeen is insurmountable. I have befouled my family's name and I disappointment my Lord. For this, I am no longer privileged to exist among the living.

My great grandfather was found dead on December twenty-seventh, nineteen seventy-nine. He hung himself from a beam in the dilapidated cabin where he was living. Inside the left breast pocket of his frayed flannel shirt was a letter he had written. The letter recanted a treacherous story of murder and conspiracy committed by the German government. I was twenty years old, not much older than he was when he witnessed the acclaimed events. As I stared into his lifeless green eyes, I saw traces of the truth within them. I cut the rope and watched paralyzed as his tall and lean frame toppled onto the worn oak floor with a dull thud. I carried him outside, trudging through three feet of snow into a wooded corral where I laid his body to rest next to my great grandmother's. I placed his letter into my own breast pocket and set out into the night, vowing to one day make things right.

....

Snow whirled all around me. The air was coarse, the wind unforgiving. I was foolish to not seek shelter; there was not a single soul around me. Everyone had retreated inside to the warmth of their fireplaces. My lips were quivering, my body had turned a muted shade of blue. I stood frozen, staring at the vast memorial before me. So ironic. It had been built around lies and deception. I knew the story to be true: my great grandfather would not fabricate such a travesty, nor would he have made unfounded accusations about his country without significant proof. He had been there, he saw what really happened. He had been a part of the evil. I patted my left breast pocket, recalling my oath.

Luxembourg was exactly as I had remembered it: cold, unwelcoming and foreboding. It had a sense of pre-eminence to it; as though still plagued by fear and intimidation. I wrapped my scarf tightly around my numb nose and cheeks. I longed to be inside savouring a glass of holiday eggnog, stretched out in front of the fireplace. My original plans were to return to Germany in the early spring. The winter thaw was one of the more pleasant aspects of the country. Streams and creeks glistened in the sunlight as though filled with millions of tiny crystals. Animals and birds awoke from their long winter slumbers and could be seen romping freely in the forests and hillsides. Hints of foliage sprung out of the earth creating vast green patches as far as the eye could see. The temperature was moderate; a light jacket would have been all that was necessary. Standing in the middle of a harsh wind tunnel, my extremities completely lifeless, I was surrounded by great white masses and I could not help but resent myself for choosing to come back to the city in mid December.

The twenty-seventh was a meaningful day for me. I wanted to avenge my great grandfather's spirit by silencing the bloodline which had destroyed him. Both Laudenbach and Hitler were now deceased, yet their lineage still carries on. After the damage Hitler had done to Western Europe, his remaining descendents changed their surname and fled to other parts of the eastern hemisphere. It is rumoured that the bloodline still exists in Poland and Turkey, however, it is next to impossible to verify let alone trace such information. Laudenbach on the other hand, had ensured his family name would remain illustrious by fervently moulding and educating his descendents in the hopes his family name would once more run the gamut. His hard work paid off considerably; his great grandson was now the country's Kanzler.

Belser Frankel Laudenbach was a mirror image of his great grandfather. Arrogant, egotistical, sadistic and multifaceted, Belser was everything former Chancellor Lutz Frankel Laudenbach had once been, and he too shared his rudimentary views on race and religion. Although more subtle about his misdeeds than that of his great grandfather's, Belser had still secretly acted to cleanse Western Europe and eventually the entire world of all those unworthy. Former insiders have claimed that he hired a team of scientists whose soul mission was to resurrect the methods and machines Hitler utilized during his tenure as Chancellor in the nineteen thirties and forties. Despite countless national inquires and United Nations inspections into Belser's extracurricular activities, no such equipment had ever been located. However, the wise know that just because something cannot be found, does not necessarily mean it does not exist. To this day, many people believe the Holocaust did not occur. Six million lost lives prove otherwise. Another cataclysm such as the one the Nazi regime had invoked would be devastating, not to mention a slap in the face to our pledged unity. If permitted to continue with his furtive campaign, Laudenbach could literally wipe out billions. If things go according to my regimen, the Chancellor will only be enjoying his powers and privileges for another one hundred twenty hours.

The memorial before me was built as a tribute to all German allies throughout the duration of the first World War. It depicted two bronzed Armed Forces members shaking hands whilst smiling widely. They were perched on a bronze platform approximately three feet off the ground. Engraved all around the platform in neat, tiny rows were names of the fallen. Lutz Laudenbach had ordered the construction of the memorial immediately after the war had ended. In nineteen forty-two, Hitler had reconstructed it under the fascia that it was deteriorating and needed to be reinforced to ensure its fortitude. In the past I had heard stories that the memorial itself contained Laudenbach and Hitler's methods of purification. Should the platform ever be destroyed, the inside of it was said to house notebooks full of both Laudenbach and Hitler's ideas and processes. A pretty ingenious plan on Laudenbach's part: to pave the way for others to follow in his footsteps. He had supplied his successors with all the necessary tools. It is unknown whether he had the original plan to gas Jews, or if that was a creation of Hitler. There is no historical evidence to suggest that Laudenbach had a hand in any misdeeds and very few individuals have knowledge of his close relationship to Adolph Hitler. Those who did have first hand knowledge of Lutz Laudenbach's motives were either forced into silence or disposed of. As history has written it, Laudenbach was a noble, fearless leader who nurtured and loved his country. Like any person in position of power, he was subject to supporters and to insurgents. He, as his grandson, had more allies than enemies, thus making it very difficult to expose him for what he really was.

Was the story about the memorial true? Did it really house such horrific secrets? Were there notebooks full of Laudenbach and Hitler's ideas sitting dormant inside this great symbol of unity? Secrets just waiting to be unleashed upon the world...These questions burned in my mind, and the more I analyzed my grandfather's letter, the more plausible the story seemed. Both Laudenbach and Hitler were diabolical enough to encase something so evil inside something so good. I found myself studying the memorial very closely. I examined every inch of it in search of a possible opening, or some sort of confirmation that it housed something destructive. I ran my purple fingers over the seemingly endless rows of names. I inspected every irregular patch of metal I came across. I noted the markings on the statue's uniforms, felt their weapons and utility belts for push trigger buttons. It wasn't until I rubbed my hand over the German Soldier's left arm sash that I realized I may have found something. The immaculately engraved German flag was slightly raised on the sash, unlike his ally's. Upon further inspection of the sash, I found a thin groove all around the emblem, as though it had been cut out and then stuck back into place. I fumbled in the pockets of my trousers for my small knife. I opened it and carefully pried on the edges of the flag. I heard a tiny grinding noise, and within seconds, the four inch emblem fell into my right hand. I gaped at what I discovered hiding beneath the emblem. An equilateral cross with arms bent at angles stared back at me. It was carved an inch deep into the statue and had been hollowed out as though a perfectly shaped puzzle piece would rest inside of it. I knew I had found the entrance that was said to have never existed. Excitement flowed through my body, filling me up and perhaps even warming me a little. I dared a haphazard guess as to what I may find on the inside. Books? Journals? Weapons?

"It is no use without the key son."

I jumped and pivoted on my left foot. My eyes wide, I deftly shoved the emblem and knife into my pocket. An old man was staring grimly at me. My first impression was that he looked like an old shaggy dog. His grisly salt and pepper hair was mangy and unkempt. The whiskers on his wizened face were stark white and had begun to curl under their length. His dark brown eyes were wide and full of sadness.

"Err... Excuse me?" I sputtered.

"I said, it is no use without the key." His voice was gruff and he shuffled towards me with surprising agility. He pointed a severely frostbitten finger at the statue behind me which I had been attempting to conceal. "The key, son. The swastika that unlocks the chamber."

"The chamber? I said flabbergasted. This old dog knew of the rumours.

"Don't be coy. The chamber, Hitler's gas chamber son! It's within these walls. It's been here since nineteen forty-two when he ordered the reconstruction of the statues. Look," he said grabbing my arm and steering me into the soldier's arm. "See that? See these numbers? It's a key and numbered combination."

It took me several seconds to realize what he was pointing so adamantly at. All around the inner side of the cavern were numbers, very miniscule engraved numbers. Surrounding the numbers were dozens of equally tiny slots. Confused as to what their purpose served, I stared fixedly at them. The numbers ranged from zero to nine and were spaced equally all around the engraved swastika.

"How does this work?" I said more to myself than him. I was enthralled, yet slightly terrified by the mechanism.

"First, you need the key: the swastika that fits inside this space. Upon it or inside of it you will find a series of numbers or a clue leading to the series of numbers which will open a fissure right here."

The old man bent at the waist and placed his right hand on the back of the platform.

"But...how? How do you know all this? Where can I find the key? Who are you?"

Was this for real? Had I really come across the opening to Laudenbach and Hitler's horrors? Or was this old man just another crazy who had long since lost his marbles? I had my trepidations about the man. He had appeared out of nowhere and seemed to know an awful lot about the inner makings of the memorial. A little voice inside my head was telling me to leave now and to never return, yet another voice was telling me to trust what the man was saying.

"The key is currently in possession of the Kanzler. Of course no one has seen it upon his physical being or in his custody, but he has knowledge of its whereabouts and guards it dearly. I trust you know the tales of Lutz Laudenbach and Colonel Berowald Hitler?"

I greedily nodded my head in accord.

"Well then you should also know the history of this memorial. No? Kanzler Laudenbach had it built to mask his own involvement in the ally killings. He then placed his diaries and transcripts inside the statues for his prodigy Adolph Hitler to one day utilize. Hitler was so fascinated by what Laudenbach had done, he decided to store his secrets within it as well. The key was given to the Laudenbach bloodline by Hitler himself. He knew upon his downfall that his own remaining descendents would make every effort to rid themselves of his tainted image. Given Lutz's track record, Hitler had the utmost faith that his teacher's family would do everything in their power to guard the secrets and one day finish what their predecessor had started."

"How do you know all this?" I whispered out of sheer terror. There was something eerie about his words. He knew too much, yet I was certain he was being truthful.

"I assisted in the reconstruction of this memorial, son. I have been inside of it. I fabricated the key and locking mechanism. Find the key and you will be able have your vengeance."

Completely frightened now, I shuttered, chills running down my spine. The old man smiled at me. He placed his hand into his raggedy jacket. I couldn't help but feel as though I may have just met my end. I wanted to run but my legs were rooted to the snow covered ground. I swallowed dryly, attempting to gather myself together. I bore directly into the old man's eyes, transfixed by their darkness. He slowly withdrew his hand from his jacket.

I closed my eyes. *Why are you not running, you idiot?* The little voice inside my head was frantically urging me to flee. I waited for the sound of the gunshot or for the plunging of a knife. But nothing came. After several long, gut retching seconds I opened my eyes. He was still smiling. I looked at his purple hands. He was holding a folded piece of paper in them. He handed it to me and I cautiously opened it. I was gazing into the eyes of at least fifteen men. They were all crammed closely together, wild eyed and grinning merrily. Their black and white uniforms bore left arm sashes embossed with three horizontal stripes: the German Army. Most of the men were young, no more than twenty, and they all seemed to be gathered around a strong looking older gentleman. Next to this man was perhaps the youngest of them all; a tall, thin, dark haired boy. He didn't even look old enough to drive, let alone serve his country. I gazed at this boy, completely paralyzed. It was like peering into a mirror. His nose and jaw line resembled my own. His dark hair was plentiful and he was built like I was. We could have come from the same mould. My great grandfather didn't have a care in the world.

"Where di--did you get this?" I whispered, my eyes still fixed on the photograph.

I glanced towards the spot where the old man was standing, but he had vanished. I spun wildly in search of him, yet like my saviour in London and Corfu, he was nowhere in sight. He had gone as quickly as he had come. I looked at the photo in my hands. Where did it come from? Who was that man? My head swam with questions. How did he know who I was? Had he been watching me? Surely he must have been. How else would he have known I was a descendent to the man in the photograph? Did he know about what I had done? Maybe he knew my family. He was far too young to have fought in World War One. But he had said he had assisted in refurbishing the memorial in nineteen forty-two. Did he know Hitler? He had to of. His knowledge was far too great to be just a theory... I absentmindedly turned the photograph over. In the lower right hand corner were the words *Holos Kaustos*. I gasped in horror. Understanding dawned on me, and for the first time in my life, I was thankful my mother had forced me to take Greek lessons in school. *Holos* meaning "completely" and *Kaustos* meaning "burnt". I smiled hungrily. I knew, or hoped I knew where the key was. Downright frozen, I pulled my collar tighter around my neck, stuffed my frozen hands into my jacket pockets and hiked up an icy Kitzscher Street in search of a place to stay.

My encounter with the old man both excited and thoroughly petrified me. I spent all night replaying our meeting in my head. He was so nonchalant in the way he spoke of the chamber. It was as though he was speaking of the weather; something entirely blasé. He was oblivious to how uncomfortable his actions had made me, or perhaps simply he enjoyed playing the role of intimidator. Either way, I knew I would be haunted by his image and by his words for the rest of my life.

I spent Christmas Day alone in my hotel room with the heater running full blast. The weather had worsened considerably. The temperature had dropped below negative thirty Celsius. The streets, rooftops and cars were blanketed by three feet of thick, shining white snow. The city would have been elegant had it not been inundated with ancient gloomy buildings. It was reminiscent of death becoming. Even the people looked and acted as though their days were numbered. Very overcast, despite the holiday season. Luxembourg was very depressing and it was contagious.

My plan was simple: retrieve the key, create some sort of diversion, and dispose of Chancellor Laudenbach. Simple, yet full of holes and potentially problematic situations. Obtaining the key would be easy. I was almost one hundred percent sure I knew its location. My great grandfather had mentioned a woodland in his letter, one that had been set on fire purposely. If my suspicions were correct, the key was in the ruins of the old church or buried with Berowald Hitler in the forest. The only downfall to the key's whereabouts was its inconvenient location: Cambrai, France. *So much for disposing of Laudenbach on the twenty-seventh.* It was a day by train from Germany to France, plus an additional two days to reach the forest in Cambrai and retrieve the key. Add another day of travel back to Luxembourg and one final day to set my plan into motion. Then there was the possibility that the key may not even be in Cambrai, but in some other forest. I was relying on my intuition and merely banking on the Laudenbach bloodline wanting to further spite Colonel Hitler. Provided I retrieve the key, what's to say my diversion does work? It had to be something dramatic, something that would detach Laudenbach from his family and administration. It had to be personal. It had to draw him to the memorial.

Chapter 18

The village of Cambrai is well noted for its seventeenth century architecture, the infamous battles of nineteen seventeen and eighteen, and for its rich religious history. Originally part of the Spanish Netherlands, Cambrai was ceded to France in sixteen seventy-eight by way of the Nijmegen Treaty. The village thrived for centuries on the coal mining industry but took a severe economic hit during the first World War. To this day, it still suffers socially and financially.

Now a commune within the administrative division of the French Republic, Cambrai's thirty-three thousand residents share a simple life whilst attempting to regain control over its steadily declining economy. It was a shame to see such a historical landmark fall to pieces, but alas, its peril is a testament as to how morally desensitized our governments have become. Gazing at the crumbling cobbled streets and decaying Caen stone structures, it was difficult to imagine that this village had once been a symbol of true classicism. Known for its creamy-yellowish colour, Caen limestone was utilized during the seventeenth century as a means to brighten a village and its inhabitants during the gloomy winter months. Years of neglect had taken its toll on the village and the once elegant fixtures had become gray and dispirited.

Strangers were not taken kindly to in the village. As I strolled down Rue Poirier, the stern faces of Cambrai's residents could be seen peeking through windows and small cracks in their front doors. They lingered for a moment, long enough for their unspoken message to sink in: *You are not welcome here.* I trudged along to the outskirts of the village. Wading through two feet of gleaming untouched snow, I wished I could have simply taken a taxi into the heart of the forest. The land was barren; seemingly endless open ground leading to a vast sea of snow covered trees. The harsh winds were merciless and after an hour of fruitlessly searching for the church ruins, I took shelter amongst the trees. I was certain the key was with the Colonel's remains. His grave was in the heart of forest, and I knew it would not be visible to the common passer-by. There would be clues or symbols marking it. This was a certainty, as Belser Laudenbach prized himself a master of symbolisms. Also, he would have needed to be able to locate the key easily.

Once in the centre of the woodland, I proceeded to examine every single tree for potential signs of the Colonel's remains. I found a cross carved arbitrarily into an aged pine tree which looked promising. I read the inscription below it and knew I was in the wrong place:

D.B. 1974-1996

Long after Colonel Hitler. Whoever D.B. was, he or she must have gotten lost in the forest and died from exposure to the elements or perhaps starvation. I examined what seemed a hundred trees before I caught a break and came across a frail looking pine laden with a series of bullet holes. At first the holes appeared to be randomly sunk into the bark, but after some thirty minutes of examining them, they appeared to have formed a crude symbol; a distorted cross with bent arms. *Retribution was about to be paid.* My primal instinct was to dig the tomb up with my bare hands. I wanted to savagely push the snow away from the base of tree and bare my hands into the frozen forest floor. I didn't care if I broke every single finger in my attempts to unearth the Colonel. I wanted vengeance and I wanted it now. Unfortunately, I did not have the tools, nor the daylight to exhume the grave, so I was forced to exercise control and make plans to return to the site upon daybreak.

Night had begun to fall and I quickly found darkness creeping up on me. The hike back to the village was cold and troublesome. What if I was wrong and the key was not buried with the Colonel? What if I had wasted a trip? Fear and apprehension flooded my mind. One moment I was experiencing an incredible high, the next, I had become deflated. A light snow had started to fall as I reached the fringes of the village. *Charming.* Flurries were all I needed. Another potential roadblock. I stepped over the invisible threshold back into the village and glanced over my shoulder: my tracks had already begun to diminish.

The inn was stuffy and untidy. Like all of the other establishments, it too bore the signs of once-upon-a-time grandeur, but had long since been neglected. The oil paintings and Victorian furniture were encrusted with grime and the carpets were so full of dust, my footsteps were muffled as I approached the check-in area. The innkeeper was equally as shabby. His tailored suit had to be at least sixty years old and it reeked of mildew. He was gaunt, yet an undertone of feistiness shone in his grey eyes. He was reluctant to board me for the evening. I assured him I would only be staying for one night; I would be gone by dawn. After much grumbling in both French and broken English, he beckoned me up the ancient stairway. Cobweb strewn lanterns lined the walls and the smell of fungus was prevalent in the air. I noticed the innkeeper was limping. Probably an old war wound. He looked as though he could have served in the French Military fifty years ago. He stopped in front of room 1605 and blindly stuffed an old skeleton key into the doorknob. With a creak, the door swung freely on its hinges and the innkeeper stepped aside, sweeping his hand in a sort of bow, permitting me to enter the room.

The room was just as untidy as the rest of the hotel and the cherry four post bed looked as though it had seen better days. I was uncertain if its ancient frame would even hold my weight. I placed my travel bag on the mattress and watched the dust rise out of the bedspread. The red velvet tapestry was unclean and had become discoloured over time. I'm sure it was once as magnificent as everything else in the place. I sat down in an armchair; my body instantly sank to the floor. I closed my eyes in attempt to develop some sort of plan. I did not have a shovel, so I would have to *borrow* one per say. Hopefully I would be able to locate one without too much trouble. I worried about being seen, about being followed, about not being able to locate Colonel Hitler's grave once more.

I slept off and on throughout the night. By four o'clock I had abandoned all efforts to slumber so I moved to the window ledge where I sat perched listening to the wind howl and watching the snow fall rapidly. Just before dawn, I quietly slipped out the hotel's exit into the icy street. It didn't take me very long to locate a shovel; every business and residence had come equip with one. I cautiously ambled onto the front doorstep of a crumbling two-story, snatched the tool, and hiked as quickly as possible towards the barrens.

By the time I reached the inner most part of the forest, I could not feel my cheeks or nose. The wind was so harsh and the air so bitterly cold that any exposed body part had become numb. The density of the trees offered some shelter, yet, every breath I took was short and constricted; knife-like. As I had expected, my tracks were covered in a fresh blanket of snow and the vastness of the trees had become a hindrance, as I would be forced to inspect every trunk in the semi-darkness. I stumbled around the forest feeling the elderly bark of each tree in search of the redemption. Time lapsed slowly, the sun began to trickle through the thickets, casting rays of light upon the hollow ground. The air was starting to warm up, both a good and bad thing. My extremities had thawed, however, it could be very detrimental to be spotted coming out of the forest. I had been hoping to locate the grave quickly, excavate it even quicker, and be back on a train to Luxembourg before the villagers had finished their morning tea. As such, luck was not on my side and by midmorning, I had finally found what I was looking for.

Squatting on the ground, I cleared the snow from the base of the tree directly under the Swastika and pushed it behind me. It was very important to keep the snow and dirt separated, as I would have to cover the Colonel back up. I could not take the chance of someone stumbling upon this location and discovering the grave. I sunk the shovel into the hard earth, cursing the unsympathetic December weather. My laborious efforts were callous and within minutes I was drenched in sweat. I removed my jacket, mopped my brow with its sleeve, and continued to slave. Sweat dripped into my eyes, stinging them and rolling off my chin onto my shirt. Pneumonia was anticipated, as it was unwise to allow one's body to sweat in colder temperatures. Fighting the chills crawling down my spine, I dug deeper. Each load of dirt weakening me further, casting doubts in my mind... I numbly thrust the shovel into the ground time and time again, but to no avail. I was tired, cold, hungry and my body was aching. Uncertainty crept over me; a countless number of what ifs. What if there was nothing here?...What if I was seen?...What if I'm wrong? I was beginning to doubt myself; to doubt my great grandfather. I continued to dig with everything I had left in me. *I know he is right... I know he is right.* Completely exhausted, I stabbed the shovel into the ground only to be knocked backwards by a returned pressure. I hastily crawled on my hands and knees towards the hole, at the edge, I curiously peered down into it. I saw a hint of metal some three feet below. With renewed energy, I dug up the earth around it with my bare hands.

After retrieving the key, I filled the hole and placed the snow back on top of the grave. I did not have the will to dig deeper. I was certain Colonel Hitler was down there somewhere, but I felt that he should remain undisturbed. He deserved that much. Leaving the shovel at the edge of the forest, I buttoned my coat and prepared to make the journey back to the train station. I was going to avoid the village at all costs, and to do so, I would need to travel six kilometres out of my way, on foot.

With the foremost important leg of my plan completed, I began to calculate my next steps. The diversion. So much was at stake. I simply could not attempt to do something mediocre. My first few theories involved blowing up a government office or sending Laudenbach a letter stating I knew what he was up to and I knew the contents of the memorial. Very trivial theories once I had really thought about them. How would blowing up a building draw Laudenbach to the memorial? I'm sure he would run for cover with his family. Sending him a letter would take too long and he probably had a member of his staff open all of his mail anyway. I was certain hate mail, threats, and just plain bizarre substance would be disposed of before reaching Laudenbach's eyes. I needed to send a personal message; something which would draw the public's attention, yet would only be meaningful to Laudenbach himself. I mulled over all the possibilities the entire trip back to Luxembourg. One would think that after ten hours of continuous thinking, a solution would have been reached. Nevertheless, when I stepped onto the chilly arctic platform, I was no closer to a remedy than when I was back in Cambrai.

Sleet had begun to fall, brining with it bitter winds and an additional eight inches of snow. I sat huddled by the fire in my hotel room, replaying potential plans over and over in my mind. The train ride yielded no answers for me, and thus far I had been unable to develop something plausible. I was resigned to push my predicament out of my mind. The answer I sought would come to me in time. And until it did, I would remain in my room, getting well rested for my next efforts.

The key, as it had transpired, was the easiest puzzle to solve. I had forgotten about it and not until I opened my travel bag in search of a pen, did I remember I still had to figure its secret out. The swastika was made from a heavy stone, much like concrete. On the back there were tiny slots cut into each arm, as though serving as a guide. There was an inscription as well: two little words, Trotz Er. *Despite Him.* As soon as I read it, everything fell into place. I knew what I had to do.

Everything made sense now. Colonel Hitler was the one to be spited. They carried on Lutz Laudenbach's philosophies to ill will the Colonel for divulging the truth to his men. I reached into my left breast pocket and removed the twenty-year-old letter I had been carrying with me. My eyes darted to the bottom of the page, falling upon the last paragraph.

For sixty-two years I have lived with this guilt. A guilt which has consumed me. The shame I feel when I reflect back upon the events of the twenty-ninth of September, nineteen seventeen is insurmountable. I have befouled my family's name and I disappointment my Lord. For this, I am no longer privileged to exist among the living.

September twenty-ninth, nineteen seventeen. The day the Colonel died; the day Laudenbach was exposed for what he truly was.

2-9-9-1-9-1-7

Armed with this new knowledge and a renewed spirit, I set out early on the thirtieth to make preparations. I decided that the public need not be put into a frenzy, so I opted for one of my original theories. Of course I would need to refine it, as to be certain the message would reach Laudenbach.

....

The office was plush, very lavish, and it reeked of power. Many men had sat within its walls; relishing its stature, feeding off its supremacy. Belser Frankel Laudenbach was one of those many men. He had spent his entire tenure as Germany's High Kanzler believing that the office's rich political history coupled with his family's esteemed name would render him invincible. He was protected from persecution and shielded from culpability on the sheer principle that he occupied this office. All the cover ups, the misdeeds, the treason, he would never face a tribunal. Anything that happened within the walls of this office was cosseted. No one would ever know the truth, his secrets were buried.

Staring in awe at the single piece of paper upon his desk, Kanzler Laudenbach could not help but feel like the walls in which he had relied so strongly on had come crashing down. Everything he had done—all the secrets he was certain were impenetrable, were now starting contemptuously at him. Over the years, he had received his share of hate mail; not everyone was enthusiastic about how he ran his country. He had been sent death threats, marriage proposals, resumes, even nude photographs of both men and women. During his first year as Kanzler, he had made it a habit of opening every piece of mail he received. Good or bad, he wanted to know what his people really thought of him. When the letters became more graphic and threatening, and words of encouragement had become hard-pressed, he enlisted several assistants whose sole daily task was to open his heaps of mail. He had another team of assistants who would then respond to any positive letters. Under strict instruction, the assistants were to only forward letters they felt were truly life threatening or completely bazaar in nature.

It had been over two years since he had received any corre-spondence from the general public. When his assistant Kirsa called his private line to inform him that she had something important to discuss with him, he became excited, not to mention very aroused. A six foot blonde with a tight, slender body and perfect breasts: she was slightly dense, but remarkable between the sheets. Their fourteen month affair had been out this world: strong and wild. They had made love in every inch of his office. Nothing was too sacred. No parts of their bodies left unmapped. She had made every one of his fantasies a reality. She had had no choice really. When he approached her and told her what he wanted, she was appalled and threatened to expose him. No one would have believed her and he would have made sure her career took a spiral downwards, never to recover. So she obliged him. Eventually she grew to enjoy it, and more often than not, she came to him first. It was always the same type of call. "Kanzler, I have something I feel is very important to discuss with you." By the time he buzzed her in, he would be stripped down to his undergarments, erection at the ready. Sometimes she would tease him, taking her clothes off and swaying her body rhythmically. Other times she would push him into his chair and ravish him whilst ripping her own clothes off. It was always something different with her. She never ran out of ideas to please him. He had gotten bored with his previous assistants in a mere three or four months, but Kirsa was a tiger. He was going to keep her around a little while longer.

Deciding to play the uninterested role today, Belser sat fashionably in his thrown-like leather chair, spectacles upon his nose, engrossed in a meaningless memorandum. He buzzed her in and waited for the soft thud indicating she had entered his office and for the familiar clicking of her high heels upon the floor. The clicking of her stilettos drew nearer, and out of the corner of his eye, he watched her approach his desk. Slow, sophisticated and sexy; she was wearing a low-cut blouse, and tight black pencil skirt. He loved the skirt above all else and could not wait to place his hands on her firm buttocks. Mouth already starting to water and a euphoric sensation between his legs, Belser did not know how long he could resist her. She stopped in front of desk and softly cleared her throat. Even something as mundane as this stimulated his genitals. He waited for her to make the first move but she stood before him, silent. Belser peered up at her; she had a strangely odd look upon her face, a cross between quizzical and frightened. He looked at Kirsa's hands which were firmly grasping a white envelope and a single piece of parchment.

"Was ist dieses?" He said arrogantly in harsh German.

This was all part of the game. Make her beg and plead before she gets her pleasure. Kirsa placed the envelope and parchment on his desk before sitting down in front of him.

"I am not sure what it is Kanzler, but it is so bazaar in its nature that I thought you may want to take a look at it." Picking up the piece of parchment, Belser immediately felt his heart stop. All colour drained from his face. His lips parted slightly, but speech had lost him. He swallowed dryly, regained his composure and tossed the parchment aside.

"Ah, this is nothing to be alarmed about Kirsa. Just some sort of prank, I'm certain. However, I thank you for your bringing it to my attention. I know you have nothing but my best interest at heart."

He had hoped his throw away behaviour was believable. He glanced into her green eyes. She didn't believe him. "Kirsa, you will have to excuse me. It is ten o'clock and I have just remembered I have an important call to make."

She rose, and with one last concerned glance at the Kanzler, left his office, her firm buttocks swaying menacingly. Groaning hungrily as he watched her walk away, Belser looked down at the horrifying image which lain upon his desk. *This better be some sort of sick joke* he thought beseechingly to himself. But as his erection diminished, and all traces of arousal left him, he knew it was the real thing and he knew he should be very alarmed.

And now I wait. I sat crouched in the bushes some five feet from the memorial. He would come. I could feel it. He knew that someone knew his secret and he would do anything in his power to silence that person. I expected a bribe of sorts. Probably a sizable amount of Deutsche Marks to buy my trust. It would be foolish of Laudenbach to send someone after me. I had proven that the key is now in my possession, so he will take every necessary step to retrieve it. And he would do so quickly and quietly, without anyone else knowing.

The night was calm. The harsh weather was still forcing residents to remain in doors. I had been crouched amongst the bushes since dusk, waiting patiently for Laudenbach to appear. A light snowfall was working to my advantage, covering all traces of movement around the memorial and surrounding areas. From a distance, I had seen what I thought may had been the old man I had encountered several weeks prior. His stooped shadow was lurking somewhere near, mutely keeping his ears and eyes peeled. With each movement, I became more aware of my surroundings. Car doors shutting, passers-by braving the elements to take a night-time stroll. Children bundled up like abominable snowmen, running through the streets hurdling tightly packed snowballs at one another. Their shrieks of delight carried through the thin air, echoing in my ears.

Darkness had completely fallen by nine o'clock and all sources of commotion had ceased. I did not expect Laudenbach to appear until well into the night, so I was pleasantly surprised when I heard movement a mere six feet ahead of me. A tall figure had approached the memorial and was studying it with great concentration. I was bursting with anticipation. I was certain this was Laudenbach. He seemed to know exactly what he was doing. I heard a rustle, and then the distinctive pop as the flag emblem was removed from its place. I knew it was him and I knew I needed to make my move.

I crept out of the bushes, and via the cover of the darkness, I pounced. Before Laudenbach even knew what had hit him, I had wedged his body against the statue and placed him into a well executed sleeper hold. My hands compressed his carotid arteries, collapsing his jugular veins almost instantly. It took less than twenty seconds to render him unconscious. When he fell to the snowy ground, I immediately retrieved the key and my flashlight from my pocket. Time was of the essence. I knew that in a mere forty seconds Laudenbach would wake, and although placing him in another chokehold would be simple, I did not wish to remain exposed outside the memorial longer than necessary.

I pushed the swastika haphazardly into the hallow of the sash. Using my flashlight to guide me, I jammed my finger in between the numbered slots. 2-9-9-1-9-1-7. Nothing happened. *No! This can't be happening. It was suppose to open. Why the Hell wasn't the door opening?* Laudenbach had begun to stir. I shoved my hands into my jacket pocket and produced the rope and scarf I had packed. I deftly bound and gagged the waking Kanzler, before returning my attention to the memorial. I tried the combination once more, but to no avail. Each passing second was critical. Someone could discover us. *Shall I just kill him here?* Time had stopped, everything had come crashing down. *What the Hell am I going to do?* Out of nowhere, I saw a figure move towards me. Before I could react, it was next to me, pushing a decrepit hand into the hollow with great force. Within seconds, a muffled rumbling noise occurred and the rear platform wall had begun to shift.

"Get in son, quickly!"

I dropped to my knees and entered the black abyss.

I was falling, and fast. My body was being retched to and fro, like a rag doll and my head kept rolling uncontrollably. I collided with something hard, and with a numbing thud, I was forced onto my back. Several more thuds and a deafening slam followed in my wake. I felt what I was sure to be a human body lying next to me in the darkness. I turned on my flashlight and gasped in amazement. My eyes adjusted to the site before me. As my mind struggled with comprehension, a flood of emotions had begun to wash over me. I was in a concrete cell. No more than thirty by thirty. I glanced above my head. The ceiling had to be at least ten feet high. It too was built of solid concrete. Suspended from it was a huge, dusty chandelier. I fumbled in my pocket for my matchbook. Upon striking a match, I tossed it into the centre of the chandelier and watched everything around me come to life.

The walls were lined with shelves stretching from the floor to the ceiling. Books, old parchment, chemistry sets, telescopes, knives, pistols, shot guns, corked vials of black liquid and mysterious boxes covered these shelves. I was inside the chamber. It did exist. Completely awestruck, I choked back tears of certainty. I had the proof and most importantly, I had Laudenbach. I moved towards the shelves of books and began to leaf through them. Endless pages of tiny writing filled the pages. There were notes on Cambrai, drawings of what appeared to be torture devices and odd astrological symbols. I was overwhelmed and speechless. I sat down on the cold floor and placed my head in my hands...

A low groan followed by a sharp whack was omitted from somewhere in the corner of the chamber. I strained my eyes towards the far side of the room and saw the old man struggling to stand upright. Laudenbach, it appeared, had been knocked out once again and lay nearby.

"You did it, son," I heard him croak. Looking as shabby as ever, the old man smiled weakly and slowly moved towards me.

"I am Kohl. Tavin Kohl," he said sliding down the wall and onto the floor next to me. "I do not know your name, but you are an angel. For so long I have waited for this day to come. I cannot even begin to tell you how much this means to me. To Germany, to Colonel Berowald Hitler."

I glanced sideways at the old man, he had closed his eyes, hands folded in his lap. Not really knowing what to say, I decided now was as good a time as ever to introduce myself.

"I'm Wilhelm Miller."

The old man opened his eyes and stared at me contently. He had a cut across his forehead and his left arm was rather limp.

"You look like him," he whispered. "Your grandfather, that is. Perhaps he is a great grandfather. He used to come to the memorial quite often. He, like so many others, were convinced of its secrets. For hours he would sit transfixed in front of statues, examining them, writing things in a small notebook. Then one day, he just stopped coming."

I did not interrupt him. Obviously, this man had things to tell me, important things. Things about the past. I stared blankly ahead of me; fighting back tears and trying to ignore my aching body.

"Nineteen seventy-nine was the last time I saw him. He had come to the memorial for what I assumed was another attempt to penetrate its secrets. Instead, he placed a piece of paper at the base of the platform and merely walked away. I retrieved the photograph which is now in your possession and I immediately recognized the face of Colonel Hitler. I had been under his grandson's command for over ten years and I knew those strong features well. Over the years, many men, and sometimes women, had come to the memorial. They all seemed to study the statues in the same sort of curious fashion. They each bore strong resemblances to the men in the photograph your grandfather had left behind. I always watched them from afar. Certain as to what they were looking for, but uncertain as to whether they had strength enough to accept the truth and act upon it. In nineteen ninety-five, I decided to show myself to a young woman whom had been frequenting the memorial. Her great grandfather had served alongside Berowald Hitler, and the story had been passed down through her bloodline. She said her great grandfather had died full of shame and she wanted to make the Laudenbach's and their pedigree face their demons. I told her what I knew and she set out, but never returned. I am not sure what became of her, perhaps she gave up. She may have even died trying. She was a pretty young lady, full of life, determined. I pray night after night for Danielle's safety, although in my heart I am certain she is with the Lord."

The old man sighed heavily and closed his eyes once more. Something triggered in my brain. Like a picture book, I saw a large old pine tree with the letters "D.B. 1974-1996" etched upon it.

Already certain as to what Danielle's fate had been, "What was her surname?" I murmured.

"Beich," the old man replied softly.

He did not have to tell me. I knew the grave in the forest of Cambrai belonged to the young woman he spoke of. Tears were leaking from the old man's wrinkled face as though he knew too. Wiping his eyes on his tattered sleeve and gently blowing his nose with his handkerchief, the old man pointed towards the bookshelf on his right.

"You should be going, son. Before someone sees the open platform," he whispered hoarsely.

I did not understand what he meant. I peered all around me. I was trapped. The old man slowly got to his feet and walked over to Laudenbach who was still unconscious. Prodding him with his foot, the man rolled the Kanzler onto his stomach and untied the rope.

"He will be out for quite some time. I kicked him rather hard in the head. Lucky him, things are about to heat up down here."

I stared bewildered at the old man. What was he planning to do? I walked around the chamber in search of a way out, but there appeared to be nothing but bookshelves and solid concrete walls. Panic was starting to sink in. *I just may die down here...*

"Listen, son, you need to leave now. See that bookshelf behind you? Pull the lever in the back, left hand side, and it will open up a secondary shaft which leads into the bushes. There is an iron ladder built into the concrete wall. Climb up it and shut the chamber straight away. Just turn the key counter-clockwise and push it inwards."

Flabbergasted, I stammered, "You're--you're not coming with me?

The old man bore directly into my eyes and shook his head firmly. "No, I am not coming with you. I am old, I am tired, and it is my time. Go, I will make sure Laudenbach gets his justice. He will burn like so many had during his bloodline's regime."

"But—but what about you? You shouldn't have to die with him. Just come with me. I'll carry you if I have to. Please come with me," I pleaded, tears falling uncontrollably down my face. He was going to kill himself to ensure that Laudenbach met his end. I could not allow this to happen. I did not understand.

"I will not die with him, son. Yes, my body will burn, but I will not die from the flames. Now please, go. You have done your part, let me do mine...With honour," he added.

Comprehension dawned on me. The old man's words sunk in and I glanced at the rope he held firmly in his hands. There were still so many unanswered questions. So much more to the story. I wanted to know everything. I needed to know everything...

As thought reading my mind, the old man placed his frail hand on my shoulder. "There is much more I could tell you: minute details, tales of my own misdeeds, things I had overheard in the past. None of these things will help you now, nor in the future. Your great grandfather, along with Colonel Hitler and his men have now been avenged. Their stories have been validated and now you must move on as they would have wanted you to."

He walked over to the bookshelf, placed his hand behind it, and stepped back as it swung open on its hinges, revealing a manhole. I hesitated for a few moments before climbing into it. I looked back to see the old man dumping the vials of black liquid all around Laudenbach and on the shelves. He awkwardly climbed onto the third topmost ledge of the bookshelf and used the rope to lasso the chandelier towards him. Knowing what was to come, I turned and began to make my way back up the shaft. As I rose, heat and smoke pursued me; faint at first, but it gathered momentum quickly. I crawled out of the chamber onto the cold, wet ground, and immediately thrust myself through the dense bushes towards the statue. I blindly found the key and turned it counterclockwise. I pushed the swastika inwards with all my strength, all the while praying for God to accept Tavin Kohl's soul.

The mysterious disappearance of Belser Frankel Laudenbach had spread all across the country the minute his administration had become aware of his absence. By noon, all of Eastern and Western Europe were marvelling over where the Kanzler had disappeared to. His entire staff were subject to lengthy interviews, and piece by piece, his last known movements were strung together. German Police determined his assistant Kirsa Neustadt was the last individual to see Laudenbach alive. She recited the conversation which took place in his office a little before ten o'clock the previous morning. She spoke of the bazaar letter he had received. The photocopied image of a stone swastika with the words "Trotz Er" upon it and below, in clearly a man's pen, the numbers 2-9-9-1-9-1-7. Kirsa explained Laudenbach's reaction to the letter, how he at first appeared frightened by its presence, but then quickly cast it aside as a mere practical joke. She told police that he seemed tense, worried even. When he asked her to leave his office because he needed to make an important telephone call at ten, she was certain he was being untruthful.

A team of investigators conducted a methodical search of the Kanzler's office in search of the letter, but nothing of the sort was ever located. The call log for Laudenbach's private line was seized, where it was also discovered that he placed only one outgoing call that day at sixteen minutes past eight o'clock to his wife's mobile device. Every square inch of his office and administrative building were searched, but no traces of him or any sort of malice acts were found.

It was later concluded that High Kanzler Belser Frankel Laudenbach had lost his mind due to the amount of pressure he was under and left the country to enjoy a quiet life off the coast of New Zealand or perhaps even Aruba. Of course, I believed neither story. I folded my newspaper and got up from the bench I had been resting on. I shouldered my travel bag, took one last glance at the memorial and began to trudge back up Kitzscher Street; the next quest ablaze in my mind: Sonni.

Chapter 19

Kishiwada, Japan
7 July, 2000

Is this kid ever going to stop vomiting? We were cruising at thirty-five thousand feet. The air in the cabin was thick with the stench of fish; remnants of our feeble meal. The strident buzz of the 747's wings was almost deafening. Somewhere near the front of the cabin, two babies were wailing very unhappily. The child strapped in the seat behind me kept kicking my chair rhythmically... As if these distractions weren't irksome enough, the young boy in the aisle seat next to me had been bringing up his dinner at fifteen minute intervals for the last two hours. *Hurry up and land this damn thing before someone gets hurt.* My patience was waning. Seven hours of non-stop commotion and it appeared as though I'm in store for another three more. No matter how hard I tried to block the racket out, no matter how hard I tried to ignore the constant pressure and throb upon my lower back, no matter how hard I tried to breathe through my mouth to obstruct the smell of vomit from my nasal passage, I just could not do it. My inner ears had become overpowered by shrill noises which were banging on like crazed drummers. My back was absorbing each kick like a sponge; the pain had long since become dispersed throughout the rest of my body. My nostrils were full of the heavy, sickening scent of rotten fish and spoiled milk. It was creeping down my throat and into my stomach, further nauseating me. I had to get off this plane...

For over three hundred years the residents of Kishiwada, Japan have been enjoying the yearly festival known as Danjiri Matsuri. Originally created by the Lord of Kishiwada, all of the districts within the city would build Danjiris to parade around the city as a means of praying for an abundant harvest. Hand carved of zelkova wood and embellished with portraits of animals, past wars and fallen heroes, no Danjiri is twinned. Weighing upwards to four tons and measuring 3.8 meters high by 2.5 meters wide, each Danjiri is to be pulled by one thousand men throughout the city streets. The festival is attended by hundreds of thousands of individuals from all across Japan. The intricate designs on each Danjiri, along with the master craftsmanship required to construct such a work of art are astonishing. One would be hard pressed to find an individual who was not mesmerised by them. This yearly celebration is so historic, it is not to be missed. Even the Prime Minister himself would be in attendance.

"As Senior Advisor of your staff, I do not recommend you attend this year's festival Prime Minister. It is not safe for you to be in the public eye. What with the thousands in attendance and a previous attempt on your life, we simply cannot keep a constant visual on all of your surroundings."

The two men were seated in a posh, Victorian style office smoking fifty-dollar Cubans and sipping thirty-year-old scotch. The Prime Minister was sitting gingerly in a high-back winged leather chair, while his advisor was seated some six feet away on a less impressive piece of furniture. The Prime Minister preferred it this way; it made him feel important, daunting. He wanted his staff to know whose hand their lives were held in. In this room, even his childhood friend was to show the highest respect.

Puffing leisurely on his cigar, the Prime Minister appeared to take no heed to what his Advisor had said. This, however, was a front. In fact, his attendance at the festival was all that was on his mind these days. He would be expected to attend. It was his country's most revered celebration. For over three centuries men, woman and children had gathered in the streets of Kishiwada to pay tribute to this great country: it was his civic duty to be there.

"Please, Prime Minister, I beg you to hear me out. If something ever happened to you, this country... it would crumble. Attending the Danjiri Matsuri is plain reckless. Think of your supporters. Think of this nation. Think of your wife and children."

Dropping to his knees, the Advisor crawled to the base of the Prime Minister's chair. "Takada, we have known each other since we were schoolboys. I am asking you... begging you... as your friend, not your Advisor, to rethink your presence at this event."

The Advisor was close to tears. The concerned look in his eyes and the slight twitching of his body was genuine. He had known the Prime Minister for forty years. Through thick and thin, he had stood by his side; always faithful, never wavering. When the Prime Minister was caught committing an adulterous act in nineteen ninety-three, it was he, the Advisor, who had to calm the political storm, not to mention the war which had erupted at the Prime Minister's home. In nineteen ninety-five, the Prime Minister landed himself in the limelight when he was accused of selling and exporting children to the United States, Australia and Canada. Once again the Advisor had to meticulously execute cover-ups and disposed of individuals who held damaging evidence against the Prime Minister.

Then just two years ago, the Prime Minister was involved in an experiment conducted by his own government which cost the lives of over seventy thousand people. Although the Advisor was able to smooth things over by convincing the country's mutinous residents they had been attacked by terrorists, the truth was their own government had fucked up. Hundreds of barrels containing biohazardous materials had been improperly labelled: instead of disposing them in a safe manner, they were dumped in the city of Sako's water supply, wiping out ninety percent of its inhabitants.

Of course, the Prime Minister went on as though nothing had happened. He made hundreds of speeches claiming such buoyant things as the country of Japan will not be overtaken, will not be manhandled in such a manner, will not succumb to the forces of evil. His followers lapped it up and called for mass attacks on Kosovo, Iraq, Iran and Saudi Arabia.

Despite the number of messes the Advisor had to clean up, no matter how many times the Prime Minister's integrity had been put in question, the Advisor remained at his side. Yes, there were times when the Advisor wondered whether or not the Prime Minister even appreciated all that he had done for him. On numerous occasions he had thought about resigning. *Let the next schmuck deal with Takada and all of his bullshit.* He could retire to Spain, get a dog, fish off the coast of La Palma, enjoy the fresh air and marvellous scenery. No politics and no messes. Yet, he knew those days would never come. Someone had to hold the Prime Minster's hand. Since there was no one willing to do it, he who was bound by a four decade year old friendship, was the only man for the job.

"Takada, my old friend, listen to reason. It is unwise--" The Advisor ceased speaking as the Prime Minister had raised his right hand to silence him.

"First of all, you are in no position to tell me what may or may not be unwise for me. Forty year old friendship or not, you will not speak to me in such a manner and you will not address me by anything other than Prime Minister. I am a man who is to be respected and I will get the consideration I so rightly deserve." The Prime Minister sat a little higher in chair, a smug look upon his face.

"My sincerest apologies Prime Minister, I merely--"

"Secondly, do I appear to be a man who can be easily intimidated? I will not be bullied by tyrants or terrorists. I WILL NOT! DO YOU HEAR ME? Let them come to the festival. Let them try to get past my men. IT WILL NOT HAPPEN!" roared the Prime Minister.

Exhaling heavily, he stood up. Dousing his cigar and draining the remains of his scotch, he turned to his Advisor and said in a harsh undertone, "We are political men, Senichi and in politics, friendships do not matter."

The dates of the Danjiri Matsuri celebrations had been set, September thirteenth and fourteenth. Although I had arrived in Japan more than two months in advance, I was wary of the short time frame. There was much to prepare for. My first attempt on Nakamura had failed despite nearly six months of planning. I was apprehensive as to whether I could pull this execution off in a mere eight weeks. Granted, this time around I would be surrounded by a mass of people and the execution would be from afar; I still needed to take every precaution to ensure my efforts would be successful and my escape clean.

The Prime Minister was not a dim-witted man. I was certain he would put in place every man he had available to him for protection. Everything had to be perfect right down to the most miniscule of details. I had sworn to never harm the innocent; however, in this case, it was necessary. If saving a million lives meant killing fifty people, than so be it. Given any other option, I would take it. It seemed the only way to eliminate Nakamura was to take out his protectors as well.

The explosive device would be placed in between the top and sub floors of the Prime Minister's Danjiri. My camera would act as the detonator. One day prior to the festival, I would set the explosives in place. All of the Danjiri's would be put on display in Osaka where they would be open for public viewing. Although each Danjiri was different from the next, it would be quite simple to spot the Prime Minister's from the rest: the most majestic of them all would be his. I was confident everything would fall into place as it should. My only concern was getting the bomb into the

Danjiri. I would be using my camera to house the components of it, however, setting it up and implanting it without being noticed would be difficult. And even if I succeed in doing this, there was a possibility a security sweep would uncover it. With the basics worked out, I could concentrate on the more complex tasks.

Throughout the remainder of July and the first part of August, I gathered all the materials I needed: copper wire, gun powder, compressions, and metal fittings. I had never constructed a bomb before, but with the help of several books I found in Kishiwada's public library, I was able to assemble one fairly easily. *And this is why we live in a world of chaos. Information such as this is right at our fingertips...*My device was nothing elaborate, in all actuality, it was very crude. The detonator would operate off of my camera's battery. It was to send a small electronic signal to an antenna-like tower which I encased inside a large shoebox, along with the rest of the components. The copper wire would act as an electrical conductor. I tied one end of it to the top of the antenna and draped the exposed end over the gun powder. The signal would cause the antenna to light up, therefore creating an electrical charge. The electricity would pulse through the copper wire; spark the gun powder, and then goodbye Takada Nakamura.

To ensure my device would function properly, I created a smaller one to test out. On a cloudy, misty night in August, I decided to take a midnight stroll. I grabbed my jacket, flashlight and all my supplies and headed to a wooded park not far from the shelter I was staying in. I was completely alone except for a junkie propped up against a large tree. His body was convulsing wildly and he was surrounded by his own vomit. *What a waste.* I hurriedly moved past him.

I trekked deeper into the woods, weaving in and out of the large trees whilst plunging further into the darkness. I had no idea how vast the thicket was, but judging by the density of the trees, I was in the heart of it. I shone my flashlight over the ground in search of a large flat rock. The ground was strewn with pebbles, litter, twigs and leaves; no flat rocks. *Great.* I would have to dig with my hands. I dropped to my knees and sunk my hands into the earth. It was cool and moist. In no time I had dug a foot deep hole. By the beam of my flashlight, I assembled the bomb, enclosed it within a shoebox, and gently placed the device into the ground. I tightly packed earth around and on top of the box and once again covered the area with leaves. I removed my camera from my bag and walked forty paces away from the device. I turned my flashlight off and took a slow, deep breath.

My success depended on what would happen once I clicked the green 'capture' button. Trembling with excitement, I powered on my camera and with an unsteady index finger, pushed capture. In seconds I heard a muffled boom and was splattered with leaves and soil. Brushing myself off, I ran over to the site. Switching on my flashlight, I saw a hole slightly larger than the pre-existing one. Resting inside, a small piece of copper wire and antenna fragments were visible. I grinned broadly.

....

"Members of the press, this way please! Members of the press, over here!"

I looked up to see a charming young lady standing on a platform beckoning the media towards her. Her English was immaculate, with a smooth transition between her Japanese and English tongues.

"Identification badges out please! If you do not have a press badge, you need to be in the other line!"

I hastily placed my HNN identification badge around my neck whilst joining the queue of journalists and photographers to my left. I had worked all night on my I.D. Today I would be Raul Bolanos, an international photographer from the Honduras News

Network. Equipped with an employee access number, barcode and smiling self portrait, I was confident I could fool the keepers of the Danjiris. The lined thinned and I found myself standing next to the girl on the podium. She peered down at me and smiled warmly.

"Are you American?" Her voice was more demanding than quizzical. I shook my head. *No.*

"Then where are you from? Do you have a press badge? If not, the public line is over there."

She pointed effortlessly towards a sea of people which seemed to never end. I could not help but smile, her tones reminded me of my little Pakistani friend. I clutched my badge and leaned towards her.

She whistled lowly, "Honduras... wow. You are a long way from home. I would have never imagined the festival to be an attention seeker in your country. We get a lot of Americans and Brits, but wow, I think you are the first person from Central America. I mean, I have been volunteering for five years and never came across one."

She was speaking as though I was some sort of exotic species. Coming across such a thing once in a blue moon was intriguing. Truth be told, her charm was starting to wear off and I was starting to find her rather annoying.

"It will be a few more minutes before you can go in. We only allow five people in at once. What's the point of offering an exclusive tour if there are swarms of people around, right? Have you been here before? No? Well you are in for a treat. The public only gets to view a fraction of what you are going to see. You will be given the opportunity to photograph the more sophisticated and important Danjiris; like our Prime Minister's. Hey, where are you from in Honduras anyway?"

Thinking of the first city that came to mind, I flatly said in a poor Spanish accent, "San Antonio."

She had a rather confounded look upon her face. In fact, it was quite comical. "San Antonio? Is that near Tegucigalpa?"

I shook my head. "No, it's many hours north of it."

"Oh, well Tegucigalpa is the capitol and it is the only city I know of. Just thought I would ask. Anyway, I can see the other tour heading back now, so if you would just stand to my right, the guide will be with your group in a moment. Enjoy yourself!"

And with a wave of her hand she was off blabbering in Japanese to some other unfortunate soul.

The girl was right about one thing: I was getting an exclusive tour. Myself along with three photographers and one journalist, were guided towards the back of the lot, out of the public's eye and into a dome shaped building. Inside there were six magnificent Danjiris; each handcrafted to perfection. The tour guide was speaking rapidly in Japanese. I only caught such phrases as the "pride of the festival," "honour," and "spirit." After several minutes, the rest of the group branched off and went about photographing the Danjiris. I saw one gentlemen enter the temple, so I assumed we were permitted to do so. *This is going to be easy.* An old female journalist was standing alongside a particularly stunning Danjiri. She was running her fleshy hands over the carvings whilst speaking casually into a tape recorder. Something about her behaviour sparked my interest, so I made my way over to her. She glared up at me for a second as though I was invading on something private. I started to walk away, but stopped suddenly as I felt a soft tap in the middle of my back.

"You are gentleman from Honduras, No? I help if you wish. I come every year for fifty-seven years."

I smiled at her and shook my head. *Yes.* Deciding to go out on a whim, I said in a warm voice, "I saw photos of this festival when I was a young boy. I told myself I would one day come to Japan to view these masterpieces. Tell me, who sits on top? Will they not fall off?"

I tried my best to appear confused, interested and cumbersome all at once. She made a half croak, half chuckle sort of noise.

"The Danjiri creator is given the honour of dancing on top. They work hard for an entire year and deserve the notoriety. Inside, our country's most important men sit. They are pulled through the streets by many hundreds of men."

Speaking more softly, she glanced around before saying in a hushed whisper, "Prime Minister Nakamura is to sit in this one."

Feeling slightly guilty for using this woman, yet hungry for more information, I said in an equally hushed voiced "How do you know? They all look the same."

She beckoned me towards her and placed her right hand delicately over the carving of an oddly shaped animal.

"This ancient Japanese symbol is only bore by the Prime Minister. It represents nobility, honour and courage; all things empowering of one's soul. You will not find this one on the other Danjiris."

Slightly awe-struck by her knowledge, I gently ran my fingers over the symbol. I felt my fingertips penetrate the deep groves. I turned towards her, but she was gone. I saw her some thirty feet away engrossed, hands moving effortlessly over another Danjiri. I slipped inside the temple and hastily started to disassemble my camera. There were no windows, so I was forced to assemble everything blindly inside the shoebox. I removed a small multi-tool from my trousers pocket, and as quietly as possible, shimmied a floorboard loose. I placed the box down onto the sub floor and carefully replaced the top board. Everything had to be exactly the way it was, as to not attract suspicion. I stood up gingerly, reassembled my camera and pretended to take photos of the inner temple. I exited with ease and continued "snapping shots" of all the other Danjiris. It was tedious and boring: I wanted nothing more than to leave, but apparently, each tour was on a specific time limit.

The old woman found me, grasped my arm and said, "Did you like? I hope you got enough photographs. The tour is over, time to go."

We left the dome arm in arm, parting ways at the entrance to the lot. She waved genially to me before disappearing into the sea of people.

....

I had been pacing the length of my room for the last two hours. Sleep came late and ended way too early. In just a few short hours time, Prime Minister Takada Honjo Nakamura would be dead, and my mission would be complete. I was nervous, but also very excited. My body pulsed with a jumbled mix of all these emotions. To have come this far...it was no easy feat. I was proud of myself. My accomplishments had been far greater than any other. To do what I have done, to have the courage to stand up to our governments, to fight back...I was overwhelmed.

After checking my camera for what seemed the millionth time, I stowed it in my travel bag alongside my clothing, fabricated Canadian passport and pocketbook. I threw the HNN Badge and the pages I had written the bomb instructions on into the waste-basket and proceeded to light them on fire. I gathered up the excess copper wire, bound it all together and made a mental note to throw it in the dumpster outside the building.

I bustled out into the street where I was shocked to see it was already crowded with people. Neighbouring residents had set up lawn chairs and were chatting animatedly amongst one another. Rapid bursts of Japanese swelled around me. I weaved my way through a particularly large congregation of people and continued my march up the street. It would be foolish of me to detonate the device so close to the place where I had been staying. Although I had been cautious by only coming in contact with a few other men who stayed across the hall, I could not take the risk of attempting the execution here where I could identified. The further I plunged into the depths of the city, the more congested it became. The streets were literally flooded with onlookers. It was quite spectacular. I nestled into a spot on the corner of Nihon and Kyoto Street, bracing myself for the upcoming action. There were masses of men, women and children in every direction, as far as the eye could see. I played the part of the photographing tourist well, constantly snapping photos from different angles. If my camera would have been functional, I would have captured some beautiful photographs. There were men and woman in costumes parading in the streets whilst singing and dancing. Vendors selling food, knick-knacks and beverages were enticing customers with succulent samples of their goods. Had I not work todo, I would have sat back and enjoyed this three hundred-year-old celebration.

In the distance I heard the booming of a siren, followed by the whoops and cheers of the crowd around me. *It had begun.* Everyone around me fell silent with anticipation. Several minutes passed, and then we saw it: a massive twelve foot temple being pulled by at least a thousand men. The dancers on top of the Danjiri were jeering and basking with pride as their creation was being displayed before millions of people. The noise of the crowd had increased tenfold. No one was paying any attention to anything other than the pieces of artwork before us. One by one, the Danjiris glided past us. Some at breakneck speed, others more leisurely. I held my camera up as though taking more photos. So far, sixteen Danjiri had passed. None of which were that of the Prime Minister. My eyes were glued to the elaborate designs on each Danjiri. I was in search of the ancient symbol the old woman had shown me yesterday. Surely I had not missed it. The Prime Minister would want to save the best for last. I was certain of that. Then I saw it rounding the corner: the unmistakable oddly-shaped animal carved just inches below the rooftop. My heart was soaring with anticipation. The Prime Minister's Danjiri was just as magnificent as ever. The dancers were adorned in black and gold dressings. The ropes fastened to the temple were twined with gold ribbons. Simply marvellous. It was a shame to ruin something so gorgeous, something so meaningful. But it had to be done. This was the only way to get Takada.

As the Danjiri drew nearer, I raised the camera. My index finger was shaking just as it had the night I was testing my device in the park. Beads of sweat started to pop along my brow. The noises of the people around me were deafening. I was focused only on the fast approaching Danjiri. I held my finger over the green button. The temple was almost aligned with my camera... I knew what was going to happen. If I went down with the Prime Minister, than so be it. I smiled blissfully and with warm thoughts of Sonni, I thrust my finger downwards. It happened in a millisecond: the blast, the heat, the screams of shock, the terror. I felt something hit me hard on the head. I surrendered, falling to the ground in a haze of darkness.

When I awoke, it was to find that I was indeed not dead. I was in a room full of people, some laying in beds, others sitting in chairs holding various body parts. I touched my head softly and glanced around the room. I was in a makeshift hospital tent. Doctors and nurses were buzzing all around me, their hands full of gauzes and syringes. I tried to elevate myself, however, I wasn't but six inches upright before the pain sucked me back down. I glanced into the bed next to me; a small child was laying unconscious, her left cheek covered by a large bloody gash. All around me, people were shaken. Some sat with their families, holding hands and praying. Several black body bags were laying on gurneys in the far corner of the room. The soft crying of a child flooded my eardrums. *This is what I had caused.* I felt horrible. My heart was aching with remorse. I did not intend for this many people to get hurt. All I wanted was Takada dead. All of these innocents. *God forgive me...*

Despite the pain, I had to leave. I needed to get out of the public eye and I needed to get away before the police started to infiltrate the area. I clutched my left ribcage and slowly swung my legs over the side of the bed. I was about to stand up when an angry voice hit me like a ton of bricks, blasting away in Japanese. Taken aback, I froze, uncertain as to what I should do.

"Ah, yes, Canadian," said the voice. "You are not going anywhere. You have suffered major head trauma and you have broken three ribs."

For such a strong voice, the woman behind it was rather miniscule. She was wearing a smock, but her pants suggested she had been one of the dancers in the street. They were a vibrant shade of blue and silver sequins.

"What happened? Who are you?" I inquired bewilderedly. I could not act as though I knew too much. I needed to get out of here undetected and to do so, I must co-operate fully.

"We found you unconscious on Nihon Street. You were right in the middle of the blast. I must say, Sir, you are lucky to be alive and you are equally lucky your injuries are somewhat minor. Others, I am afraid, were not so lucky. We have recovered twenty-one bodies so far. One, being Prime Minister Nakamura. It appears as though someone planted a bomb." Her eyes were misty, as she choked on her last words.

This last statement hung in the air. I did my best to appear upset and confused as the nurse checked my blood pressure and listened to my heart.

"I am going to give you something for the pain. It will make you drowsy, but you could use the rest anyway."

"When can I leave? I am only here for the Danjiri, I must return to Montreal."

"In your current state, I would say five to seven days. You must give your body time to heal. Now lay down, get comfortable and enjoy your sleep."

I was surrounded by complete darkness the second time I woke up. My head was throbbing, my ribcage was on fire. I listened for a few moments for any sign of movement, but heard nothing. I really needed to get out of this place. My body did not wish to, but I knew I had to. I stifled a moan of pain as I propped myself up against the pillow. If I was going to leave, better to do it now whilst everyone was peacefully asleep.

Once again, I swung my legs over the side of the bed, carefully drawing myself up to full height. I walked several paces before my foot snagged on something. I winced as I bent down to untangle my foot. Surprisingly, my hands grasped the worn leather strap of my satchel. They must have brought it in with me. That would explain why the nurse assumed I was Canadian. Thanking the Lord for this small miracle, I shouldered it and walked as fast as my body would allow towards the exit. I didn't know where I was going; all that mattered was I got far away from Kishiwada.

Chapter 20

Bangkok, Thailand
26 September, 2000

"Your documents please, Miss," murmured a thick female accent.

I stared benignly at the wall in front of me, sweat dripping from my brow and completely exhausted. I had been waiting in line for four hours. My feet were aching and were so swollen they were ready to burst from my shoes. My side was killing me softly and my breathing was extremely irregular. Each breath felt as though I was being stabbed: sharp and swift....mercilessly. I needed a warm bath followed by a hot meal, a rather large nightcap and a comfortable bed. I shook my head in disgust. *Why do I punish myself in such a manner?* Why was I anticipating these things when I knew full well it was going to be at least another four to six hours before I would be able to enjoy such indulgences, for there had to be two hundred people ahead of me.

I was standing in a tiny glass box surrounded by dozens of weary travellers and sober customs officials. I had initially decided on Thailand due to its affordable cost of living, low key nature and nonchalant immigration laws. I could get lost in Bangkok while taking the time I needed to recover from my injuries and enjoy the calm. So far, it was shaping up to be a dreadful trip. My entire body was beginning to throb and the room was so crowded I felt as though I was a marshmallow in a nutcracker. With each squeeze I was becoming more intolerable; my insides were about to rupture at the seams out of sheer annoyance. I was hot, I was hungry, I was tired and I was in no mood nor physical condition to stand around much longer. Thailand was really starting to piss me off...

When I stepped off of the plane and meandered through the gates, I was nothing less than thrilled. Finally it was done. My mission had been successful. I could now rest before making my trek back to England. I had high hopes of spending a year in Bangkok; taking in the city, enjoying its festivals, food, culture and basking in its vastness. I looked forward to lazy days and tranquil nights. I had longed to lounge around on a high- rise rooftop where I could overlook the city completely alone and completely at peace. What I would give to be doing that now.

The line slowly diminished and after several painstaking hours, I was next in the queue. The young man in front of me got caught trying to smuggle a grumichama, a Brazilian cherry, into the country. After several minutes of ruckus involving him trying to plead ignorance of the Food and Agricultural Import Regulations, and then when all else failed, he dashed towards the exit. He was finally apprehended and wrestled to the stone floor where he was restrained and removed from the room, all the while kicking and screaming, professing his innocence. The red light directly in front of me flashed green and I hastily moved towards the counter where a young, arrogant looking gentleman awaited me.

"Documents," he grunted staring blankly at me. I removed my passport from my travel bag and placed it on the counter before him. He picked it up, turned to the page where my photo was and scoffed. "Can-a-da." I simply nodded. I did not want to give anything away and I was very leery of my accent. I had travelled all this way and it would have been a pity to be denied entrance into the country.

"Business or Pleasure?"

"Beeziness Monsieur," I replied with a heavy French-Canadian accent.

The young man peered up at me for several minutes. He kept glancing to and from my photo. It was as though he knew something didn't seem right. He held my passport up to the light. Frowning slightly, he called out in Thai to the agent next to him. He was brandishing my passport, speaking very quickly. The same thick female voice responded and held out her hand. He handed her my passport and she in turn held it to the light above her head. She smiled, spoke rapidly to the young man and thrust my passport into his chest. He grunted and turned to face me, his features full of superiority. *I've been made. Try to stay calm.*

My heart was beating a million times a minute, the pain in my side and feet had been long since forgotten. All I could think about was being detained right here and chucked into Suan Plu Immigration Detention Centre. I would never make it out of that place alive...

"I repeat, how long is your stay?"

I blinked. The agent was peering down at me quizzically, a rubber stamp clutched firmly in his left hand. My thoughts quickly strayed from prison. I gazed confidently into his eyes and responded with an accent so accurate, I fooled myself:

"Seekz-teen weekz Monsieur."

He nodded in acknowledgement, thumbed through the pages until he found a fresh one and firmly rooted a tourist visa stamp upon it.

"Go through those doors," he said hitching his thumb over his right shoulder. "Down the hall and take the escalator to the main level. You will have no problems finding the exit from there. Enjoy your stay Mr. Lecavalier."

"Merci. J'espère que vous avez une bonne nuit." *Thank you. I hope you have a good night.* I replied in perfectly rehearsed French.

He slid my passport across the counter. I scooped it up, placed it back into my bag and made my way to the exit.

As the agent had said, I found the main level with no trouble. The Thais were very good about displaying signs in both their native language and in English, so in no time I found myself outside the main entrance and staring off into the night. There wasn't a cloud to be seen and a million little stars lit up the purple sky brilliantly.bbBangkok was one of the most magnificent cities in the world and I couldn't wait to explore it. However, my adventures would be put on hold for this evening as my primary concerns were finding a place to stay and obtaining some substance to satisfy the roaring in my stomach. I spotted several taxicabs clustered together about two hundred yards in front me. I started to make my way over to them when I drew back, crestfallen. I only had fifty euros and eight thousand yen in my pocketbook. The Baht was Thailand's official currency; of this I had none. My hopes of acquiring a hot meal and a hotel had just been shot down as I was certain no driver nor hotel would accept my money. I hitched my bag over my shoulder and set out on foot. Perhaps I would get lucky and find a currency exchange shop that was still open this time of night.

The air was chilly yet pleasant, especially after being cooped up in the stuffy customs building. I walked a mere half block before I realized that my feet were aching again. I suppose the pain never really went away, I had just become sidetracked with the customs procedures and finding accommodations for the evening. Sighing heavily, I backtracked to the airport entrance. I didn't want to have to do it, I promised myself I would never live like this again, but I had no choice: I was going to have to spend the duration of the night in the airport.

Frustrated and ashamed of myself, I hobbled back through the main doors and took an immediate left towards the escalator. I found a seating area on the second level and decided that it would have to do. The cushions were thin and worn, but at least I would be elevated. Sleeping on solid ground is most uncomfortable. I removed my shoes, placed them into my bag and gently rubbed my feet. They were so tender, I winced at the slightest amount of pressure. My ribcage was throbbing and my stomach was now booming like a beast. I propped my lumpy bag against the arm of the chair and stretched my tired legs out over the remaining three seats. I was so hungry, so tired and so sore. My body wanted to crash, yet the disturbance in my stomach had now reached its peak.

I felt tears in my eyes. I let them flow; there was nothing I could do to stop them. I knew I was being foolish. In just a few short hours, the shops would be open and I would be able to change my money over into Bahts. I suppose it was the principle of things; I had made a promise to myself that I would never have to seek shelter or go hungry again. Yet here I was, completely helpless. I knew that I should be thankful I was safe inside an airport, yet, I could not help but feel humiliated. My thoughts drifted to my past life, and when I awoke six hours later, my face and polo sweater were tear stained.

The sounds of hurried footsteps were all around me. For a moment I had forgotten where I was. I pushed myself up and dug the sleep out of my eyes. I peered around the airport. Everything was in full swing: travellers were hurdling past me speaking various languages whilst lugging huge suitcases behind them. I could hear the buzzing of the baggage carousel and the airline flight status announcements over the intercom system. I slowly removed my shoes from my bag, and with some effort, rose from my seat. My eyes darted in every direction in search of a restroom, and when I spotted one, it was with purpose to which I walked towards it. After washing my face and relieving myself I hopped on the escalator and rode it down to the main floor.

Bangkok during the day was just as stunning as it was at night. Although the city was still feeling the aftermath of the Asian Financial Crisis; it was very much alive. I had to fight my way through the heavy foot traffic as I ventured downtown. The shops were buzzing with the sounds of patrons; mostly tourists who were speaking delightfully in their native tongues, all the while snapping photographs of the scenes around them. I came across several currency exchange establishments, however, I moved past them. The city was so captivating, I wanted to explore every inch of it. Baiyoke Tower II, the grandest building in all of Thailand, could be seen from any crevice of the city. It was the most ingenious marriage of steel and glass I had ever laid my eyes upon. The tower had a mysterious elegance to it. I was bursting with anticipation and could not wait to discovery the amusements inside of it.

Succumbing to hunger, I entered a tobacco shop where I was able to exchange my Yen for approximately twenty-three hundred Baht. I could have gotten over twenty-five hundred Baht, but the shop's wizened owner looked as though he could use the extra funds, so I did not complain. I also purchased a small bag of mixed dehydrated fruit, a map of Bangkok and its districts and a Thai dictionary. If this city was going to be my home for the next twelve months, it was imperative that I become familiar with it. I walked leisurely down the streets, consulted my map from time to time, munching delightfully on the dried fruit. I found Lumphini Park; a magnificently manicured green oasis, where I spent a few hours stringing together phrases in Thai and watching cyclists beat along the lake's track. It was such a breathtaking spot. I knew there would be many days to come where I could relax in this sliver of nature's Heaven.

Twenty-three hundred Baht would not get me very far. This was not going to be a year of luxury. I needed to make all that I had stretch. I would have been foolish to think that I could live an entire year off of what I had in my pocketbook. I knew that at some point I would have to find employment. I was confident that acquiring a job wouldn't be too difficult. I would just have to adapt to Thailand's customs and learn their language much sooner than I had anticipated.

With the help of the dictionary I purchased, I was able to secure a place to stay on a week to week basis. The space was nothing to boast about; one tiny room and the use of a community shower and lavatory. From what I could tell, the place's sole occupants were drug dealers and prostitutes. The hallway was lit by a single fixture, the walls were grimy and had what appeared to be dried blood smeared on them. Many of the doors had been kicked in; some were hanging off their hinges. The smell of sulphur was strong and when I stopped in front of room 519, there were unmistakable bullet holes in the door. *How charming.*

After wading through all of the junk piled up at the front door, I entered my new home and looked around. It was just as grimy as the hallway—if not worse. The carpet was threadbare and almost completely covered in stains. The sleeper sofa wasn't in much better shape. It sagged in the middle and the brown patterned material was laden with rips and burn holes. The small kitchen was set in a corner of the room next to a cracked window overlooking the parking lot. I opened the cabinets to find syringes, elastic bands, prophylactics and tiny brown pellets, presumably rat droppings. I would deal with that mess later. My sole attention was going to be getting the sofa in a fit state to sit and sleep on. I found a scrub brush and a bottle of concentrated cleaner under the sink. Within minutes I was attacking the sofa vigorously. When I finished some thirty minutes later, I started in on the carpet and the droopy window coverings. I obtained a waste basket and a box of trash bags from an unlocked utility closet at the end of the hallway and proceeded to clear out the rest of the debris. Six long, disgusting and tiring hours later, I had finished decontaminating the place. I used a can of wood putty I also found in the closet to fill in the holes on the door. It was a far cry from a professional job, but it did the trick and would have to suffice. The place wasn't entirely liveable, but it was better than what it was and it was the only thing I could afford at the present time.

Red Herring

....

My first month in Bangkok was devoted to sleep and wellness. I bought a small microwave oven and a mini refrigerator from my landlord. Neither of them were in working condition, so I spent my first week repairing them. It seems foolish to have purchased these non-functioning appliances, however, my gluttonous landlord was not about to let them go for nothing. After haggling with him for nearly an hour, I purchased the items for two hundred fifty Baht. I found a grocer nearby where I could purchase food and toiletries. I bought enough tea bags and noodles to sink a ship along with the most cost efficient dinnerware and utensils: plastic. My room only had one light; no television or radio. Very spartan. I bought ten paperback novels from a thrift store for forty Baht. These would serve as my means of entertainment until I was well enough to travel around the city. I spent my days puttering around my room, reading Edgar Allan Poe, Ernest Hemingway and Jane Austen literature. I loved history and I absolutely adored Hemingway's novel entitled *The Sun Also Rises*. It reminded me of my own life; the love, tragedy, isolation and emotional issues within it. I felt connected to the characters, as though Hemingway wrote this masterpiece just for me. I had read this novel so many times; I could recite it almost verbatim.

Five months into things, I obtained employment as a bagboy for the grocer who was located near my place. His name was Pham and his family had been operating in the same spot for over forty years. Although I was still learning the language, Mr. Pham spoke surprising fluent English. And when he asked me if I was interested in working for him, I gratefully accepted. He said that he could not pay me a lot, but I did not mind. All I wanted was enough to pay my rent each week, purchase food and supplies and have a little set aside to explore the city more thoroughly. We agreed on two thousand Baht each week. Both of us were most pleased with this.

Before I knew it, eleven months had passed. I had become so caught up in my new life; working at Pham's, travelling around Bangkok on my days off, taking cooking lessons, reading, and writing, I had forgotten that my intentions were to only stay here one year. It was with a heavy heart when I informed Mr. Pham that I would be leaving.

"Where will you go from here?" he had asked.

I told him I was going home to England, back to my old life, back to my family. Of course none of this was true. I was indeed returning to London; it was the only place I truly felt connected to. I was at rest there. London was where I needed to be, where I needed to die.

....

The trip back to London was long and uneventful. Parting from Bangkok was such sweet sorrow. I did not want to leave, but I knew I must. When I stepped onto the train, it was with reluctance and I remained subdued for the duration of the journey. I was sick of flying, sick of travelling in general, sick of being alone. I no longer wished to carry this burden...

The train slowed to a halt, I stood up to remove my bag from the overhead compartment. I dawdled on purpose, not wanting to exit the compartment. Part of me was still in Bangkok and it took every ounce of strength I could muster to not purchase a return ticket back to Thailand. I wanted to confess, I needed to. Yet for the first time in many years, if ever, I had started to second guess myself.

Maybe I should go back to Bangkok, spend a few more years in city. I went twelve months unnoticed; I was perfectly capable of enjoying a quiet life there. I could work for Pham, see more the country, pick up Asian cooking lessons again... As much as I wanted this for myself, I knew that I could not have that life. I had to stick to my plan. I set out to purge the world of all things that were evil, and in doing so, I had committed sins for which I must now pay for.

I exited the station and made a beeline for the currency exchange booth across the street. Upon leaving Bangkok, Mr. Pham had given me an envelope. Inside was fifty thousand Baht. When I asked him what it was for, he told me that he wanted me to have it. He said that he wished I could stay, but he understood that I could not, so this was his gift to me from his family. I told him that I could not accept such a generous gift, but he insisted and told me that I had been severely underpaid for seven months and to consider it a bonus. He said he did not care what I used the money for, as long as I used it for "good." I fought with him, tried to return it, but he said I would insult him and dishonour his family if I did not take it. I resigned to take his gift, but I would only use a small fraction of it.

I changed thirty thousand Baht to Rupees, and the other twenty thousand Baht to Great Britain Pounds. I walked three blocks to a stationary shop where I purchased a single envelope, and a notepad. I stowed the items in my travel bag and I hailed a taxicab to take me to St. James Park in Westminster. It was my favourite spot in all of London for it boasted over fifty acres of paradise, two islands surrounded by a lake, hundreds of waterfowl, vast green trees, hand carved stone fountains and a stunning view of Buckingham Palace. It was completely blissful. I hoped Heaven would be similar to it.

I paid the cab driver twenty-one pounds, shouldered my bag and walked serenely into St. James. The Park was just how I remembered it, picturesque and welcoming. I found a picnic table near the east corner of the park. It was shaded by two large oak trees which nestled me out of sight. I placed my bag on the table and removed the notepad and pen from its inner compartment. I grasped the pen firmly in my left hand and closed my eyes. *What to say...* It had been over five years. He was a man by now. Would he have remembered me? I had rehearsed my correspondence to him out in my head a million times. I knew exactly what I wanted to say. Suddenly, I was at a loss for words. All the things I wanted to say just didn't seem fitting. I decided to listen to my own heart and before I knew it, my pen was etching rapidly across the notepad without thought.

My dear friend Nouman,

I hope this letter finds both you and your family well, as a number of years have passed since we last spoke. By now you have grown into the noble man I know you are. I am confident that you have made your mother and father proud. You were destined to do great things, and I trust you have embraced the gifts of courage and intellect which have been bestowed upon you.

Before our lives divided, I promised you we would one day see each other again. It is with the deepest of regret I write to inform you that this will be my only correspondence to you. I extend my sincerest apologies to you, Nouman, for I knew I would never return to Pakistan. I will understand if you despise me; I broke a promise I made to you. Although there is no excuse for my deception, I want you to know that my intent was to do you no harm. You were simply too young to comprehend what was really going to happen to me.

When our paths first crossed, you were a mere young boy. Your family took me in, fed me and clothed me, and ultimately kept me in good health. When you found out my true reasons for being in your village, you were all too eager to assist me. You had seen and experienced evil firsthand and you sought revenge against the government which had terrorized your family for so long. I permitted you to assist me, and together we succeeded in eliminating Zafar Amini.

The time came for me to leave and I saw the sadness in your eyes. You asked me if you could come with me, but I could not allow it. You were only

Red Herring

thirteen years of age and you belonged in Pakistan with your mother, father and sister. Tears streaming down your face, you begged me to one day return to the village. "Even if it is just for a second, will you come back to see me?" you had asked. I could not deny you, Nouman, so I told you that I would return. Your eyes lit up like beacons and a wide smile instantly spread across your face. Wanting to remember you this way, I swallowed my guilt and allowed you to believe that I would one day come back.

So I walked away, my head down in shame of the lie I had just told you. I am not a man of regrets; however, there is not a day that passes when I do not reflect upon what I said to you. In hindsight, yes I should have been honest with you. Please trust me when I say that I wanted to tell you the truth. I just could not bring myself to do it. You are older now, much more capable of comprehending irrefutable truths, so I am going to tell you what I should have told you on the country lane that day.

I have come home to England to die. I always knew I would. I had no intentions of living once my mission was complete. I know this seems crazy, dramatic even, but it is the truth. At the tender age of thirteen years, I did not feel you were ready to hear those words. I am a simmer, Nouman, just like the people I murdered, and I must face my fate. I must pay for what I have done. Even though my acts were for the greater good, I still perpetuated an evil. The only thing which separates me from those whose lives I took is that I did it out of necessity. Nonetheless, the Lord's word is law, and under His law, I must be punished. In time I hope you will forgive me, and in time I hope you will understand the reasoning behind my words. I am so very sorry, but this is how things must be.

Along with this letter, you will find 63,000 Rupees. Please distribute it amongst yourself, your mother, father and sister. I vowed to one day repay your family. This by no means excuses the debt to which I owe, but it is all I have to give. Give your family my regards and may you always be blessed. You will forever be in my thoughts.

My utmost sincerity,
Wilhelm

Wiping my eyes hastily on my sleeve, I folded the letter in half and tucked the Rupees inside of it. I placed the note in the manila envelope I had purchased and sealed it tightly. Sighing heavily, I got on my feet, stowed the letter safely in my bag and left the park.

I shuffled my feet along Queen Ann Street, not really knowing where I was headed. My heart ached. All I could think about was Nouman's reaction when he finds out I deceived him. Would he understand? All these years I had known I would never see him again, yet I led him to believe the reverse. I had started many letters to him, but could never seem to finish them. He was just too young to fully grasp everything that my mission entailed, to understand my own sacrifice...I expected him to be angry and I expected him to be bitter. I prayed he was merciful enough to understand forgiveness...This fear carried me all the way to High Street where I stopped at a Post Office to mail my letter. I quickly scrawled Nouman's name and address on the envelope and gave the formidable looking postmaster five pounds for postage.

On Rotherdam Avenue I nipped into a run down housing complex to see about leasing a flat for thirty days. A small step up from my old place in Bangkok, the flat I was interested in bore all the signs of neglect, however, it was blood stain and bullet hole free. I was also most pleased to find out that I would have my own lavatory. I paid the filthy landlord three hundred pounds and pocketed the small metal key he gave me.

He kept eyeing me up suspiciously. As I turned to leave his makeshift office he said brusquely, "I don't usually let blokes lease monthly. If you decide to stay longer, you will have to give me three months in advance."

"I see," I said smirking slightly. "Well, I won't be staying here more than thirty days."

"Are you some sort of drifter then? Because if you are, then I don't want you here. You can give me back that key!"

His features had darkened and there was a defiant look upon his face. *How odd.* What did this chap care? He had been paid. I suppose it was his job to know his tenant's business, so I chalked his rudeness up to purely meddlesome.

"No, I am not a drifter," I said smiling sardonically. *This bugger isn't going to get any information from me.* "I will be staying here for thirty days—only thirty days. I have business to attend to in London and I will not have use for this flat beyond the fourteenth of September."

"What sort of business?" He asked blatantly. "If you need any help, I can assist you," he added sugary. *He really wants information badly. Absolutely no couth; shameless.*

Deciding to disappoint him, I turned my heel and called over my shoulder, "Very kind of you, however, I know my way around the city quite well and you do not want to go where I'm going...at least not yet."

Chapter 21

Scotland Yard, England
14 September, 2001
8:42 a.m.

For years I had planned my confession. Although I had taken every precaution to hide my identity whilst on my mission, I never intended to conceal my true self forever. In earlier years, I had envisioned myself sauntering leisurely into Scotland Yard and nonchalantly revealing myself. I had foreseen myself being taken into an interview room where I would be permitted to candidly speak of my travels and my mission. The inspectors would be enthralled by my tales. They would be eager with anticipation and I would facilitate their hunger with my phenomenal stories. I had dreamt of being put on a podium where I could tell the world of my good deeds, where I could present my gift to humanity. I relished upon these delusions, for in mind I knew them to be such. Nonetheless, even wise men are permitted to fantasize.

I woke up early on the morning of September fourteenth. I deftly dressed myself in the most tasteful articles of clothing I owned: a dark green polo and neatly pressed black slacks. I swiftly combed my hair, rinsed my mouth and applied shaving foam to my jaw line and chin. As I glanced at my reflection in the mirror, I took notice to how much I had aged. My features were no longer youthful; my once sparkling blue eyes were dull and full of despair. My short sandy hair was generously streaked with gray. I had the tell-tale signs of an over worked individual. Deep creases lined my forehead and jetted out from under my eyes. Sighing heavily, I was resigned to face the irrefutable truth; I was not the man I once was. I finished shaving and wiped my face with a frayed hand towel. I put my socks on and proceeded to slip my tired feet into my brown weather-beaten shoes. I moved blindly towards the outlet and with one last glance around my spartan bedroom, I placidly shut the door behind me.

I walked serenely down the hallway, meeting no one on my way to the stairwell. My footsteps echoed as I made my way down the cluttered steps and out into the street. It was a mere ten minute walk to the bus stop four blocks away, however, I took my time. I was in no rush. I absorbed the sights and sounds around me. The sun was shining brightly and a lightly blowing breeze carried the sweet smell of jasmine. I walked past a park where young children were playing in a sandbox. Their mothers sat chatting amongst themselves on nearby benches. The children's laughter was like music to my ears: joyful, carefree and pure. Not yet had these children been corrupted by a pitiless society. I would have pledged anything to be that young again and to be given the gift which I have given them. I wondered if they knew just how fortunate they really were. I had saved them from a life of tyranny. Their lives from this point on would be nothing but harmonious. They would not be forced to suffer at the hands of their government as so many had before them. Each breath they would take would be saturated with freedom and each step would be forward, not backward.

I walked on. I made my way through the thicket of corporate-types on Heere Street. They were always in such a hurry: hustling from point A to point B, talking animatedly on their mobile devices all the while oblivious to their surroundings. They always appeared to have the weight of the world on their shoulders, as though they were the only reason the sun rose and set each day. Such a far cry from the truth––they allowed themselves to believe this as a means of making their acts excusable. These people neglected their families, became consumed with the next big project, and had forgotten that there were more important things than constructing a new nightclub or selling five hundred thousand company shares for some new miracle drug. They would never know what they had lost until it was completely gone. Their financial burdens were mediocre compared to what I had carried my entire life. I took no pity on them.

In front of a magazine shop on Cadogen Street, two aged gentlemen sat on rickety old shipping crates immersed in a game of backgammon. They had to be at least eighty-years-old. Their worn, vein covered hands shook every time they grasped a game piece. Their calculated movements were sluggish, as though their arms were not permitted to move at a faster pace. One of the gentlemen was so weak he could not hold his pieces properly, so he merely pushed them across the board. I watched them for a few minutes, my heart full of impervious ache. I truly felt anguish for these men, for they were the individuals whom have suffered the most at the hands of our leaders. They endured a great ordeal: wars, depressions, recessions, terrorism, communism...They had seen and experienced it all. These men were very near their end and they would not have the opportunity to flourish in this new world, to see its new face or to experience its new found unity. I slowly moved past them, deeply sorrowed.

I arrived at the bus stop a few short minutes later. I sat down on an iron bench in wait for my transportation. The minutes gradually ticked by. A young adolescent sat down next to me. He had vibrant green hair, which he had spiked to a point, and was wearing numerous chains and what appeared to be a dog collar around his scrawny neck. His clothing was jet black, grimy and about five sizes too large for him. His skin was covered in tattoos and piercing. I glanced down at his ink covered left arm. One of his tattoos was that of a swastika. I turned my head in disgust. Obviously, this boy did not understand the power of that symbol or perhaps he was just too ignorant to care. The terror it invoked, the lives it tore apart; the swastika meant blood and the evil that existed within it. It represented he plight of the people Hitler and his Nazi's terrorized. This young man knew nothing of sacrifice and had no idea how much his freedom had cost. Yet he proudly displayed this image upon his arm as if it were a badge of honour. I was repulsed by this.

The bus soon drew upon us and came to a halt. The young man rose and joined the queue of people waiting to climb on. He thrust a middle aged woman out of his way, and when she cried out in objection, he made an obscene hand gesture and told her to go to Hell. I climbed the stairs and took several paces before parking myself in a seat by the window. After witnessing what I just had, I found myself wondering if sacrifice was just a thing of the past. Did it really impact the future? Will *my* sacrifice be dignified? These skepticisms burned my insides for the next forty blocks.

....

I stepped off the bus into the blinding sunlight onto Broadway and Victoria Street. Scotland Yard was a massive five story building. Its humongous gyrating sign did not go unnoticed. The place had hundreds of windows and resembled a perfect rectangle. I climbed the front steps and pushed the revolving doors inward. I found myself inside a smartly decorated lobby. It had photos of the original Scotland Yard, the London Underground and numerous portraits of important men and women ranging from the 1800s to present day. To my left was an elevator shaft, along side it a staircase. Directly in front of me was an oak desk occupied by a rather large and harassed looking male Constable. Since I did not know where I was going, I approached him. His name tag bore the surname "Hughes". He merely glanced up at me before returning to the newspaper he was reading

"Can I help you, Sir?" Hughes inquired, peering over his newspaper, his voice full of boredom.

"I would like to speak to an inspector with regards to numerous murders I have committed throughout the Eastern and Western Hemispheres."

My hands twitched slightly at my sides, my voice was rather shaky. I looked up at Hughes, but he was once again buried inside the pages of his paper.

"Sir?" I inquired.

He raised his head slowly above the newspaper as if completely disinterested in the words I had just said. "Murders you say? Well you are in the right place. Enlighten me, Sir, *whom* have you murdered?"

"I am to be held responsible for the murders of eleven politicians along with twenty-six civilian men and eight civilian women. I can give you their names if you desire."

Smiling widely, "Oh please do share this information with me, Sir. I am bursting to hear it." Hughes sarcastically crooned. His eyes were full of antagonism as he had folded his newspaper and laid it upon the desk.

"I murdered Prime Minister Antokolsky Orlov Golovin of Russia, Prime Minister Charles Benjamin Addams of England, President Robert J. Redding of the United States, Prime Minister Pierre Gervais Moreau of Canada, Prime Minister Baradine Thompson of Australia, Prime Minister Alexious Theodoridis Karras of Greece, Prime Minister--"

"That will do, Sir," Hughes interrupted. The smile had vanished from his face and was replaced with an abstinent frown.

"Everyday, a good half dozen people walk through our front doors, just as you have, staking the same claim. Now, you and I both know damned good and well you have not committed any crime against any of the individuals whose names you have mentioned. Whether you are here in search of fame, whether you are here just to be here, or whether you're just plain crazy, our facility does not have the man power nor the patience to be dealing with wannabe celebrities. It would be in your best interest to turn around and walk back out the doors from which you came."

With that, Hughes abruptly picked up his newspaper, turned to the page he left off on and continued reading. I watched for a few seconds as his eyes darted from side to side along each line. It was clear, however, that he was still interested. His eyes were jetting to and fro at an inhumanly possible speed; his head was inclined slightly as though keeping an open ear.

"Please, Sir, I kid you not. I murdered thirty-four people and I am here to confess my sins and take responsibility for my actions. I beg you, please allow me to speak to someone." My hands were shaking uncontrollably, I could feel the perspiration beginning to line my forehead.

Hughes rose, slamming his paper on the desk. "Sir, if you want to confess your sins, go find yourself a priest! We are not a church upon which you can walk into leisurely for a chat with God. We are a police station! Leave now, before I am forced to place you under arrest for disturbing the peace. Go on, there's the door," he said pointing a stubby finger at the exit.

"No! You—you don't un—understand," I stammered. "I did it. I am, I am—"

"No, Sir, you don't understand. I don't give a damn if you're Jack-the-bloody-Ripper! Get the Hell out of here before I make good on my word!" Hughes bellowed, red faced, pointing once again towards the revolving doors. The purple veins on his forehead were now feverishly pulsing.

He didn't believe me. Things were not quite going as planned. I did not expect to run into *this* obstacle. Although I knew that there may be complications, I never expected to be laughed at and turned away. I had to speak to someone. My crimes were weighing on my chest and shoulders as though I were being constricted by a massive boa.

Hughes had settled down a fair amount and the colour in his face was normalizing. A wild thought came into my mind. I looked at Hughes, smiled bleakly, and started to turn away. "A wise decision sir," I heard him say. I walked several paces towards the door before violently turning and gunning it for the stairs. I was halfway up the steps screaming like a lunatic before Hughes knew what happened.

"STOP HIM! SEIZE HIM!!!" Hughes was yelling.

His cries, however, were drowned out by my own. I was blaring with as much stamina as I could muster. "I KILLED ALL THOSE WORLD LEADERS! I DID IT AND I DON'T REGRET IT. I MURDERED THEM! I HUNTED THEM DOWN, EXECUTED THEM AND I RELISHED IT!!!" I continued with my ear-splitting screams all the way up the stairs. At the top, I found myself in an open space chocked full of bewildered inspectors and civilians. *Excellent.*

Everything was at a standstill. Inspectors loosely clutched telephone receivers in their hands; their parties left abandoned on the line. A Sergeant who was fingerprinting a suspect was absentmindedly pushing the man's ink covered fingers onto a white index card, all the while gaping at me. Computer screens went blank as they went into hibernation mode. Now that I had gotten their attention, I simply stood hunched over clutching my side, trying to catch my breath. I was still rather weak from the injuries I had sustained in Japan. A forceful hand grabbed the back of my neck and I heard Hughes hiss into my right ear. "You are going to regret doing this asshole."

I smiled at him. After what just happened, after what I had just claimed, I could not be denied a chance to speak.

Once order was restored and the inspectors commenced to work again, I was taken by a young inspector. He escorted me to the elevator, pushed the upwards arrow and we waited in silence as the unit slid down the shaft. We stepped over the threshold, the doors clambered shut and he punched the number five. The ride to the top was peaceful. I was still trying to get the painful stitch out of my side and the inspector merely gazed above our heads at the floor level numbers. The doors rattled open and we were off. We stopped a mere twenty feet past the elevator, the young man swiped his identification badge through a slot in an unmarked door on our right and gruffly pushed me into the room. There was one small window to my left and in the centre of the room, a steel table and three chairs were set up. A wall-sized mirror was on my right, but I knew it to be only masking as such. I knew it was really a one-way window. I was in a suspect interview room.

The inspector pointed towards the chair in front of me and told me to sit. I obeyed and proceeded to occupy the seat. He sat down as well, pulling a pen and notepad out of his left breast pocket.

"What is your name, Sir?" he said.

I noticed that he was trembling slightly, yet his voice was steady and uncompromising. His first assignment perhaps? He simply wanted to appear tough. We had something in common. I was attempting to mask my trepidation as well. I wanted to confess, in fact, I yearned to do so. I wanted everything to go off without a hitch, to be perfect. My story was so spellbinding and mesmerizing and I wanted to do it justice. My fears were that I would be unable to properly serve it.

Alas, I spoke. "My name is Wilhelm Radulfus Miller." The inspector began to scribble my response on his notepad.

"Thank You," he said lightly. "Mr. Miller, my name is Inspector Matthew Yates. I am going to be speaking to you about the events that just occurred in the lobby."

I nodded in agreement. Maybe my confession will be as grand as I had imagined after all.

"Mr. Miller, can you please provide me with your current address, telephone number and place of employment? This, of course, is just for good measure in case we need to speak to you again after today."

Trying not to sound impolite, "Inspector Yates, this information will not be necessary for you to obtain, because after today, you will be able to contact me at the prison," I said.

Yates had a quizzical look upon his face. Clearly he did not think that I had done the things I claimed to have done.

"Prison?" He chuckled half-heartedly before scribbling on his pad once more. "Okay then, Mr. Miller, we'll get to that information later. Why don't you go ahead and tell me exactly what it is that you have done?"

Where to start? I had so much to tell this young man, so many things lead up to this point. It would be ill-mannered of me to take up too many hours of his time, yet it was pertinent that every single detail of my story be heard.

I started at the beginning. I took Inspector Yates to the streets with me, walked him through Hans' murder, told him how I had witnessed the Russian Prime Minister and his two henchman execute him out of sheer amusement. I explained to him that the Metropolitan Police arrived on the scene, only to immediately close the case. Yates inquired as to who exactly Hans was; he said that he would launch a full investigation into his death, but we both knew he would do nothing of the sort. Hans was murdered over seven years ago by a man who was now deceased. There was nothing left to solve.

Yates sat silently scrawling on his notepad as I rehashed the last seven years of my life: the things I had done, the places I had been, the people I had met along the way. He granted me full forum, and not once did he interrupt me. It took over four hours to tell my story and by the time I finished, Yates was looking at me with wide eyes and a blank expression; his notepad lain forgotten on the table in front of him. I restfully exhaled, re-crossed my legs for what seemed the hundredth time, folded my hands in my lap and waited.

Now it was Yates' turn. He said nothing for close to five minutes. It was as though he was trying to absorb all of which he had just heard. I could imagine the gears in his brain churning as his mind frantically attempted to register my words. After what seemed an eternity, he gathered his thoughts, closed his eyes and softly groaned. Yates abruptly stood up. "Stay put," he said anxiously before darting through the exit, the clicking of the door's self-locking mechanism drowning out his footsteps. *How ironic*, I thought. Nonetheless, I did not move from my chair. Another thirty-five passed before I heard the familiar swish and buzz as he swiped his badge through the slot and re-entered the room.

Yates looked dishevelled, agitated even, yet a curious expression was upon his face. He looked down upon me with his dreary green eyes, shook his head at nothing in particular and pulled his notepad towards him as he reclaimed his seat.

"I have just spoken with my superior, Mr. Miller," Yates said in a submissive voice. "He would like me to go over your account of these events an additional time, and if you please, could you provide me with some more detailed information."

It was quite clear that listening to me recount my story was the last thing Yates would like to be doing. However monotonous it may be, he lazily flipped open his notepad and clutched his pen firmly in his left hand.

"What sort of detailed information would you like, Inspector?" I inquired in a soft, airy voice.

I knew that his superior had sent him back in to speak to me with the hopes of obtaining the most intimate of details. Yates believed me to be a murder, nevertheless, his superior did not. I was prepared to tell Yates anything he wanted to know, for I was not going to walk out of Scotland Yard in anything less than shackles and chains.

"Anything will do, Sir," he said. "The most minute details, something only *you* would know."

"Something only *I* would know, you say?" My lips were parted ever so slightly, a smile forming upon my face.

"Yes, Sir, that is correct. You see, my superior does not believe you to be capable of committing these crimes. On the contrary, you state otherwise, so he would like you to provide him with additional information. Whether it be the clothing the victims were wearing, any tattoos or birthmarks they have... you get my drift, right? Give us something, Mr. Miller, because if you don't provide us with what we need, we'll have to release you."

"I do believe I can accommodate you and your superior, Inspector Yates," I said unable to contain my broad smile.

Smiling also, Yates straightened his posture and glanced briefly over his shoulder. I knew what he was doing: I had no doubt that there were other lawmen, possibly the prosecutor for the Crown, huddling around a speaker inside a tiny room behind the mirror. Yates was signalling to them as to say, "He's about to talk, turn the speaker on."

The presence of an audience did not intimidate me in the least; rather, it heightened my spirits. I ever so passionately wanted to give this story the recognition and validation it deserved: the more individuals who heard it, the better. They were apt to spread my story. There was no better way for it to reach humanity.... Caught up in my reverie, it was a full five minutes time before I awoke, so to speak, and become aware of my surroundings. Inspector Yates had a curious expression upon his face as he sat unwearyingly waiting for me to bestow upon him the information I claimed to possess. Although it was extremely ill-mannered of me to keep Yates waiting, part of me was savouring it. I held all the cards. Both he and I knew that it was I who was in control. If I chose not to speak for another eight hours, than so be it. Yates would still be sitting next to me clinging to the hope that I would give him what he needed soon. I was the fish, he was the fisher-men. Without me, he had nothing. Yates needed my information; even he could not deny such.

"I only got close enough to two of the politicians: President Gomez Salazar Cervino of Spain and President Ivana Simona Vladislava of Czechoslovakia. I only saw the remaining nine leaders I disposed of whilst tracking their movements and the vast majority of the time, they were only visible to me from a long distance. President Gomez had a tattoo of his country's flag on his upper right thigh. It was in black and white and about the size of a business card. I know this because I saw the marking when I castrated him."

Scribbling furiously, Yates merely nodded and said, "Go on. How did you know which hotel the President was staying in? And more importantly, why were his screams not heard by any of the hotel's staff or visitors? Removing his genitals would have caused him to suffer great discomfort."

"I watched the President's movements very carefully for close to three months. He had a liking for young girls. Only he and his assistant knew this, of course. Once per week I witnessed his assistant's grey Mercedes leave their office building and travel across the city. It was always to a hotel. One day I followed him into the Villa Brazos disguised as a flower delivery man and I watched him go into a suite on the hotel's highest level. A young girl, no more than fourteen and dressed like a whore, turned up at his door approximately ten minutes later. About an hour later she left the room looking tousled and smelling of sex and sin. I knew she would be my ticket into his suite. Although he never had the same girl, I was banking on being able to persuade one of them to assist me. There was no way those girls could have been happy giving up their innocence to a man who cared nothing for them; who used them and took advantage of them.

A few weeks later, I found myself once again outside the President's suite waiting patiently for his prey to arrive. I stopped a young girl just as she was about to enter, and I explained to her that what he was doing was wrong and that he must be punished for it. I promised her no one would ever know she was involved; the Spanish government would make the President's excuses for him and even in death, his secret would be protected. Surprisingly, she was eager to help. So, I explained to her what I needed her to do: blindfold the President and bind his hands together as though they were participating in sadomasochism behaviour. She obliged and everything went off without a hitch. I quietly entered the room; she was teasing him with a feathered whip, and doing a superb job of making loud, pleasurable noises. When I reached the bedside, she covered his mouth with her hands and removed her body from on top of his. He was erect and very much enjoying her dominatrix role. I took out my dagger and castrated him. He started wailing instantly, however, I placed a pillow over his face to drown out the sounds. I'm certain he suffocated before he bled to death. The young girl put her clothes back on, embraced me tightly, called me an angel and left the room. A few short minutes later, I exited as well and vanished into the streets."

Yates' eyes were wide and his mouth was gaping. His notepad was full of tiny illegible writing. He glanced at his notes, parted his lips as to speak, but no sound came out. He wiped his brow with his right hand, opened his mouth once more and emitted a low barely audible, "Wow." I seized the opportunity; Yates was still looking rapt, so I launched into details of the Czechoslovakian President's murder.

"President Ivana Simona Vladislava was perhaps the most effortless target of them all. She loved to be pampered and everyday at precisely two o'clock in the afternoon she called for a massage: always the same outfit, different therapists. Her patterns were to have the therapist set up at one forty-five—exactly fifteen minutes prior to her appointment. She would enter the room at five minutes to two o'clock, remove her clothing, lie on the table and ring a bell to signal the therapist that she was ready. Her massage would last for exactly one hour and thirty minutes. She was always alone with her therapist."

I swallowed dryly. My throat was aching and my mouth felt like it was full of cotton. I asked Inspector Yates for a glass of water and a short break if he did not mind. He said that this would not be a problem and left the room for a second time to fetch me a refreshment. I hummed lightly to myself and gazed up at the ceiling: I was on cloud nine. I was finally telling my story and it felt magnificent. I was euphoric, completely elated and when Yates re-entered the room, I was only too eager to continue with my narrative. I hastily gulped down the water he brought me before picking up where I left off.

"I paid the therapist five thousand Czech Koruna to give me his uniform, table and bag full of oils and scents. He, like the young girl in Spain, was more than happy to assist me. I asked him to give me the run down on how things operated; at one forty-five I was given the nod by Vladislava's security personnel to proceed into her private quarters. I set the table and candles up according to the therapist's instructions and I left the room. Precisely fifteen minutes later I heard Vladislava ring the bell. I entered the room to find her face down on the table, her buttocks covered with a white towel. She merely glanced at me as if I were vermin, rested her head back down on the table and said in a cold authoritative voice, "Dělat svou praci dobre nebo budu mit vas vyhodili."

"She said what? What does that mean? Do you speak Czech?" Yates was about to jump out of his seat with excitement.

It means, *Do your job well or I will have you fired,*" I said. So I approached her, placed my hands upon her skin and within a little over an hour she was dead."

"But....but I don't under— How the Hell did she die?! She just didn't drop dead on her own accord, what did you do to her? You must tell me!"

"I poisoned her, Inspector—with Hemlock, an ancient plant which can kill upon skin contact. I mixed it with the oils the therapist had and rubbed it throughout her body. I, of course, wore latex gloves so that I would not be contaminated."

"Didn't she notice you were wearing gloves? I mean, surely she must have felt the rubber come in contact with her skin."

"Ivana was a very vain, not to mention cruel, woman. She treated her assistants with the utmost disrespect. They were her puppets, always at her beckon call. She cared for no one but herself. She thought anyone who was beneath her, which incidentally was the entire country of Czechoslovakia, to be unclean beasts. She made everyone who worked for her or provided a service to her wear latex gloves. Her security personnel forced everyone who walked through her doors to sterilize their goods and their clothing by use of an antiseptic spray."

"I see," said Yates. "Is there *anything* else you may have forgotten to tell me Mr. Miller?" He put a strong emphasis on the word *anything* and was checking his notepad again, all the while scratching his chin with the end of his pen.

"Yes, Inspector, just one last thing: President Vladislava had a six to eight inch scar on her lower back, right side. It was an odd shaped scar. A medical procedure would not have caused it. Perhaps an accident or self inflicted: I do not know. Nonetheless, it resembled a pitchfork."

"A pitchfork? That *is* rather odd. Alright, Mr. Miller, thank you very much for your information. I need you to stay here once more while I confer with my superior. Is there anything I can get you? Perhaps another glass of water? A cup of tea? I'm not quite sure how long I will be gone and it is my wish that you are comfortable."

"Oh, no thank you, Inspector. I am quite comfortable as is. I will see you upon your return."

Yates turned to leave, his hand had grasped the doorknob when I exclaimed, "Inspector, are you not going to inquire about the other murders? I have only given you information on two of the eleven leaders. I can give you a detailed account of the others as well."

"No, that will not be necessary, Mr. Miller. However, I will know right where to find you should I require that information." And with that, he left.

....

"What do you suggest we do, Sir?" Yates looked tired, his voice weary. "I have no doubt he murdered these people. Surely there must be a way to verify the information he has given us."

"Oh, there is a way to verify what he has told us. What you must understand is that we have to be certain that this Miller bloke is the perpetrator. This story will be seen on the international news. We cannot just go around arresting the first nut job who claims to have committed these crimes. Scotland Yard is in the limelight enough these days. We do not need the negative backlash if he is the wrong man," the Chief Inspector said.

"I am certain he's the one, Sir. I can feel it. My gut is telling me that we have the right man. We mustn't let him slip from our clutches. You were not in that room with him. The way he talks, the way he presents himself...It's him, Sir, I would bet my life on it."

"Inspector, leaving something as important as this up to a 'gut feeling' is completely ludicrous—not to mention unacceptable. It is not the way I run this facility. We cannot detain Miller until we are absolutely certain he's done what he claims to have done.

Now, I'm going to give you two options: release him or go back in there and retrieve further information on the other murders."

Scowling at his superior, Yates begrudgingly returned to the interview room.

I was waiting for him. I knew Yates would return. He had yet to ask me about the other politicians' murders. As soon as he stepped into the room, I could tell his meeting with the Chief did not go well. He looked displeased; the colour had drained from his face. Yates slumped into his chair and slammed his notepad open. He roughly flipped through the pages until he found a fresh one.

"Mr. Miller," he began through clenched teeth. "If you please, could you give me a thoroughly detailed narrative of the other crimes you have committed?"

I glanced down at his left hand: his knuckles were pure white from grasping his pen so forcefully. Feeling sorry for Inspector Yates, I went into a long-winded reminisce, a fully detailed portrayal of the other executions. By the time I had finished, Yates looked as though he wanted to murder himself. His black hair was standing on end. He was slouched so low in his chair, only his shoulders and head were visible over the table top. This time he left the room without saying a word.

Matthew Yates' blood was boiling. He had spent close to eleven hours with this suspect and he was nearly at the end of his rope. He knew the man was guilty. He could sense it. The accounts of the murders were spot on. Yates knew that at least half of Wilhelm Miller's claims were true. He had followed these murders so closely over the last seven years. He read anything and everything he could get his hands on which pertained to the named politicians. His brother-in-law worked for INTERPOL and he had a cousin who had married a German diplomat. He had some inside information which he had promised to never reveal. If only he could explain this to the Chief, Miller would be arrested in the blink of an eye. However, Yates knew he could not betray his sources, so he had to follow protocol and do things the Chief's way. He entered his superior's office, slid the notepad across his handsome cherry wood desk, and sat down.

"Well?" said the Chief Inspector.

"It's all there, Sir. Everything. Miller's full account of his crimes. He confessed to every murder but the Laudenbach disappearance, which in my opinion, he is guilty of, but for some reason not disclosing details. And if I must say, we should stop wasting time and start making phone calls before it's too late. By now I am certain the public knows we have a man in custody. At least twenty-five people heard Miller's outburst. The Global Times will be all over this. You know how they are, Sir; can't report a solid bloody fact. We need to wrap this up before the rumours start to fly."

The Chief Inspector seemed to weigh Yates' words for a moment before he sighed, all the while sinking a little deeper into his leather armchair. "Call INTERPOL. See what they turn up on this bloke. Fingerprint him as well. Also, put a team together. I want someone to contact the Central Intelligence Agency in the United States, the French, Spanish, Russian and Australian Police Bureaus, the Royal Canadian Mounted Police and Governor Symond at Her Majesty's Belmeade Prison."

"You want me to call the Governor, Sir? May I ask why?"

"I want him made aware of the situation. However, do not disclose any particulars to the Governor. Simply inform him that we *may* be processing a highly dangerous prisoner into his facility this evening and that he *may* want to make the necessary preparations for his arrival."

"May, Sir?" It sounded to Yates as though the Chief Inspector wasn't expecting Miller's information to pan out. A little frantic, Yates anxiously looked towards the Chief to explain himself.

"Inspector, we cannot arrest this Wilhelm Miller bloke until we have solid proof that he is our man. If the information he gave you checks out, we will take him into custody. Until then, I need you to get that team together. Oh, and be sure to tell the other inspectors that this is priority number one. You are correct, Inspector Yates, we do not need The Global Times reporting anything other than the truth."

....

I sat silently, resting my head on my chin. Inspector Yates had been gone quite some time; this had to be a good sign. I glanced at my watch: it was nine fifty-two in the evening. I had been here for close to thirteen hours. I wondered vaguely what Yates and the Chief were doing. No doubt calling all over the world trying to verify my story. A Constable had come into the room to obtain a copy of my fingerprints. I was positive they were being run through INTERPOL at this very moment. The urge to sleep had long since passed. In fact, I was wide awake. I wished Yates would return soon. I had to use the restroom relatively urgently and my stomach was consumed by hunger pains. I had gotten used to the hunger pains whilst on the streets. After a while, they are fairly easy to ignore. My full bladder was another story. The minutes ticked by at an incredibly slow, painstaking pace. Finally, around midnight, Yates returned. I abruptly stood up and informed him that it was urgent I find a restroom. He escorted me out of the room and down the hall, where he waited for me as I relieved myself in the urinal. I washed my hands and met him just outside the restroom door. He took me back into the interview room. This time, we were not alone.

A formidable looking older gentleman was standing at attention next to the table. He had thinning grey hair, high cheekbones and a prominent chin. He reminded me of Hitler; minus the tidy little moustache. This had to be the Chief Inspector. Yates put some downward pressure on my left shoulder. I took this as meaning to sit down, so I did. The Inspector stood rooted in his shoes as he pulled a notepad from his breast pocket. He opened the notepad and started skimming through the words that were written on the paper. I recognized that pad to be Yates'. The tiny messy writing unmistakably belonged to him. The Chief cleared his throat. I had expected him to speak, but he did not. It was Yates whose voice I heard.

"Wilhelm Miller, I am placing you under arrest for the murders of Charles Benjamin Addams, Pierre Gervais Moreau, Robert J. Redding, Savard Guillory Leblanc, Zafar Amini, Takada Honjo Nakamura, Alexious Theodoridis Karras, Baradine Thompson, Antokolsky Orlov Golovin, Ivana Simona Vladislava and Gomez Salazar Cervino. You will be escorted to Belmeade Prison where you will stay until you have been arraigned by a justice of our legal system. Do you understand the words I have just spoken to you? A simple yes or no will suffice."

"Yes," I said in a weary voice. *I understood completely.*

Chapter 22

HM Belmeade Prison, England
Cellblock E5
15 September, 2001

Her Majesty's Belmeade Prison is a maximum security facility in Thamesmead, in the south-east city of London. At any given time, the prison houses approximately twelve hundred inmates. The vast majority of Belmeade's population have been detained in connection with terrorist related offences. Some of Europe's most dangerous rebels and insurgents call this place home. The building itself resembles a small reddish-brown brick box with minimal windows and a fenced-in grounds equiped with barbwire and snipers. An underground tunnel connects the prison to Woodbridge Crown Court. This court has been in operation since nineteen ninety-one and is primarily used for high profile cases. The tunnel was established as a means to safely and discreetly transport defendants from the prison to the courthouse. I would no doubt walk the length of that passageway many times.

I was escorted from Scotland Yard by two sergeants and placed into a navy unmarked car, where I was then transported to Belmeade. I arrived at the prison around two-thirty in the morning. Completely exhausted and fighting my hunger pains, I incoherently allowed the guards to process me into the prison. My mind and body were so numb; I merely nodded my head in concurrence to everything they said. I was stripped of my clothing, forced to endure a highly embarrassing cavity search and was left alone for a measly thirty seconds while I dressed myself in the putrid orange jumpsuit and skimpy footwear the prison had issued me. My hands were placed in shackles and my feet were bound by chains. I was then escorted down a long windowless hallway. The guards came to a halt in front of a pitiful looking set of barred doors. I had a thin blanket and a lumpy pillow thrust into my arms and was aggressively rotated on the spot so that I was facing the cell doors. The guard on my left nimbly shoved a key into the lock and with a loud clang, followed by a soft, yet agitating creaking noise, the doors slid open to reveal my new home. I felt a large powerful hand push me over the threshold into the room. Immediately, the doors were shut and bolted down behind me.

"Welcome to Cellblock E5," an unsympathetic Scottish voice said. "Enjoy your new slice of heaven. Don't bother us and we shall not bother you."

I did not respond, but stood frozen in the middle of the cell. The only sounds were the echoes of the guards' heavy boots as they trekked back down the corridor. I took a few moments to absorb the space around me. It was pathetic. A small cot and night table were flush with the east wall, a toilet and sink occupied the corner of the south wall, and a small writing desk with a three legged stool tucked beneath it stood alone on the west side of the room. I sat down on the mattress, it felt like it was stuffed full of rocks. I succumbed to my exhaustion and drifted off some time later, thinking only for a moment about what I would be served for breakfast in a few short hours.

Six o'clock came early—way too early. It felt as though I did not sleep one wink. I was awoken by the opening of my cell doors and the swift slamming of them as my breakfast was hastily placed upon the floor. I scampered out of bed, as a young child would do on Christmas day. I fell to my hands and knees and ate the food the guards had brought right in that very spot. The eggs were cold and runny, the toast was hard and the sausages were vile, however, I was starving. I ate every bite, even little bits of egg that had fallen off the plate onto the cold stone floor. It felt as though I had not eaten in a hundred years. I was deeply saddened when my plate had been cleared; I was still rather hungry.

Mid morning I was paid a visit by the Governor of the prison. I was laying on my cot when the most curious scent filled my nostrils: wood infused with oranges. The fragrance became stronger, and by the time it reached my cell doors, I was gasping for air. I heard soft footsteps approaching. I sat upright on my bed, peering towards the iron doors. I heard a male voice; a very cold and astute voice, yet there was no one standing before me.

"Good morning and welcome to Her Majesty's Belmeade Prison, Mr. Miller."

Rubbing my eyes, I looked hard at the doors. Were my eyes deceiving me? Surely I was not dreaming this. Someone was standing outside my cell, attempting to converse with me. I was not imaging it. However, no one appeared, and after a few short moments I uttered an apprehensive, "Hello?"

"Hello to you as well, Mr. Miller. I trust that your first night here at Belmeade was pleasurable?" His voice was less than sympathetic and even far less concerned. It was no doubt prison procedure that the niceties be acknowledged.

Still bewildered as to why this gentleman was hiding himself from me, I replied with a simple, "Fine, thank you."

"Superb," he said dryly. "Allow me to introduce myself; I am Thomas C. Symond, the Governor of this institution. At this time, I would like to take a few moments to familiarize you with the rules and regulations which you are expected to abide by whilst you are here."

The Governor embarked on a long, monotonous and what I am sure to be a well rehearsed speech. Lights out every night at ten o'clock; no exceptions, five minute showers were permitted every four days, three meals would be provided to me each day and I would be granted leisure time only if I earn it through good behaviour. Fighting with his staff or other inmates would land me in solitary and any contraband found in my cell during random inspections would lead to discipline and/or a lengthier sentence.

"So, that about sums it up. I trust you comprehend the policies and procedures I have set before you?" the Governor inquired.

"Yes, Sir. I understand," I responded dully. This was a high security prison, not an amusement park. I had expected nothing less than the most stringent of rules.

"Very good, Mr. Miller. I hope that your stay here is enjoyable. Please feel free to take advantage of our inmate education program. I am confident you will find it rewarding. Good day to you."

His footsteps dissipated as quickly as they had arrived, and before I could get a look at him, he was a mere shadow at the end of the corridor. I saw the outline of his figure: tall and lean. He was walking swiftly and carried himself with substance. I knew he was not a man to cross.

Later that afternoon, I was removed from my chamber and shepherded down three flights of stairs and into an underground hideaway; the entrance to the tunnel linking Belmeade to Woodbridge Crown Court. It was long and narrow, smelled of moss and was faintly lit by miniature electric torches. The soft orange glow accompanied by the echoing of our footsteps gave the place a feeling of approaching doom. Myself, as well as two armed guards, trudged down the path for what seemed to be an eternity. The shackles and chains made it difficult for me to walk at a fast pace, each step was slow and calculated so I would not trip. The loud thud-clang of my restraints was almost maddening. When we started to ascend, relief swept over me.

At the top of the stairs, one of the guards knocked gingerly upon a steel door. A small window was framed into it and within seconds, a wizened old face peered cautiously back at us. He blinked nonchalantly, but did not move.

"We are accompanying this prisoner to his arraignment at four o'clock, Reginald," the guard to my right said.

Reginald gave him an approving nod and disappeared. We stood in stillness for a moment. The guards seemed unaffected by Reginald's absence, I on the other hand, was quite perplexed. Suddenly, the door swung open on its own accord and I was steered through it. I peered around; another corridor. To my left was a second entrance. A huge windowpane permitted me to see inside the room. A desk, armchair, computer, telephone, refrigerator, sofa and microwave cluttered the small space. Reginald was sitting at the desk--apparently napping. I glanced over my shoulder at the door. It had closed itself and upon further inspection, I noticed a security panel and a series of unmarked buttons. The door must be linked to a timing device, which would explain why Reginald had disappeared.

We moved down the corridor as fast as my chained legs would allow and entered an elevator shaft. The heavy iron gates banged together noisily, once more, we were moving upwards.

I stepped out of the elevator into a magnificently ornamented foyer. The mosaic tile floor was breathtaking. The Venetian brown walls were covered in oil paintings, flags and replicas of our nation's independence documents.

"Do you have any idea which courtroom he is required to appear in, Daniels?" The guard who had spoken to Reginald was facing his co-worker.

"Number four," grunted Daniels. He was a beefy man who always bore the look of downright incomprehension upon his face. I was quite surprised he was capable of speech, let alone providing us with any useful information.

"Ah, Justice Evans," said Daniel's colleague to no one in particular.

Outside the huge oak courtroom doors, I was released from the guards' clutches and put into the custody of a bailiff. He directed me into the courtroom and pointed towards a table and chairs on the left side of the room; the defendant's sitting place. I walked up the aisle by myself and sat down in the chair nearest the window. To my right was the Crown's table. Both seats were already occupied by a pompous looking middle-aged man and an attractive, yet professional looking female. They gawked at me shamelessly for a few moments before placing their heads together, conversing in low whispers. Straight ahead of me was the justice's bench. It was beautifully handcrafted of mahogany and donned our nation's flag and a portrait of the Queen on the wall behind it. It wreaked of prestige; of high importance.

We were instructed by a representative of the court to rise out of respect for the Justice, the Court and the Queen. Justice Evans drifted out of his chamber and stepped onto the bench. He was a well matured man of approximately seventy years of age. His features were delicate, yet there was sternness to them brought about by his steel blue eyes. He looked at me; I could feel my soul being penetrated. The court representative informed us of why we were all congregated on this day. I was expected to enter my plea to the court and my possible terms of release, if any, were to be negotiated.

"Where is your counsel, Mr. Miller?" Justice Evans inquired. "You have been made aware that you are permitted to have an attorney present at these proceedings, have you not?" He glanced reproachfully in the direction of the Crown as though blaming them for the absence of my attorney.

"Yes, Your Honour, I am aware of my right to counsel, however, it is my wish to represent myself."

Confused, Justice Evans repeated, "Represent yourself, come again, Mr. Miller?" There was no hiding the look of shock on his face.

"Your Honour, if it would please the court, I would like to represent myself. I would like to enter a plea of guilty and I would also like to be held without bail and returned to Belmeade Prison."

This time there were gasps being omitted from the Crown followed by a hasty,

"We will accept this plea and respect the defendant's wishes to return to Belmeade, Your Honour." Wide smirks were etched on both the Crown's faces. It was clear I had made their job easy. Justice Evans, however, was not smirking; more like frowning disdainfully.

He held up his hand to silence the buzz that had filled the courtroom and peered at me as though I were a piece of artwork. He was trying to figure me out; attempting how to best handle me and my situation. After several minutes of restless silence, Justice Evans spoke.

"Mr. Miller, I strongly advise you to contact an attorney to aid you with these proceedings. Generally a defendant does not just waltz into my court and plead guilty. Nor does a defendant ask to be held without bail. If it is not feasible for you to hire counsel, this court will gladly provide you with someone who is capable of assisting you. Since it is imperative that we enter your plea and make bail arrangements today, I will accept a plea of not guilty and I will accommodate you by allowing you to return to Belmeade prison. Are you in agreement with this, Mr. Miller?"

"I suppose so, Your Honour," I said resentfully.

Justice Evans turned towards the Crown; "Mr. Jenkins, is the Crown satisfied with this as well?"

Slightly crestfallen, Jenkins gave a feeble nod and said, "Yes, Your Honour we are."

"So be it. Mr. Miller, I have entered your plea of not guilty and I am instructing the bailiff to have you released back into the custody of the guards who serve Belmeade Prison. I am also going to have my clerk allocate you counsel. Furthermore, I would like a full psychiatric evaluation performed on you as well. Adjourned."

I was immediately escorted out of the courtroom by the bailiff, relinquished to the guards and lead back to the prison.

....

An attorney came to see me shortly after I arrived at the prison. Barrister was a more appropriate term to describe him. There was an air of arrogance to him: he carried himself in such a conceited manner. When he spoke it was with an unctuous, yet condescending tone. MacLeod was his name, and he was an Eaton graduate. He stood before me in his tailored navy suit, handmade Italian leather shoes, a Rolex upon his right wrist. It was clear he thought he walked on water. I instantly had distaste for him.

He said he had been appointed by the court to aid in my defence.

"What defence?" I had asked him.

I did not wish to participate in a trial I told him. I *was* guilty. *I* committed those acts and *I* was prepared to face *my* fate. I asked him if he could arrange for me to receive the needle as soon as practical. He informed me that under English law, I am presumed innocent until proven guilty and that I must stand trial and be convicted of a crime prior to being sentenced. Even then, there was no guarantee that I would receive the death penalty, as a separate hearing was necessary to determine how severely I would be punished. I told him that I wished to waive my right to a trial. I would plead nolo contendere, as there would be no need to refute any of the evidence against me. We could skip that step and go straight to sentencing, I said. Again, he said that this could not occur. I *must* stand trial.

He droned on for some time about my case. He was going to utilize the insanity defence. I informed him on more than one occasion that I was not insane, yet he was adamant I was. He told me that I would be evaluated by the Crown's psychiatrist, and once the prosecuting attorney heard my story, they would instantly release me to a mental hospital where I would receive treatment for my illness. Again, I informed him that I was not insane, but he would just not listen.

He put on his coat, collected his paperwork and smiled at me. "No one wants to admit they are sick Wilhelm," he said placing his papers into his briefcase before fastening it shut. "We will get you the treatment you need. Leave everything to me. For now, just concentrate on preparing for tomorrow's psychiatric evaluation."

I was thankful when he left my cell. We had gotten off to a rather rocky start as he clearly did not understand my needs. I made a mental note to convey my wishes more plainly to him at our next meeting.

Chapter 23

Psychiatric Ward
HM Belmeade Prison, England
17 September, 2001
1:30 p.m.

"Tell me about your life Wilhelm," she said.

Her voice was soft and full of concern—almost mother like. With great effort, I lifted my head to look at her. My heart skipped several beats, my breath became short. She was young; no more than thirty, virtuous and pious-like. I knew instantly that I had to be in the presence of divinity.

Am I in Heaven? Surely I must be, for I have never seen such beauty before. Almond shaped hazel eyes, radiant waist-length auburn curls: this must be what angels look like. I gazed absently into her eyes, her warm smile was comforting. I felt at peace. If this was death, it wasn't so bad after all. I became completely consumed by her aura, as though I were under her sovereignty. And for the first time in my life, I spoke of my past...

"My mother died of Leukaemia when I was seven and a half. My father was an abusive alcoholic whom I rarely saw. I grew up on the south coast of England, in East Sussex, a small fishing town called Rye. My mother ran a floral shop. She used to let me help her arrange bouquets every day after school. She loved tulips. Red ones were her favourite. She always had a freshly cut one stuck into the pocket of her apron. I try not to think of her too much, just her eyes. She had striking blue eyes. I could get lost in them for hours. She was a beautiful soul and I loved her dearly. Her kind face bore signs of her burden and of a life spun full of hardship. We didn't have much. All my life she had to fight for everything we had, and she kept fighting up until the very end. She was a strong person, but her illness took its toll. On August twenty-forth, nineteen sixty-six, her suffering ended and she left this world.

My father fancied himself a fisherman. My mother and I knew better. All he did was drown himself in the bottle, and spent my mother's hard earned money on scotch and prostitutes. When he *did* manage to go to work, he would waste the day away down at Jack's Pub, where he would tell old war stories and drink himself into a comatose state. I can recall countless times when his fishing buddies would drop him off on our doorstep: passed out, smelling like a distillery and stale tobacco. My mother and I would drag him into the house, get him cleaned up and wait for the alcohol to wear off. He was always at his worst when he was coming back down. The lack of "sauce" in his system made him violent, and we were always subject to beatings whenever he was sober. I liked him best when he was drunk. He would disappear for days at a time, sometimes weeks. Personally, I always hoped he would disappear permanently, but like a stray, he always found his way back to our front doorstep sooner or later.

During my father's periods of absence, my mother and I would relish the peace and bask in one another's company. Her one true passion was gardening, so we spent most of our time in the little six-by-six wooden paddock she built in our back yard, tending to her tulips, working the soil, and weeding the beds. The time spent with her in her "Earthly Heaven," as she called it, were the happiest times of my life—I would not trade a single moment. When I reflect back on those times now, I can't help but feel guilty for not opening up to her more. We never really said too much to each other. We didn't have to. Both my mother and I knew how much we loved one another, and we both understood that simply being in each other's presence was good enough. Thus, words were not necessary to solidify our bond. She was truly an angel, a gift from God.

By the time she died, she weighed eighty-two pounds and was completely bed ridden. We couldn't afford medical treatment, so she just wasted away. I remember coming home from school to find my father passed out and my mother lying in a pool of her own vomit and sweat. She suffered greatly, and I will forever despise my father for not helping her. He just disappeared. He showed no signs of concern for her decaying health, and gave her not one ounce of love. The last few days of her life, she did nothing but beg the Lord to take her. My father did nothing but get drunk and fraternize with the whore who lived three doors down. She died alone in her bedroom, while my father was deep inside Angelina the prostitute. He later said that was his way of coping.

My mother knew her death was coming, so she sent me to Vera's Bakery to buy a loaf of bread. I pleaded with her to let me stay—she needed me. She needed to know that she wasn't alone, I was with her—the Lord was with her. But she sent me away, and when I returned, I found her. I sat with her for hours; I didn't want to let her go. She was my heart. She was the only person who ever loved me. I foolishly clung to a small ray of hope that God would bestow a miracle upon me and wake her, although I knew she was never coming back. She taught me many things, among which the terms of life and death.

"You will one day die, Wilhelm," she had said. "In fact, the moment you were born, your physical being began to diminish. But do not worry; it is your soul that is of greater importance, for it will live on forever."

Years later, when I finally permitted myself to reflect back upon her death, I recalled how peaceful she looked. Her face was youth-like, with no traces of her sickness, and there was not a single agonizing burden left upon it. She looked angelic, content even. And although it still pains me to go through life without her, I know that she is truly at rest, and that I will one day see her again."

I fell silent. I had said too much. I have never spoken of my past before; I had vowed not to. It meant nothing to me. The only thing of any importance, the only thing worth remembering, *was* my mother. So for years, I forced myself to believe that I *had* no past. I repressed any memory of my father, savoured the sweet memories of my mother, and tossed everything else out like a piece of trash. What was I doing telling a stranger about my life? Who was she to ask me? What did she care? I became defiant. I was no longer going to speak with this woman. Goddess-like or not, I could not allow her in. I could not allow myself to share the hatred I've held for so long. I gazed at the white wall in front of me, my eyes fixed upon a discoloured spot.

Close your mind, I kept telling myself. *Do not let her in. This is nothing. Your past doesn't exist. Stay resilient.*

"After your mother passed away, what did you do? You were still quite young, did your father take a more active role in your upbringing?"

Her voice was so soothing, yet I kept averting her eyes. I had to...The minutes ticked by. I remained silent. Every now and then I would steal a glance her way. I found myself wondering what her name was. I was certain it was just as beautiful as she...

"Wilhelm, please," she said. She softly touched my right arm. Her skin was smooth, her touch gentle and warming. I felt comforted. I felt loved. I felt...my mother. Maybe this is what she meant when she said our souls live on forever...

I had to know. "What is your name?" I asked her. She hesitated, and for a moment I thought she may not answer.

"My name is Doctor Alexandra Tulpen-Grake."

Tulpen? "Dutch for *tulips*," I whispered in horror.

She smiled at me, her hazel eyes were dancing, as though full of life. Once again, I became subdued and obliged her...

"After my mother died, my father became nonexistent. He was still living, but he meant nothing to me. I hardened myself beyond giving a damn about him. I was angry, I was bitter, I was spiteful and many a times, I wished he'd just drink himself into his own grave. We had no relationship, although there were times when he tried fruitlessly to get close to me. I hated him. He abandoned me and my dying mother, and for what? A few minutes of euphoric pleasure with a whore? A forty of scotch and his lowlife alcoholic friends? He was never there for us. I didn't need him while my mother was alive, and I sure as Hell didn't need him after she died. He was a pathetic excuse of a parent. I guess one could say he was my father; I could never have another, but that was as far as it went. He was still prone to periods of absence, so I raised myself. Necessities like food, clothing and shelter didn't mean anything to him, so by the time I was nine, I had my first part time job. I worked gutting fish for an old Nazi down at the boat docks. I made twenty dollars a week, which in my opinion, should have been tripled. I never complained though, I had to eat.

I grew up fast: my youth was stripped away from me. When all the other children were fishing and playing football, you know, all the normal things that ten year olds should be doing, I was watching jealously from my work station. My heart ached for a family, for some sort of normalcy. But sadly, my requests went unanswered and I was left completely alone. Well not completely alone, I should say. There was an old woman who worked down at the public library who would talk to me. She had a couple of grandsons that were my age, so she would sometimes give me their old clothes and comic books. I was thankful for anything I ever got. I needed it, and when you have nothing to begin with, you come to cherish and appreciate anything that is given to you despite what state it may be in. I'm not sure what happened to her. I moved away from Rye when I was fifteen.

The old man finally died in nineteen seventy-four, October the third if my memory serves me. He was found face down in a ravine a couple miles outside of town: two empty bottles of single malt scotch and an old fishing rod and reel lying nearby. When I heard the news, it was like hearing of the death of a stranger. I didn't care. I just remember packing my clothes and a few items that belonged to my mother into duffel bags and leaving. I didn't know where I was going, but I knew I'd never return to Rye.

I floated around for a number of years. I lived in a youth hostel in Luxemburg, Germany for approximately sixteen months. I always loved the smell of freshly baked bread, so I ended up working in a bakery for a while. Due to monetary reasons, I was forced to move on. I lived in Paris for about three months. I didn't speak the language and found it very difficult to adjust. I moved to Trieste, Italy when I was twenty-two. I found employment working on the Rivabahn, a transalpine railway which facilitated freight traffic around the city's port.

From there, I travelled to Budapest, Hungary. It was known as the "Capital of Freedom." How quite the contrary. With the Soviet military's presence, it was anything but a happy place to be. I saw many wicked things. People feared their government. They were forced into showing loyalty, or be subject to political terror and police brutality. The standard of living was low: farm animals had better living conditions then seventy-five percent of Budapest's residents. Slums were put on a pedestal. Needless to say, I didn't stay there very long.

In nineteen eighty-three, I found myself hopping off a train in Naestved, Denmark. My mother always spoke of Gavno Castle, an establishment known predominantly for its vast collection of artwork and endless gardens of tulips. I got a position maintaining the Castle's one thousand, two hundred acres of agriculture. I had a small flat where I lived a simple, yet fulfilling life. I convinced myself that this very well could be the place for me, so I began to socialize within the community. I took Danish lessons every Tuesday and Thursday from a man whose wife I worked with. I even met a young German woman whom I allowed myself to get close to. Claudia was her name. We spent two glorious years together; completely in love, oblivious to the world around us, and to the people in it. Or so I thought. I came home from work one sunny May afternoon to find a note lying upon my pillow. She had left me. Just picked up and left me. She gave me nothing but excuses for her behaviour, no explanation of any kind. From that day on, Naestved didn't seem like the place for me. So yet again, I took another train.

This time I ended up in London. I will never forget the cold December day when I stepped foot off the train. I stopped dead in my tracks. It was as if I had walked into a brick wall. It wasn't the weather which immobilized me, but the people. The air was full of arrogance, unfriendliness, and I had a sinking feeling this place was no good for me. Yet something made me stay. To this day, I'm still not sure what drew me in. But for whatever reason, London was my home for the next eight years.

I wandered the streets for what seemed a lifetime. The architecture and parks were breathtaking, not to mention plentiful. I spent my first week touring monuments and visiting various parks and gardens. I found a flat in the south of the city on Cannon Street. I acquired a janitorial position with the London Underground. I did all the up keep at the Mansion House Tube Station from nineteen eighty-six to eighty-nine, at which time it was shut down temporarily due to reconstruction. From there, I went to work as a busboy for Michael's Restaurant down on the north end of King William Street. The job didn't pay very well, and how quickly I found myself falling further and further behind.

By mid nineteen eighty-nine, I had been evicted from my flat on Cannon Street along with the place I had rented on Gracechurch Avenue. I didn't have two pounds to my name. I held up in a shelter near St. James for a while, still working at Michael's, but my situation wasn't getting any better. I lost my job in nineteen ninety. Michael's moved to a new location in the ritziest part of the city, at which time I was informed by my manager that they no longer had a position for me. Completely broke, I shuffled from business to business seeking any kind of work I could get. Nothing ever panned out. And in March, when the doors to the shelter were bolted shut, I found myself standing on its doorstep dumbfounded with no place to go. Countless others were in my position as well. Penniless, hungry and cold, I took to the streets and that is where I lived—if you can call it living, for the next four years."

I talked for hours. Two turned into three, three turned into four, then five. Alexandra wanted to know every single intimate detail about my life. Where were you born? What was your childhood like? What was your family like? Do you have any siblings? How did you cope with the loss of your mother? Do you still have ill feelings for your father? What was it like to travel the world? How did you feel when Claudia left? What was life on the streets like? She even asked about my mission. What made you do it? Did I regret what I had done? She asked me dozens upon dozens of questions, but I did not mind sharing my life with her. She seemed truly fascinated by me, and I could have sat in that room with her for an eternity.

Chapter 24

Governor Thomas C. Symond's Office
HM Belmeade Prison, England
17 September, 2001
7:15 p.m.

"After nearly six hours of conversation, what have you concluded, Dr. Grake?" The Governor's voice was abrasive and highly authoritative.

"He is not crazy, if that is what you are asking, Governor."

"Then *what* exactly is he, Dr. Grake? Wilhelm Miller has confessed to murdering no less than thirty-four people. He strolled into Scotland Yard and professed this in front of seven inspectors and a dozen civilians. He has described these murders with utmost intimacy... Crazy cannot even begin to hold a candle to what he is."

"Wilhelm Miller knew precisely what he was doing, Governor. He relentlessly pursued and studied his victims, as an animal would its prey. He adapted to their lifestyles and cultures. He learned new languages; he infiltrated their lives. This man is nothing less than a genius. He may very well be one of the greatest masterminds this country has seen this century."

"Be that as it may, Dr. Grake, which I highly doubt it is, he is not an idol. He is not someone that should be looked upon with reverence. Miller will not be put on a podium for all to worship. He is worse than scum and he, like others before him who have committed murder, will face the needle. I assure you, Dr. Grake, Wilhelm Miller has done not one ounce of good for this world. And when he is burning within the gates of Hell for his sinful acts, not one living soul will be praising him!"

"Sir, I was not implying that what he did was right. I was merely giving you my op—"

"Dr. Grake, I do not care to hear your opinion on this matter. You are not paid by our government to give your opinion on whether or not Miller's acts are justifiable. You are paid to determine his mental state and you are paid to determine if he has the capacity to adequately aid his attorney with his trial. So with that being said, does Miller have the mental capacity to stand trial, and furthermore, does he have the legal capacity to aid in his own defence?"

"Yes, Sir, he does."

"Thank you, Dr. Grake. I will notify Justice Evans straightaway. That will be all. Please shut the door on your way out."

....

Barrister was back. This time he had two other nitwits in tow. I sat dispassionately in my cell, listening to his fervent-like tones buzz on and on about my upcoming trial. He was very unhappy with Alexandra's psychiatric evaluation, and he said that I would be evaluated once more by a doctor whom he had hired.

"This is to ensure we get a favourable determination of your mental state," he had said. He was convinced he could have me sent away to a psychiatric institution based upon the grounds that I have a severe mental defect.

"Wilhelm, you are sick. And the law says that someone who is determined to be mentally unstable cannot be sentenced to prison or be put to death because they do not have the capacity to understand the seriousness of what they have done."

I merely sighed. *This guy just didn't get it.* I turned my head to look at him. He was so mediocre; sitting in his chair like an anxious schoolboy anticipating recess. For someone who was supposed to be properly educated from Eaton, he was rather dim. Countless times I had told him that I did not wish to be tried under the insanity defence. I wanted to scream "I AM GUILTY, YOU BASTARD! STOP TRYING TO SAVE ME!" All I wanted was to leave this world, to be reunited with my Creator and to see my mother again. Why wouldn't this idiot necessitate me? I did not wish to be sent to St. Andrew's Hospital or the Stone House Institution. I was not a lunatic. I did not need to be locked away for the rest of my life in some derisory asylum; to spend the rest of my days playing with children's toys and keeping company with fools and crazies.

I wanted to die. I wanted to feel the needle being pushed into my veins. I longed for the afterlife. Finally, after two hours of agony, the Barrister grew tired and left my cell, but it was not without informing me that I was due to appear before Justice Evans and his court the following morning at nine.

"Mr. Miller, you do realize the repercussions of what may occur should I grant your wish, thus permitting you to remain at Belmeade for the duration of your trial?" His steel blue eyes were full of apprehension, yet his voice was stern and quizzical. "It is your legal right to be present at your own trial, to aid your attorney with your defence. I strongly recommend you to renounce what you have just asked of me."

I drew myself up to full height and bore directly into his eyes. "Your Honour, I have a full understanding of what I have just asked of you. I do not wish to be present during these proceedings. I am confident my attorney can adequately handle my defence whilst I am absent. I wish to remain in Belmeade Prison."

"Your Honour, if I may speak," the Barrister said. "My client is not mentally capable of determining what is best for himself, or his defence. I beg you not to take a word he has spoken for more than face value. Regardless of what he has just told you, he truly does not understand what he is asking of you."

"Counsellor, I have been a part of this country's judicial system for more than forty-five years. I have seen and heard many things. Your client is not the first person, nor will he be the last, to make a request such as this one. Now, it is my belief that Mr. Miller *does* have an awareness of how detrimental his absence from these proceedings may be. I cannot deny him his right to stand trial, nor can I deny him his right to not attend his own trial. Counsellor, your client has put his faith in you. He is certain you are competent enough to defend him sufficiently; therefore, I must also put my confidence in you. Mr. Miller, you will be returned to Belmeade, where you will stay throughout the remainder of these proceedings."

Trying to contain my excitement, "Thank you very much, Your Honour," I said.

I was elated, grateful to be permitted to stay in my cell. The Barrister, however, looked livid.

"Your Honour," he began, "I would like it to be noted that I do not support my client's decision to not be present during his own trial." He glanced at me: his eyes were full of distaste.

"So noted, Counsellor. Proceedings will commence on Monday the twenty-sixth of September at nine o'clock in the morning. I trust both the Crown and the Defence will be prepared. Dismissed."

With that, everyone rose. Justice Evans swept down from the bench and floated through a door on his right into his chamber. I was shackled and removed from the courtroom. The Barrister was barking orders at the same two idiots who visited me in my cell. They had not spoken a word as of yet, and I could not help but wonder what exactly their purpose in this trial was going to be. Probably just lapdogs. The Barrister ran the show. It was quite obvious; for he was not going to allow anyone to steal an ounce of his thunder. I chuckled slightly to myself, *thunder*. If he only had the wits to begin with...

I did not see the Barrister again until mid October. Things were not going as well he had hoped. The prosecuting attorney, Edward Jenkins, had done a stupendous job of painting me out to be a homicidal maniac, and had made a fool of Barrister's star defensive witness; the psychiatrist. It turned out that the good doctor forgot to renew his license here in England, so his testimony in its entirety was thrown out by Justice Evans immediately after the discovery had been made. The jury was only permitted to take into account Alexandra's testimony, which amounted to that I knew exactly what I was doing, and that I showed no remorse for killing those people. *Perfect.* I only hoped that the juror's minds were not too polluted by *our* doctor's statements.

He spent half of our meeting trying to convince me to take the stand.

"Let the jury know the real you."

I wasn't going to fall for that. He simply wanted to parade me around and showcase me as a certified psycho. That was not going to happen, and after threatening to terminate him on more than one occasion that afternoon, he got the hint and begrudgingly moved onto the next topic.

"Good news," he said. Since there was no evidence against me, other than my signed confession and a few intimate details of the murders, he was going to try a new platform. He said he was going to attempt to have my confession thrown out because the detectives at Scotland Yard did not follow protocol one hundred percent. They should have allowed me to have counsel present when they questioned me. As for the details, he would now be arguing that I read about the murders in the newspaper and on the internet, thus permitting me to know many things about the victims. All of which were hearsay, information accessible to the public and I was now only "slightly crazy." What a joke this guy was. Justice Evans was right about one thing; I did have confidence in him. Not the confidence to acquit me, but the confidence to mess everything up and have me sentenced to death.

He kept asking me why I was in such a great mood. I informed him that I was extremely happy with the way he was handling my defence, and that I had faith in him. Smiling like a giddy child, he collected up his documents, placed them in his briefcase, and snapping it shut said, "That's the spirit. See you next week."

He bustled out of my cell, prancing ever so slightly and whistling all the way down the corridor. I relaxed back on my cot, eyes closed, arms folded behind my head. *That's the spirit, indeed,* I thought to myself before blissfully drifting off to sleep.

Over the course of the next few weeks, I sat in my cell reading Poe and sifting through mounds of mail. I had developed a fan base of sorts; mostly young men and woman who were political activists. They thought that what I did was heroic; some of these people literally worshiped the ground I walked on. I even had one gentleman ask if he could write an autobiography detailing my life and times. Never before had I seen such vast support. It was humbling. Finally, I felt as though I was someone my mother could be proud of. All these people kept thanking me, telling me that I had done a great thing for mankind. My fruitless labours would be forever cherished and recognized. I was elated.

Of course, not everyone who wrote to me was pleasant. I also received a large portion of hate mail, mostly do-gooders and Christians who simply told me that I would burn for my sins.

"God will reject you, Wilhelm Miller. He will reject you and you will rot in the fiery depths of Hell where you so belong." This particular piece of literature made me smile. Hell was the last place I would be going. God would not punish me. Obviously, this person did not understand my sacrifice for humanity. Her ignorance must be her bliss.

I continued to read well into the night. As it was, I had nothing better to do and the letters served as company. No one other than the Barrister had been to see me and I only caught a glimpse of the guards who brought me my meals. The letters were human-like to me. I had stacked my favourites on my night table and I reread them until I could recite every word verbatim. I tried to imagine the person behind the pen.

One letter I received was from a woman who called herself Olivia and claimed she resided in Yarmouth. She said she admired me and applauded my efforts. She also said that she one day hoped to have the courage that I had to stand up to our government. It was odd reading her letter the second time. At first, I thought nothing of it. She seemed like a sweet woman. Probably in her early to late twenties, uncertain what she wanted to do with her life, but smart enough to know that the government would always have control over it. As my eyes swept over the text and my mind soaked up what she had written, I felt a strange sense of connection to her. I was unclear as to why this may be. She was a stranger, someone I would never meet. I brushed it off on the outside, but on the inside, she lingered.

Chapter 25

Cellblock E5
HM Belmeade Prison, England
19 November, 2001
4:45 p.m.

"Congratulations. You got your wish, Wilhelm."

I peered groggily through the bars of my cell. I had been napping off and on all afternoon. The Barrister was standing before me, tired and dishevelled, unable to stand without the aid of the cell bars.

"My wish?" I asked him sitting up enthusiastically. His statement had peeked my interest.

"Your wish to die. You were found guilty on all thirty-four counts of murder. The jury voted unanimously for the death penalty. Your execution is scheduled to take place on January the nineteenth, two thousand seven at 12:01 in the morning. I trust you won't need me to appeal the verdict?"

There was a hint of sarcasm in his voice. He looked at me with his tired eyes. I shook my head, *no*. He smiled weakly before walking away, his footsteps thudding behind him.

"Thank you, Mr. MacLeod," I said aloud. He had succeeded. Although he did not get the outcome he had gallantly hoped for, I could not have been happier.

....

The next six years went by quietly. I was moved to Belmeade's death row unit a mere forty-eight hours after the verdict was reached. It was a small, dingy place, but I didn't mind it. I could actually see the inmate in the cell across the corridor from me. It was a nice feeling. I kept my letters, they comforted me. I received three meals a day and was permitted thirty minutes of outdoor leisure time each day as well. I was very grateful for this. I missed being outdoors: the trees, the flowers, the sounds of people, automobiles and birds. One develops true appreciation for these simple things when they no longer are privy to them. I missed these things most of all.

On December the nineteenth, a guard approached my cell and informed me that I had a visitor. He opened the doors, shackled me and proceeded to lead me into the visitation room. He grunted and pointed towards a table at the back of the room. A young woman with short blond hair sat patiently staring at the clock on the wall, tapping her fingers lightly on the table. I hesitated, but eventually made my way over to her.

She stood up when she saw me. She was tall and slender and her face was heart-shaped. She wore sun glasses. I found this to be very odd as it was the middle of December and the room was dimly lit to begin with. She smiled at me and pointed to the chair across from her. I pulled the chair out and sat down, still very confused as to whom this woman was and why she was here. We sat in silence for a moment before she finally spoke in hushed tones.

"My name is Olivia."

My eyes grew wide. Surely I had heard her incorrectly. This was the Olivia who had written me the letter? It couldn't be. I was speechless. I imagined I looked like a deer caught in headlights to her. All I could do was sit there, paralyzed.

"I had to see you," she said. She was still whispering, but there was something about her voice that was familiar to me; very kind and exceptionally warm. I sat frozen in my chair, unable to speak.

"Wilhelm, I want you to know that I have nothing but the deepest and utmost genuine admiration for you. What you did for this country—for this world, was nothing shy of greatness. You have truly saved us all. In a world of cosmic political warfare and intense governmental control, you stepped up, a lone man, and did something to make this place better for the rest of us. I am truly thankful, as will be the rest of society when they see the good which has become of your acts."

She stood up as if to leave, I rose as well, but she did not move. She stretched out her arm and grasped my right hand. I instantly felt calmed...loved. I whispered the single word, "Alexandra."

She lowered her sun glasses. Beneath them I saw those unmistakable almond-shaped hazel eyes. She quickly pushed her glasses back up.

"It was you." I gasped. "You were on Schultz Avenue that night and you were in Greece. It *has* been you this entire time. Hasn't––hasn't it? But why?"

Alexandra smiled at me, and squeezed my hand gently before releasing it. I watched in wonderment as she floated towards the exit. She *was* truly divine.

I was taken back to my cell, still in awe of the events that had just occurred, but jubilant, nonetheless. I curled up onto my cot; Alexandra's face swam in my mind. It comforted me as I allowed myself to drift into the most peaceful of sleeps.

Chapter 26

Death Row
HM Belmeade Prison, England
18 January, 2007
11:00pm

When you are confined to a dark, dank cell with no company and no luxuries to speak of, it is quite peculiar how ones' senses take over. You acquire the ability to hear things you have never heard before, smell things you have never smelt before. The stench of death is almost overpowering in the Belmeade Prison Death Row Unit. It is a rotting scent, but when mingled with fear, it is almost sweet. This smell constantly fills my nostrils.

Many of the inmates here are not ready to expire. I, on the other hand, am fully prepared to die. I am at peace with myself and I am ready for the Lord to take me. I sit in my damp, mouldy iron box listening to the sounds of my fellow inmates. Their pleas are deafening, and how I wish they would come to accept their end. They sit day after day in their pitiful chambers gorging on the fantasy that their case will be overturned or a miracle from above will be bestowed upon them. Clinging to these small rays of hope has caused many of these men to lose their minds. Some have been here for over twenty years; rotting inside the decaying walls which surround them. They are only alive because their shrewd attorneys manage to obtain continuances and stays of executions, thus prolonging the inevitable.

I despise them for this. They need to acknowledge their fate as I have acknowledged mine. The few men who have embraced their death sit quietly awaiting; further decomposing as their dates have already been set in stone. Others who fear the needle sit smoking like chimneys, hoping to die of lung cancer and can be heard wailing like children, repenting to the Lord with full vocals. Praying will not help them. God cannot save the wicked, but I do not have the heart to tell them this. They have been filled with evil for so long that there is not one ounce of good in them. They will go to Hell.

My last meal was fit for a king. I feasted upon prime rib, herb roasted potatoes, steamed vegetables, warm butter rolls and a single glass of Denbies Red Wine dated 1966 —the year my mother died. I sat waiting for the guards, overcome with the most euphoric sense of calm. Not even my rapidly approaching death could have tarnished this moment. While slowly sipping the Denbies, I reflected upon my life for what seemed an eternity. My thoughts strayed to my mother. I found myself wondering if she would be where I am going. I would very much like to see her again...My mind swelled with her image: long, flowing brown hair, crystal blue eyes, her soft warm smile...such a wonderful, astonishing, loving woman, who did not deserve her fate. She did everything she could to ensure I would have a "glorious" future full of hope, dreams, family and friends. If she could only see me now. I wonder if she would be proud. Would she have understood why I have chosen this path?

My meal ended at precisely eleven thirty. The guards came for me shortly thereafter. With one last look around my feeble cell, I dimly thought, *I'm going to miss this place.* It had become a home of sorts, a shelter from the storm. It was dismal, chilly, and musty, but it served its purpose and I was indebted to have a solid roof over my head. For so long I had lived like an animal, exposed to the elements, using twigs and tatty newspapers for shelter. This place may not have been much, but it was most pleasurable to spend my remaining days in a dry place.

With my head held high, I was escorted down a long, narrow hallway, past my fellow inmates. I was permitted to make this walk without shackles or chains; almost as though I were a free man. My footsteps echoed behind me. I could not help but smile, for each step I took brought me closer to the end. This elated me.

"You have exactly five minutes," said a gruff voice into my right ear.

I turned slightly to find the guard on my right pointing to a door which was slightly ajar. Where a nameplate should have been, there was a cross engraved. This was unquestionably the prayer room. I stared at the door for a moment, the feeling of trepidation had come over me. I hesitated a few more seconds before finally stepping into the candlelit room.

Immediately I was engulfed in warmth and I could feel the powers of God flowing through my body. It was a calming and comforting feeling. I was wholly at peace with myself. I gazed up at the photo of Christ, dropped to my knees and began to pray...

I did not take notice of the Priest who was standing a mere five feet away from me until he spoke. His voice was soft and soothing.

"Repentance is the key into the Lord's Kingdom, my son. For only the deepest atonement will save you from the horrible fate which you face. You must repent and continue to repent, for only then will your sins be washed away."

I ignored him. He knew nothing of my relationship with Christ. I was most thankful when I heard a stern knock on the door behind me.

The guards were back; my time had expired. They led me down two flights of stairs and along another narrow hallway before finally stopping in front of a second door. I knew instantly that I had arrived at the entrance to the execution chamber. Behind this door, my fate awaited me.

Chapter 27

The Execution Chamber
HM Belmeade Prison, England
18 January, 2007
11:50 p.m.

The execution chamber was a meagre thirty by thirty foot space nestled in the back of the prison, out of the general public's eye. The concrete floor and walls were about as welcoming as the plague. Damp, dingy, and bitterly cold, the room had a morgue-like feel to it; death becoming. As I stepped over the threshold leading into the dimly lit room, I felt the unmistakable feeling of anxiety. Surely not I; for years I have been preparing to leave this world. This moment was the only thing which sustained me these past thirteen years. It was all I dreamt about. I relished the day when I was to be reunited with my Creator, to worship Him and to become one of His eternal children. A lifetime with Christ, what was I to be afraid of? I then realized that it was not death, but my meeting with the Lord which terrified me. Suddenly, I felt like a child on my first day of school: nervous, yet full of excitement. What if the Lord did not find my work to be satisfactory and condemned me to a life in Hell? This painstaking thought swelled inside me. I knew subconsciously that I was being foolish. How could I be denied by the Almighty? My work was done. I had succeeded in securing mankind's future, and I did it in the name of God and all His people. In just a few short minutes, I would be welcomed into the Kingdom of Heaven with open arms.

Once inside the room, I looked to my left to find two men dressed in white smocks standing at attention: executioners. Both were middle-aged and bore the classic signs of men who had been doing this job a long time. Stern faced, narrow eyed and straight backed, I knew the instant I saw them that it would be they who stuck the needle in my arm. The eldest of the two, a tall, thin, balding man with wire-rimmed glasses shifted a few feet to the right. Upon doing this, my eyes became focused on a medicine cabinet directly in front of me. The cabinet's dingy shelves were stocked full of numerous bottles of which I knew would aid in my death. The guard on my right shifted awkwardly causing his keys to clatter softly, as though to announce their presence. The second man, gray haired, stone faced and slightly shorter than his colleague—but just as austere—turned toward me. His piercing hazel eyes swept over me, as though sizing me up, as a beast would its prey. I returned his gaze and for a moment we lingered, our eyes transfixed upon one another. It felt as though time had stopped. For an instant, I stood frozen, completely thoughtless and oblivious to my surroundings. Not until I felt a hard jerk on my right elbow was I awoken. The guard whose keys had jangled was now directing me towards the far corner of the room. I shuffled my feet allowing him and the second guard to steer me. They pushed me into a wobbly old chair, perhaps using more force than necessary. I glanced at the clock on the wall above the door. It read 11:54 p.m. Not long now...

Upon further inspection of the room, I noticed a thick, black velvet curtain hanging on the wall to my left and a makeshift stretcher with worn leather straps stationed against the wall to my right. The straps, I assumed, were to be used as a restraint. Next to the stretcher was an intervenes drip and a vital statistics machine. Overall, the room was very sparse. I vaguely thought to myself, *this is it?* As time ticked by, I became fascinated with the black curtain. Pondering what could be behind it, I stared aimlessly at it, my mind slipping in and out of consciousness. Caught up in my reverie, I did not notice a fifth gentlemen enter the room. But I smelt him; a sharp woody scent with a soft mixture of moss and citrus. As soon as the scent hit my nostrils, I knew who had entered the room. His cologne had almost smothered me when I first arrived here.

Governor Thomas C. Symond had changed very little over the years—if at all. A tall, fit and rather handsome man, the Governor ruled Belmeade Prison with an iron fist. Now in his mid sixties, he still had the air of a man who meant business. Firm and unsympathetic was his dictum. He feverishly followed all the rules and any misconduct in his prison would cause a man to meet his end sooner than expected. His lust for the justice system was sickening, as he felt more love for the law than he did for his own children.

I looked up at the Governor and became quickly consumed by his acute green eyes, prominent chin, square jaw and thin, expressionless lips: features I had been pondering over these last six years. He took several steps towards me, bent slightly at the waist and whispered the words, "It is time."

His voice was cold and shrewd as ever, but as I gazed into his eyes, I saw sadness in them. It was unlike the Governor to show this sort of emotion. For a brief moment his lips parted as though to speak, but no words came out. As though coming out of a trance, he hastily straightened himself up to full height, turned his heels and exited the room with his usual demeanour of importance.

The two guards pulled me to my feet and escorted me to the stretcher where the executioners were waiting. I was heaved up onto the mattress. Immediately my legs were tethered down with the heavy, thick leather straps. A second strap was thrust across my chest to completely immobilize my arms and upper torso. Thankfully, my wrists were left unbound. The guards left the room; the hurried sound of their boots mimicked my heart beat. I was elevated to a sitting position and my chest was exposed. Cold, clammy hands grasped my upper right arm and instantly I felt a needle piercing my veins. A second set of hands worked diligently equipping my body with electrocardiograph pads to detect my heart's electrical activity. These pads were then connected to the EKG monitor next to me. A second intravenous needle was inserted into my left arm. Whilst doing so, the older man smiled callously and said, "This is a backup line."

I simply nodded in acknowledgement. I had spent many hours reading up on lethal injection procedures and I knew what was to come. Next the drips would be started and a saline solution would be sent pulsing through my veins. This insures the drug mixture stays separated and does not block the needle. Sodium thiopental would then be inserted, sending me into a glorious unconsciousness. Tubocurarine, a muscle relaxant would follow, leaving me paralyzed. Lastly, potassium chloride, the most deadly of the three, was to be fed into the line. And with one final, painless breath, my heart would go into cardiac arrest and I will exit this world.

I heard a door shut behind me and the Governor's unmistakable voice instructing that I be brought to face the black curtain. The executioners obliged. I was quickly moved into the centre of the room. With a stiff nod and a glance at the clock, the Governor cleared his throat, turned toward the black curtain and spoke.

"Ladies and Gentlemen, you have been congregated here on this eighteenth day of January, two thousand seven, the year of our Lord, to bare witness to the execution of one Wilhelm Radulfus Miller. At this time, the condemned will be permitted to speak any final words. I will now remove the curtain."

With an effortless swish, the curtain was drawn back and the blank expressions of half a dozen men and women stared back at me. Their faces were unfamiliar to me: I was grateful for this.

"Mr. Miller you are now free to address the panel."

I drew one final confident breath, looked into the eyes of the panel and spoke the words I had been yearning to speak for so long...

"The streets of London are always blistering cold this time of year. Dark, damp, freezing and barren, they have an almost cruel-like way of consuming a person. If one can survive a winter there, they can survive anywhere. Each day and night that passes feels like a thousand years and it leaves a person hollow and dejected. Most people are driven mad during their first forty-eight hours on the street. They lose all sense of feeling and emotion. They become consumed with painful memories of their past lives, and more often then not, they are left to face their fears and demons alone.

There are over half a million people who call the streets of London their home: vagabonds, vagrants, hobos, junkies, rejects and prostitutes. They are mostly good people who have felt the wrath of an evil, Godless world. Down on their luck, they are simply looking for help; a friendly face and a hot meal. Ninety-five percent of these people will die whilst looking for this. They walk the streets not understanding why they are there; not understanding why no one will aid them. For they have been cast away by a society who thinks they are some form of mutated life—beast like, not worthy of their attention or concern. Passers-by forget that these people are still of man and they fear them as though they are an unspeakable, perfidious being; some sick, filthy animal whom cannot be trusted, whom deserves this fate.

I know these things because I was there. I have firsthand knowledge of what it is like to lose everything, to feel numb, to be treated like vermin. I know what it is like to be hungry, to have constant roaring pains, to be unclean and to have to fight for the makeshift shelter we squatters call home. Many nights I spent gazing up at the London sky wondering why God chose to punish me in such a merciless way. I can recall praying that it would all end and hoping that the Lord would take me away from what seemed a condemned life of misery. Death would have been better than this. But the Lord never came, and for many years I lived in a box, ate out of dumpsters, and drove myself to the brink of insanity with my idle thoughts of better times to come.

I got through the days and nights by dreaming of another place. I dreamt of a warm bed under a dry roof. Nothing fancy, just a small space to shelter me against Mother Nature. I thought of all the things I never got to do, of my stolen youth, and I vowed to one day get my life back. I saw many things on the streets, none of which were pleasant. There is pure evil out there. It lurks in every alley, around every corner, and it has a sickly sweet habit of consuming people. I have seen starvation. I have seen disease. I have seen murder, rape, and suicide. This monstrous beast we call the Universe harnesses these evils and it feeds itself upon them. It is ever mounting, and each time more vicious than the last.

I will never forget the twentieth day of February, nineteen ninety-four. It was the day I vowed to change this world. I pledged to make the rest of the world see that our governments and leaders were responsible for our downfall. We were not the cause of it; for we merely fell *with* it. The world's most prominent men and women were not willing to live harmoniously, as each sought to have unwavering power over their people. For this, we suffered. Nuclear attacks, cyclones, hurricanes, mass epidemics: each tragedy far worse than the last. And as each event unravelled and went overlooked, more men, women and children lost their homes, their families, their lives.

Suddenly, it seemed as though the streets had become flooded with people. Something had to be done. I begged the Lord for his help, but it never came. Things got worse. My fellow men were dying from disease and hunger right before my eyes. Women and children were being used in patriotic revenge missions. Smaller countries were losing half their population trying to fight losing battles against the United States, Britain and China. Death, destruction and disease had become a very natural being. This world was crumbling, and for mankind's sake, action needed to be taken.

Although my allegiance to Christ is immeasurable, I knew that he could not fix this world. I decided to shoulder the burden myself. I took the trouble out of God's hands and placed it into mine. I did this willingly, freely and without regret..."

"Do you have anything else you wish to say?" asked the Governor.

"No, Sir, I do not."

"Very well. Wilhelm Radulfus Miller, you have been brought here tonight to face your death at 12:01 a.m. the nineteenth day of January, two thousand seven, by method of lethal injection. Under English law, you have been convicted of thirty-four counts of murder, spread throughout nine different countries. You must now realize punishment for the acts which you have committed. May you find redemption in Christ and may he have mercy on your soul."

Epilogue

23 April, 2042

    The sleek, black body was as flawless as it had been the day it was purchased. Long and slender; it sat picturesque, perfectly poised, waiting for its owner to return. Thirty-five years had passed, a reunion unlikely, yet there it stood unyielding. Housed in an antique oak cabinet, it took its place between a tattered sheet of parchment and a severely battered guitar case. Its caretaker had shown great compassion: had flown it over mountains and across oceans. And he too was waiting...Waiting for the day when the calm would die.

Acknowledgements

I have many people to thank for assisting me in the creation of this publication. Firstly, I must give my gratitude to my husband, Nick. Your encouragement and support is appreciated and will forever be cherished. A huge thank you must also go out to my family and friends. Each one of you have enriched my life and inspired me in your own way.

Many thanks to my editor and very good friend, Marie. She has a gift of seeing things that others cannot, and her lust for creativity and etymology are most appreciated. I must also thank Dave Bardwell for his stupendous work on the cover design. And Dave Bowen, I thank you for taking time out of your studies to journey across Nova Scotia in search of the "perfect" photograph. Darin Casier and Jason Clark, your support and assistance is graciously acknowledged; I am privileged to have both of you involved with this project.

No story, whether it be a work of fact or fiction is written solely based upon the author's creativity and knowledge. Although my novel is fiction, there were certain aspects of which I had chosen to keep factual. Many hours of research and firsthand accounts of others were utilized throughout. The colourful Cajun life in Louisiana, the harsh tundra of Russia, and the impoverished villages in Northern Pakistan are all very real. I was fortunate enough to hear the tales of these lands from individuals whom had experienced life in them first hand. Francis, Ivanka and Nouman; thank you so very much for sharing your experiences with me. It was a privilege and an honour to hear them.